BOOKS

Tales of Ravenloft

Edited by

Brian Thomsen

TALES OF RAVENLOFT

First Printing: September 1994
Printed in the United States of America
Library of Congress Catalog Card Number: 94-60102

9 8 7 6 5 4 3 2 1

ISBN: 1-56076-931-9

TSR, Inc.
P.O. Box 756
Lake Geneva, WI 53147
United States of America

TSR Ltd.
120 Church End, Cherry Hinton
Cambridge CB1 3LB
United Kingdom

CONTENTS

The Crucible of Dr. Rudolph van Richten

David Wise

As Darkon's heavens deepened past indigo, receding beyond the ruddy backward reach of dusk, sinewy vapors slid between the trees and churned into dim mirages on the old forest road. Shadows lost their confining edges, merged, and thickened. To scorn shelter in the land of the Mists after sunset was deadly folly, but for one traveler, the promise of a bright hearth and a warm bed had already slipped into darkness.

Dr. Rudolph van Richten turned and grimaced at the burden lashed to the rump of his horse: the stiffening corpse of a dark-haired young man.

"We may both be ghoul meat tonight, but I'll catch your people before the flesh eaters find me, Vistana!" he spat with a great deal more conviction than he felt.

The lean, middle-aged herbalist searched the diminishing horizon ahead, desperate for any sign of a brightly painted vardo. He'd ridden hard since morning, yet the gypsy caravan had somehow outdistanced him anyway. There was no other route they could have taken from Rivalis, but he had seen no sign of them all day. Still, Van Richten rode on doggedly, as fearless of the impending night as a lamb of the chopping block. The Vistani had kidnapped his beloved child Erasmus, and all the torments that might descend out of the night were nothing compared to that loss!

As Tasha trotted along the eclipsing lane, Van Richten scanned its overgrown borders. He spotted a slender oak branch that hung by a feeble tether of bark; the bough snapped off cleanly in his hand as he guided Tasha past it. Draping the reins over the saddle, he trimmed and peeled the wood into a crooked pole about as tall as himself. Then, grasping the coarse linen shirt of the lifeless Vistana, he ripped free a wide swath, which he wrapped about the end of the staff and tied off, fashioning a long torch. Now for the courage to light it.

Overhead, the leafy ceiling cast a net of opaque shadow over the horse and rider, reducing the gritty road to a colorless strip that withered into void just ahead. A deathly hush smothered the forest, and the lonely staccato of Tasha's hooves rose in the silence, growing painful to Van Richten's ears. He vainly wished she could walk above the ground so they might slip through the woods without sound, but with every step, even her saddle creaked in betrayal. All creatures of the day were deep in their lairs, while things that creep in the night were just rising, pricking up their ears at the isolated *clip-clop* in the spreading blackness.

The anguished father wondered if he could keep the path without a torch. They were alone, and he wanted to remain so. Dr. Van Richten was just a peaceful herbalist from a small village—no match for danger—and only the torturous vision of Erasmus drove him on. *A man who braves the Darkon night,* went the saying, *will see wondrous things before he dies.* Until now, that had been an old preacher's proverb, spoken with a chuckle . . . and behind safely bolted doors.

The merest suggestion of a queer noise implanted in Van Richten's ear, and a cold shiver wrung his spine. A dim wisp of light flashed in the nearby underbrush—or so he thought. He ogled the dark spot, but spied nothing beyond the murky flank of the road. A shadow flitted by Van Richten's stirrup. His eye darted after the motion, but caught only a snatch of gyrating mist. He blinked and squinted at the depthless surroundings, then shivered again.

"Perhaps it's only the echo of light a man sees when he closes his eyes," he murmured hopefully.

Tasha expelled a tense, low whinny and turned her sleek head in the same direction.

She had seen something, too.

Another phantom spark flickered in the eaves of the weald, then faded. With a start, Van Richten turned toward it. A scattering of pinpoints ignited nearby, dying as quickly as he looked their way. He glanced to the other side of the road, where more pale fires kindled beneath the brush. Their numbers multiplied, and soon a greenish glow slithered through eerie silhouettes of thicket, illuminating the undergrowth in a faint pall.

Another shadow rolled by underfoot, spooking the horse, and the rider nearly lost his balance as she shied from it. "Easy, Tasha, easy girl," he urged, soothing the mare with a stroke on her gray dappled neck. "It's only mist and faerie fire."

Tasha threw back her head and snorted anxiously, stamping one hoof and then another.

"I suppose I *must* light the torch," Van Richten muttered, putting down the reins once more and reaching into the chest pocket of his wooly coat for a small, spring-loaded spark block. He squeezed the roughened strip of steel against the small flint bar, compressing the spring, then released it. The file scraped across the surface of the block as the spring uncoiled, releasing a flurry of brilliant sparks.

"I hope we're alone, girl," he remarked to Tasha. "This torch will—" Van Richten caught his breath and held his tongue.

Something had whispered in the mist below.

Tasha's ears snapped forward, angular and trembling, and her muscles went taut between Van Richten's legs. A blood-chilling, unnatural moan fluttered the horse's muzzle, inducing an ominous tingle under the man's skin. Instinctively he pocketed the spark block and caught up the reins. Then Tasha's ears went down flat—

With a sharp heave her equine scream splintered the silence, piercing Van Richten's heart with icy dread. The mount reared up and leaped as if she would climb into the air, nearly flipping onto her back. Van Richten madly flung down the torch, seized her mane with both hands, and leaned into the cringing saddle, clutching with all the strength his four limbs could muster. The unhinged animal bucked and spun in blind, reckless hysteria, filling the air with shrieks that wound higher with every convulsive breath. Meanwhile, the Vistana corpse behind Van Richten flailed wildly on Tasha's haunches, striking the doctor with blows from its floppy limbs. With each thrash, Tasha's sturdy mane slipped further through Van Richten's fingers. For a moment he experienced a queasy weightlessness, until he and his mount collided with a barrier of pine trees, brutally knocking the wind from him. Tasha writhed against clawing needles and lunged away with another scream, leaving the doctor entangled in the branches, ripping free of his clasping legs and wheeling out of sight while he plunged head-long into a pulpy thicket.

For a long and dizzy moment, Van Richten lay oblivious in the wet and thorny bed, but fear that Tasha might whirl back and trample him provoked him into action. He rolled out of the bushes and into the road, now illuminated in the subtle blaze of faerie fire. He frantically searched around him for stampeding hooves, but Tasha rampaged in another direction. The thought struck Van Richten that she might bolt back to Rivalis and leave him stranded, so he crawled stupidly toward her, still unsure of his feet.

The mists suddenly parted, and a bolt of horror shot through him—Dr. Van Richten abruptly drew up on his knees and threw his hands to his mouth.

Even as Tasha ferociously pitched herself into the air, a swarm of short, pudgy humanoids leapt and clung to her! The lunatic horse squirmed and kicked furiously, yet the little fiends only vaulted in greater numbers. Beneath Tasha's piteous screeching, a babble of clicks and hisses passed between the diabolical villains as they hopped along the ground, fearless of her hooves, and flung themselves upon her. They hung from her legs and shoulders and haunches by their teeth, their stumpy, digitless limbs twitching as she vainly sought to shake them off. The miserable beast began to sway and founder, until at last her forelegs folded. She buckled to the ground with a rough heave, and the horde swept over her.

Van Richten clutched at his heart and cried "Tasha!" in spite of himself. In response, a half dozen of the unnatural creatures turned and looked at him, kneeling in the middle of the mist-swirled road.

With gigantic, bulbous eyes creased by slitted pupils, they gazed at the man. Noses did not protrude between those bulging orbs; their mouths were nothing more than holes from which tubular black tongues spat, lizardlike, and their horrid faces were sewn with cruel stitches into hooded body suits of heavy cloth. They were *constructs,* the doctor perceived through his haze of terror; grotesque manikins infused with the baleful life-force of some malevolent power. He shook uncontrollably under their glassy examination. Both repulsed and fascinated, Van Richten gaped into the raptorial eyes of the dolly abominations, and they in turn regarded him stonily.

The sinister fabrications began to hop toward him.

"Think, Van Richten, think!" the man sputtered, falling back to his posterior and crawling away, crablike. The little creatures fanned out and toddled closer, chattering to one another with short clicks and pops of their spitting tongues. As the nearest doll-beast bobbed on its stumpy legs and prepared to leap, Van Richten clawed at the cold dirt behind him, his will teetering. Then by chance his hand fell upon the torch. Instantly his fingertips recognized the object, and renewed hope spurred him to motion.

Gigantic eyes like theirs were *obviously* designed for perfect darkness. If he could light a fire . . .

The doctor rolled to his knees and scrambled to his feet, seizing the pole as he rose; the length of the shaft slid through his grasp until the knot of rags butted against his fist. With a clumsy pivot, he turned to face his foes and shoved his fingers into the pocket that housed his spark block. The bobbing predator sprang like a flea, landed face-first upon Van Richten's lower leg, and thrust its mouth against him. To his horror, he felt a spiny point wriggle and probe its way through the thick cloth of his trousers, seeking the meat of his calf. The intruder found a soft spot and thrust inward, sending Van Richten into a frenzied dance, yelping and kicking his distressed limb outward, each snap of his knee growing more forceful than the last. Finally, with a *pop* the tiny creature dislodged and tumbled into the bushes.

A second assailant bobbed frenetically and lunged at Van Richten, but he swatted it aside before its tongue could impale him. Two more leapt, but he snarled and swung the base of his staff, connecting with one in midair and sending it end over end in the opposite direction; the other he grabbed by the hood and flung into the woods. Now the man no longer waited for his enemies' advance, but charged into their moon faces, kicking one on the run and sweeping his weapon across the shoulders of two more. At the end of the charge, he spun and faced them again—this time with the spark block in his hand. He lowered the torch head, raised the block, and squinted against the imminent burst of sparks.

Without warning, an impact from behind sent Van Richten sprawling to his face; the rest of the pack had interrupted its repast upon poor Tasha to bring him down. They tackled the human with surprising force and sent him forward, his arms outstretched before him. A feeble streak of crackling flint embers arced through the air, but none of them caught on the torch. The doctor struck the ground heavily, and the shock of the blow bounced the spark block from his fingers. Tiny bodies stormed like rabid vermin across Van Richten's back, and a dozen fleshy drills rent his clothing and bit into him.

Agony sliced through him like blistering-hot wires, wrenching a scream from his astonished lips as a host of wriggling intruders burrowed and squirmed under his skin. Still he crawled forward, scratching at the dust as still more tiny monsters piled on and pierced him with their dagger-tongues. Desperately he swept his arms back and forth over the ground, until finally his searching fingers fell upon the spark block. As his thumb fumbled for the file, his other hand drew the rag knot closer. The mounting torment on his back began to unhinge his mind. His extremities numbed as his head began to swim. His thumb slipped clumsily across the steel file, and the tool flipped over in his hand.

A jabbing probe lanced his spine and spasmed inward, eliciting a sharp, involuntary arching of his punctured back. Every muscle in his body locked, and he clenched the spark block in his palm, squeezing the file tight against the flint, then snapped his fingers wide. The steel strip scraped across the stony block as he freed it, sending up a fountain of light.

The probing tubes within Van Richten's torso hesitated. He gasped with hope, then clutched and released the spark block again. A bright shower of kindled stone skittered across his palm and the torch beside it. Blisters swelled on his skin as the sparks found soft flesh, but he began to pump the firemaker zealously, generating a dazzling display of light bursts. Soon the burning welts on his hand supplanted the torture on his back, and he realized that the invaders had fled his body. Still he raked at the flint until at last the linen torch flared to life. Van Richten climbed drunkenly to his knees, planted the tip of the staff in the road, and pulled himself to his feet. His smoky torch sent up a dirty ribbon of soot and cast a yellowish glow over the bushes around him, jittering with scurrying foes. He stared dazedly after the movement until the pounding in his ears subsided. Slowly the internal cacophony diminished, only to be replaced by a grating shuffle behind him.

Van Richten weakly turned about and squinted through the torch light, only to crumble back to his knees and groan hopelessly at the approaching faces of two walking dead men!

"He who braves the Darkon night *indeed* sees wondrous things before he dies," Van Richten moaned. The zombies' waxy skin sagged from the bone beneath their eyes, puckering about the neck and cracking at the folds. Their splintered teeth were clogged with dirt beneath wide-cleft, blackened lips. Brittle hair tangled in wiry chaos atop their seeping heads, sometimes bordering upon an encrusted patch of sloughed-off scalp, and rotten clothing clung pointlessly to meatless bones wrapped in torn, leathery skin.

"Whatever you are," he pleaded, "I beg of you. Raise me to living death if you must, but leave me the will to avenge myself upon the Vistani. . . ."

The dead men halted and hovered silently over him, radiating frigid oblivion, then spoke, moving their lips in unison. "I am the voice of Lord Azalin," they croaked through moldering vocal cords.

The Wizard-King! Here? "L-Lord Azalin?" stammered the man.

The king was a powerful wizard, but to detect the plight of a subject at the very borders of his domain, let alone come to the rescue, was astounding. He must have used his magic to animate the dead men and make them perform his will.

"Identify yourself," the dead ordered monotonously.

"I am Rudolph van Richten."

Another corpse joined the pair from behind—this one a female, with her throat torn open. "I know you," claimed all their flayed lips together, some with a hiss, others with a croak. "You are a physician of Rivalis."

"Yes, Lord Azalin. Thank the gods you are here!" exclaimed Van Richten, fighting down the rush of bile in his mouth at the sight of scrolling eyes and air-dried bones.

"Do not rejoice, Van Richten. There is no mercy for those who defy curfew. Only one thing stays your death: curiosity. What are the Vistani to you?" Another zombie shuffled up and joined the chorus. Van Richten stared dumbly at the ribboned stumps of its fingers, worn away from digging free of the earth.

"Speak! What are the Vistani to you?" they all asked in sepulchral tones.

The man's gaze sank to the ground as the story formed in his head. "They came yesterday, to my house in Rivalis, and demanded that I treat one of their tribe: Radovan Radanavich—that man there." Van Richten pointed a trembling finger at the raven-haired Vistana, who lay in a heap beside Tasha's scored, crimsoned haunches. "But he was too sick. I couldn't save him."

Van Richten's throat constricted as the memories focused. "He was the son of their leader. She accused me of letting him die, and she threatened to curse me. I told them they could have anything of mine if they would withhold their terrible powers. And when I awoke this morning, I found that they had chosen to take my *son!*" The doctor halted, swallowing his rage like a shard of broken glass.

"Old Belandolf—my neighbor—saw them go west," he finally growled. "I've chased them all day, but they're faster than I expected." More zombies lumbered into the simmering circle of faerie fire, which now outshone the dwindling embers of cloth on the torch, and he could hear the graceless shuffle of even more approaching.

"The Vistani do not travel the roads," intoned the raspy chorus. "They travel the Mists. Most likely they are in Barovia by now, for they are Strahd von Zarovich's toadies, and he grants them asylum."

"Barovia? But that must be four or five days' ride from here."

"For them it is not an hour's walk."

"Then my son is lost!" moaned Van Richten.

"Most certainly," returned the manifold voice of Azalin. "So, how would you avenge yourself, if you could?"

"I—" He paused, unprepared. "I don't know, but I'd figure something out."

"Would you . . . *murder* them?"

"I am a doctor. I don't know how to kill anything! I . . . I hoped to simply steal back my son. I may have seen more than forty winters, but I can still move quite stealthily."

"You cannot even follow the Vistani at a distance, let alone approach them unnoticed," retorted the undead assembly. Still others were arriving; there must be twenty or thirty of them now.

Van Richten felt a prickle of irritation. "How can I know what to do when I haven't done something before. Without knowledge, one can learn only through experience—"

"And thus are foolish mages killed."

"I'm not a fool, I'm a desperate father! Besides, Lord, I learn quickly, and as a doctor I am sure that knowledge is power."

The forest echoed with the throaty laughter of desiccated vocal cords; the doctor felt spiny icicles form in the pit of his stomach. "Indeed, Van Richten, it is the purest power, but one must wield it only when one has acquired it."

Van Richten blustered with ill-acted bravado and claimed, "I *am* here, after all!"

"Well said. I am of a mind to help you to your revenge, for I cannot tolerate the devil Strahd's gypsy poachers in my lands. Besides, it will be interesting to see if this dead Vistana of yours can guide you through the Mists."

"You can restore his life?" cried the doctor with sudden hope and awe. "That would be perfect! Surely the Vistani will return my boy if Radovan is returned to them!"

"I did not say I would restore his life. . . ."

The chorus began to whisper, first in unison and then in dizzying counter-rhythms that blended into an acidic hiss. Ebony coils of smoke belched from their mouths and slithered across the ground, coalescing into a shiny, scaly cord that wormed its way into Radovan's mouth in search of his unbeating heart. When the ebony tip curled and sank between his lips, the chanting subsided and Radovan's eyes fluttered open. He wobbled to his feet and stood crookedly, for his spine had snapped when Tasha had fallen. The youth's slack-jawed, listing face was flushed with chalky blue, and his chestnut eyes rolled back, white, while his swollen tongue punched between his teeth and waved in the air as if it were lapping at the remains of the inky smoke that had animated him.

"Fetch the bridle of the horse," commanded Azalin's multitude.

Too numb to question, Van Richten stumbled to Tasha and knelt beside her still head. Her icy blue eye lay open wide in motionless terror. He stroked her jaw, shot with oozing sockets, and mumbled, "I'm sorry, girl." A pang of guilt stabbed him as his hand caressed the velvety lip. Gently he unstrapped the bridle and slipped it off her muzzle.

"Put the bit into the mouth of the Vistana," ordered the voices.

Van Richten looked at Radovan, perplexed. "You want me to put the bridle on him?"

"Correct."

" . . . Will he not attack me?"

"By my will, no unliving thing may touch you this night."

Van Richten squinted at Radovan, then at the mortified congregation. Finally, he scanned the darkness around him. "And what about the ghoulies in the bushes?"

"Your perceptions are sharp, Doctor. The blood hunters are indeed *not* undead. But all things in Darkon, living or otherwise, are at my command and will not accost you. Now, obey me!"

"You have even *that* much power, Lord Azalin?" uttered Van Richten, stricken by the thought. "How do mortals possess such omnipotence?"

"Obey me!" commanded the multitude.

"Yes, Lord." Van Richten stood before Radovan and searched the lolling, dark irises; they returned his gaze in a cadence of movements, but no glimmer of sentience shimmered behind them—nothing except perhaps some instinctive craving for some forgotten thing, long gone. Gingerly, the doctor reached out, grasped Radovan's cold chin, and forced the bit of the bridle between his crusty lips, pinning back the wagging tongue. He slipped the muzzle strap over the top of Radovan's head and cinched it behind, letting the rest of the harness and reins dangle to the ground.

The deathly voice of Azalin instructed, "Obey me! Hold this minion's reins and he will heed your commands. Learn if he can guide you through the Mists. Report to me, Van Richten, if you return."

Dr. Van Richten reluctantly took up the reins. "Radovan?" he whispered, but the gypsy made no reply.

"Radovan," he repeated, louder. "Take me to your people."

The zombie lingered a moment longer, then turned its back on the doctor and paused again.

"Radovan! Damn you, take me to your mother!" With that, the bridled, emaciated scout staggered forward, and as one, the undead mob turned and followed. Gray tentacles of mist embraced and drew them all into a blind fog, leaving the netherworld of faerie fire and blood hunters behind. Van Richten's walk among the dead stretched into a time-trapped phantasm, a shuffling nightmare in which his leaden feet slavishly ignored the constant, desperate urge to flee. There was little to see as he trudged squeamishly behind his ghoulish beast of burden, and all he could hear was the funereal shuffle of the lifeless herd, so he stared glumly at Radovan's broken back, unwillingly reliving the Vistana's last moments of life.

"I didn't kill you, Vistana," Van Richten asserted. "Blood on my hands washes clean! *Find your people,*" he growled. "Find them *now!*"

In response, a breeze swelled and broke the mists, swiftly scattering them to reveal the foothills of an unfamiliar, mountainous region. Van Richten searched the terrain around him and wondered at stark, keen-ridged peaks to the east, carving a jagged horizon in the starry sky. The heavens behind them were vaguely blue, portending morning's advance, but dawn was at least an hour off.

Slowly, the size of the undead horde around him dawned on Dr. Van Richten. A great host of them—perhaps a hundred!—stood by in a huge crescent. They gibbered with ravenous urgency while their mindless presence pressed against Azalin's invisible barrier, grasping for a seam with an unconscious, unliving will of their own. Only Radovan looked away from Van Richten, to the south, along a grassy road that led over a knoll. His tongue began to writhe under the bit of his bridle, rattling the metal rod against his yellowish teeth.

"You've found them, haven't you?" breathed Van Richten, and as if they understood his words, the legion of corpses turned and lumbered toward whatever lay over the ridge.

What to do! The undead would shred any living thing they found. What if a farm lay beyond the ridge? Even if the kidnappers were there, was this what he wanted? What if the zombies should attack Erasmus?

Van Richten dropped Radovan's reins and jostled through the moving throng of undead. They groaned hungrily at him, but let him pass. He crested the hill and looked down a short expanse, into a glade of poplars, where he spied the twinkle of a campfire. The leafy cover of the glade around the bivouac did little to hide the rounded roofs of three large wagons.

It was the Vistana caravan.

The undead mass lurched forward, grasping with their claws and grumbling in incoherent agitation, but as they neared the camp an alarm went up. From within the advancing mob, Van Richten watched the gypsies rush about, casting glittering dust into the air and making frantic gestures. Two dark-haired men swung thick staves at the first zombies to reach the camp, beating them to the ground. Another cadaver cast itself upon a defender and the two of them went down. The man began to scream as it bit into his shoulder. A young girl snatched up a heavy staff and jabbed it sharply against the ghoul's ragged skull, knocking the head from its shoulders. Meanwhile, the dead circled the encampment, but their inward progress halted as the gypsies completed a warding circle.

Sharp commands rose above the grunts and sighs of the thwarted zombies as they huddled on the perimeter. Van Richten sought their source and finally sighted a hunchbacked old woman. It was Madame Radanavich, rushing among her people, snapping out orders and reinforcing the perimeter with somatic hexes of her own. As he looked upon her frightened yet resolute face, Van Richten seethed in vexation. Without a plan, he parted the wall of undead and crossed the warding line. Two of the tribe moved to halt him, but fell back amazed when they recognized him.

"Madame Radanavich! Thief!" he charged.

"Dr. Van Richten!" gasped the wrinkled woman. "How came you to Barovia? Have you set these flesh-eaters upon us?"

"Where is my son? Give me my son!" he cried in answer.

Radanavich looked over the zombies, then back at Van Richten with hardened eyes. "No! The boy is forfeit by your own agreement *and* by your own incompetence."

"Return him to me or I'll—I'll unleash the dead upon

you," the doctor threatened.

Two burly males seized the doctor, and the old Vistana laughed cruelly. "Your brainless minions cannot touch us, Van Richten," she sneered. "We know their ways better than you."

"I want my son, *witch!*"

Madame Radanavich hobbled up to the prisoner and gazed into his pale blue eyes. "We sold the giorgio child for fair profit. He now belongs to Baron Metus." She gestured to the east with her head. "If you want the child back, deal with him."

"Sold Erasmus?" gasped Van Richten. "Why, I will—I will—" He struggled against the rough hands that held him. The old Vistana laughed.

"What will you do, little doctor? Your companions can't reach us, and it's a wonder you even found us—" She paused and frowned. "How *did* you find us? Only the Vistani can travel the Mists."

In spite of his predicament, Van Richten realized it was his turn to smile. "Radovan showed me the way," he replied, grinning enigmatically.

"Radovan?" she sputtered, taken aback. "My Radovan?" She began to cast worried glances toward the undead. "Dr. Van Richten, where is *my* son?"

"Call him," whispered Van Richten coolly. "Call your son."

"No!"

"Then I will. Radovan! Radovan, come to me!"

The dead Vistana pressed to the fore and halted at the warding circle. The gypsies who held Van Richten cried out and released him, backing away from the sight of their lifeless fellow, who weaved like a broken doll, a horse's bridle in his mouth. Madame Radanavich wailed and wrung her hands, moaning, "Black gods, black gods, my poor son!"

Van Richten rushed to Radovan, seized his reins, and snarled, "Here's your son, witch! Don't you want him back? I've brought him for you!" The doctor flipped the reins over the dead gypsy's head and began to pull him across the invisible barrier. Radovan's feet remained planted where they were, but his body folded unnaturally from his severed spine—he seemed to look at Van Richten as if to plead not to be pulled so, but the man tugged harder. Finally, with a stumble, the zombie crossed the line.

"He is inside the circle!" yelled a young Vistana girl. Now Radovan staggered past Van Richten and moved toward his mother.

"Stop!" she cried, making a sign against her son, but he continued toward her.

Van Richten caught the reins and held them, and Radovan paused. "Tell me where to find my son!" demanded the doctor, and the entire army of undead pronounced it with him. "Where is Erasmus?" they asked in unison.

Madame Radanavich's expression changed from fear to horror and finally to fury. She pointed two fingers and a thumb at the doctor and hissed, "I *curse* you, Rudolph Van Richten, with all the power I have to lay you low! Live you always among monsters, and see everyone you love fall beneath their claws, starting with your son!

"Erasmus is the slave of Baron Metus, and he will be forever." She laughed hysterically and cried, "The baron is a *vampire!*"

"No!" cried Van Richten in horror. "No! A vampire! NO!" Hatred burst his heart, transporting him beyond reason, and he blathered, "You curse me, Madame Radanavich? *You* curse *me?* I say, feel the power of that oath redoubled upon you—I curse *you!* I *will* have my son back, as you have yours!" He threw down the reins and cried, "Go to her, Radovan!"

Van Richten turned upon all the terrified gypsies and screamed, "I curse you all! Living dead take you as you have taken my son!" To the zombies he bellowed, "Take them! Take them all!"

The army of undead writhed on the circle, pressing against it with inflamed determination, until one of them suddenly broke through where Radovan had crossed. Then another penetrated the ward on the other side of camp. Screams of alarm went up among the tribe as the circle collapsed and the mass of voracious corpses swarmed over the camp. Some of the living futilely swung weapons or tried to flee before collapsing under the rush of starving, oblivious carnivores. The Vistani's terrified wails rang through the countryside as the ghouls chewed upon their raw human flesh. The stench of fresh meat thickened the air, and slowly it penetrated Van Richten's delirium of rage—he gaped in shock as Radovan tore the bit from his mouth and began to devour his own mother before her bulging eyes.

"Stop!" he shouted, but the feeding frenzy was long beyond control. "Stop!" he bawled again, then ran from the butchery, leaving the undead to finish their human repast with smacking lips and licking tongues. He careened down a footpath, away from the carnage, crashed into some bushes, and lay there retching in utter misery. Soon his dry heaves gave way to sobbing, and he wept until dawn.

"I am a murderer," he confessed woefully, "and I will never be the same."

When the sun began to cast its beams among the peaks of the mountains, brightening their snowcaps with blue-white radiance, Van Richten sat up and wiped his eyes and mouth. There, in the wilds of Barovia, far from home, he realized that he had survived the night. It was more terrible than he could have imagined, yet still he lived.

Dr. Van Richten looked toward the east. Somewhere out there, his son remained the prisoner of a vampire. It was said that those creatures must sleep by day, and if Erasmus had somehow survived the night as well, perhaps Van Richten might still find him! Weakly he stood, then staggered off to climb the rocky slopes. He would find this Baron Metus, and *nothing* would daunt him, *ever* again!

* * * * *

It is with some measure of trepidation and yet infinite resolve that I, Rudolph van Richten, begin this journal as I begin a new life—if "life" I can call it. In truth, I am more like an undead creature, for all that I knew of life is gone, and I am most assuredly a foul murderer.

Madame Radanavich's tribe is slaughtered by my hand, for I set doom upon them like vicious dogs upon a fallen beast. My son, whose rescue was my only chance for vindication—for redemption itself—is dead, again by my hand, for he was transformed into a monster by the vampire Metus, and it was I who drove the killing stake through his tender heart. My beloved wife Ingrid is dead, and still again I am to blame, for I threatened Baron Metus before fleeing Barovia, and he preceded me to Darkon and vented his wrath upon her!

I should have died that night on the Ludendorf Road, when the blood hunters attacked, and perhaps I did, for all that is left of me is hatred and malice, which inflame my spirit beyond mortal limits! Because of Metus, I have dipped my hands into blood whose taint shall never leave me! I am forever lost to the night, belonging only among those whom I would obliterate with my own bare hands!

If Death will allow me to be its champion but once—if I may only live to see Baron Metus delivered into everlasting darkness—I will gladly yield what "life" remains in me. I'll make no claim to heroism in the assassination of the fiend, but if even one person is spared my agony by the destruction of Metus, then I may rest in peace. . . .

Rudolph van Richten
Rivalis, Darkon
King's Calendar, 735

The Vanished Ones

Chet Williamson

It's not easy being a lycanthrope, especially if you want to do more with your life than rip apart red-blooded creatures. I've told you already how I got the bitter venom of lycanthropy in my system, how the blood of the creature I slew dripped into my eyes and polluted my bloodstream, turning me into a beast during every full moon or when I become enraged.

A damnable situation, particularly for one like me, Ivan Dragonov, who has dedicated his life to fighting evil in all its dreadful forms. Now here am I, a creature of evil myself—or potential evil. I'll let you be the judge of that.

My first inclination as I left the chilly domain of Lamordia was to visit the one man I knew who could possibly release me from the curse. Well you know of Hamer, priest of Stangengrad. I was weary from battling Victor Mordenheim's monster—blast both their dark souls—and another flesh golem, from whose master's tomb I stole weapons and coin.

But then the thought occurred to me that a lycanthrope could be a ferocious *enemy* to evil, even more so than a strong warrior, such as I had been. So I postponed my visit to Stangengrad and, instead, continued my crusade, seeking out villainy in all its forms in order to destroy it.

I learned to deal with my disorder in the weeks that followed. I sought out deep caves during the full moon, and when I could no longer find any, had a ropemaker weave me a rope with silver strands woven through the jute. I wind myself up in it before nightfall, and tie knots that my lycanthropic side cannot undo. Those nights are filled with terrible pain, but they keep me from killing.

I also have to avoid traveling in any party, for if it were attacked and I changed into a beast, I might not stop at destroying our enemy, but might savage my companions as well.

So I've traveled alone, and I've come across my share of evil creatures. With every battle, the werebeast within me has come out and triumphed, far more easily than I would have if fighting as a mortal man.

I was in Lekar when I heard rumors of an evil that the soldiery had not been able to deal with in the town of Chateaufaux. So I rode quickly to the domain of Dementlieu. I hoped that I could put aright whatever was amiss before the next full moon.

I arrived in Chateaufaux just before noon, and stopped at a large inn. I ordered a haunch of venison and a mug of tea, at which some of the drunkards made stupid remarks, but my fierce look quickly quieted them. Before too long I fell into conversation with a pair of soldiers. When I told them my name, I learned that they had heard of me, and they eyed me with more respect than before.

When I remarked that rumors had spread of doings darker than usual in their city, one of the soldiers, a stout, honest-looking fellow named Jacques, was quick to give me the details.

"You need not tell us, Monsieur Dragonov. We've seen comrades, and in my case my brother, disappear."

"Or we *haven't* seen them disappear," said Henri, the other soldier, "but they're gone nonetheless!"

Jacques nodded. "For the past six months, men of Dementlieu have been vanishing, one every few weeks. The first was a mill owner named St. Just. Three weeks later a cobbler who left behind a beautiful wife and two children. Then a blacksmith, a tailor's apprentice, and a merchant who was also a member of the town council."

"That got some action, that did," Henri added. "Town council came to the army then, sure enough."

"Asked us to solve the mystery," said Jacques. "And

a mystery it was."

I didn't get the point. "But men run off all the time," I said. "Women, money problems, wanderlust—a whole slew of reasons."

Jacques's face grew rigid then. "Are you saying my brother would desert?"

One thing I didn't need was a brawl in an inn; it's not a good place to turn into a werebeast. "No, by the gods, of course not. But what about these other men?"

"They vanished without taking along a thing, and the horses were always found of the ones who rode away," said Jacques, apparently pacified. "None of the men owed anyone money, and each man already had a wife or sweetheart whom he loved, except for my brother."

"And," said the slightly drunk Henri, "do you think any man in his right mind would leave a woman such as *that?*" He pointed toward the door, which had just opened.

You know that I'm not the kind of man whose heart beats faster at the sight of a female. Never had time for them, battling evil for most of my life. But when I saw this creature walk into the inn, my jaw swung down, my eyes got wide, and I thought every woman I'd ever seen before didn't deserve the name.

This was a *woman;* no doubt about it. Hair red as flame, falling down the back all the way to her . . . well, pretty long hair anyway. A face like an angel's, with cheeks red as the rose and eyes so deep you wanted to fall into them and never come up. She was dressed modestly, but it was hard for even the heaviest cloth to disguise the lushness of her figure. And I found myself thinking that maybe I'd wasted too much of my life without the companionship of such females, though she was unique.

Then she looked in our direction, called Jacques's name, and came swiftly toward our table. "Monsieur Legrange," she said with a voice as sweet as honey, "have you news of my poor husband—or of your unfortunate brother?"

"None, Madame, I regret to say. But pray, allow me to introduce a gentleman who has heard of our plight and

whose curiosity has brought him far: Ivan Dragonov.
Mister Dragonov, this is Gabrielle Faure, the wife of
Roger Faure, who was the first man to vanish."

She turned those incredible eyes on me then. "Monsieur," she said, "your reputation precedes you." I saw
her gaze run over me, taking in my size, my weapons,
my warlike attitude, my hair and beard nearly as flame
red as hers; as you know, I present quite an impressive
picture, and I felt certain that she was sizing me up as a
potential ally. Her next words proved me right.

"Could I beg you, Monsieur, to assist us? I have done
little but tremble in fear and worry during the past six
months, ever since my dear husband disappeared. I
know that he would not have deserted me, and even if
my judgment is wrong, he would not have left his thriv-
ing business behind. You have in the past exposed many
evils and righted many wrongs, Monsieur Dragonov. Will
you not have pity on me and on the other poor wives,
families, and sweethearts who have been left lonely and
distraught by these disappearances?"

Well, I mean, what was there to say? How could I
refuse such a beautifully phrased—and flattering—
entreaty? So I gave a little bow, feeling silly as I did it,
and said I'd be happy to do whatever I could to help find
her husband.

We were all colleagues then, and I think Jacques was
also pleased that I would be trying to help find his
brother as well. The four of us sat there for nearly an
hour. Gabrielle and I drank tea, Jacques nursed a glass
of wine, and Henri fell into a drunken sleep.

Gabrielle told me about her husband's disappearance.
She said he had ridden toward town one morning from
their country house near the mill, and was not seen
again. No one reported meeting him on the road, but
many hours after he vanished, a soldier found his horse
roaming in the fields halfway between the town and the
Faures' home. There was no trace of blood on the saddle,
no signs of violence at all.

Then Jacques told me as much as was known about
the other missing townspeople. Quite simply, they had
gone off on errands at different times of the day and

night, and never reappeared. The mounts of those who rode away were always found, but with never a trace of evidence that suggested violence.

"And then they assigned my brother to find the men, or their bodies . . . you'll pardon me, Madame. He meticulously interviewed families, friends, fellow workers, but learned little. Then one night he told me he had some new evidence to gather, but would say no more, and rode off. I have not seen him since."

"But they found his horse?" I guessed.

"They did," said Jacques. He excused himself then; he had to go back to his barracks.

I felt uncomfortable left alone with Gabrielle. Although my manner is rough, I seldom feel ill at ease with either man or woman; they can take me or leave me as it suits them. But this woman was different, as I say. Beyond doubt I was drawn to her, but she showed no sign that she had conquered me. Instead, she asked me if there was anything she could do to help in my investigation.

I thought that, since her husband had vanished somewhere between his house and the town, it might be worth my while to look around the mill and see if I could find anything. Oh, not the kind of evidence that the law and soldiery look for on their hands and knees, but signs of monstrous habitation—the spoor of cursed night-creatures who might be swooping down and plucking men out of their saddles, then flying away to devour them at their leisure—or worse. I've found more than one hellspawn lurking in a remote mill.

She seemed agreeable enough and promised to show me over the grounds of the house as well. So we rode out together. By the time we got there, it was nearly time for the three men who were crushing grain to leave for the day, and Gabrielle dismissed them early. I couldn't help but notice the looks that they gave her as they left, as though they dreaded leaving the glory of her sight. And these were men with wedding rings on, too. She just had that effect on anything in trousers.

I got my attention off her long enough to prowl around the mill. The grounds didn't have many places for creatures to skulk. I found a dry well, but she told me that they used it for garbage, and after I got a whiff of the stench coming from down there, I believed her.

We looked in the mill then. "The only place within that is not in constant use is the cellar," she said. So I told her to stay upstairs while I went down with a lantern in one hand and the hilt of my sword in the other. I needn't have been so cautious. There wasn't a thing down there except for some staved-in barrels and some empty wooden boxes, none of which was long enough to harbor a vampire. Even the dirt floor had been long undisturbed.

I used the time alone down there to think about my situation. My emotions, really. I hadn't come into close contact with a woman since my blood was profaned by lycanthropy, so naturally I started to think that this . . . baser feeling toward her might be the result of it. If this were true, then the best thing I could do would be to avoid Gabrielle now that I'd gotten as much information from her as she could give.

I was just about to bid her good-bye, as much as it hurt me to do it, when she asked me if I'd be willing to come and dine with her, that she had a few more things she wanted to tell me about her husband— "things hard to say," as she put it.

I should have refused. I should have gotten on my horse and ridden back to Chateaufaux and never seen her again. That was what I wanted to do, for I feared for this woman to whom I was so attracted, this woman whom I feared I was actually starting to love. Imagine that: me, who had never known love except for the concepts of goodness and purity. But what if that love for her grew into a passion that bore away Dragonov the good man, the slayer of evil, and the beastly side of my nature took over?

But I could not say no to her, no matter how much I wanted to. I believe I would have done anything to remain by her side. So I agreed to dine with her.

As we rode the short distance toward the house, I suddenly drew up my mount and raised a hand for Gabrielle to do the same. She did, looking at me curiously, but I only listened.

Finally she asked, "What is it?"

"Nothing, I guess," I said. "Just thought I heard something." What I did not tell her was that it was not hearing as much as sensing. My years of hunting and being hunted by foul beings has given me a sixth sense, in most cases at least, and my lycanthropic blood has increased the sensation. I can feel the presence of a stalker, and I knew that there was something watching us from the thick trees that surrounded the open space in which we rode. I did not want to alarm Gabrielle, however, and since I couldn't tell where the watcher was hiding, I rode on. After a moment I thought that maybe there was nothing there at all, that my sensing an unseen enemy was just a manifestation of my own unease at being alone with Gabrielle.

At the house, she ushered me to a large dining hall and told a servant that there would be two at dinner that evening. I was placed at the end of the large table in the middle of the hall, and she at my right, a very intimate setting in spite of the size of the room. The ceiling was a good thirty feet high, and richly embroidered tapestries hung from nearly every wall.

Two servants brought the dinner and waited on us as we ate. The food was plentiful and delicious, though I could scarcely take my eyes from the woman long enough to eat. We talked of this and that, and she didn't bring up her husband until after she had dismissed the servants for the night, and we were alone in the room, lit by firelight and candles.

Then she walked toward the fireplace, turned, and stood there looking at me. Her gaze might just as well have turned me to stone. During dinner, she had looked at me politely, and reacted with interest when I spoke, but now the look she gave me was that of a lover, intimate and searching.

"Monsieur," she said huskily, "I have told you that there is more to the story, and there is. My husband Roger and I did not share the happy marriage you might have imagined. I do wish to find him, that is true, for he is my husband, and for that I owe him the loyalty of a wife. But when I saw you and spoke to you, I knew that you were . . . different from other men."

She had me there, no doubt about it.

"I could tell this to no one before, but I feel certain that you will understand. My husband, despite his public face, was not a kind man to me. He did not know how to treat a woman. But you, I am sure, do."

I felt unaccountably hot, not only because of the blazing fire whose red-yellow glow illuminated the room, making Gabrielle's hair shimmer like red mist, or, I fancied, a swirling cloud of blood.

"I prefer to be frank, Ivan Dragonov. I will say it once and once only, and if you do not wish to hear it you may leave and I will never speak of it to you again. But I have never felt about a man the way that I feel about you. I see in you the lover and husband I wish I might have had. And I sense that you feel the same emotion toward me."

I could scarcely breathe. I felt passions and longings I had never known I was capable of.

"There is no one else here," she said. "The servants are dismissed for the night. I beg you, Ivan, come to me. Take me in your arms. And love me as I have never been loved before."

I had no choice. I stood up, completely weaponless. I had not even my will to stop me from going to her embrace. Her moist lips were slightly parted so that I could see the pure whiteness of her teeth in the bright firelight. Her bosom rose and fell with the quickness of her breath, and I knew that she longed for my touch as greatly as I did for hers. She held her arms out toward me, and I ran into them as though blown there by a strong wind.

I had not held a woman in my arms for many years, and the heat of her body pressing close to mine excited me beyond reason, seared my very soul. I sank into her embrace as though drowning once more in the Sea of Sorrows. But this time I welcomed the sensation, preparing myself to dive into the blissful oblivion this sea of love would bring me. We kissed, and the heat from her mouth was like a furnace, a heat that annealed, molded . . .

Transformed.

I felt myself begin to change.

True horror is not knowing that something is going to destroy you. No, true horror is just the opposite, knowing that *you* are the evil, the monster, and that in another few seconds you will be destroying the only person you have ever loved—and are unable to stop yourself. True horror is when the monster looks out of your own eyes. That, my friend, reduces all other horrors to bedtime tales. And that is the horror in which I found myself immersed.

I first felt the transformation in my face, the teeth pressing outward against my gums, lengthening into points that cut into my lips until they, too, expanded and grew, pressing outward along with my snout as the very shape of my skull changed, becoming long and beast-like. Then my muscles expanded, my back broadened, and I closed my eyes and struggled desperately to keep from crushing the air from Gabrielle's lungs. I became taller too, and thought I could feel her flaming red hair gliding down my chest as my head grew nearer to the dark ceiling. I knew that in only seconds my claws would thrust out of my fingertips, piercing the flesh of my gentle love.

There was still enough of the human left in me to realize that if I pushed her away, I might still be able to turn and run out of the house before the beast took over completely and rended her dear body to pieces. But when I tried to push her back, I discovered that she was still clutching me tightly, even tighter than before, holding in her arms a lover who was turning into a murderous fiend.

That startling fact alone actually stopped the transformation for a moment. The overwhelming trust I thought the woman must have in me nearly returned me to my human self, goodness overcoming evil. Or so I thought.

Then I realized that it was not soft arms wrapped around my widening back, but the hairy, long, and wiry legs of a gigantic spider.

My dear Gabrielle was a creature like myself, a shape-shifter, a deadly red widow, queen of spiders who seduces men and then drains the life from their bodies.

But this knowledge did not come to me then, for the sudden danger dropped my lycanthropy over me like a spider's web, and in an instant I was transformed into a raging, furious beast, knowing only that it was being attacked, that it must kill to live—and that it lived only to kill.

I remember, though, as if my human mind was looking out through those blood-rimmed eyes. I saw what was trying to hold me. A round body larger than an ale barrel, coated with crimson hair. From its bulk eight great legs grew like small trees, wrapping themselves around me, drawing me closer and closer to the hideous head. Two rows of shiny eyes glared at me, and gleaming fangs protruded from two hairy sheaths.

Suddenly the head thrust itself toward me, and before I could pull away, the fangs buried themselves in the thick fur of my neck. Poison that would have killed a man instantly pumped into my veins, and it was as though my blood caught on fire. All my beast-mind could think of at that moment was escape, and ease from the pain that burned every inch of my flesh, muscles, and bowels.

With a tremendous burst of strength, I hurled the hideous thing from me and screamed until my pain was bearable. It took but a few seconds, and I can only guess that my lycanthropic blood, already tainted by unimaginable evil, could not fall prey to the red widow's otherwise fatal poison. But all I knew then was that I must destroy whatever had hurt me, and I leapt toward the giant spider-thing.

It was quicker than I and scuttled on its eight great legs into a corner, displaying the telltale black hourglass on its bloated back. It didn't pause, but went right up the wall until it reached the thirty-foot ceiling, where it hung looking down, as if wondering what to do next.

I didn't wonder a thing. I simply acted without thought, following it into the corner and using my steely claws to climb up the tapestry, shredding the sturdy cloth as I went. When the hangings stopped, ten feet beneath the clinging spider, I leapt at it. My preternaturally strong legs carried me up into the corner, where, at the apex of my jump, I sank my claws into the red, rotund ball and dragged it from its perch, so that we both fell heavily to the stone floor. I did not let the monster escape again, but grasped it with both of my feral hands, and kicked the claws of my feet against it, spraying yellow ichor over the gray stones.

It gave a screech pitched so high that my human ears could not have heard it. But my animal ones did, and the sound drove nails into my brain, distracting me just long enough for the thing to break my grip. It scuttled away from me toward the fireplace, dripping whatever it used for blood.

Again I launched myself at what Gabrielle had become, and caught it just as it reached the stones in front of the vast fireplace. I was on its huge, bulbous back now, but within seconds its wiry legs threw us both over. Those legs cut through the air like steel whips, and the fat, obscene body twisted, pressing me cruelly against the floor. But still I would not release my savage hold. At last the red widow rolled to the right so that we were both on our sides, and turned so that her multi-eyed face and leering mouth were nearly against me. The fangs came toward me, but I dodged them even more quickly, opened my own great muzzle, and closed my fangs upon the giant spider's head.

My reward was a mouthful of foul ichor and a scream that made the others sound melodious. I kept my jaws fastened upon that section of the head that comprised several of the eyes and a corner of the mouth, and bore down even harder, until more of the vile fluid gushed over my mouth. The momentary limpness of the widow's body told me that I had struck a mortal spot, perhaps even what served the monster as a brain. And as its body slumped, I relaxed for a split second, just long enough for the creature to yank its head away from me and scuttle back blindly, directly into the flaming logs of the fireplace.

There was an awful hissing sound, like that of a large chunk of fat falling into a fire, and the red flames became one with the crimson hair of the spider's body. The legs burst into flame as well, igniting like dry twigs, and the creature tried to scramble out of the fire. But the burning legs crumbled beneath her like sticks of charcoal, and the flames mounted as the body fell full upon the blazing, wrathful coals.

The fire licked up around her, making the fluids within her sizzle, and she twitched as though she were already being prodded by the cruel spears of all the fiends of the pit. Her rotund shape began to diminish, burning greasily away, the hot ichor spitting in final defiance from the mouth of the fireplace. Within minutes, she had been reduced to a smoldering, sparking mass of crusted fur in a puddle of bubbling putrescence.

My enemy defeated, I felt myself becoming human again, and mortal relief flowed into me as beastliness flowed out. The transition took only seconds, and as I stood, my clothing ripped and torn by the expansion of my frame, I happened to glance in one of the two large mirrors that hung on each side of the fireplace, and saw behind me a pale, ghostly face at the glass of the doors that led out onto a terrace.

I swung around and saw that the shocked visage belonged to none other than Jacques Legrange, the soldier at the inn. My true nature had been discovered, and I knew I could not let him flee. So I dashed to the door and yanked it open. He stood there, possibly petrified by fright, not knowing what to do. Nor, to tell the truth, did I. I could not kill a man for his knowledge, but if he made any rash move against me, I might have no choice. Then his hand tentatively started to move across his body toward the hilt of his sword, as though he intended to attack me, but feared to:

"Do not fight me," I said as sincerely as I could, trying to keep down the killing rage. "As you love life, man, do not anger me or try to fight me, for I may do what I would not wish to."

He seemed to understand, then nodded and let his hand fall back to his side.

"You followed us," I said. "You were the one hiding."

He cleared his throat roughly. "I was. I suspected her. There was a look . . . between her and my brother . . .

and that night he rode out and did not come back."

"You suspected her, and you didn't say anything?"

"I could not be sure, and to accuse a lady . . ."

He left it unfinished, and I shook my head in disgust. "You fine gentlemen of Dementlieu," I said scornfully. "So did what you saw this night confirm your suspicions well enough?"

He swallowed heavily and nodded. "A red widow, was she not?"

"A red widow," I agreed. "One of that hellspawn that mimics the appearance of a scarlet-tressed beauty, lures men to intimate privacy, and then reveals her true, hellish self, killing the poor love-struck fools, and then draining their corpses over several days until not a drop of fluid remains. Such indeed was Madame Faure."

"And . . . and *you* . . ." Jacques said, his voice trembling.

"A lycanthrope," I said. "What good to deny it after what you've seen?"

"And will you . . . slay me now?"

"I slay only the evil—or have been able to until now." And I told him how I had acquired the curse, and how I had been using it. "So keep the secret to yourself," I concluded, "and live. And let *me* live."

"I think you speak the truth," he said. "If not, you would have no reason to let me remain alive." He gave his head a sharp nod. "I swear that your secret is safe with me."

"Glad to hear it," I said gruffly, annoyed that I had to depend on this man's silence. "Now let's find what that hag didn't want me to see."

It didn't take long. What remained of the corpses of the missing men were in the large attic of the mill, whose locked door I easily battered in. "In constant use, indeed," I said, remembering Gabrielle's words as we entered.

Jacques uttered one word only, "Louis . . ." and then was shocked into silence. I could well understand why. His brother's dried and desiccated husk lay on the attic floor amidst the others. There was still enough left of their faces to tell who they were, but I knew Jacques's brother from the uniform that still clung to the fragile, husklike body.

For a long time we stood there among the dead men, and then Jacques stepped forward and looked into each withered face in turn. At last he stood up and spoke. "My brother . . . the cobbler, the smith . . . they're all here but one."

I nodded, for I knew. "Her husband," I said. "He was the first one chosen here. He would have been the mate. So we'll seek him somewhere no one would ever have reason to go."

I led Jacques straight to the dry well, remembering the smell that had come up from it. There I looped a plain hemp rope under my arms, and Jacques lowered me down into the pit. I clung to the rope with one hand, and with the other held a lantern at my side.

As I suspected, Roger Faure was at the bottom. At first I thought that he had not suffered the fate of the other victims, for his body seemed full and plump, almost swollen. But when I drew my sword and prodded his body, Gabrielle's children scurried from beneath their dead father's clothing so that he instantly withered into a foul matting of rags, parchment skin, and brittle bones.

The repellent nest of spiders, hatched within Roger Faure's pitiful corpse, attacked me then, but the change did not come over me, for it was butcher's work I now did, efficient and yeomanlike, hacking them into bits one at a time as they tried and failed to bite through my heavy boots and scuttle up my legs. After I had dispatched the six, I searched the dry well thoroughly but found no more of the creatures.

"Haul away!" I shouted, and looked up to see Jacques's white face high above. I thought he might be tempted to leave this humble lycanthrope at the well's bottom, but he was a man of honor.

At the top I turned and spat back into the hole. "Another half a year, and six redheaded beauties would have crawled up out of that hole to go their separate ways and drain the men of this domain. But no more. You might fetch that poor fool's body out when you return with soldiers for the cleaning up."

"You're not riding back to town?"

I shook my head grimly. "No. Tell them what you will. Tell them you killed her yourself, if it'll advance your rank. I don't care. My work here's done, and there's something ahead of me that will wait no longer."

I bade him good-bye and rode here, straight to Strangengrad. For I knew that what I feared has come true. When I held that thing in my arms, even before she had begun to transform into her true monstrous self, I felt my own self changing. Had she been what I then thought she was, a true woman filled only with love and passion for me, I know that I would have killed her. I felt the beast escaping, that beast that yearned for hot blood and torn flesh.

And I knew then that I must suffer the cure for my dread disease. I must try to scour this curse from my spirit, whether the attempt drives me mad or kills my body. For I cannot live on knowing that my spirit is corrupted by evil.

So, Hamer, good friend, good priest, I stand before you a sinful penitent, stuffed full with undesired iniquity. You have heard my story. Tonight is the full moon. Lead me into the chapel, bind me, and do your best to drive this curse from me. And if my blood remains impure . . . if the change comes . . .

Well, you have a sword, and it is silver. You will know what to do.

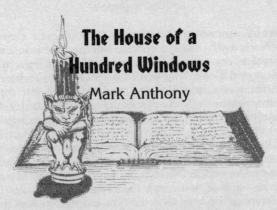

The House of a Hundred Windows

Mark Anthony

"Three . . . four . . . five . . ." Clarisse Harrowing murmured, counting windows as she wandered through the ancient, dust-dim air of Evenore's grand hall.

It was here that her game always began, in the gloomy, rambling room that sprawled across the entire front half of the manor's first floor. Here the high, narrow windows were easy to count, each opening like a keyhole onto a leaden sky, nestled between smoke-stained beams arching overhead like the ribs of some dread leviathan from the deepest sea. Seven windows on the west side of the hall, seven on the east. Fourteen in all. But that was just the beginning.

The House of a Hundred Windows. That was what the old Vistana woman in the village below—the woman with eyes as small and black as a raven's—had called the manor, even though Clarisse had only ever been able to count ninety-nine. Of course, had it been so simple, it would not have been a game at all.

Clarisse moved into the library, her gown of dove-gray silk whispering across the worn stone floor. Heads of boars, stags, bears, and feral beasts she could not name snarled down at her from high walls, each draped in a shroud of cobweb and dust, as though wearing a funeral veil. She tried not to look at them. She concentrated on the windows. They were smaller here, trickier. Some hid behind the corners of overburdened bookcases, and others were all but obscured by tarnished suits of armor or tapestries whose idyllic hunting scenes had been darkened by years of soot and dust. Carefully she counted each window, making certain she peered into every alcove, every recess. The dreary afternoon light made her game difficult. It looked as if a storm was brewing.

After some moments she nodded. Yes, nine more. That was what she always counted in the library. But then, it might be that there was a window here she had yet to find.

Clarisse sank into a chair of blood-red velvet to consider this thought. She had played the game a dozen times or so—always when Lord Harrowing was away, of course—and at first, each time she searched, she had found more windows than the time before. Many of them were small and obscure, and easily overlooked. But on the last few occasions, Clarisse had counted only the same windows she had discovered before. Ninety-nine of them.

She frowned, a fine line casting a shadow across her smooth, pale forehead. She thought of her encounter with the old Vistana, as she did with curious frequency of late. It was the day Clarisse had dared to tell Ranya, Lord Harrowing's red-faced housekeeper, that she would walk to the village herself to purchase candles and salt. On her way back, in the middle of the village's one muddy street, she had come upon the old woman, clad in shabby rags that swirled on the cold wind like dirty feathers. The shriveled Vistana had gazed at Clarisse with those hard black eyes, and had pointed with a crooked finger toward the manor house, perched like a dark bird on the tor above the village.

A window lets in darkness as easily as light, the old woman's cracked voice whispered once again in Clarisse's mind. *Forget that not, child, if you would dare live in the House of a Hundred Windows.*

Clarisse sighed, wondering if she should give up her game. Perhaps the old woman was mad. Gareff had often said that all the wandering Vistani were, what with their fate-scrying cards and their magic crystals and their strange, wild music. But no, she couldn't give up. Not yet, at least. The game was all she had to stave off the vast loneliness of this place when Gareff was away.

And he was so often away, doing what she did not know, for he never spoke of it.

Clarisse wondered if this was what her father had meant for her, this desolate existence in a country manor, so far from the bright, candlelit ballrooms and opulently gilded opera houses of the great city of Il Aluk. But no, all that had mattered was that his daughter married a lord of ancient and honorable lineage. Clarisse's father was one of the wealthiest merchants in all of Il Aluk, but he had learned that there was one thing all his gold could not purchase—noble blood. Thus it was that when Lord Gareff Harrowing came to call at their fashionable city redstone nearly a year ago, Clarisse's father had welcomed the suit for his daughter's hand, even though the suitor himself was more than twice her age, and lord of a provincial estate over a fortnight's journey from the city.

Clarisse, of course, had been given no voice in the matter.

"The choice of whom to marry is not ours to make," her mother had explained as she had basted up the hem of Clarisse's antique lace wedding gown.

"I don't see why," Clarisse had replied crossly.

"Men are better at making decisions, Clarisse." Her mother's voice had sounded flat and weary. A look of resignation had shone in her eyes—eyes that years of meekness and subservience had washed utterly of all color and emotion. "Men are stronger and smarter than we are, Clarisse. Do try not to forget that."

Clarisse had only bit her tongue. She knew she was smarter by far than most of the flighty, foppish noblemen who frequented the city's ballrooms and theaters— and most likely stronger than half of them. But there was no use in saying it. Her mother had given up long ago. Now Clarisse supposed she would do the same. It was, after all, what was expected of her.

The next day Clarisse had wed Lord Harrowing in the largest cathedral in Il Aluk. Then, while her mother wept silently, her father had lifted Clarisse into a carriage with her new husband. As the horses lurched into motion, Clarisse had gazed back through the carriage's small, tear-drop-shaped window to see her father smile. With a start, she had recognized the satisfied expression. It was the same smile her father always wore after a profitable business venture. Apparently he had finally bought himself what he had always desired. A spark of hatred had flared in Clarisse's heart then, so hot and sudden that it frightened her. She had turned her gaze from the window, trembling.

Now Clarisse stood and smoothed her gown, as if the memories could be brushed away like dust. The gloom was steadily gathering in the library. What little light the day had managed would fade to night soon, and then her game would be over. Swiftly she moved through the parlor, the ballroom, and the kitchen, with its cavernous stone fireplace large enough to cook an entire roe deer. She made her way quickly up the great, sweeping staircase to the manor's second floor and there went from bedchamber to bedchamber, pausing to count the windows in each. Finally her game brought her up to the attic rooms. Here Ranya and Evenore's few servants resided, though most of the small, haphazardly arranged chambers had been given over to storage, each filled with a maze of shabby furniture, ancient trunks, and portraits of long-forgotten Harrowing ancestors.

In the last of the storage rooms, Clarisse sat upon an ironbound chest and ciphered in the thick dust that covered a worm-eaten mahogany serving table. Fourteen windows in the grand hall, and nine in the library. Six for the parlor, and twenty for the ballroom, and five more for the kitchen. Then all the bedchambers, and the servants' quarters, and the storage rooms. Carefully she checked her numbers. At last she leaned back, brushing the dust from her hands, gazing at the numbers drawn upon the table.

Once again, she had counted ninety-nine.

Clarisse sighed, and for the first time found that her game had left her lonelier than before. She caught a pale glimmer out of the corner of her eye and turned to find herself gazing into an old mirror with a gilt frame. A pretty young woman stared back at her with wide green eyes. Her dark hair was pulled back from her high fore-

head, and a tear-drop pearl glistened at her throat. The
mirror's ornate frame made her face look like a painting—just one more object of delicate beauty purchased
to decorate the rambling manor called Evenore.

Sudden rage flashed through Clarisse's breast. Was
that all she was, then? A mere thing to be bought and
sold? Without thinking, she snatched up the mirror and
smashed it against the floor. The gilt frame cracked and
splintered, and the glass shattered into a dozen jagged
shards. Clarisse clapped a hand to her mouth, her anger
turning into cold horror. From each of the shards, a fragment of a pale, wide-eyed face stared up at her in mute
shock. What had she done?

Quickly she snatched up an old rug and threw it over
the broken glass, concealing the disturbing images.
Then she moved toward the door. She needed to wash
her face. Gareff could return at any moment, and she
didn't want him to wonder why there were cobwebs in
her hair and dust on her gown. She reached to turn the
porcelain doorknob.

A single spark of ruby light touched her hand.

She gasped, snatching her arm back. Then, tentatively, she reached out once more. A small circle of
crimson light danced across the back of her hand. Small
motes of dust swirled on the air, transformed briefly into
tiny glowing suns before vanishing. It was a beam of
sunlight.

Clarisse looked up at the storage room's sole window.
It was utterly overgrown with ivy, letting in only a dusky
green illumination. But that meant the light must come
from . . .

"The hundredth window," Clarisse whispered, her
pulse quickening.

Fascinated, she stood and began moving slowly
through the room, keeping the ruby spark of light on her
hand, tracing the beam to its source. It led her to the far
side of the chamber. Here the wall was covered by a
faded tapestry, its images so murky with time and
neglect that Clarisse could not make them out. The
edges of a small, moth-eaten hole in the tapestry glowed
as if on fire. Holding her breath, hardly daring to let her-

self hope, Clarisse reached out a trembling hand to lift the tapestry.

Suddenly a voice rang out from far below.

"Clarisse!"

She froze. Footsteps sounded on the stairway.

"Clarisse, where have you gone?"

Gareff! Swiftly, Clarisse let the tapestry fall back. She whirled and sped from the room, brushing the cobwebs from her hair. She dared not keep Lord Harrowing waiting. He might ask what she had been doing, and she would have no choice but to tell him. And she did not want to tell him. The game was hers, a private thing. Smoothing her gown, she dashed down the stairs to greet her husband.

She found him standing before a window in the parlor, handsome despite his gray hair and mustaches, elegant in his old-fashioned frock coat and breeches. He gazed outside through rain-spattered glass.

She knelt beside him and clasped his hand, as was expected of a wife. "Welcome home, my lord," she murmured softly.

"Ah, there you are, Clarisse." He stroked her dark hair with the same absent fondness he always displayed when petting his favorite hounds. She tried to suppress a shiver, and did her best not to recoil from his touch. Then he turned his gaze back out the window as the storm that had threatened all afternoon finally loosed its fury over Evenore.

It was only then that a queer thought occurred to Clarisse. If it was raining outside, from where had come the crimson ray of sunlight in the attic room?

*   *   *   *   *

Clarisse reined the gray stallion to a halt at the top of the heather-blanketed ridge. The beast tossed its head and snorted, its hot breath casting faint ghosts on the damp air. Countless droplets of mist, glistening like tiny pearls, beaded the woolen cloak she had thrown over her riding gown. The somber landscape marched below her in endless, dun-colored waves, broken only here and there by a hedge of dark thorn or a crumbling stone wall.

Crimson blossomed in her pale cheeks as she dared to laugh. She knew she was a fool to have spurred her mount so swiftly. Riding sidesaddle was precarious enough; and the irregular ground made it absolutely treacherous. Yet that was a great part of the excitement. Sometimes there was a part of her that secretly, almost darkly, hoped she would have a horrible accident. She knew that a throw from the back of a horse and a hard landing on cold ground could snap the bones of her neck like dry kindling. It would be a terrible price for freedom, but one she was not entirely certain she would be unwilling to pay.

Of late, the airs she took about the countryside were all that gave Clarisse a sense that she was alive. Even her game had given her no comfort these past weeks. After that day she had discovered the strange beam of sunlight in the attic storage room, it was nearly a fortnight before Gareff's mysterious business once more took him away, and she was able to resume her search. To her dismay, she had found the storage room door locked. Somehow, Gareff must have learned of her private amusement. No doubt the hateful Ranya had told him.

Whatever the cause, Clarisse knew it was best that she forget her window-counting game. True, she had learned where Gareff kept a skeleton key that worked all the locks in the manor—she had spied Ranya stealing it once to open the wine cellar and snitch a bottle—but Clarisse did not dare use it. In his wrath, a lord might rightly punish his wife for such a disobedience. Of course, Clarisse thought with disgust, a lady had no such recourse should her husband betray her.

The gray stallion gave a snort, pawing the damp ground with a hoof in agitation. Startled, Clarisse looked up to see a man approaching. By his ragged clothes and the bundle of firewood slung over his back, she took him to be a villager. He doffed his cap when he reached her and smiled, baring a handful of yellowed teeth.

"Milady is a brave one, yes?"

Clarisse frowned. The villager's thick country brogue

was difficult to fathom.

"I wouldn't know what you mean," she answered coolly.

"Aye, don't you, milady?" The man winked with one bulbous, palsied eye. "Lord Harrowing is gone wandering. And so has milady, yes?"

Clarisse's slender eyebrows knit in a scowl. "Lord Harrowing's affairs are his concern," she said sternly. "As my own affairs are mine."

The villager hopped a step backward, his peculiar eyes bulging in alarm. "Aye, milady, just as you say. Begging your pardon and not meaning to presume. It's just . . ." The man clutched nervously at his threadbare cap. "It's just that it isn't safe for you to be out riding by your own, what with the shadows and all."

"Shadows?" Curious, Clarisse leaned forward in her saddle.

"Aye, shadows." He lowered his voice to a coarse whisper. "The kind as sneak up on a foolish man who sets out for home too late to make it afore sundown, and then he never makes it at all. I heard old Madam Senda say a goblyn lord conjured them, and her being Vistana and all, I suppose I'd tend to listen."

Clarisse shivered and drew her cloak more tightly about her shoulders. "It's just a story," she said flatly. But she felt a strange tingling of excitement in her chest all the same.

The haggard man pulled his cap back over his head and hefted his load of firewood. "As milady wishes," he said. "I'm certain she'll be troubled not by man or shadow this day." He nodded his head in farewell. But as the villager turned away, Clarisse saw a strange look in his eyes. It was a fearful look, and one of pity.

Finding the dwindling afternoon light suddenly menacing, Clarisse spurred her mount and rode in the direction of Evenore.

She returned to find Gareff pacing before the fireplace in the library. Three black mastiffs lay sprawled asleep by the hearth. He spun around at the rustling of her silk gown.

"Clarisse!" He set down a glass of wine and strode

toward her, his snow-white eyebrows bristling. "Where
have you been?"

"Why, out riding," she said breathlessly, taking off her
mist-damp cloak.

Lord Harrowing shook his head. "I should have
known." He sighed deeply and took her by the shoulders. "Clarisse," he said sternly, as if speaking to a child.
"You must promise me that you will not go riding out on
the moor any longer."

"By why?" Her heart fluttered in her chest. "Is it because . . ." Her voice trailed off. *Is it because of the goblyn lord?* she had almost said. But she didn't dare.
Gareff would laugh at such foolishness.

"Please, Clarisse. You must promise me."

For a giddy moment she almost considered defying
him. Without her sojourns across the moor, she had
nothing. But the fierceness of his blue eyes seemed to
bore into her. Finally she cast her face downward. "Of
course, my lord."

Gareff lifted her chin with a finger and smiled at her.
Then he leaned down and roughly kissed her forehead.
"Come," he said briskly. "Let us see what Ranya has set
out for our supper."

Clarisse swallowed the bitter taste of bile in her throat
and followed after him as the shadows gathered outside
the library's windows.

The days that followed seemed as dreary to Clarisse
as the ancient air that filled Evenore's chambers. She
tried to content herself with matters about the house, but
to little avail. A day of trying to tame the manor's garden
left her hands burning with nettle stings, and she quickly
gave up that pursuit. Nor, she found, did she have the
patience for embroidery or sewing or other domestic
pursuits. It helped matters little that Lord Harrowing was
away more than ever, at times leaving in the middle of
the night and not returning for days on end. When he did
return, he seemed haggard and distracted, hardly noticing Clarisse except to kiss her cheek fondly now and
again.

Finally, one chill autumn day, Clarisse sat down to
pen a letter to her father. Gareff was off on one of his

mysterious journeys again, and Ranya had walked to the village that morning to visit an aunt taken ill.

The storm-swept sky outside the library's windows was dark and angry, and Clarisse was forced to light a candle to work by, though it was only midafternoon. In smooth, delicate script, she wrote of how lonely the country was, and how dark the manor, and how desolate she felt so far from the city. But when she lay down her quill, she knew she could not post the letter. Her feelings meant nothing to her father. He had bought his nobility with her, and he had obviously found the price more than fair.

Slowly, she stood and carried the parchment to the fireplace and placed it carefully in the flames. She watched as its edges darkened and then caught fire. The letter blackened and curled in on itself like a dying spider. Then it was gone.

Clarisse stood, sighing. She paced despondently before the fire for a time. Then, almost without thinking, she moved to a bookcase on the far wall. She counted five shelves up from the floor and then ran her finger along the gilded spines of the tomes. She pulled a small volume bound in green leather from the shelf and undid the brass hasp. Inside, the pages of the book had been cleverly hollowed out into a small recess. Nestled within was an iron key.

Gareff's skeleton key.

Clarisse did not allow herself a moment to pause and consider what she was doing. Suddenly she was burning to know what lay behind the tapestry in the attic. She grasped the key and returned the book to the shelf. Swiftly she ascended the stairway, glancing back over her shoulder. She had to be careful. Ranya might return at any time.

Moments later found her breathless before the attic storage room. Hand trembling, she fit the key into the door's lock. It turned easily. She slipped within and pressed the portal quietly shut. A flash of crimson light caught her eye. There—she had not imagined it. The ray of sunlight danced across the bodice of her gown as she approached the tapestry. Swiftly she pushed aside the threadbare weaving.

It was a keyhole.

She could see no doorway, but there in the middle of the stone wall was a lock. It was from this that the ray of light emanated. A thought struck her.

"It can't be. . . ." she whispered to the silent air.

She lifted the skeleton key and brought it to the keyhole. It slipped easily within. She held her breath for several heartbeats, then turned the key. There was a faint *click*. With a gust of stale air, a section of the wall swung inward. She blinked against the flood of crimson light that poured forth. Hesitating only for a moment, she stepped inside.

Clarisse had found the hundredth window.

It dominated the entire far wall of the small room, a chaotic mosaic of jagged, colored shards that made her dizzy to gaze upon. Sunlight streamed through the nightmarish stained-glass window, tainted by the colored glass, and only dimly did Clarisse remember that, when last she looked, the sky outside had been dark and brooding, concealing the sun. The writhing patterns of the window dazed her. Then her gaze locked upon an image in the center of the window. It was a man.

Slowly she approached, fascinated. He seemed a noble, clad in a coat of black velvet and golden breeches. A red ribbon held back his long, raven-dark hair. The portrait was exquisitely done, tiny fragments of glass rendering his grave, handsome features in perfect detail. She supposed it was only a trick of the light, but there was a fire in his eyes of smoked glass. It was almost as if he were gazing at her . . . gazing at her with passion. She shook her head. It was a look she had never seen in Gareff's eyes.

"Who can this have been?" Clarisse mused aloud. "He seems so . . . so melancholy."

"Indeed, my lady," a rich, masculine voice spoke behind her, "he has good cause to be."

Clasping a hand to her mouth to stifle a scream, Clarisse spun around. There was no one else in the room. All she saw were the patterns of light thrown upon the far wall by the stained-glass window.

"Who's there?" she called out, trying to keep the fear from her voice. "Where are you?"

"Why, I stand here before you . . . Clarisse."

Impossibly, Clarisse watched the patterns of colored sunlight on the wall swirl and move. Suddenly she realized what she was seeing. It was the man. The light coming through the stained-glass window cast an image of him upon the wall. And that image was moving. Even as she watched, the ghostly man on the wall bowed to her. He straightened then, and smiled. Clarisse felt her heart racing—from fear, yes, but something else quickened her blood as well. A strangely disconnected thought passed through her mind. She had never before seen a man so handsome.

"Who . . . who are you?" she managed to speak. She took a step toward the wall. "How is it that you know my name?"

"I am Domenic," the glowing image of the man answered. His smile deepened. "And I know much about you, Clarisse. I have waited so long for you to find me here. But I knew that one day you would come, that one day you would free me from this prison in which I am wrongfully bound."

Clarisse shook her head. This was maddening. Yet she felt a powerful, dizzying excitement as well. "How can this be?" She gazed to the window, and then to the image of the man on the opposite wall. "Your portrait in the glass does not move, but your image upon the wall does."

Domenic spread his hands. "Glass is brittle, Clarisse. It does not flow. But sunlight. . ." He laughed, a sound like horns. "Ah, sunlight flows like water."

His laughter seemed to catch her, buoy her, and set her adrift. She found herself laughing as well, for the first time she could remember since coming to Evenore.

Domenic's laughter faded. "Now, Clarisse, will you release me?" he asked intently. "There is a way."

She shook her head. Why was it so hard to *think?* The crimson light seemed to fill her mind. "I . . . I don't know."

He appeared to reach a hand toward her, though his

image was confined to the flat plane of the wall. "Set me free, Clarisse, and I will set you free as well. I can take you away from this—from this lonely manor, this bleak countryside." Her heart skipped a beat. "And yes, Clarisse, away from *him*. I'll take you back to Il Aluk, if you wish it, and each night we will dance in a different ballroom, until we have made them all our own."

She took a step nearer the glowing wall. "But how . . . how did you come to be imprisoned so?"

"It was a wicked man, Clarisse." He shook his head sadly. "A man of evil, and a wizard. I dared to stand against him, and he bound me in the glass with a spell. But do not fear. When you free me, I will deal with him." Domenic's smoldering eyes bored into her. "Go to the window, Clarisse."

Before she even thought of whether to do as he asked, she found herself standing once more before the hundredth window.

"Look through the glass, Clarisse. Tell me, what do you see?"

Clarisse leaned forward and peered through the colored shards. She expected to see the village huddling meagerly at the foot of the tor below, or the endless, rolling moor. She saw neither.

It was a sea of monsters.

She felt a scream claw at her chest, but her throat, constricted by horror, strangled it. A thin sheen of sweat broke out on her forehead. She should look away. She knew she should look away. But somehow she could not. The creatures beyond the glass held her morbidly in thrall.

She could see no land, if indeed the beasts stood upon such, for the throng of creatures blotted it out entirely. They were shaped like people, but people from a nightmare, for their skin was a sickly green, and their bloated heads far too big for their twisted bodies. Those closest to the window turned as if they could see Clarisse, glaring at her with mindless, hungry eyes as hot as coals, baring fangs as sharp as shattered glass. Some were clad in rags that might once have been clothes, and here and there Clarisse saw the glint of a silver ring or a gold necklace. It was enough to make her wonder if these things had once been . . . human.

"What . . . what are they?" she finally managed to whisper.

"You needn't fear them, Clarisse," Domenic answered from behind. "Every great lord must have servants. These are mine." His voice seemed to coil around her like a soft cloak. "Now, Clarisse. Reach up to the window. Take my hand."

She shook her head. "But how?" Fear made her entire body tremble. Or was it desire?

"Just reach into the window, Clarisse," Domenic urged gently. "Take my hand. Do it, Clarisse—if you love me."

She could resist no longer. The fear in her breast melted into a powerful, heady warmth. Domenic was so handsome, so compelling . . . so utterly unlike Gareff.

She reached toward the window. Her fingers brushed strangely slick glass. Then suddenly her hand closed about warm, living flesh. She backed away, not loosening her grip, and as though he was surfacing from deep, murky water, Domenic stepped from the glass, a living man.

"Ah, my Clarisse!" he cried. "At last, I am free!" He swept her into his strong, encircling arms and kissed her passionately. His burning eyes seemed to light a fire in her. She clung to him fiercely, kissing him back again, and again.

Domenic whirled her about, and a faint, disconnected fragment of Clarisse's mind noticed that they were no longer in the attic chamber, but in the ballroom downstairs. Yet too much had happened for this small thing to disturb her. Domenic waved his hand, and suddenly a quartet of musicians played upon the dais, clad in coats of the finest red velvet. The musicians began a lovely, lilting waltz, and Domenic spun her about the ballroom in a sweeping, dizzying dance.

"We shall dance together forever, Clarisse," he said joyously. "Forever!" For a terrible moment, his smile was the mirror image of her father's.

"What have I done?" Clarisse whispered, but her

words were snatched away by the sweet strains of music. She gripped Domenic tighter as they danced, spinning about the ballroom until she forgot herself in a sweet, burning dream.

* * * * *

"Clarisse!"

The cry shattered the air of the ballroom. Domenic halted the dance abruptly, and Clarisse's momentum spun her breathlessly away. She looked up to see Gareff in the doorway, his blue eyes blazing. He threw down his rain-soaked riding cape and strode into the hall.

"Domenic," he hissed with contempt. "I should have known you would find a way to free yourself. And I see you have brought your foul goblyns with you."

Clarisse followed Gareff's gaze and gasped in horror. She saw now that the four musicians upon the dais were not men at all, but creatures like those she had seen beyond the glass. The beasts threw down their instruments and leapt to their feet, baring jagged teeth in hungry leers.

"Begone with you!" Gareff cried, waving his hand in an intricate gesture. The four goblyns screamed as each burst into flame. They writhed for a moment in agony. Then the flames died, leaving only four small piles of greasy soot.

"Clarisse, come to me," Domenic beckoned urgently, holding out a hand toward her.

Gareff quickly interposed himself between them. "Stay back, Clarisse," he warned. "I know you have heard rumors from the villagers, rumors of a goblyn lord. Know, then, that Domenic is he."

"In the flesh," Domenic bowed with a flourish. He and Gareff began to circle each other warily.

"Years ago Domenic ruled these lands with fear, Clarisse, capturing villagers and transforming them by unspeakable means into goblyns." Gareff's voice shook with loathing. "But finally I put a stop to him, imprisoning him in the window. Since that time I've traveled the land, hunting down and destroying the last of his vile creations. I tried to conceal it from you Clarisse, to protect you. I see now that I was in error."

"You defeated me once with your trickery, Harrowing," Domenic spat. "You will not do so again." He spread his hands apart. Crimson light crackled between them. "This time you'll discover what it feels like to be transformed into a goblyn yourself." The shimmering energy between his hands arced toward Gareff. Clarisse screamed, backing up against the wall.

Just as the livid, blood-red fire reached him, Lord Harrowing crossed his wrists and chanted in a strange, dissonant tongue. A circle of green light flashed into being before him, blocking the crimson radiance. Domenic swore violently.

"Your magic has diminished during your confinement," Gareff goaded. He muttered the queer incantation again, and the circle of green light grew until it surrounded him completely. Then an emerald tendril began to reach out, pushing back the searing crimson magic streaming from the hands of the handsome goblyn lord.

"And you are a weak old fool," Domenic said between gritted teeth. Scarlet fire crackled around his entire body now, reaching out to entwine itself about the green glow conjured by Gareff's incantation.

Clarisse shook her head in horror, watching as the two wizards assailed each other with all their powers. Sweat poured down Lord Harrowing's face, and Domenic's brow was furrowed in supreme effort. Halfway between them, emerald magic met crimson in a sizzling fount of sparks. Gareff was growing paler, his bushy eyebrows knit in concentration, and Domenic was trembling. Yet the violent juncture of their magics stayed even between them. It was a stalemate.

"Clarisse!" Domenic cried. "You must help me!"

The anguish in his voice rent her heart. She took a hesitating step toward him.

"No, Clarisse!" Gareff shouted. "You must not listen to him. I beg you, come to me. You can help me defeat him once and for all."

Clarisse froze, gazing from man to man. Magic

charged the air with the acrid scent of lightning.

"You are my wife, Clarisse," Gareff grunted sternly. "You must do as I tell you. Come to me!"

"No, Harrowing, she is yours no longer," Domenic gasped. "Her soul is mine. I own her now."

Clarisse shook her head. "No . . ." she whispered, backing away from the two wizards.

"You will never have her, Domenic!" Lord Harrowing cried furiously. The emerald magic surged forward. "Clarisse is *mine!*"

Crimson fire leapt from Domenic's hands, countering the green incandescence. "No, Harrowing. She is *mine!*"

Clarisse let out a wordless cry of anguish. Clutching her gown up above her ankles, she turned and fled the room. She ran down shadowed corridors, leaving the desperate shouts of the two men behind. She made her way through the grand hall. Portraits of Harrowing ancestors seemed to glare down accusingly at her from the walls. Afraid she had gone mad, she ran on.

Abruptly she stopped, blinking in surprise. The stained-glass window shone before her. She didn't remember coming here. But that wasn't important, for now a thought struck her, a horrifying thought, yet terribly compelling all the same. She knew she could not choose between Lord Harrowing and Domenic. One form of imprisonment was no better than another. Each man believed he owned her soul.

But neither did, Clarisse knew now. Her soul was her own, to do with what she would. She would pretend to be weak no longer.

"There is one more choice," she murmured softly, approaching the hundredth window.

She gazed through the shining, colored glass—glass she sensed was older than Lord Harrowing, older than Evenore, ancient as the bleak and shadowed countryside itself. She reached out and thrust her hand into the window. The glass did not shatter. Instead, it was as if she had plunged her arm into warm, ruby-colored water. She felt the touch of a dozen cold, clawed hands on her own.

Clarisse smiled.

Moments later, she stepped through the door of the ballroom to see the two men still locked in their magical duel. Both were gray and haggard with exhaustion.

"Clarisse, you must choose between us!" Lord Harrowing gasped grimly when he saw her.

"Yes, Clarisse." Domenic's rich voice was now hoarse. "Who will you give yourself to? Him or me? You have to choose!"

Clarisse approached the two men, her silk gown rustling. "Indeed?" she said mockingly. "I must choose which of you will possess me like a common brood mare?"

The two men stared at her in shock.

"Isn't that all I am to you?" she went on, her voice hard. The men shook their heads, dumbfounded. Their shimmering magic wavered. "All my life I have been treated as so much chattel—by my father, by you, Lord Harrowing, and yes, by you, Domenic. An object to be sold and bought, or a prize to be seduced, won, and used. But no more." She laughed, a cold, crystalline sound. "You wished to hear my choice, gentlemen. This then, is it: I choose neither of you."

Before either man could react, Clarisse held her arms aloft. "Come to me, my friends!" she called exultantly.

Suddenly a chill mist poured through the doors and windows of the ballroom. From the fog leaped dozens of hunched, twisted forms; eyes glowing ravenously. Goblyns. The creatures circled about the two wizards. Both crimson and emerald magic flickered and faded as Clarisse watched in satisfaction.

"Clarisse, no!" Gareff shouted.

"Please, my love!" Domenic cried.

Their words turned to screams as the goblyns fell upon them.

*　*　*　*　*

The day hung drearily over Evenore, but Clarisse did not mind.

She banished a knot of trembling peasants from the doorstep of the manor, though not before throwing the wretched throng a few coins. She shut the massive mahogany door and turned to wander through the grand hall, running her hands lightly over ancient vases and expensive tapestries. She reveled in the ornate beauty of the hall. It was hers now. All of it. The folk in the village below had taken to calling her the Lady of Evenore. Clarisse supposed the title suited her well enough.

Humming dreamily to herself, she made her way upstairs. She found herself in a room on the third floor, a chamber that had only recently been enlarged and furnished. She approached a black velvet curtain and pulled a golden cord. The curtain lifted, and crimson light poured forth, shimmering off the pearl at Clarisse's throat.

The stained-glass window glowed despite the dimness of the day outside. In the window, intricately portrayed in glass mosaic, two men struggled, locked in a mortal embrace, their faces wearing expressions of frozen, ceaseless anguish.

Clarisse laughed softly as she released the golden cord. The curtain fell back in place, concealing the window, as the Lady of Evenore turned to leave the chamber.

Song Snatcher

Elaine Cunningham

Larson had been a traveling bard for fourteen years, almost half his life, but none of the lands he'd visited could rival the dark beauty of Kartakass. From his perch aboard the riverboat's top deck, he had a fine view of the rugged landscape. Forests of deep, velvety pine covered much of the land, punctuated by a scattering of snug villages. In small, well-tended holdings, farmers wrested crops from rock-strewn soil. Watching over all were the Balinok Mountains. Purple clouds gathered around the craggy peaks even on the fairest of days, brooding over the mountains as if trying to fathom the secrets hidden within a labyrinth of caverns. Larson's hazel eyes drank in the wild beauty with an appreciation that was deep and passionate. He sang softly to himself as the riverboat made its way north.

The sun hung low over the mountains when the village of Skald finally came into view. The young bard let out a whoop of delight at the sight of his long-awaited goal. Grabbing a passing sailor by the waist, he spun her around the deck in an exuberant dance. After her first startled shriek and salty oath, the woman fell into step with the ease of frequent practice.

"And what might we be celebrating this time?" she demanded when the dance spun to a finish.

"What else?" replied Larson gaily. "We're almost to Skald!"

The sailor turned and squinted upriver. High stone walls surrounded the town and cast long shadows onto the silver water. Beyond the walls loomed the ruins of an ancient, fire-ravaged keep. She harumphed and stepped back, folding her arms and regarding the young bard with a mixture of exasperation and amusement.

"Aye, that rubble heap has long been a favorite of mine, too," she said dryly. "Now get below, afore the night falls."

Larson grinned and picked up his viola da braccio, a small viol slightly longer than his forearm. "I'll go to my cabin," he agreed slyly, "but only if you'll join me. You Kartakans need to stop fearing the nights and start enjoying them!" He tucked the instrument into the crook of his elbow and began to play a bawdy little ballad.

The sailor harumphed again and stalked off, trying to hide her amused chuckle. Larson blew her a kiss, then he brushed back a lock of his wind-tossed, dark hair and once again set his bow to the strings.

The sound of a single distant fiddle stilled his arm. Larson lowered his viol and hurried to the rail. Tangled vines and bushes lined the shore and hid the musician from his view, but, oh, the music! Melody that throbbed with acute, searing pain, then soared into a wordless song of such hope and longing that even the gruff sailor paused to listen, her eyes moist with remembered dreams.

Larson hummed along as best he could. When the song ended, he took up his viol and tentatively began to play. He captured most of the melody, if not the magic or the pathos. As he played, the haunting song again reached out to him from across the water, joining him in an impassioned duet.

The music faded into a moment's silence. Bushes parted near the shore, and a dark-eyed woman stepped out onto the rocks. A mass of black curls tumbled over her bared shoulders, and a battered gypsy fiddle was tucked under her arm. She smiled at her handsome partner. Larson returned the smile with a roguish wink and a courtly bow.

"When the moon rises, we will dance," she said casually. She turned and disappeared into the forest.

Larson shook his head in disbelief. "Am I dreaming, or

was I just invited to a Vistana campfire?" he murmured incredulously. The gypsies—or Vistani, as they preferred to be called—were as wild and elusive as their music. They could not bear to remain within walls, nor would most villagers welcome them. Finding the camp would not be easy, but Larson vowed to try. Outsiders were seldom permitted into the Vistani's circle. An opportunity to learn Vistana music was nearly as precious as the one that had brought him to Skald.

In Kartakass, almost everyone sang. There were songs for all occasions, and each season had its own musical contests and festivals. For many months, Larson had been content to wander from village to village, collecting songs and stories. In recent months, however, all talk had turned to the spring festival at Skald. Of even greater interest to Larson was news of a notable bard and teacher who had retired to the village. Larson was eager to learn all he could from such a man.

As evening shadows crept over the river, other, even more elusive musicians began to sing. Mournful and mocking, the cry of wolves came from mountain caverns and forest glades. In Kartakass wolves were as plentiful as seabirds, and nearly as bold. The people lived in dread of night attacks. Even aboard ship, in the center of a broad river, no one felt truly safe. Each night torches were lit before the sun disappeared, and the crew set watch for any creature that might swim for the boat. Larson had never seen this happen, but many a night he had seen the eyes reflecting back torchlight from the not-too-distant shore. Sometimes they were so numerous that it seemed a cloud of watchful red fireflies stalked them along the river.

The sky had faded to silver when Larson's boat docked at Skald. Dock hands sang as they secured the boat. The urgent rhythm of their work song sped their movements in a race against the approaching darkness.

Larson joined the stream of latecomers hurrying for the city gates. Once inside Skald, he made his way down the cobblestone streets, taking in his new surroundings with the trained eye of a storyteller. He saw little to suggest the presence of a festival. Skald looked much like any other large village: rows of sturdy wooden structures topped by thatched roofs and decorated only with bright blue or green shutters. The buildings huddled together, silent and wary. Each narrow window was shuttered and barred from inside, so tightly that not a bit of light escaped.

Then he turned a corner, and the Fireside Feeshka Inn shone like a beacon in the center of a large, stone-paved courtyard. The inn was a vast and sprawling complex, crafted of thick stone and crowned with deep red tiles. Light streamed from its narrow, tiny-paned windows, and the sound of music and laughter beckoned Larson.

Inside the inn, chaotic merriment ruled. A dozen or so musicians played a reel. Everywhere small circles of dancers kept time with the rollicking tune. Even the doves perched on the steeply pitched rafters broke into occasional swirling flight. Barmaids with wheat-colored braids carried trays laden with mugs and steaming trenchers of beet soup. The air was fragrant with the mixed tang of borscht, sourdough bread, and meekulbrau, a bitter local brew distilled from berries. Small tables were scattered here and there so that patrons could enjoy the simple fare in comfort. On one of these tables, a woman danced in an uninhibited testimony to the meekulbrau's potency. Larson smiled and began to ease his way through the crowd toward the bar.

There was but a single discordant note to mar the revelry. Near the bar, a solitary man slumped over a table, staring at his hands. Larson noticed a glint of silver between the man's fingers. As he took a stool at the bar, Larson studied the lone figure with a mixture of sympathy and curiosity. His face was sharp-featured and strikingly handsome, but lacking animation, with skin nearly as pale as the thick, graying blond hair that spilled carelessly over his shoulders. He did not move; he barely breathed.

The barkeep tapped the meekulbrau Larson ordered and slid the mug toward the bard with a flourish. Larson thanked him and nodded toward the solitary man.

"Who is that?"

"Him? That's old Quintish."

This news turned Larson's first sip of meekulbrau into a sputtering cough. "Not the *bard* Quintish!" he said, as soon as he could speak.

"See you anyone here who isn't a bard?" the barkeep retorted. "Even I've been known to tell a tale or two." He raised a single eyebrow, inviting further inquiry.

"I hope you'll share your stories with us," the young man murmured absently. He left his mug on the bar along with a few coins, and hurried over to the bard's table.

Larson made his introductions with a deep bow. "I have been searching for someone like you for years, Master Quintish." He nodded to the empty chair. "May I?"

He waited politely for a response. When none seemed forthcoming, he took the empty seat and carefully placed his viol on the table. Quintish's eyes settled on the instrument, and he gently stroked the polished wood with fingers that were tapered and supple. "What do you want from me?" he asked without looking up.

The voice was a thin, dry whisper, and Larson struggled to hide his dismay. *This* was the master he had long sought? "Will we have the honor of hearing you sing later this evening?" he asked tentatively, hoping he had been misinformed.

Quintish turned his gaze to the tavern window, as if an answer could be found there. The sky had darkened to black velvet, and the moon had yet to rise. "No, you won't hear me," he said emphatically.

The man's voice was stronger this time, and in it Larson heard the resonant bass timbre for which the bard Quintish was famed. The young man leaned forward eagerly. "If you no longer perform, Master, surely you still teach?"

Regret—the first emotion that Quintish had shown—flickered in his eyes. "No, no more students." As if eager to end the discussion, he resumed his study of the silver object.

Larson glanced at it, wondering if therein lay the key to the bard's strange behavior. He held out a hand. "I'm very fond of silver jewelry. May I see it?"

Quintish's hand clenched possessively, and for the first time he met Larson's eyes. He recoiled, as if shocked by the unfamiliar act of making contact. Larson smiled encouragement, and after a moment the older bard relaxed. His eyes seemed to take on more focus, and he handed his treasure to Larson.

It was a small locket. Larson opened it to find a skill-fully rendered miniature of a woman. The painting was faded by the passage of years, but Larson could see that she was a Vistana, a beauty with rippling dark hair and enormous black eyes.

"My Natalia," the bard said simply. "She died one night bearing my son. The babe followed his mother ere morning broke."

"I'm sorry," Larson said awkwardly. There seemed nothing to add. He closed the locket and handed it back.

Quintish nodded acknowledgment, and a strange light dawned in his eyes. "I'm going to her soon," he said with certainty.

"But you said—" Larson broke off, for the bard was no longer listening. As he studied the older man, he noted that Quintish apparently paid little heed to much of anything but his ancient sorrow. Not only was the master bard distracted and unkept, he was painfully thin.

Larson caught a passing barmaid's elbow. He ordered borscht and bread for Quintish, and asked for an empty goblet. When the meal came, Larson produced a small flash from his travel bag.

"This is a specialty from my homeland," he said cheerfully. "In the monastery where I trained, the priests kept bees and brewed a fine mead—dry and full and scented with raspberries." Larson carefully poured a measure of the brew and, cupping Quintish's hands around the goblet with his own, he helped him take a sip.

The strong drink seemed to rally Quintish, for he emptied the goblet and avidly devoured the soup. When the meal was finished, however, the older bard turned his attention back to the locket. Larson made a few attempts at conversation. Finally, regretfully, he crept away and left Quintish to his sorrowful meditation.

"That was kindly done," observed a silver-toned voice at his elbow.

Larson spun and looked into a woman's upturned face. Like most natives of Kartakass, she had fair hair and delicate features. Her pale face was dominated by dark blue eyes, as vivid as violets blooming in snow. She nodded toward the grieving bard.

"It is a sad thing. At last winter's solstice, Master Quintish was brilliant. Now he has forgotten all he knew of music and lore. What is left for such a man?" she said with deep compassion.

"Has he seen no physician, no priest?"

The girl gave a short burst of humorless laughter. "There are few of either in Kartakass."

Larson thought of the pendant he wore under his tunic: the symbol of Oghma, patron of bards. It had been given him in his tenth year, when he first came to train at the monastery. "Perhaps I can do something for him."

Her smile brought rare loveliness to her face. "I wouldn't be surprised. Such compassion is rare in this land. You are different from most men of Kartakass," she mused. Her violet eyes searched his face. "You haven't the look of a Kartakan. From whence have you come?"

Larson paused, wondering how best to answer this. "I came from a land called Cormyr," he said slowly. "How far it is from here, I do not know. As a scholar and bard, I travel much. One day while I was rowing a skiff, a strange mist covered the river. When it lifted, I found myself—"

Slender fingers sealed his lips, cutting off his words. "We have many superstitions in Kartakass," she said lightly, but there was real fear in her eyes. "It is best not to speak of such things within walls."

"Ah." Larson bowed an apology. "But dancing is permitted?"

"Encouraged," she responded with a smile.

Ellamir—for that was her name—was graceful in his arms, and as they danced, her expressive eyes warmed with invitation and promise. Larson knew he should thank Oghma for his good fortune, but his gaze kept straying to the table where Quintish sat. The older bard listened to the dance music with a mixture of puzzlement and longing on his ravaged face.

When the dancers stopped, happy and exhausted, they settled down to drink and listen to the singing of ballads. Two tales were sung, then someone called for Ellamir. Murmurs of approval and anticipation rippled through the crowd as she picked up a small harp and made her way to the center of the circle.

She put her slender hands to the strings. A sad silver melody flowed from her fingers, and then another, and then the two entwined in a complex, compelling dance. Larson had never acquired more than the bare rudiments of the instrument, but he considered himself a fair judge of harpers. Seldom had he heard Ellamir's equal. Despite her youth, she was a harper of uncanny skill.

Then, when Larson was convinced that never had music been so exquisite, Ellamir began to sing. Her silvery soprano floated through the room like the chime of fairy bells. He listened entranced, forgetting for the moment even his concern for Master Quintish.

Then the words of Ellamir's song caught Larson's attention. It was a woman's lament for a lost love, a bard who had scorned her. She died, but her obsession did not. From her shattered dreams rose the *Lhiannan shee*—

"Silence!"

The indignant baritone command shattered the silvery web of Ellamir's song. The village meistersinger leapt to his feet, his blond mustache quivering with rage. Many of the bards in the circle shifted uncomfortably. Some made signs of warding. Ellamir's hands dropped to her lap, and two bright spots of color flamed on her pale face.

Larson cleared his throat to break the uneasy silence. "I am a stranger here," he said slowly, "but I don't see how Ellamir has done wrong! The song was lovely and her voice superb, even by the high standards of Kartakass."

"It is not her bardcraft that we fault," the meistersinger

said severely, "but her judgment."

"But what is a . . . lanan she, that you fear it so?"

"Enough! That is something of which a bard should never speak. In this land we have a saying: Be careful what you call, for you might receive an answer!"

"Wise advice," Larson said gravely, but he caught Ellamir's eye and winked. A small, grateful smile touched her lips.

Hoping to change the mood of the crowd, Larson rose to his feet and lifted high a mug of meekulbrau. He then drained the bitter brew without coming up for air.

"Feeshka!" he shouted, and tossed the empty mug to a burly, sandy-whiskered balalaika player. The man caught the mug, accepting the challenge with a grin. In the language of Kartakass, "feeshka" meant "little lies," and these tall tales were a passion in this land of long winters and dreaded nights.

As the evening wore on, many mugs were drained and tossed as the bards strove to outdo each other in absurd storytelling. Larson was delighting the crowd with a ribald story of elves and satyrs when he saw Quintish rise abruptly. With quick, fevered movements the older man made his way toward the back door, and then out into the night.

Larson improvised a quick ending to this tale, then he slipped away to follow the bard. The courtyard was brightly lit, but Quintish was not to be seen. The only sign that the bard had passed through was the sharp staccato of boots on cobblestone. The sound was fading away quickly.

For a moment Larson paused, uncertain what to do. Calling for help would be effort wasted, for few Kartakans would venture outside during the night. Yet he could not let the bard wander alone. Taking a deep breath, Larson sprinted off in pursuit.

The city walls shrouded the streets in shadow. A scant half-moon had crested the mountains, but it cast little light. Larson ran as fast as he dared through the dark streets. Once, he stumbled over something he sincerely hoped was a night-prowling cat. Then the sound of Quintish's footsteps stopped, and the city was eerily silent. Larson was beginning to despair when he heard the shriek of wood against wood. He raced down an alley toward the sound.

There was Quintish, heaving at a thick board barring a door in the city wall. Before Larson could reach the bard, the door gave way and Quintish was off. He hurried through the field, as unerring and unwitting of his surroundings as a sleepwalker.

A distant howl sliced through the night, and again Larson hesitated. He remembered the Vistana camp that lay nearby. For some reason, wolves seemed to avoid gypsies. Armed with that scant assurance, Larson followed the older bard through the field and into the forest.

Quintish came to rest in a clearing, a place of quiet and unearthly beauty. Faint moonlight played on the ripples of a small stream, and moss formed an inviting, velvety cushion along the banks. Larson crouched behind a copse of trees some hundred paces away, waiting to see what had lifted the master bard from his strange lethargy.

A dark-haired woman stepped lightly into the clearing. She was a compelling beauty with an oddly familiar face. Recognition hit Larson like a fist, and he sucked in a quick, startled breath. It was the woman in the locket, the long-dead Vistana whom Quintish mourned!

Larson watched, barely breathing, as Quintish buried his hands in the rippling mass of the woman's hair and drew her close. She pulled playfully free of the bard's embrace and leapt onto a rock in the middle of the stream. There she seated herself, arranging her skirts seductively as she spoke words that Larson could not hear.

Quintish began to sing, and his celebrated bass voice lifted in a wrenching declaration of love that seemed torn from the fabric of his soul. Larson listened with awe and longing. Only once before had he heard such a fevered, passionate song. It ended far too soon. The raven-haired beauty leaned toward her bard, offering a kiss in reward for the tribute.

A cloud passed over the moon, casting the clearing into darkness and granting the lovers a moment's privacy. When the cloud passed, the woman was gone.

Quintish lay face down in the stream.

Larson leapt up and ran into the clearing. He dragged the bard onto the mossy bank and turned him onto his back. A silver chain caught the moonlight as it slid from the master bard's limp fingers. Larson picked up the locket and absently thrust it into his own pocket. He bent down and put his ear to Quintish's chest. The bard's breathing was shallow, his heartbeat weak and slow. Larson shouldered the older man and half-ran, half-staggered back toward Skald. Urgency quickened his steps: he had come too far to lose Quintish now!

It took all Larson's eloquence to persuade the owner of the Fireside Feeshka to open the door for them. Once they were inside, the village meistersinger took over. He had Quintish carried to his room, and the inn's herbalist roused from slumber. Many suspicious glances were sent Larson's way, but he answered questions with a frank, open manner. He told them that he'd been distressed by the bard's confused state of mind and unwilling to let him wander alone in the night. He described the gypsy woman, but out of respect for Quintish he omitted the tale of a long-lost love. When all the questioners were satisfied, Larson hurried upstairs and took up a vigil outside the master bard's door.

It was there that Ellamir found him. She had listened to Larson's story with a growing sense of dread. Quintish had once shown her a picture of his long-dead wife, and the Vistana woman Larson described sounded far too much like Natalia for Ellamir's peace of mind. The words of her own song haunted her, and she felt as guilty as if she had summoned—

"A Lhiannan shee," she breathed.

Ellamir shook her head in self-recrimination. Why had she not seen it sooner? It would explain the strange malady that had stolen Quintish's songs and drained him of life. Sometimes called the Ghost of Obsession, a Lhiannan shee was an undead vampiric spirit that feasted upon living bards. The creature could appear in any form that might appeal to its chosen victim, usually that of a beautiful woman or half-elf. Once enspelled, a bard could think of nothing but his nightly meetings with his love. An enthralled bard willingly, eagerly gave up his essence to the seductive creature, one kiss at a time.

A door creaked, and the herbalist stalked into the hall. Larson rushed forward and demanded news of the bard.

"Dead," the herbalist muttered as he brushed past Larson. "Poisoned."

Relief swept through Ellamir. Death by poison was a sad end to the master bard's life, but infinitely less fearsome than the one she had imagined. She turned to Larson. The naked anguish on his face stunned her.

The young bard sank to the floor. "Too late," he mourned. "To travel so far, all for naught!"

Ellamir knelt beside him and encircled his shoulders with her arms. "I share your loss," she said sincerely.

"You cannot know what I have lost," Larson murmured through his hands. "All that Quintish knew, the wealth of songs and stories!"

An ugly murmur rose from the taproom below. Ellamir rose to her feet, her lovely face creased with worry. "What now?" she muttered, and quickly fled down the steps. She returned but a moment later. "Some of the men will go to the Vistana camp at first light to seek the woman you described. They will demand justice."

"Master Quintish is dead, for all that," Larson observed dully.

"And that is a great loss," she agreed. "Still it is not so grim as it might have been." She quickly confided her fears to Larson. "Think of it! At a gathering such as this, a Lhiannan shee could choose any bard here as her next victim."

Larson stared at her for a long moment. Slowly the light returned to his eyes. "Thank you, Ellamir," he said fervently, and drew her into his arms. "In my land we have a saying: There is no night so dark that morning will not come."

To a woman of Kartakass, such words of hope were as rare as roses in winter. At that moment, Ellamir lost her heart to this man, so different from anyone she had known. She framed Larson's face with her hands. "Morning will come, but not for a while," she whispered.

* * * * *

The sun's first rays stole across Ellamir's face, awakening her as if with a kiss. She stretched like a cat, smiling as she remembered. A moment passed before she realized that she was alone in Larson's room. Puzzled, she threw back the covers and quickly dressed.

Once she was in the taproom, however, Ellamir could not bring herself to ask anyone about Larson's disappearance. She could not bear the ribald jesting usually directed at festival liaisons. Reluctantly, she accepted an invitation to join several other bards for morningfeast. A sleep-eyed barmaid brought to their table small loaves of freshly baked bread, soft cheese, berries, and ale.

Ellamir broke open her loaf without much interest and idly watched the fragrant steam rise. As she lifted her eyes, she saw Larson walk through the front door. He seemed deeply distracted; she called his name several times before she got his attention. Instantly his charming, boyish smile lighted his face. He came over to the table and claimed half of Ellamir's loaf. While they shared morningfest, he regaled the group with amusing, irreverent stories of his early life in a monastery.

After all had eaten, the tables were cleared and pushed against the walls to make room for the dancing. One of their morningfest companions took up a viol and played the first few measures of a popular rondeau. He called for Larson to join in.

A puzzled expression flickered in Larson's eyes, so quickly that Ellamir was not entirely certain she had seen it. Surely she was wrong; after all, hadn't he played that very rondeau just the night before? Suddenly Ellamir thought of Quintish, and there was a horrifying logic to Larson's night-time walk and seeming forgetfulness. Ellamir's hand flew to her mouth. She held her breath and silently willed Larson to play the song, to dispel her fears.

But the young bard slipped an arm around Ellamir's waist and begged off, saying he preferred to dance.

"Don't you know that tune?" Ellamir prodded.

Larson dropped his arm. "If you don't care to dance,

you need only tell me."

She drew back, startled by his harsh words. But Ellamir's passions ran deep, and her concern for Larson far outstripped her hurt. To her knowledge, no one had ever escaped the spell of a Lhiannan shee.

Ellamir recalled the night before, and her delicate face hardened with determination. Though she did not command the compelling magic of an undead spirit, she was, after all, a living woman. She would do what she could.

All that day, she remained at Larson's side. He was a charming companion, but as night approached he grew increasingly restive. In desperation Ellamir enticed him up to his room, hoping to detain him with wine and wiles.

Faint moonlight lit the bard's room, and he drew her close in a tender embrace. For the first time, Ellamir began to hope. When he handed her a goblet of mead, she drank deeply, savoring the ripe with the taste of summer fruit and the warmth of Larson's intense hazel eyes. Setting down the cup, she entwined her arms around her lover's neck. As he returned her kisses, she began to drift into a dark, sensuous haze. Larson lifted her in his arms and carried her to the bed.

Her violet eyes drifted shut as he lowered her. With a sigh of relief, Larson eased out of her embrace. Once again the strong sedative in the raspberry mead had done its work. He only hoped that he had not misjudged the dose this time.

Larson began preparation for his next trip to the forest clearing, and every other consideration fled from his mind. All he could think of was the mysterious woman he had met there last night, and his aching compulsion to see her again. For the third time, he hurried out into the night.

She rose as he entered the clearing, and even though there was no wind, the gossamer layers of her gown swirled about her slender form. The woman looked a bit like Ellamir, but she far surpassed human beauty. Silvery hair, purple eyes, delicate features, and elegantly pointed ears proclaimed her fey race.

The lovely elf beckoned him close. Larson took her hand reverently, and it seemed to him that the scent of flowers rose from her cool satin skin. As she swayed closer to claim her second kiss from Larson, he steeled his will and drew a powerful amulet from his pocket. He raised it high. Blue light burst from the amulet, and the young priest of Oghma began to chant the words of a powerful sacred spell.

The elf's eyes widened in terror. She tried to wrench her hand away, but Larson's magic held her fast. The amulet in his hand hummed with power and silent song, and the lost, lilting dance tunes of the Kartakan festival flowed back into his mind. The elf began to dissolve as he reclaimed the songs she'd taken from him. Her features melted and flowed into a new shape. She writhed in anguish as her body became more lush and compact, and screamed when her silvery hair burst into a rippling, dark mass of curls. Suddenly, Larson found himself gripping the slender bronze wrist of a Vistana woman. The elf he had loved to the point of madness was gone. Though his heart nearly broke with grief, Larson continued to chant.

More music flowed into him: the aires, laments, and dances of Kartakass that embodied the essence of the bard Quintish. Again the Lhiannan shee changed form, this time into a beautiful, flame-haired vampiress. From her the bard wrested songs of passion and dark hunger that no human voice had ever sung. A dainty farm girl pleaded and wailed as Larson's magic drained from her the ancient tunes of a shepherd's pipes. A beautiful half-elven minstrel yielded up songs in a language Larson had never heard, but understood, nonetheless. On and on the magical battle raged as Larson took stolen songs from the undead creature.

The light of his amulet flared into an explosion of power that rocked the forest clearing and cast Larson to the ground. Through the thunderous roar, he heard the creature's cry of denial and rage. The magical force dissipated, and with it, the last incarnation of the Lhiannan shee.

For a long moment, Larson clutched the ground,

dazed and nearly blinded. When he could draw breath, he groped for his amulet. The light and the power that had led him to the Lhiannan shee had faded; the creature was truly gone.

Larson remained in the clearing until the moon set behind the mountains and the sky flushed with the first pink of dawn. There he regained his strength and savored his triumph. Hundreds of stolen songs resounded through his mind, stretching it to limits of musicianship he had only imagined possible. Nearly all his life he had studied and stalked the Lhiannan shee, but nothing he'd learned in the monastery of Oghma had prepared him for this night.

He had first encountered a Lhiannan shee in his fifteenth year, when he heard a victim sing in the throes of enchantment. In that moment, the fledgling bard found his life's quest. He studied all the arcane lore on the Lhiannan shee, and his faithfulness—or, as some named it, his obsession—was rewarded by the priests with a holy amulet. With it, Larson could restore a bard's stolen essence. The first test of this power changed Larson's life.

One night some men brought an enspelled bard to the monastery, bound and drugged. Larson began the sacred chant, and felt for the first time the rush of music and power as the amulet reclaimed the bard's stolen essence. All the bard's songs, all his memories and experiences and tales, flooded Larson's mind with an intoxication greater than that of any wine. Drunk with the music, he willfully neglected to cast the last, vital part of the clerical spell, that which would restore the afflicted bard. Larson kept the stolen songs. The bard died, and his unknowing companions did not fault the young priest.

But one bard's life was not enough. From that day, Larson sought those who'd fallen under the spell of a Lhiannan shee. In ten years, he had found only one other. Then came the trip through the mists, to a land of dark enchantment that seemed uniquely suited to his purpose. Yet even in musical Kartakass, such creatures were rare. Quintish was the first afflicted bard Larson had found, and Larson had nearly ruined his chance with a too-generous dose of poisoned mead.

Ellamir's words the night before suggested another way. As she pointed out, the Lhiannan shee would seek a new victim. Why should Larson mourn the loss of an enspelled bard, when he could go directly to the source? Draining the Lhiannan shee had brought Larson success beyond his dreams, and more songs than anyone could learn in a lifetime.

But once again, Larson found that it was not enough. There was so much still to learn, so very much. Already he hungered for the kiss of another Lhiannan shee.

At first light Larson returned to the inn, deep in thought. He was startled by the sight of Ellamir in his bed. She sat up slowly, fighting off sleep and still groggy from the potent mead.

Quickly recovering his composure, he sauntered into the room and greeted her with a kiss. "I thought you would never awaken, my love," he said cheerily. "Too much wine last night, I fear."

He saw the relief cross her face, and suddenly he realized that she suspected his involvement with a Lhiannan shee. Well, there was one sure way to convince her that she was wrong.

Much later, they nestled in each other's arms and spoke of things that could be said at no other time. "I feared that I'd lost you," she confessed, a little shamefacedly. "First Quintish, and then it seemed that—"

Larson stilled her with a kiss. Ellamir was lovely and loving, but her intensity was becoming a bit much. The festival lasted but four days, and though Ellamir was a pleasing diversion, he had no interest in the enduring passion her violet eyes promised.

As if she sensed his thoughts, as if she feared her serious tone might be displeasing to the lighthearted youth, Ellamir gave him a gay smile and shook a finger at him in a teasing parody of warning.

"Do not toy with me, Sir Bard," she said with mock severity. "For I would surely die for love, and come back to haunt any lady you chose over me!"

Her words hit Larson with the force of inspiration.

Once again, Ellamir had suggested a solution to his problem! He might not find another Lhiannan shee in Kartakass, but perhaps he could *create* one!

He doubted not that Ellamir's heart was his for as long as she lived. If all went well, after her death he could possess her songs, perhaps even her skill with the harp!

The young man's slow, charming smile returned to his face. He took both of Ellamir's hands, and fervently vowed his undying love for the talented, beautiful bard. But as he spoke, his eyes strayed to the table where stood his flask of raspberry mead.

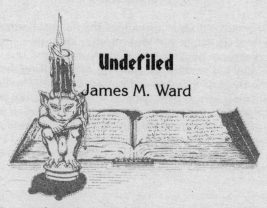

Undefiled

James M. Ward

Fire ran through the knight's veins, burning his body in the pain of his struggle. His legs blazed from the constant effort to keep upright, to keep moving, and his arms felt like two hot pokers pressing into his shoulders as he held the unconscious form of his sister. Each breath ripped spikes of fiery agony into his lungs.

A vampire!

His mind raged at the thought of the attack. For the hundredth time, he mentally reviewed the battle. Guilt caused him to wonder if there was anything else he could have done to save his sister from the coma the vampire had forced on her.

In his mind's eye, he again saw the battle, saw himself drawing the sword:

Leaping from his bolting mount, the knight had activated his weapon's magic to slay the vampire with sorcerous fire and enchanted steel. The sword struck the vampire's side, and the creature hissed and turned away from the still form of his sister. Rising with bloody fangs, it stepped back. The knight would never forget the red glare of the undead monster's eyes.

"Leave the woman and go," the creature growled.

Its words tried to beguile; the vampire's magic prodded at the knight and commanded him to flee . . . but his sister's life was at stake.

He raised his sword again and uttered a word. A blast of intense mystical heat bathed the vampire in flames. The creature must have had some type of magic of its own, because it stood proudly in the flames, flames that had turned many a previous monster into ash.

"Your puny weapon's magic can't hurt me."

Despite his words, the vampire was favoring the side where the enchanted sword had first struck. Maybe the magical flames weren't effective, but the cold steel of the blade had done its work well.

"Begone, foul creature. I've holy water and the cross of my god to protect us." Filled with energy, he raised the silver cross. The flames of the sword were an afterthought, but they worked well to cast the shadow of the cross on the undead thing.

The creature's flesh erupted in fire, causing the monster to swirl into a man-shaped green mist.

"As the sun sets, Knight, I will be back with the strength darkness gives me. Prepare to feel my fangs when your sword and cross mean nothing," warned the creature's disembodied voice.

The green mist had blown away with the wind.

The remembered words of the monster sent new strength into the knight's legs. He had to find somewhere to hide before night fell. He wondered if he should again try to wake Larom, but before nothing had roused her from the unnatural coma. Holy water, healing potions, even gentle slaps had failed to open her eyes.

As the mists lifted before him, the answer to several prayers appeared ahead in a large valley. At the valley's center was a walled city.

Surely within the walls of that place there would be protection from the vampire.

* * * * *

The duty of the first speaker was to get the congregation quiet and ready for Friar Whelm's sermon. During the first speech, people could still walk in, as latecomers often did, but when the White Friar spoke, no one was allowed to disturb his message. Though he demanded absolute attention, Friar Whelm never gave a long sermon, for he believed temple pews and worshipers' bottoms weren't meant to be long in contact. First speakers, on the other hand, often weren't as merciful: today's first speaker, a merchant, rambled on pointlessly.

"Estrangia, my brothers and sisters, is a dark, gloomy city cowering behind its tall walls. Fear has governed the people of the city for centuries. Fear's name is Crave, a vampire who considers our metropolis his dinner plate and has feasted well for over four hundred years.

"In the past, those bold enough to attack the undead monster have found themselves transformed into his minions. Today, such bold folk are gone from the dreary streets of Estrangia.

"In the past, those brave enough to try to move elsewhere found themselves drained of blood before they left the valley. Today, there are no brave people rousing the populace with talk of stakes and crosses.

"In the past, those stout of heart enough to remain in Estrangia prospered. And they are we: enduring, hardy souls living under the fear of the vampire. Today, Estrangia grows, filled with the lucky and not so lucky as the vampire Crave feeds once a week.

"Our Temple of White Hope presents the only bright spot in our lives. Legends tell of the founding of the temple, even before the coming of Crave. One day a white-robed friar came within the walls of the city and brought hope and love with him. From that time on and down through the centuries there has always been a single such friar serving the needs of the growing city.

"Our temple is now the oldest building in the city. Its white marble walls glow with a holy power, even in the darkest part of the night. Its single spire rises above the gray and black buildings around it, and nothing is taller. The bell in the spire brings worshipers to the daily service. Ringing clear and heavenly over the other sounds of the town, the bell welcomes the middle of the day.

"No matter how large the city grows, there always seem to be enough benches to welcome worshipers into the spotless temple walls. Not everyone in Estrangia worships at the temple, but everyone respects the good friar who works here. Whenever Crave takes a victim, the good friar visits the families, even if they don't believe in the God of White Hope. His comforting words make things seem better somehow.

"Let's raise our voices in song as the last of us enter to hear the words of the friar."

In reply to these words, the congregation began to sing, and the melody filled the temple to overflowing.

Once the parishioners finished singing, they sat. It was the normal crowd of people today. The poor tended to rest in the back where no one could see their threadbare clothes, while the rich took up positions in the front for just the opposite reason. Kids, being kids, fidgeted beside their parents. Sometimes they were put on their mothers' laps, and that would quiet them. Sometimes a caring father would give them a sweet to nibble on during the service.

There was one special white pew right at the front of the temple.

It was for the friar's favorites.

Every service, several distinguished worshipers were ushered by the friar himself to the front of the temple. All sorts sat up there at one time or another: rich, poor, meek, mild, young, old—though for some reason there weren't many old people in the congregation.

Those sitting in that special pew were smiled upon by the faithful. At each service, Friar Whelm explained the act of kindness that entitled each worshiper to a place of honor on the front pew. Sometimes a child had been kind to his little sister or had helped around the house. At other times someone had given gold to a soup kitchen. Always, the person's good deed had aided the community.

On rare occasions during the service, a spark would emerge from the friar's eyes or hands and float out to one of the people sitting in the special pew. The spark was a sign from the gods that the person was being blessed. It could happen anytime during the service, though lately it had been occurring right after the first hymn. While Friar Whelm was speaking, a white light would flow from him and touch one of the people on the special pew. The person would fall over, unconscious, and others, hoping the spark would touch them, would joyfully catch the lucky soul. That person would awake tired but happy a few minutes after the pale spark

spewed out. It was also said that these blessed individu-
als looked older and wiser from the touch. Parishioners
tended to be nice all week long with the hope of sitting in
the special pew and being recognized by the gods.

Now all eyes turned eagerly toward the front of the
temple, where Friar Whelm stood in long, flowing white
robes, preparing to speak. To his right, in a pearly marble alcove, stood the ten-foot-tall statue of the God of
White Hope. The snowy, cold stone robes of the statue
were just like the pearly ones Friar Whelm always wore,
robes that remained clean no matter what work the good
friar performed. The short, snowy hair and balding head
of the god resembled those of Friar Whelm as well.
Some said this was the merest coincidence. Others
whispered it would be grand if an incarnation of the god
actually serviced their temple. Many were oblivious to
such talk, but proclaimed for everyone to hear that the
friar gave a damn good sermon.

He began to speak, and his pure voice reached out to
everyone; he never needed to shout. Today the talk cen-
tered on lost ones.

Three days ago, Crave had taken a little girl, and her
family sat in the special pew for this service. Their grief,
clearly written in their tired eyes and slumped bodies,
was shared by many around them. Several times during
his sermon, the friar approached them and repeatedly
prayed for the little girl. He spoke eloquently, almost
wistfully about the unsullied innocence of the lost
daughter. Speaking with the sound of grief in his voice,
Whelm sermonized about the little girl, about the intelligence in her eyes and the energy in her tiny body. He
reached out to the parents and touched them, tears
rolling down his full cheeks. Both parents began to
quietly sob, bending over with exhaustion and grief.
Ever louder, ever more vigorously, he eulogized the
power of this family and their strength in loss.

Just when he was coming to the main point of his sermon, the doors burst open at the back of the temple. A
huge warrior, outfitted in plate mail, strode boldly through.
In his arms he carried a beautiful, unconscious woman.

"Someone please help us!" The knight took three

more steps and collapsed from exhaustion. Even then, as he fell, he made sure the woman took no harm.

Men rose to remove the warrior from the sacred place, but Friar Whelm waved them back. "He seeks aid, and he could not have known of the weapons ban in the temple. What is your name, Sir, and what has happened to you and this fair one?"

The warrior threw off his ebony helm and revealed a care-worn face, rugged and handsome. "I am Lord Tenet. . . . A vampire attacked us. . . . Our horses went wild with panic. They threw us. . . ." He gasped in exhaustion. "I fought the creature, but it seized my sister, Lady Larom. . . . Help her, please!"

"Rest easy, young warrior. I'll do what I can, with my god's help. Did you kill the vampire?"

"No, damn me for a weak fool. My sword cut deeply into it, but the monster turned into mist and floated away, leaving me to tend my sister. Cease this questioning! Can you help her, or must I . . . " He was too weak to continue.

Lifting Lady Larom up as if she were a weightless child, Friar Whelm placed her on the snowy marble altar. The white of the stone matched the ashen color of her flesh.

"Pray for her, my people," Friar Whelm asked as he examined the huge bruises on her arms and face. He noticed several hidden pockets in her crimson gown, holding what he took to be mage's spell components.

Lord Tenet needed help to rise and come to the side of his sister. "She's only seventeen. If anything happens to her, I don't know what it will do to me."

"I feel the same way about my flock. Don't worry, I can take care of most of her wounds. Lady Larom—is that her name?"

"Yes, that's right. Her friends and I call her Lar."

The friar closed his eyes and stroked his hands over the unconscious woman's tangled hair. Her pallid expression marked her blood loss as did the fang marks in her neck. Even near death, her beauty showed through. There was an energy and power in this woman that the friar very much appreciated.

Several of the more helpful parishioners gathered behind the warrior at the altar. They noted the woman's pallid skin and wan movements. Her eyes opened, but there was no intelligence behind them. "Crave's work for sure," some of the watchers whispered. Most of the congregation held little hope for her survival. Looking at the brother, some of the parishioners backed away at the thought of having to tell him about his sister: it was common to stake the heart and take the head of someone bitten by Crave.

A smile filled Whelm's face as he chanted words of hope and love. His hands moved deftly and swiftly, circling over the still form of the woman. A chalky mist spewed from his palms and drifted over the bruised flesh. Frosty blasts of air hit everyone in the congregation.

Truly their friar worked a miracle this day.

In seconds the woman was lightly covered in snow.

"What insanity is this?" Lord Tenet reached for his weapon, but didn't have the strength to draw the blade. "Stop him, someone stop . . . " The warrior fainted. He'd done too much that day, already, and his body collapsed into blessed unconsciousness.

Friar Whelm stopped his hand motions and lightly blew the snow from Lady Larom's body. The flakes of frigid whiteness wafted throughout the temple and melted as they touched the worshipers. Each one singled out by these cold flakes sighed in wonder, touched in a mystical way by the icy flakes.

Most of the snow, however, fell on the warrior. His bruises and fatigue melted away with the flakes. Where wounds were, now only chalky, undefiled skin remained on brother and sister.

The healing took a toll on the friar. He looked visibly older. One of the congregation moved to steady the friar, but was waved off.

Reaching down, the friar helped Lady Larom rise from the altar. She shook her lovely head, and a cascade of raven-black hair moved in a tumble down her shoulders to her supple waist. Life and intelligence clearly returned to her.

"Where am I?"

"You're in a house of hope and light!" Friar Whelm said, loud enough for everyone to hear.

"Hope and light!" The congregation chanted back, all with mindless smiles on their faces. *Miracles!* They'd seen wonders to tell their grandchildren. Truly wondrous occurrences filled their hearts with joy.

Lord Tenet woke, surprise filling his face. A born warrior, he knew how long it should have taken to recover from the exhaustion of the vampire battle. Stretching his whole body, he found himself free of pain and full of vigor. In the past, he'd never had much use for friars and their talk of peace and brotherhood, but this cleric had saved his sister and healed him.

"Brothers and sisters, let us welcome Lord Tenet and his sister, Lady Larom."

Awe and respect filled Lady Larom's face. "I've never met anyone like you. What did you say your order was?"

"I serve hope, the light of truth. If you will permit me, we can talk of the faith in the weeks ahead as you rest and recover."

"Rest!" interrupted Lord Tenet. "That's just what we *can't* do. We're going to ride out of this valley while there's daylight!"

"You will be attacked by minions of the vampire in countless numbers, numbers even too great for your magical blade and battle skills."

"Then I'll lead you and some of these other men to kill the creature," Lord Tenet said. "I've killed vampires before. We must go, now!"

Many in the congregation shook their heads. They knew what the knight was feeling.

"My order and my people are of a peaceful nature. None of us can stand against the might of the undead Crave. With faith in the light and enough hope in your heart, the monster won't come and attack you again. Won't you believe, Sister?" The friar took Lady Larom's hands in his and smiled down at her.

A shining glow of faith filled her pale face as she turned toward her brother. "Tenet, I feel so weak. I can't help you with my magic. Won't you wait until I'm stronger?"

"I've weakened the creature. I know it. Now is the time to strike. Won't anyone help me?"

Everyone's head bent down. No one could look into the bold eyes of this powerful man.

"My congregation, be not ashamed that you don't go with this man. None of us are warriors, but all of us do what we can for our families and city. Lord Tenet, if you must go—and I recommend against it—you'll find the creature in the cemetery north of the walls. Crave is guarded by minions who don't fear the light, and by cunning traps. It will know of your coming and will be prepared. May hope and light go with you, my son."

"Hope and light," The congregation intoned without conviction.

Lady Larom turned, trying to leave with her brother, but the good friar held her back. "You can't go with him. I have restored his strength, but you are still weak."

One hand went to her brow, and a rush of fever overtook her.

"I, I *do* feel faint. Please, where can I lie down? I need to rest."

The friar took her into his study, and the congregation let itself out. Lord Tenet stood for a moment, worried about his sister. He couldn't think of a safer place for her than behind the walls of a temple. Holy ground was usually safe from most foul creatures, and especially the undead. Grasping the hilt of his sword with grim determination, the warrior went to kill the foul beast that dared to harm his sister. Looking at the sky overhead, he saw the sun come out of a light scattering of clouds and took it as a good omen.

*   *   *   *   *

Lord Tenet easily found the tumble of toppled gravestones that marked the cemetery beyond the walls. Warrior's senses, sharpened from hundreds of battles, searched the area for traps and enemies. Several large mausoleums dotted the fenced area, but a large one in the center caught and held Tenet's attention.

"Why is it always the center one?"

As he had expected, skeletons, zombies, and ghouls leapt out at him as he approached the vampire's lair, but his sword of magical flame made short work of these lesser foes. Holding his flaming blade aloft, he charged the crypt door with quick steps and an armored shoulder. The ancient wood gave way with a splintering crack, and he was inside.

"Crave! I've come to kill you!"

The light of day and the fire of his sword revealed a huge stone sarcophagus in the room beyond, and on the far side of the room, a set of stairs spiraling down into the depths. There was no doubt where those stairs led, but a sound of crying came from beside the stone coffin, in this very room.

As Tenet carefully maneuvered the area, heading toward the sound, he noticed that the lid of the coffin was carved into the shape of a warrior at rest. The stone man in plate mail had a comely form and bold manner. Tenet couldn't help thinking it was in just such a noble coffin that he would like to be buried when the gods saw fit to grant him death.

He rounded the corner of the sarcophagus and discovered a little girl curled up into a ball, sobbing, her hands covering her face.

"Don't hurt me, don't hurt me!" She screamed in panic.

"The vampire must have been keeping you for a snack. You're not large enough for a full meal." Tenet sheathed his sword and tried to get the spratling to uncurl. "There, there, little one. No one is going to hurt you. We'll get you back to your parents, but first let's get you into the sunlight, where you'll be safe."

A gravelly voice erupted from the tiny fanged maw, "No!" Talons reached for the knight.

Suspecting something like this, he'd kept a stake in his hand. Lashing out, in one strike, he put the little one to rest for eternity.

"You won't find me so easy to destroy."

Lord Tenet whirled as Crave floated into view from the stairway. The foul stench of rotting flesh and ancient blood wrapped around the monster in a dusky mist while dark clouds rolled out from it and blocked the sun's rays.

Twirling in the air, the vampire floated to the top of the arched vault and glared down at Lord Tenet.

The knight drew his sword and blasted flame at Crave.

"I thought we'd decided your magical fire couldn't hurt me," the creature hissed with a smile. "Now it's my turn."

With a few gestures and words, the vampire cast black bolts of energy from its talons, striking the knight in the chest. His armor glowed white for a second, then dimmed. The knight appeared unharmed.

"A magical sword and magical armor? I had no idea you were such an enchanting fellow. I guess we'll have to do this the old-fashioned way." The monster hurled itself down on the knight. As it fell, its talons, muscles, and fangs grew larger and larger.

Flaming sword out, the knight pierced the breast of the monster as its talons ripped and tore at his armor. With every blow, the vampire raged at Lord Tenet, but the knight grasped his sword with two hands, causing it to tear and burn at the vitals of the undead thing.

"Yes, it hurts! Yes, it burns! But you'll be dead before your blasted weapon kills me!"

The vampire ripped off the shoulder plates and helm of the knight and sank its fangs deep into his throat. New energy filled the vampire as it hurled away the sword that had caused it so much pain and ripped apart the body of the human who dared to use the weapon.

In one gruesome moment of raining blood, the knight was unmade.

For hours after the battle, the vampire lay gasping for life on the cold stone floor. Shards of the sword were still buried in its flesh, preventing it from regenerating to full health.

Crave could hardly think, the pain was so terrible. It needed more food; it needed the sister and knew where to get her.

Many hours later, it gathered enough energy to turn into mist, then floated into the city, seeking a meal seasoned with revenge.

*   *   *   *   *

Sitting by herself at the funeral, Lady Larom seemed fully recovered from the previous day's attack. Several congregation ladies had donated their clothes and other accoutrements to properly outfit her for the temple service. An ivory shawl draped a snowy blouse and creamy, form-fitting skirt. It was obvious to the women that Lady Larom looked good in white things.

Many had sadly shaken their heads at her hair. The lustrous, dark tresses of yesterday were peppered with gray today, and the sheen of her hair was also gone.

"It must have been the horror of the attack," some had said behind concerned hands.

"The loss of a loved one can often do that, too," others had added, thinking of times when the friar had come to their houses.

But now, all the voices were silenced, for Friar Whelm was beginning his eulogy.

"We are here today to honor and mourn a brave man. Some would argue a foolishly brave man, but I would never say that." Whelm's hand reached out and touched the now-graying hair of Lady Larom.

Looking up, her devotion and respect plain to read in her face, Larom shed a single tear.

"This wonderful lady took up the faith of hope and light, taking it into her bosom. That strength comforts her in this sad hour. The vampire must have taken her brother as it has taken others down through the centuries. But she sits here, a shining example of what hope can do. Pray with us, brothers and sisters."

The service was simple and quick. Friar Whelm made sure Lady Larom went home with respectable people, people who would feed her well and take care of her, people who would show her the ways of the city and help her learn how wonderful it was to be a part of the temple.

Friar Whelm wanted her around for a long, long time.

Filled with vigor it hadn't known in centuries, the friar-coraltan closed the doors of the temple, warding them from entrance. The portal wasn't locked, but anyone coming to the doors would suddenly find something else to do.

It needed to rest after feeding so well. It wondered if it should have used an energy spike on the woman: the herd expected such things. But the undead thing was so full that the thought of taking more energy during the normal feast time made it nauseated.

Then it felt a presence in the warded temple, an energy source it hadn't felt for centuries.

"Crave?" the coraltan asked the empty air. "Didn't I tell you never to come in here after your first foray into the city?"

Turning from mist into monster, the vampire gasped in pain while leaning against the altar.

"I had to!" Fear and anger mixed with a plea for help in the sound of the vampire's voice. "Part of that warrior's blade is still in me. It burns; the pain is unbearable. Do something, or I'll perish and you'll be left to your own devices."

"Perish? You can't do what you've already done, and perishing is something we all do but once. Go back to your comfortable dirt before I become angry."

"I want the sister. You've sensed the energy in her. I must have her, and I will. Today. Now!"

The coraltan shed its robes like a snake shedding its skin. Standing before the vampire, the creature revealed its true, undead nature, its desiccated and worm-infested body, and the vampire knew itself for the puny thing it was. Crave curled up before the transformed friar, much as the vampire girl before Lord Tenet.

"I won't hurt you while you remain useful. Come, let me heal your wounds and show you the light of truth."

A spark spewed from the tangled maw of the coraltan and sucked energy from the vampire. It used that energy to heal the wounds the magical sword had made. Judging from the damage done to the vampire, the warrior would have made a nasty foe. The monstrous friar was glad.

"Did you turn the knight into a minion, or drain him dry?"

"After the pain he caused me? His body is in pieces all

over my lair. His weapon and armor hide forever in a sarcophagus ten men couldn't open. Now, may I have her?"

"The Lady Larom is much too tasty a morsel for the likes of you. Feed, as we agreed, in your own way. I'll feed in mine."

The coraltan stroked the head of the vampire as the creature rested in his lap. A look of wearied peace was on the face of the vampire.

The White Friar started growing new robes and thought of its next sermon . . . and the need to talk again about patience.

The Briar at the Window

Roger E. Moore

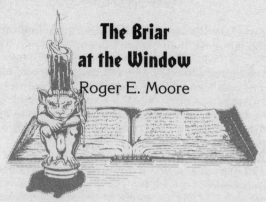

. . . Even as Lord Kromfier tear free his helmet & roar aloud in the Havok to rally his Folk, the Will of his men be break before the Daemons claws & teeth in the Darkness of Castle Harith. The Shriek of men clutch in the arms of fiery Monsters ring the Halls as their flesh be burn; bloody men beg for Succor yet be trod under-foot and crush; the Laugh of Daemons echo in the ears of the Lost. At such pass did the Wyzards of Demune lose sight & sound of the Lord in their magic Pool, yet they renew not the spell, for they see that all be Finish.

Of the Fate of Lord Kromfier & his Paladins we know No-thing, but for a Squire who be trample & be forget as dead. In the Blood of his Folk he lie, by-pass & forget by Daemon-kind. He hear in the Dark much of Awfulness, then crawl to tell all to a Lay-priest before he be perish of his many grave wounds. Before he breathe last, the Squire speak of the great Screams that—

Something tapped at a window.

Lord Godefroy looked up through his pince-nez, his habitual frown deepening. He sat motionless in the half-gloom, the old volume propped in his lap on a crossed leg, and waited. Light from the oil lamp's flame flickered once across the steady darkness.

The tapping came again, fainter now. It was from the corridor to the entry hall.

Lord Godefroy took a slow, deep breath, though he didn't need to, and exhaled through his nose in silent rage. The yellowed bookmark was carefully fitted into place, and the volume reluctantly set aside on the tea table. Lord Godefroy treasured his history books, and the early evening, after the sun had fallen and all was still, was his favorite time for reading.

He quietly got to his feet, the spell of the moment broken. Something always happened. He never got to finish that book, and he had been trying to read it for the damned knew how long.

There was but one thing to do about it.

Lord Godefroy left the room in no great hurry. He had all the time in the world these days. In the soundless hall, out of reach of the lamplight in the study, he shuffled through darkness that cloaked him like a second skin. Faint moonlight lit the bare tree branches outside on the lawn, seeping through the streaked and aged windows that opened into the old mansion.

The tapping came once more. Lord Godefroy stopped by the second of eight tall, black-framed windows. There he waited again, all patience, staring down at a dirty corner windowpane through his thin lenses.

A long, whiplike branch swayed gently into view, pushed by the cold wind and lit by the white moon. The briar swung close, then struck the windowpane with a faint tap.

Lord Godefroy reached for the briar. His right hand and ruffled sleeve, colorless as the moon's rays, slipped through the dirty pane of glass to seize the branch. He felt the thorns but no pain from their pricking, felt the wind but not the bitter cold. He was long beyond that now.

"Suffer now, dear wretch," he whispered with bared teeth to the briar in his hand, then willed his words to happen.

The briar writhed with the jolt of the Touch and tried to curl away from him, but too late. It withered and broke apart into rotting dust before it could escape his grip, reduced to blackened debris. Lord Godefroy fancied the briar even gave out a cry of agony like an animal as it did, though in a voice too small to be heard.

The entire briar bush then collapsed, its shattered

stems and leaves scattering out of sight. It was dead to its last root, a ruin that would feed no worm.

Lord Godefroy pulled his hand back through the old, streaked glass. The satisfaction he felt at the briar's demise was a cold glow inside him, new snow where his heart had been. To his discomfort, though, the emotion passed quickly and left him feeling hollow, useless. Lord Godefroy squinted out the window at the empty space where the briar had grown. His teeth clenched together in frustration.

The briar's death was not enough anymore to satisfy. It was far too easy most times to dominate and punish. His Touch would age any living being by decades in mere seconds; plants and small animals suffered and died too rapidly for him to take a lasting pleasure in their agonized struggles. People were different—their deaths were more satisfying by far. One gained a sense of genuine accomplishment in hewing them down, the treacherous and ungrateful mongrels. Humans were like waste matter, vile trash to be disposed of in vile ways. Abruptly, almost unwillingly, Lord Godefroy remembered the feel of the mattock in his hands, the smell of manure and blood, the sound as the mattock bit into her soft flesh—

Something creaked overhead. Startled, Lord Godefroy blinked and looked up at the vaulted ceiling. Only motionless shadows gathered there.

What had he just been thinking of? The powerful images had fled. He strained for the memory but caught nothing. Was he becoming senile even in this form? He looked down at the window and remembered the briar, but nothing else. Nothing moved on the lawn outside in the moonlight. Reminiscing, perhaps. . . .

With a slow look around, Lord Godefroy left the corridor. He looked behind him twice before entering the study again, then closed the double doors with a thump of finality.

* * * * *

Back in his study, Lord Godefroy stopped by the tea table next to his favorite chair and stared down at his book. It was no use to pick up his reading; his mood was spoiled by the interruption. Perhaps tomorrow night there would be time. He lifted the old brown tome in his hands and headed reluctantly for a bookcase.

I've done this before, he thought, too many times before. Each time he wanted to relax and take a few moments to himself, something ruined it. Something would pay with its life for the interruption, but then he wouldn't be in the mood for his favorite book, for which he had paid so much to that leech, Harlan Attwood. Served the old mongrel right to be run down by his own horse, laid up in bed a cripple and a pauper when he died at last.

That wouldn't happen to me now, thought Lord Godefroy. He paused before the bookcase, looking up to locate the space among the books from which he'd pulled his favorite history. Five shelves up, only three feet beyond his reach.

He willed himself up, his slippered feet leaving the faded red carpet. Not a sound, he marveled; not a sound. Flying was the easiest thing. He came to a stop at eye level with the shelf he wanted, then glanced over his shoulder and saw how small the rest of the room looked as he hovered above it, so near the ceiling.

Lord Godefroy almost smiled. Though his frame was still bent and his face furrowed with three-and-a-half score years, the aches and creakings of his once-rotting body were gone. He felt no pain now, none at all. And he could fly, fly like a leaf from a dead tree, fly like smoke from ashes.

And he had the Touch now, too. A handy thing, that Touch.

The oil lamp's flame flickered in its glass prison. Something moved in the shadows to Lord Godefroy's right. He flinched, almost dropping his book, and threw up a hand to shield his face from a blow.

No blow came. Slowly, he lowered his arm. It was just a shadow, a shadow on the wall over the coat rack. It flickered in the light as he stared at it, then was gone. A flaw in the lamp's glass, or a cobweb, perhaps.

Lord Godefroy realized he was breathing very quickly,

almost panting. Mortified, he stopped it at once. He didn't need to breathe. It was a weakness. He had no weaknesses now. Humans were weak, but not him.

He lowered himself to the floor and straightened his posture, sniffed abruptly, then turned to a wall mirror to smooth his high-necked shirt and long black coat sleeves. He glanced up at the space over the coat rack as he did. Nothing. He sniffed again and regarded his reflection severely. His behavior did not become the lord of Mordent, master of the Gryphon Hill and Weathermay estates. If he was now a god in his own domain—as he surely was—then he should act the part.

Perhaps it was time to look at his mail. It would have been delivered around noon, while he was out walking the borders of his property. He nodded to himself in the mirror and left for the dining room.

* * * * *

The mail came once a week, delivered by some means that Lord Godefroy had never bothered to divine. It merely appeared on the dining room table, neatly stacked to the side of his empty teacup and saucer. Though his appetite was long gone, he insisted on retaining the cup and saucer. Any manor lord would have done it. Old habits never died without good reason.

He made his way to the dining room, pausing only once to brush fingertips along a dusty tabletop. He had arranged for the house to be kept clean with the magical assistance of a minor spirit or two, something a business associate had arranged for him in the old days. The spirits weren't doing their jobs well, though, and being unalive were immune to punishment from the Touch. Lord Godefroy grimaced as he rubbed his dirtied fingers together.

At the doorway to the candle-lit dining hall, he nodded with satisfaction as his gaze fell upon the long, cloth-draped table. As hoped, the week's mail awaited him.

With a sigh of relief, he settled into his dining chair, adjusting his pince-nez. Perhaps now he would have the time he was cheated of earlier with his history book.

Woe to that which disturbed him now, he thought to himself. He would have his due and more.

Thin, translucent fingers plucked the first of three letters from the stack. Behind Lord Godefroy, more candles came alight, attended to by the spirits who silently looked after Gryphon Hill and its master.

"Schupert," he whispered, glancing at the envelope. He knew the spidery handwriting well. He slid a long, gnarled fingernail under the back flap, breaking the wax seal, then pulled the thin page from the envelope and read quietly.

Comings and goings, plots and plans—the usual web. Schupert was too smart to say much, too unwise to say nothing. As was his habit, the old wizard's letter was so cryptic as to be virtually meaningless, nothing more than an acknowledgment of the receiver's existence and a request for any tidbits of information that the lord might have heard. Lord Godefroy set the letter aside, only half read. He knew of no rumors for the withered fool's ear, but he would have passed none along if he had. Schupert could burn for all he cared, and with the old wizard's constant meddling in the affairs of domain lords, his burning would not be long delayed.

Lord Godefroy cleared his mind and selected the second letter, noted the handwriting. His frown faded, evidencing less disappointment than usual.

"Narvis," he murmured. "My dear Narvis." It was the first good turn his evening had taken.

Narvisek Grellar was someone Lord Godefroy understood. Dear, twisted, betrayed Narvis. His wife Viola, soft and heavy and stupid as a cow, had objected to Narvis's taste for vivisection. How like a little boy Narvis was, restless and curious, eager to see the inner workings of a still-living creature whose flesh had been entirely removed. Viola, Lord Godefroy had heard from other sources, had threatened to expose Narvis as a monster. Dear Narvis couldn't have that, so soft Viola became his next vivisection subject, right on their own kitchen table.

Narvis never spoke of Viola's fate, but someday Lord Godefroy would have to ask how long it took for soft, stupid Viola to die. He would have loved to have seen her in her last moments on the table, every nerve and muscle open and burning, a red thing no longer human.

A twisted thumbnail broke the seal on the letter, and he held two scrawl-covered pages aloft in the candle-light. Not much on his experiments this time—only reports of bad weather and his fears that he was falling ill again. Narvis was obviously preoccupied, the letter scratched off in a hurry.

Lord Godefroy finished his reading in bitter disap-pointment. He had hoped for an accounting of a recent experiment, an exciting one with a human subject. Narvis had a lovely gift for detail and understatement, though his script and grammar stank. The letter was set aside with a sneer of disapproval. Narvis was capable of much better.

In an ill humor, Lord Godefroy picked up the last envelope. His narrow gaze fell on the cursive handwrit-ing on the cover.

Wilfred.

Time stopped.

Wilfred.

The name filled his eyes and head. It was all he saw and thought.

Wilfred.

No one living called him Wilfred now. No one ever had. No one but Estelle.

Lord Godefroy clutched the letter like a serpent's neck and saw her again, the earlier memory now in full bloom:

The wide, dark eyes on her pleading face. Hair like oily black smoke. His open hands and the red explosions on her pale skin. The dancing shadows in the barn, the frightened horses. Her white blouse. *She had looked at another man.* Her upraised left arm, fingers splayed. Black strands of hair thrown violently across her face. *She had looked at another man and wanted him.* The mattock by the hay bale. *Wilfred, dear gods above, no, Wilfred, no.* The mattock's swing like the flash of an insect's wing. The red on her blouse. Screaming, the screaming—*Wilfred, Wilfred.* The mattock high again. *She had wanted another man. Wanted another man.*

The mattock's swing an endless blur, the blouse all red, all red, all red, all.

Wilfred, said the envelope.

An automaton, he opened the seal. He pulled the single scrap of paper from within it and held it to the light.

A moment later, he flung it away with a hideous cry, unaware of the strength with which he threw himself back from the table. His chair was dashed to the floor. Candles throughout the room flickered; some went out. The scrap of parchment lay on the tablecloth beneath a wavering candle. Its words were clear even from a distance in dim light.

What became of the lord when they caught him at last?

"No!" Lord Godefroy roared at the room. "You are—it is not—not possible!" He struggled with the words as he wrung his hands, ridding them of the feel of the letter. "You are not alive! You cannot do this to me, you filthy whore! You damned whore!"

But he knew there was no reason she couldn't do it.

What was good for the gander was good for the goose.

He fled so quickly that one of his shoulders passed entirely through a door frame. It wasn't proper, but he never noticed.

The candles in the dining hall swayed with his flight.

Then, one by one, they began to go out.

* * * * *

He regained control of himself at the foot of the grand staircase. He was breathing again with rapid, shallow breaths. Stop it, he ordered himself, clasping the post and railing. Stop it at once. I am the lord of Gryphon Hill. I am the master of Mordentshire, sovereign of life and death. Nothing can take that away from me. Nothing can take anything away from me. No power in this world or beyond. She cannot even hurt me, much less kill me.

Lord Godefroy broke into high, brittle laughter. He had killed *her,* not the other way around! She had no power over him, even if she had come back from the grave herself. He was being a fool. She could not kill him now.

His pale hands clutched the stair railing until they resembled white crab claws. With an effort, he loosened his grip, slowed his breathing, and, coughing loudly, forced himself to stop breathing altogether. Then he settled back on the stairs to regain his composure.

Well, so she was back. If she was back, maybe . . . maybe Amanda was back, too. It wasn't unreasonable, though the reason for the miserable child's return was beyond him. Amanda had counted for nothing in his life. A girl erroneously born in the place of the boy who should have slipped from Estelle's womb. Amanda had betrayed him by her very existence. He remembered her, too—not as clearly as Estelle, but he remembered the face in the background, the bowed head, her whimpers as he beat her with his belt, time and again. A worthless child, though beating her did bring pleasure, after a fashion.

Amanda had been there in the barn, too, hiding. Screaming. She had rushed him. He'd fallen back, surprised, while the child cradled her mother. Her hair was like strands of gold in the lantern light. He even recalled her last words—*I hate you, I hate you, you evil old man.* She threw something at him while he was still holding the mattock. *I hate you,* she screamed, clutching the body of her mother on the dirt floor of the barn as the shadows danced.

It was strange that he didn't remember actually killing her. There was nothing to it, not even passion. Afterward, he had covered up her death as he had Estelle's: the bodies dragged into the stall, the pistol fired by the stallion's head, the great horse dancing in fear on the wet bodies. Shooting his best horse was the only way out. No one had argued over it; everyone knew his temper and his grip on power. Case closed. He lived alone after that. It was better than living with a whore and a whore's worthless daughter.

Lord Godefroy put a withered hand over his face, as if to cover his eyes from a light. His pince-nez fell and dangled from their ghostly white chain.

There was something more. Something more had happened.

It would not come to him now.

He flung his hand down and in a rage stood up on the stairs. His mind was playing tricks on him. He was still lord of Gryphon Hill. He would be its lord forever. If Estelle wished to confront him, by the Mists of this cursed land, he would give her what she wished.

He had the Touch.

Perhaps it would work on the dead as well as the living. Perhaps he should find out. It might be worthwhile.

The master of Gryphon Hill set his pince-nez in place, then set out for the stables, teeth clenched. Let the little trollop frighten him *now*. She had started it all. She had looked at a stable hand, looked at him with undisguised lust. She had betrayed her lord and husband. The whore had started it all. Now her lord would finish it.

The halls passed. The kitchen. The drawing room on the right. The back entry hall. Candles lit at his approach. Damn those magical bastards, they had *better* move when he appeared. He was the lord of Mordentshire, the colossus of Gryphon Hill. He did not wait to open the door at the end of the hall. He strode right through it.

"Light!" he roared, entering the stables. Light sprang up from a lantern ahead of him, shedding a weak radiance over the remains of the stables. Gray wood stalls, dirt and rotting hay underfoot, bridles and ropes disintegrating on their pegs on the wall.

He saw the mattock against the wall, seized it, and swung it high with the strength of a young titan.

"Estelle!"

Quick echoes answered him. Scampering noises came from all directions. Only field rats.

"Estelle!" Louder now. The walls rang.

Nothing. No one.

"You dirty whore, come out! I command you as your lord and husband! Estelle, you crawling slut, come face me!"

The scampering faded. Nothing else was heard.

He whirled.

No one appeared.

He held the mattock high over his head for several

minutes more, until he slowly lowered it and held it in front of him.

Nothing came.

He kicked at the stall doors. Rotten hay. Dried manure. A hoofprint. Nothing.

Silence.

The mattock swung at his side, in one hand.

"Bitch," he said under his breath. It was just like her. But . . .

Maybe it hadn't been Estelle after all.

He considered this, standing by the dim lantern. There was no Estelle here, no Amanda, no trace of either of them. Had the letter been a trick itself? Had someone, another power in this land, made him a fool? Or was a darker motive in store—a power play? A takeover? Gryphon Hill was not undefended; the lord of Mordent-shire was hardly weak.

He didn't know.

He would have to go back and look at the letter. He knew Estelle's handwriting. He'd been a fool and worse not to have checked it.

He hefted the mattock in his thin-boned fingers, looked around at the wreck of the stables, then set the tool aside where he'd found it. She wouldn't come back where the mattock was kept, anyway. She knew it all too well, much too well, he was sure.

Lord Godefroy drew himself up. He checked his shoes, even knowing it was unnecessary, then went back inside the house. He opened the door this time, too. Old habits.

In the stillness of the stables, the lantern's flame faded away. It grew very, very cold.

* * * * *

The candles came to life in the dining hall as he came through the doorway. He walked up to the table where the paper and envelope lay and reached down for them with a quick hand.

He froze. Ashes. The candle by the letter had fallen over as it had melted. The flame had consumed the paper, lightly scorching the tablecloth below. The letter was just ashes now.

He stared, then touched the ashes with a pale fingertip. They crumbled.

That was that, then. He'd never know. Still . . .

He left the hall, walking thoughtfully toward his study. He knew what he had to do. As is given, so return. Repay a blow in equal coin. Look for a gift in the market where a giver found his gift for you. Lord Godefroy's study held dozens of papers and letters collected over the years of his new life at Gryphon Hill. It would be simple to find the guilty party with logic and deduction. It could be anyone. But he had the time for the hunt. He had lots of time.

He passed a window looking out over his estate, gave it a glance as he slowed. Moonlight fell across the grounds, the leafless trees lost in frigid autumn, the low hill not far away.

He looked at the hilltop. No sign of the cemetery. No trace of where Estelle and Amanda's coffins lay, their contents long devoured by worms, returned to the filth from which they'd been born. Not even the moon would shine there. All was right with the world.

He walked through the double doors to his study, knowing they were locked and lacking the patience just now to be proper. The lantern was lit. All was still. He walked to his desk and quickly began to shuffle through a sheaf of old papers he pulled from a drawer. He turned around with the papers in his hand and saw the history book on the tea table, fallen open.

Forgot to put it up, he thought, then remembered that he had.

He looked up at the bookshelf beyond in the lantern light. The space where he had placed the book was empty. But there had been the shadow, and he had not finished the job.

Something moved in the corner of his eye.

"What . . ." he said, and spun on his heel to see if something had crept up behind him. With a mixture of rage and dread, his dark eyes searched the room. The papers were clutched to his breast like a shield.

It was nothing. The whore and her daughter were back, perhaps. But he was still the lord of his estate.

He put his papers aside and reached out for his book. His eyes fell on the open pages, looked down at the passage there.

. . . Before he breathe last, the Squire speak of the great Screams that break the Darkness as the Daemons begin their work on the Lord, in the lonely Halls of his own Castle. And of these Screams the Squire hear no end, even in his Dreams. . . .

Something scratched at a windowpane behind him.

He whirled and saw the closed double doors.

The scratching came again, fainter now. From the hall beyond.

Lord Godefroy slowly closed the book, without looking down at it. He frowned in silence at the doors.

This had all happened before. More than once. It seemed that it was dreadfully important to him that he remember why it kept happening.

He left the book lying on the table by his chair. Adhering to tradition, he walked over, still staring at the doors. He carefully unlocked and opened them.

The dark hall beyond was empty. Moonlight crept in through the tall, old windows.

The scratching sound, from the same window as before.

It would seem that he hadn't finished the job of killing the briar. He was getting senile after all, even in this new sort of life that wasn't quite life, in a body that wasn't quite a body.

But he was still lord of Gryphon Hill. He still had the Touch.

As was proper, he walked down the hallway to the window, peered out until he saw a pale branch swing close, then stepped forward and put his hand through the streaked glass window. He caught the branch.

It was not a branch. It was an arm like ice.

Something white floated into view behind the glass and fluttered in the moonlight. He let go—too late.

Freezing cold hands clamped down on his wrist and drove nails of ice into his now-solid flesh.

He screamed with the shock of pain he had not felt in years uncounted. He flailed his arm to dislodge the clawed apparition. White fingers gripped his arm, fingers attached to bare, translucent arms.

A face came up to the window.

The face was dead. Its wide eyes were frozen open, and its black hair crackled as it pressed against the dirty glass, as if it had been walking a long time in the cold on its way down the low hill where the moonlight never fell.

Lord Godefroy howled like a wild animal. He fell back, staggering, and struck the far wall of the hallway.

He pulled the face and the body behind it through the window as he did. Its claws dug into the bones of his arm. Its wide, frozen eyes silently drank him in as the mouth opened, a black wound on a face like a snow-field.

Wilfred, said the face as he screamed.

He threw himself forward, trying to push it all back through the window. He beat at the fingers that gripped him. He swung his arm to knock the fingers off against the windowpanes. His other arm passed close by the windowpanes.

Something grabbed that other arm, the iron grip tearing old flesh. Something pulled itself into the hall as he struggled back, placed blue lips to Lord Godefroy's ear.

I hate you, it said. Its cold breath blew worms and grave rot over Lord Godefroy's fine black jacket and ruffled shirt. The lord of Gryphon Hill saw its white eyes next to his own, set in a face of cold blue stone, and he screamed and screamed and screamed, until his screaming was all there was in the universe.

Wilfred. One pulled him toward his study.

I hate you. The other pushed.

He was in his study. Four cold arms brought him to his chair. His limbs flailed. He kicked his feet at them, striking nothing, helpless as wood in a vice. Their touch made him solid. His new body was just like his old. It couldn't fly. It couldn't fade through the chair. It ached. It bruised. It was cold, cold, cold. And his Touch was gone.

They forced him down in his chair. The small, dead blue face mouthed words as it levered his right arm down against the arm of his favorite chair. Only one word issued from the black mouth of the dead white face as it pressed his other arm down as well. It was terribly easy. They had done this many times before.

In the depths of madness, Lord Godefroy now remembered the first time this had happened, ages ago, the night he had killed his wife and child. Then it all happened again, the night after that, then all the nights after that, on forever, until he escaped them at last by drinking bitter herbs he bought from the apothecary, falling into his last sleep in this very chair. The next day he had his new body and new powers while the powerless old body was buried far, far away, and he came back to Gryphon Hill to rule again. He had been free, free, free!

That freedom had lasted one day.

Estelle and Amanda came back that night, unstoppable. And they were back the night after that. And the night after that. It was too much to live with, even in death, and his mind was gone from trying to block it out.

A cold, foul breeze brushed his face. He opened his eyes for a moment. It was the wrong thing to do.

The dead faces were against his own. Their breath washed over him, suffocating him with rot. He was beyond remembering that he didn't need to breathe.

But he did remember what came next. He always did.

His mind fled. He screamed. It was a new sound, a great magnitude louder than before. It was not the scream of a lord or master or god. It was an animal's scream when it knows of an unspeakable thing and is joined to that thing forever, without end, without escape.

Dead lips touched the skin on his face. Cold teeth would touch next.

Estelle and Amanda had missed dinner ages ago.

With sightless, hungry eyes, they again began to eat.

Nocturne

Allen C. Kupfer

The black skies contained no moon this night, and apparently the stars had fled as well. Richemulot was blanketed in the darkness of midnight, except for the candlelight the citizenry provided themselves. But since most of the good citizens had retired for the night, even the candlelight was feeble, and it could be spotted only here and there throughout the town of St. Ronges.

No candle burned in the home of Klaus Nellak. He had retired hours earlier; after all, his duties as burgomeister of St. Ronges required much devotion and even more energy. His day had begun at sunrise, and he had worked hard and long until well past the dinner hour. He had debated with members of the town council, made judgments on several important civic matters, dealt severely with a couple of chronic troublemakers, and, most importantly—at least to him—raised his salary for the next year. The two bottles of wine he had consumed at dinner might have had some small effect on his retiring early, too.

He slept soundly, but some slight vibration, some minor deviation from the normal calm of his room, caused him to open his eyes for a moment, and he stared into the almost complete darkness. He felt a weight upon his chest, as if someone were pressing a hand against his heart. Bah! he thought: perhaps the physicians were correct after all. Perhaps I should not drink so much. Perhaps the wine—and the tremendous stress of his civic duties—were taking their toll on his heart. Perhaps . . .

The weight shifted on his chest. Had he not been half asleep at this moment, he would have sworn that the weight *walked* from one side of his chest to the other! He put his hand on his chest, expecting to feel his heart beating, but instead felt . . . fur, and then a stinging pain in his thumb. Something bit him! He cried out, and his cry was answered with a throaty squeak. Then the weight leapt from his chest.

The burgomeister sat upright, lit a candle, and surveyed the room. In the far corner, two illuminated eyes gazed defiantly at him. His own eyes adjusted to the light, and he realized the source of the weight, the stinging pain, and the squeak: it was a rather large, mangy rat. The creature squeaked again and dashed out of the room.

"Hell's Bells!" Klaus Nellak exclaimed loudly. "Those damnable creatures! Now they've invaded *my* home! I'll put a stop to this . . ." He yawned, closed his door and window, blew out the candle, and got back into bed. He pulled the blanket up around his neck and continued his thought: ". . . tomorrow."

* * * * *

The next morning, the St. Ronges town council was called in for an emergency meeting. The members muttered to each other, wondering what the source of the emergency could be.

"Perhaps His Lordship, the noble Claude Renier, has asked for an accounting of the town's funds," suggested one member. "God help the burgomeister if Richemulot determines the amount spent on his food and spirits!"

The rest of the council laughed, until a door opened and the burgomeister took his seat.

"And what is the source of this merriment, gentlemen? Klaus asked, reproach in his tone of voice. "There is little to be jolly about."

"And why is that?" asked the councilman who had caused the laughter.

"Vermin!" said Klaus.

Another councilman frowned. "Good sir, there is no need to refer to us in that manner!"

"No, no," Klaus corrected. "Vermin, gentlemen! Specifically, rats. They are everywhere. They have overrun this town. One of those diseased, hideous rodents bit me on the hand in my own bed last evening." To confirm his statement, the burgomeister held up his bandaged thumb.

A councilman nodded in agreement and said, "You are correct, sir. I have heard the beasts in my own abode. I haven't had the courage to visit my own wine cellar in weeks. I believe there are scores of them hidden down there."

"But there have always been rats in St. Ronges," stated another civic leader. "Rats exist everywhere. They are impossible to control, impossible to eradicate. We might as well hope to do something about insects."

Klaus weighed the councilman's words, cupped his chin in his hand, and muttered, "Perhaps."

Loud words from the rear of the chamber answered him: "Perhaps *not*."

The entire council turned to see the man who uttered these words. He was tall and handsome, resplendently dressed, and exceedingly arrogant in demeanor.

"Who the devil are you?" the burgomeister demanded.

"I, good sirs," the man answered, "am simply a wandering tradesman. My trade is the extermination of pests. It is the trade my family is renowned for. I am a piper of Hamelyn." In his hand was a crude wooden flute.

* * * * *

The rat sat on her lap and squeaked continuously. Jacqueline Renier found the rodent's tale so amusing she bellowed with laughter. The rat, too, squealed with delight. When she was able to compose herself, she said, "That was a very amusing story, my friend. I hope your bite causes the burgomeister's thumb to swell as large as his opinion of himself."

The rat leapt from her lap, ran around in a small

circle, and squealed once more.

Jacqueline pondered for a moment, then said, "Yes, I think I will go to town, but not with you, my little friend. I shall remain in my present form. My grandfather will arrive in St. Ronges within the hour. He plans a surprise visit to that odious burgomeister and his council of cretins. I want to hear all about it from him."

The beautiful young woman stood up and smoothed the wrinkles that had formed in her gown. Then she headed for the city square. "Go, my friend, go dine on more of the burgomeister's menu of cheeses . . . unless you prefer his appendages, that is!"

The rat bolted into a sewer as she headed off, amused at her own wicked sense of humor.

* * * * *

"Permit me to understand you correctly," Klaus said. "You are stating that you are the famed Piper of Hamelyn?"

The council members snickered, and one said, "And I am Lloth, Queen of the Spiders." The comment drew laughter from his colleagues.

"No, sir," the piper corrected. "You are merely a presumptuous boor."

Flustered, the insulted councilman turned to Klaus. "We must throw the scoundrel out, sir. How dare this rogue insult a member of the council!"

"Oh, settle down, Werner!" the burgomeister said in response. Then he turned to the piper. "Speak. Do you claim to be the Piper of Hamelyn?"

The man smiled. "I claim to be—and in fact I am—*a* piper of Hamelyn, blessed with the same abilities as my brethren. Like them, I possess the knowledge of magical airs and hypnotic ditties, which I am wondrously able to perform on this instrument."

Interested, Klaus asked. "So there are many pipers about?"

"Only a very few with the talent of enchantment."

"And how is it that you arrive here in St. Ronges at this particular time, when we are indeed in need of an expert exterminator of filthy rodents?"

The piper stepped toward the council. "Perhaps we should attribute it to a fortunate turn of the Wheel of Fortune, good sirs. For you and for me."

The burgomeister and the councilmen whispered among themselves while the piper relaxed and gazed around the council chamber, noticing the marvelous carpentry of the furniture, the beautifully detailed if garish design of the stained glass windows, and the finely crafted goblets the men were drinking from.

But the piper grew impatient with the men. "Sirs, if you do not wish my services, you merely have to inform me of that fact. There are, I am quite certain, many burgs not very far away that would gladly welcome me." He let his pipe slip into a small leather compartment on his belt. "But it is a shame. I assure you I could have rid you of every single rat within a ten-mile radius of this town square. My talent is infallible, my musical charms quite overwhelming."

"You are a braggart, young man," Klaus retorted. He turned briefly to the council members, then faced the piper again. "But no one hates rodents more than I. I want to see them gone. They have given the town of St. Ronges an air of decrepitude that I don't want it to have. Particularly since His Lordship of Richemulot, the noble Claude Renier, will be visiting us anon."

"Perhaps a demonstration of my musical prowess will help you decide whether to employ me or not," the piper suggested.

The burgomeister scanned the faces of the council members. They all seemed interested. "Yes. I think that is an excellent suggestion. Councilman Dragova mentioned the rats in his wine cellar before. Why don't we go there and put your alleged powers to the test?"

The piper bowed flamboyantly. "I am at your service."

Klaus and his council stood up, and they and the piper headed out the door. But two guards, both heavily armed, blocked their path.

"What is the meaning of this?" Klaus demanded angrily.

The guards separated, and Claude Renier stepped

between them.

"I am," Renier said, smiling. "My itinerary has changed, Klaus, my friend. I trust my early arrival will not inconvenience you?"

Nervously, Klaus answered, "Er . . . no, Your Lordship."

"You and your fellows seem headed on an important mission," Renier continued. "I would love to accompany you. So rarely do I get to see one of my town councils in action. What is the nature of your mission?"

Klaus tugged at his collar in order to loosen it and wondered how to explain where they were headed. "I'm afraid it's rather mundane, milord."

"Speak, man!"

"If I may be so bold, Your Lordship," the piper interjected. "The citizens of this good town are having a rodent problem. I was about to demonstrate my technique of extermination."

His Lordship smiled. "Oh. Rats, eh? And this is a major problem, is it Klaus?"

"I'm afraid it is. They will take over if we do nothing."

"Will they?" Renier laughed. "Will a rat rule Richemulot someday? Who knows? In any event, I would very much like to see this young man's demonstration, so I will accompany you. Please, lead on."

"A-As you order, Y-Your Lordship," Klaus stuttered, and the group of men set off toward Councilman Dragova's home.

As they walked through the streets, a beautiful young woman, unseen by the group, wondered where her grandfather, the Lord of Richemulot, might be headed with such a sorry group of men. She resolved that she would follow them, but would do so in secret.

* * * * *

All of the men, including Claude Renier, assembled at one end of Dragova's rather extensive wine cellar. Lighting yet another candle, Dragova himself pointed at several partially emptied bottles of port and cried, "Look. The foul beasts have eaten through the corks, damn them."

Then, unnoticed by everyone except Lord Renier, a white mist seeped into the room and moved behind several casks of amontillado at the far corner of the cellar.

"What in heaven's name is that foul odor?" the burgomeister said. "Do you keep sewage down here, too, Dragova?"

The odor faded, the mist dissipated, and, unseen by all but the Lord of Richemulot, a female human form materialized behind the distant casks. Lord Renier concealed a smile when he realized it was his granddaughter Jacqueline.

"It is time, gentlemen," the piper said. He turned to Renier. "With your permission, Sire?"

Renier nodded as the piper stepped to the center of the cold cellar and began to play. Soon, the melody of his pipe was accompanied by the squealing of still-hidden rodents. Suddenly, he stopped for a moment. "Mister Dragova, please be so good as to bring me some oil."

Dragova grabbed a container and put it down by the piper's feet. "Here."

The piper resumed his playing, and although the men found the tune quite irritating and repetitious, rats began to crawl out of all corners of the cellar and assembled practically at his feet. Klaus and the councilmen were pleased at the sight; Lord Renier watched unemotionally; and Jacqueline, still hidden, frowned.

The musician continued to play with one hand as he squatted and, with his other hand, opened the container of oil and poured it on and around the seemingly intoxicated rodents. Then he took a lit candle and dropped it in the center of the group of rats. The flame encircled them, trapped them, burned them, but the piper's song was powerful enough to keep them from running away.

Their fur, their flesh, burned, and the cellar became filled with the horrible odor of living flesh being burnt from its bones and the terrifying sound of hundreds of squealing, choking creatures.

The men covered their mouths with handkerchiefs; Jacqueline Renier, too, covered her mouth, but it was to suppress a cry of pity and anger. For among the creatures who were painfully dying were several of her friends, including the rat who had bitten the burgomeister.

The flames themselves died a bit, and through them Jacqueline saw the charred, ashy remnants of the rodents. The sight was too much for her. Her human form faded and within seconds the white mist she had become blew out of the cellar, out of Dragova's house, out into the street.

* * * * *

An hour later, Jacqueline Renier sat by the shore of the river. She tossed stones into the water and watched them splash. A figure sat down beside her and kissed her on the cheek.

"My darling girl, it is so good to see you," Claude Renier said. "Actually, I saw you before . . . at that fool's house."

She kissed her grandfather's hand. "It is good to see you, too. But I must admit I was puzzled by your presence there. That . . . musician's magic is quite amazing. It is repulsive and, I might add, dangerous. Suppose *I* had been in rat form. Would I have fallen under the spell?"

"That is difficult to know, my dear. But clearly this piper is a potential danger to you and others in our community. Would you like to take care of this matter, my dear, or would you prefer I handle it?"

Jacqueline wasted no time answering. "Grandfather, I would like your permission to give this piper a demonstration of my own magic."

Claude looked in her eyes and saw the true meaning of her words: her demonstration would rid Richemulot of the piper forever. "Very well," he said. "But allow me to pass on this information to you. After you left, Burgomeister Nellak gave the piper a thousand gold coins in advance for his services. The piper will come here—to this river—tonight at midnight, and he has promised that every rat in the community will be drawn here by his song. He further promised that, under his spell, all of them will then march into the river and drown. Perhaps you might want to visit with him prior to that."

Jacqueline kissed her grandsire's hand again. "Thank you. I will waste no time preparing for the piper's . . . surprise."

Claude Renier stood up. "I must go, my darling girl. You must come see me more often."

"I shall," she promised, standing up next to him. He nodded and winked his eye; then he mounted the horse his two guards held steady for him, and they were off.

Jacqueline turned back toward the river. She shook her head and said, "Only one creature will suffer tonight!"

* * * * *

Gauzy clouds whipped by the midnight full moon like a series of ghosts. The air was chilly by the river, and the sounds of the approaching men echoed everywhere. About a hundred yards from the river, the piper raised his hand, and the burgomeister and two of the city council members halted. "You must stay here," he instructed. "I will need full concentration tonight. I must not be distracted. And certainly you won't want to be in the path of the throng of onrushing rats."

The burgomeister's face registered disgust. "I should say not!"

"Very well," the piper continued, drawing his flute from his belt, "then I shall proceed with my task." He took a couple of steps toward the river, but stopped and turned his head back to the town leaders. "And I shall expect the other thousand gold coins when I am finished."

"Indeed," Klaus Nellak snapped nastily. "Be careful where you step. There are some dangerous bogs along the river banks."

The piper laughed and made his way to the river. He gazed up at the moon and thought how perfect the bright moonlight would be for allowing his employers to see all that happened. He looked about him; all was still; all was quiet.

He began to play. The melody this time was mellifluous and quite catchy; the men from the town found themselves tapping their toes to it—until they saw the first few rats scurry by.

The piper's tune continued with little deviation, only slight variations. Within minutes, thousands of rats lined up near him, completely still and completely silent, staring straight ahead. The piper's lips curled into as much of a smile as he could allow without hindering his performance.

Suddenly, the piper seemed engulfed in a mist that blew around him and slowly passed him. It smelled horrible, and he coughed several times. His tune was momentarily halted, but when the mist passed him, and he noticed the rats twitching and beginning to scatter, he resumed his tune. Again, the rats stood silent and faced the river.

Then a crisp but husky, alluring voice called out to him: "Your music is magical."

The piper turned his head to the left and saw a woman standing a few feet from the river's edge. She was radiant. She wore a white gown that hung low over her shoulders, nearly touched her feet, and gave her the appearance of hovering over the ground, not merely standing upon it.

"Are you a stranger in these parts?" she asked softly.

The piper nodded, his eyes taking in all her beauty, his song continuing all the while.

"Then I must make you feel welcome." Jacqueline slipped one of the straps of her gown down over her shoulder, revealing a generous sight of her cleavage. "Has it been a very long while since you had a woman?"

Again the piper nodded, blowing on his pipe while thanking the stars above for his good fortune. He smiled at her; Jacqueline recognized the lewdness in the grin and responded to it by extending her arms out to him.

Yes, she thought, come to me, you torturer! Come to me! Feel the delightful sensations I have in store for you!

The burgomeister grew nervous as he watched the piper, continuing to play his music, step toward the woman, but he dared not follow. He nudged his accomplices with his elbows and whispered, "What is the fool doing? Who is that accursed woman? I cannot see her features. Is she a witch?"

The piper was within twenty feet of her, close enough that he felt hypnotized by her beauty, felt himself sinking into her seductive, twinkling eyes. Sinking into them. Into her eyes. Sinking.

Sinking!

The cold wetness that surrounded his legs halfway up his thighs awoke him. He tried to step forward, but his motion only resulted in him sinking deeper into the bog. He struggled again, and sank deeper, before he realized that struggle was useless.

Jacqueline laughed evilly, loud enough to frighten the men from the town, who tried in vain to see—through an ever-thickening fog that now obscured their vision— what was happening. She stepped toward the musician, raised her hands to her chest, and her form quickly and smoothly changed into that of a rat. She squealed, the sound every bit as loud as her human laughter. Her rat form ran lightly over the scummy top of the bog; then she bit the outstretched arm of the piper until the instrument fell from his hand. She picked it up in her teeth and scurried back to the dry land surrounding the bog.

The piper screamed, but even that much exertion caused him to sink lower. He watched as the murky wetness climbed to his chest. Then he turned, expecting to see the rat, but looking at the beautiful woman again.

"I know a magical air myself," she said mirthfully, "though I am certain I lack your skill. Care to hear it?"

She expected no answer and received none. She began to play, fingering the pipe as if she were a little girl with a new toy. There was no logic to the progression of the notes, no recognizable melody. Yet the notes provided the desired effect: the rats assembled at her feet.

The piper's eyes grew wide in terror, and his muscles contracted, causing him to sink to his shoulders in the clammy bog.

Jacqueline's improvisation changed slightly; higher notes emanated from the pipe now. The rats turned toward the piper. Then several hundred of them dashed into the bog. They swam, crawled, even fought each other in their overwhelming desire to find an unprotected part of the piper's hands, neck, head, and face to rip into with their razor-sharp incisors.

He screamed until his lungs could scream no more as the flesh was torn from him in tiny pieces. In his last moments of consciousness, he prayed he would mercifully sink, quickly and completely, into the bog.

Jacqueline turned to revel in the reactions of the men from the town, but in this she was cheated. They were already gone, having fled when the piper's screams ripped through the fog, and were in all likelihood already shivering in fear in their beds.

*   *   *   *   *

The next morning, in the relative safety of bright daylight, surrounded by guards, Burgomeister Nellak made his way to the bog to search for . . . something. He did not really expect to find the mysterious woman—a wererat—but perhaps he would find . . . something.

What he found was a sight that sickened him every bit as much as the occurrence the night before. There in the bog, the pipe pointed straight up out of the murky liquid. One of the guards reached over and attempted to pull it out, but it seemed stuck. The guard positioned himself better and pulled again with all his strength.

The burgomeister nearly retched when he realized the instrument was wedged between the clenched teeth of what was left of the piper's face.

He backed away from the grisly sight, and the guard let go. Suddenly, the air was fouled by an offensive, loathsome odor, and the vision of all those present was blurred for a few seconds by a flowing white mist. The odor passed quickly; yet the mist hovered over the river within a few yards of them.

Then a swarm of large rats charged up the riverbank toward the men. Horrified, they ran back toward town, the sound of loud, formidable, evil, female laughter echoing through their very souls.

The Wailing

Kate Novak

The baby's shrieking stabbed into George's heart like a hot poker. He let himself burn with a murderous rage, knowing it was the only emotion that could stave off numbing cold fear.

Since he had begun tracking the old Vistana woman who had abducted the infant, the ranger had listened to the baby's distant wails, trying to gauge his plight. The first day the child seemed to be sobbing for the comfort of loving arms. The next day the sobs became howls of hunger, thirst, and discomfort, which continued through the night and into the following day. The third night, the fourth day, and last night, George hadn't heard a sound from the baby, although he knew he was still hot on the Vistana woman's heels. He hoped fervently that the old crone had finally given the child some nourishment, but he knew it was more likely that the baby had just grown exhausted and given up its futile crying.

This shrieking was a different sound, a terrifying sound. George didn't want to think about what the Vistana could be doing to the child; instead he wondered what kind of person would make a baby suffer so.

Less than a mile's travel after the baby had begun to shriek, the landscape started to change. The ground rose sharply and the lush forest thinned out suddenly, revealing the rubble-strewn slopes of a great mountain. The trees growing at the base of the mountain were stunted and twisted and leafless as if the wind ravaged them constantly, yet the air was still all about him, except of course for the cries of the baby. His horse Perseus began to whinny nervously and tried to shy back down the slope, a sign, George realized, that there was something unnatural about the mountain.

A strand of long black hair caught on a branch indicated to the ranger that the Vistana was climbing the slope. He looked upward at just the right moment and spied a flash of red and yellow through the gnarled tree branches—colors of the scarf the old Vistana woman wore on her head. She wasn't more than a mile ahead of him now. He had taxed all his skill and endurance in tracking her, fearful of speeding up, lest she use some wily Vistana trick to cover her trail, and fearful of slowing, lest she outrun him completely. Now, he felt, the time for careful tracking was passed. If he didn't hurry, the child could be dead by the time he reached his prey.

"Speed, Perseus," George whispered, nudging his mount into a trot, but Perseus reared up with a terrifying neigh and pawed at the air until George allowed it to turn about. The horse stood facing the wrong direction, shuddering, and the ranger knew that only the beast's training and love for its rider kept it from fleeing in full retreat. The horse was too sensible to face whatever lay up ahead and would have to be left behind. He dismounted and stroked the horse's neck.

Once the beast had calmed sufficiently, George rummaged through his saddlebags, shoving important gear into a backpack. With the baby's shrieking ringing in his ears, he began climbing the slope on foot as the sun touched the western horizon.

In the last rays cast by the setting sun, George spied the Vistana again. She halted before a great flat rock where she laid down the baby. Then she turned and headed back down the mountain slope.

George rushed forward, anxious to reach the rock before something or someone else discovered the baby. He lost sight of the Vistana and the baby as his path led through a denser patch of dead trees and the twilight descended around him. He hurried on, following the sound of the infant's frantic cries, forgetting caution completely, and not checking for signs of other creatures or humans who might lie in ambush.

He never saw the cudgel that swung down from an overhead tree branch and smacked him in the head.

When George regained consciousness, he was lying on his back, staked out on the ground like a sacrificial offering. The sky was gray with predawn light. He could hear the baby howling not far off, but the Vistana woman sat cross-legged beside him. Her raven-black hair framed a face lined with wrinkles, but George could see that once she had been a very striking woman. At the moment she was preoccupied laying out cards from a tarokka deck. George couldn't raise his head far enough to see the cards as they were flipped over, but it was obvious from her scowls and muttering that the old woman was not pleased with what she saw.

"Having trouble deciding the best way to kill me, ma'am?" George taunted. "I'm only a giorgio, an outsider. How hard could it be?"

The Vistana hissed and raised her head suddenly to glare at her captive. Her neck was disfigured from old scars left by some beast that had once clawed and chewed her throat.

"You are a good man, giorgio, yet you work for Soldest of Darkon," the Vistana said. Her tone was matter-of-fact, yet George could hear the slightest hesitation in her voice; she was guessing.

"No," he replied. "I don't work for Soldest." Off in the distance, the baby gave an especially ear-piercing shriek. He couldn't think of a lie that would convince the woman to release him, and he didn't think there was time to reason with her. He could only hope she would respond to the truth with her woman's heart. "I don't like Soldest at all," George insisted. "He's arrogant, vulgar, and nasty, but his wife is a nice girl. You've stolen her son. She's frantic for the child. She begged me to find him and return him to her. Whatever vendetta you have against Soldest, there must be some better way to settle it. I know you think stealing his son will hurt Soldest, but he's a callous brute. You're only hurting the innocent. You can't hold the baby responsible. It's just a little baby. Think of the baby's mother, think of her grief.

Please, ma'am, let me go, before it's too late."

"Think of the baby's mother," the woman repeated
hollowly. "I can do nothing but think of the baby's
mother," she snapped. "Soldest's wife told you the baby
was hers, did she? She lied. The baby is Asha's. Soldest
seduced Asha and then abandoned her. Still, like a fool,
she cherished his brat. Cherished it so that when Soldest
sent his men to take the baby from her, she died on their
swords rather than give it up."

"Asha was one of your people?" he asked.

"Asha, daughter of Tilda, daughter of Aliza. I am
Aliza. Asha was my granddaughter," the woman replied,
and half a sob escaped with her answer.

George was silent for a moment, judging what the
woman had said. She had no reason to lie. "I'm sorry,"
George said. "Sorry for her treatment, and sorry for her
death. But that's your great grandson crying out there. I
know your people don't accept half-blooded children,
but he still has Asha's blood in him. You can't want to
harm him. Soldest's wife wants him for her own. She
loves him."

Aliza snorted derisively. "You think, giorgio, a woman
could love the baby of her husband's mistress. You are a
ranger; you live in the wild, and you know nothing of
women."

George shifted, uncomfortable in both his body and
mind. It was true he didn't understand women well, but
he couldn't give up. "And you are Vistana," he retorted,
"you live among Vistani, and you know nothing of the
giorgio. We cherish children no matter where they come
from. Soldest's wife only wants a child."

"Soldest's wife wants only her husband's heir," Aliza
declared.

"That's not true," George growled.

"If she should have an heir of her own, she'd find
some way to rid herself of her husband's half-blood. And
even if she loves this baby, soon this baby will be a boy,
and a boy will follow his father. Better Tristessa should
take the baby for her own." Aliza looked up, beyond her
prisoner, and smiled sadly.

"Who is this Tristessa?" George asked.

"Tristessa: it means the Sad One," Aliza explained. "She was once a priestess of the dark elves."

"The dark elves? You mean the drow? Like the drow from the kingdom of Arak?" George grew agitated and worried. The drow of Arak were rumored to be exceedingly cruel, but since no human captured by them was ever seen again, the rumors were impossible to confirm. "A drow. Good gods, woman! How could you leave your grandchild with a drow?" he growled.

"How quick you are to judge, ranger," the Vistana growled back. "Listen to the Sad One's tale, and understand. Long ago, in Arak, she bore a child. The child was born deformed; it had no legs of its own, only the legs of a spider, so the drow insisted it be put to death. The Sad One loved her child, though, and would not give up her baby. The drow dragged her and her baby to the surface and left them staked out for the sunlight to burn their flesh away. Her baby perished, but she escaped death and came to this land. She wanders throughout the night, half mad, grieving for her lost child. In the day she hides in a cavern high up in the mountain—" Aliza froze suddenly. "There she is now," she whispered, and pointed up the slope.

George twisted his head to look where Aliza indicated. The sky was growing light all about them, and any moment the sun would rise. He could see now that he lay not far from the rock where he'd seen Aliza lay the baby. George could just make out the Sad One's figure moving up the mountain. Her long white hair and dark gown blew all about her slender body. A cold shiver ran down George's spine.

At the rock where the baby lay in its bundle, still shrieking, the figure stopped suddenly and looked down. George gasped. As the figure bent over and picked up the baby, the baby's crying ceased. George breathed a sigh of relief. Another shiver crawled down the ranger's spine. The air was perfectly still, now—maybe too still. The figure seemed to drift like a cloud up the slope and to the west until it disappeared behind the mountain with the baby.

Aliza sighed once sadly and looked back down at her

tarokka cards. She gathered them together, wrapped them up in a scarf, and slipped them into a pocket of her skirt. "Heed me now, giorgio. There are powers in this world, powers great and dark, powers beyond your ken. Such powers preserved the Sad One in Arak and brought her here. The tarokka says you are destined to travel much farther, and I dare not interfere with your destiny." The Vistana drew out a dagger. "But if you interfere with the Sad One, if you challenge the powers behind her, your destiny might be greatly shortened." The dagger cut through the leather strip holding George's left wrist to the ground.

The Vistana rose suddenly and dashed down the slope, disappearing like a wild creature into the trees.

George reached over to pick at the binding holding his other wrist. It took him more than a few minutes to work free the knots. He sat up and used his dagger to cut the bindings about his boots.

It took him a few more minutes to stand up and loosen his stiff muscles. Then he tried to straighten out his thoughts. He had promised Soldest's wife he would return with the baby, but his faith in the woman had been shaken by Aliza's evil insinuations. Still, could he trust a drow with the baby, even a drow who had loved her own deformed child enough to risk her life for it? He had to check on the baby's safety first. He would learn more of this drow, too, then decide what to do.

George continued up the slope of the mountain. Above the tree line patches of dead brambles competed for space with fields of browning thistles. There seemed to be no natural trails, and it took George hours to follow the route taken so quickly by the Sad One.

Once his foot crunched down on a long white bone. He discovered most of a human skeleton just down-slope, covered by brambles. He tossed a ritual handful of dirt on the skull and continued on uneasily, wishing he could afford the time to bury the remains. Had the bones belonged to a victim of the drow, he wondered, or had their owner fallen prey to some other wilderness tragedy, and the drow blameless? Later, when he spotted a second skeleton, George did not even bother with the ritual handful of dirt, and his uneasiness grew.

Near the top of the summit the thistles and brambles finally thinned out, but the climb did not get any easier. Rubble covered the slopes, and without the plant life holding it down, it shifted like sand, and every step was precarious.

The sun shone directly overhead when George discovered the mine shaft plunging into the mountain's side. Aliza had said the Sad One lived in a cavern within the mountain, and the mine shaft was the only entrance he could see. He collapsed beside it and pulled out his water flask. He was torn and bleeding from the thorns and thistles and bruised and sore from sliding on the rubble. He was also having trouble catching his breath; the air was thin this high up, and it stank from some invisible vapors.

Peering down the steeply inclined shaft, the ranger realized that the Sad One could only have traveled so quickly had she levitated up the mountain slope and then down this shaft. He'd never heard of a priestess with the power to levitate before, and he recalled uneasily Aliza's warning of powers great and dark, powers beyond his ken.

He tossed a few pebbles into the shaft and counted as he listened for them to hit the bottom. Over five hundred feet down, he estimated, unless the pebbles had hit the side of the shaft; then it might be deeper. There was a tunnel opening in the side of the shaft less than fifty feet down. He would start his search for the Sad One and the baby there.

Hand- and toeholds were chipped into the beams that braced the shaft walls, and some old rusty ladder rungs still remained in some stretches along the northern side of the shaft, but George took the time to anchor a safety rope. The sun was still high as he began his descent, and light bathed the mouth of the tunnel when he reached it. He didn't need to light his lamp until he stepped several feet down the tunnel. The lamplight glistened on silvery cobwebs that hung in thick curtains, blocking several side passages. Tattered strands of web drifted in the air along the main passage, so someone must have used the passage recently.

As George crept forward, he heard a woman singing. The melody was dissonant and eerie, and the lyrics were in some tongue the ranger did not recognize. He followed the voice until the tunnel opened into a small cavern. Just inside the cavern he halted. The Sad One sat cross-legged on the floor, rocking and singing to the baby. Presumably her song was a lullaby, but hardly one a baby could sleep to. Yet the child was still and made no sound.

George waited until a pause in the song before he spoke. "Excuse me, ma'am. I've come about the baby," he said.

The Sad One set the baby down on the floor and levitated to her feet. Her long white hair covered her like a veil, but when she raised her head, it fell back and revealed her face. George gasped, momentarily horrified. It was not her skin, as black as the darkness all around her, but her features that frightened the ranger. Her deep purple lips curled like a snarling dog's, and her bloodshot eyes bulged out and glared at him with mad rage.

Despite his fear, George's hand went instinctively for his scabbard, but the Sad One blew into him like a gust of wind. She wrenched his hand away from the sword's hilt and clenched it in her icy fingers.

A searing pain shot up George's arm as the Sad One crushed his hand with inhuman strength. He tried to yank his arm away, but the drow's grip was unyielding, and he succeeded only in pulling the awful woman closer to him. With her face near his own, he could hear her murmur some unrecognizable phrase over and over. Her tongue was as purple as her lips, and her breath was chill. His hand cramped in agony as the Sad One twisted his flesh as though it were clay. His fingers seemed to melt away, and his wrist bent backward, unable to straighten.

Finally the drow released him and whispered, "Now that you are imperfect, Jozell, how dare you come to take my baby?"

Then darkness enveloped him. George could feel the heat coming from the lantern he still held in his left hand, but he could see no flicker of light, no glimmer of a dying wick. It was a magical darkness that left him blind to the drow's movements.

Icy fingertips stroked his cheek, and where he had been touched, his skin felt as if it were sizzling beneath a hot poker. The ranger dropped his lantern and clutched at his face with his good left hand. He reeled backward, and with the stump of his right hand felt for the cavern wall until he discovered the tunnel leading to the mine shaft. Then he fled, running and stumbling in the pitch-dark underground.

Finally, gasping from the thin, poisonous air, George slowed and tried to orient himself. He didn't need to see to know he was covered with cobwebs; he could feel them fluttering about his face and shoulders in the warm breeze coming from his left. He followed the current of air until he could see a glow of light up ahead.

The tunnel opened into the mine shaft. He stood blinking in the sunlight, grateful for its warmth and light. His face throbbed with pain, and he stared with sickening distaste at his maimed hand. He'd never heard of a power that could twist flesh as his had been. One of those powers great and dark, a power beyond his ken, he thought. The drow, he realized, could probably have killed him, but she had let him live. She wanted only the baby, and she did seem to cherish it.

She was mad, though. Of that, the ranger had no doubt. He'd seen it in her eyes. Then there was the name she'd called him—Jozell—it might mean stranger or warrior, but George's instincts told him it was the name of one of the drow who'd killed her own baby. The Sad One was reliving her past, as the mad so often did. She would protect the baby from outsiders, he realized, but caring well for it might not be in her power. He had to go back.

It took him several minutes of searching for the rope he'd left hanging before George realized the tunnel he'd used to enter the drow's realm was across the shaft and several feet above him. He'd taken a wrong turn in the dark. Now he'd either have to wind his way back through the maze of passages or climb his way over and up to the first tunnel. Better, the ranger thought, to take the route I took before and stay in the light as much as possible.

He began his climb up. There weren't as many handholds on this side of the shaft, and he was unable to grip with his maimed hand, so the climb was awkward and slow. He'd made it halfway around the shaft when a rotted timber gave way beneath his weight. He began sliding down, grabbing at the dirt and timber walls with his left hand, but unable to get a purchase. He spread out his arms and legs against the wall, trying to slow his descent. It took him longer to reach the bottom of the shaft than the pebbles he had thrown in to judge its depth, but ultimately that was where he ended up.

He circled the wall until he'd reached the north side of the shaft, where there were more handholds. Before he began his ascent, though, he sat down, as much to regain his composure as to rest his aching muscles and to catch his breath.

A small pool of water sparkled in the center of the shaft, and all about the pool thistles grew thick and green. George was just beginning to think of the shaft floor as an oasis in the desert of the mountain when he spotted the gleam of a skull. He might have ignored it as he had the second skeleton on the mountainside, but this skull was different. It was so small.

George bent down to retrieve the ivory ball shape. It fit in the palm of his hand. Once it had belonged to an infant. The ranger scanned the shaft floor again. Having spotted one skull, he could now see that the floor was littered with skeletons. Some were large enough that they might have belonged to children old enough to walk, but mostly the bones were very, very small. Aliza had not been the first to abandon a baby for the Sad One to claim.

He'd observed thousands of animal skeletons during his years in the wilderness, so he was quick to realize all the skeletons were missing their leg bones. With a sickening dread, the ranger remembered Aliza's tale. The drow's baby had been born without legs of its own. With her power to twist flesh and bone, the Sad One had found a way to relive that part of her life, too, over and over. Had the Sad One then relived her grief each time one of these babies had died?

Had she arranged their deaths so she could relive that grief?

George turned and faced the shaft wall so he couldn't possibly count the skulls. He would have to move quickly now to retrieve the baby and flee before the sun got any lower in the sky. The sun would shield him from pursuit. He stood up and began climbing the shaft wall.

By the time George reached the tunnel he'd taken into the drow's lair the sun's slanting rays were beginning to climb up the sides of the shaft. Still, he figured, if he could just get in and out quickly, he'd have several hours of bright daylight left. He twisted his scabbard belt so he could draw his sword with his left hand. With his injured hand it seemed to take him forever to strike a flint for lighting a candle, but he dared not go without some light. He tied the end of a ball of twine to the rope hanging from above, stuck the ball in his pocket, and struck off down the passageway, letting the string unwind as he went.

When the candle went black, he knew he'd reached the darkness cast by the Sad One. He stepped back a few paces and smiled with satisfaction when he could again see the flame of the candle wick. Assuring himself that he still had plenty of twine, he moved back into the darkness. He counted the paces forward with his maimed hand running along the wall. At the count of eighteen, the candlelight flickered about him again. So large a sphere of darkness could be an indication of the drow's great power, George realized, or the great evil of her nature.

The Sad One was not in the cavern, but the baby lay on the floor, swaddled in blankets. George knelt beside him, holding the candle so he could see his face. The infant's eyes were closed, and he was very still, but George could see his tiny chest rise and fall and his tiny nostrils flare.

The ranger set the candle down on the floor. As he slipped his good hand beneath the baby, he sensed something was wrong. He didn't need to unwrap the blankets to confirm his suspicion, but he did anyway. Both of the infant's legs were twisted stumps, as useless as George's right hand.

George gritted his teeth. There was not time to dwell on this problem now. Somehow, after he'd rescued the infant, he'd find a way to heal it, but the rescue came first. George wriggled the baby into the space between his own chest and his leather jerkin.

He was reaching out to retrieve his candle when he heard the Sad One whisper, "Return my child or die." She hovered on the far side of the cavern. In her arms she clutched a spider the size of a house cat. She dropped the creature, and it skittered off into the darkness.

George leapt to his feet and drew out his long sword with his good hand. It wasn't his stronger arm, but he had practice using it. This time he had the sword out and brandished in front of him before the drow could close on him and touch him again.

"Do you think that I fear your weapon, Jozell?" the Sad One sneered. She lunged for George, impaling herself on the ranger's blade. Shrieking, she drew back from the weapon, but did not fall. Bits of white vapor dripped from the blade and drifted back toward her. Her form grew hazier, and the candlelight shone through her.

Finally, George understood what he was facing. The powers great and dark, beyond his ken, had not preserved the Sad One from death, they'd preserved only her spirit. And the undead spirit of a female drow became a banshee. If his weapon had not been enchanted, the Sad One would have gone right through it, uninjured, and inflicted her deadly touch on him again.

George felt a surge of certainty. If the banshee could not touch him, her only other weapon was her banshee wail, which could do him no harm while the sun shone in the sky. She might be undead, but he knew how to deal with the undead. He lunged forward and slashed through the spirit, tearing the misty form into shreds that hung in the air all about them.

The banshee drifted backward. She opened her mouth and let out a keen that pierced through George's heart like an ice blade. The sun's presence outside did nothing to lessen the paralyzing fear that gripped George—fear, not of dying here, but of what would follow his escape.

Even if Soldest's wife could cherish the child of her husband's mistress, she would not love the baby, as deformed as it had been made. She would abandon it to the rubbish, or Soldest would drown or strangle it. Maybe Soldest's wife would let it live, but come to hate it and abuse it far more than it had been abused these past five days. Then she might abandon it. There were abandoned children all over Darkon, wandering the streets, hungry and fearful, despised and unloved, without comfort anywhere. Those who survived to maturity led lives without joy, save for the few savage ones rumored to have joined the ranks of the Kargat, Darkon's secret police. He could rescue the baby, only to bring it more misery.

George felt his left hand go numb, and his sword clattered to the cavern floor. He: the baby is a he, he thought, not an it. And if no one else wants him to grow up happy, I do. He'll be mine.

George shook off the fears ripping into his heart just in time to see the Sad One flying toward him with her arms outstretched. He leapt clear just in time. Before the banshee could turn, he pulled a vial out of the emergency pocket of his backpack and unstoppered it with his teeth. As the drow spirit swooped toward him yet again, he splashed her with the contents of the vial.

The banshee howled as the holy water seared into her being. Mist rose from her form and dissipated into the darkness. George scrambled for his long sword and slashed again through the undead form.

The Sad One drifted up out of the ranger's reach. "You'll not escape my kingdom, Jozell. You will die here. When the darkness comes, I will destroy you." Then she floated off, leaving George alone in the cavern with her treasure, the baby.

Forced to abandon his candle in order to keep his sword at the ready, George followed the twine back through the darkness by winding it up on his maimed hand.

The sun still shone bright when he finally climbed over the edge of the mine shaft. Eager to flee as far as possible before nightfall, George abandoned his rope and dashed down the mountain's slope, sliding in the rubble and ignoring the prickles of the thistles and briars. He didn't stop until he came upon Perseus. The horse neighed with recognition of its master and nearly bowled him over as it nuzzled him with joy.

"Yes, I'm back. You tried to warn me about this place, didn't you?" George whispered to the beast. "You've more sense than I, don't you? Well, we're leaving now."

George mounted awkwardly and steered the beast toward the forest path down which he had tracked the Vistana last night. He slipped his hand inside his jerkin and stroked the baby's arm. He could feel the child breathing, but it remained disturbingly silent. Possibly, he realized, the infant was paralyzed with fear by the banshee's wail, as he had nearly been. The ranger wondered uncomfortably if the child might not retain some memory of the past few horrible days, stored in some dark recess to be released only when dreams stole upon him. He shook off his fears and urged Perseus into a trot.

Less than a mile down the trail, the horse halted abruptly and lowered its head. "What is it, Perseus?" George whispered. Then he felt the wind. It started as a breeze and within moments grew into a gale. Flying bits of dirt and twigs stung at his face. There was no moving forward in such a wind. George cursed and allowed the horse to turn around.

Perseus took three steps toward the road, but reared up and neighed in terror. Then the horse stood still, quivering with fear.

"You see, Jozell, you cannot escape," a voice shrieked overhead.

George looked up. The Sad One hovered at the top of the trees, the light from the setting sun piercing through her. "My winds will keep you here, Jozell, until nightfall. Then I shall destroy you."

Annoyance pushed aside George's fear of the banshee's powers. "I'm not Jozell," he declared.

The banshee said nothing. The wind continued to howl at his back. "I'll bet I don't even look anything like this Jozell, whoever he is."

"Jozell murdered my baby," the Sad One moaned.

"But I'm not him," the ranger insisted.

"You've stolen my baby," the Sad One argued. The wind howled louder.

"This baby is not yours." George unbuttoned the top of his jerkin so the baby's face peeked out. "He's not drow. He doesn't look anything like you."

"He's mine. The Vistana left him for me."

"Well, I'm not giving him to you. You'll only murder him like all the others."

"I never harmed them. They just died."

"They just died?" George asked, disbelieving, but then he understood. "You're undead. You can't nurture something alive. You can't give the baby what he needs."

"As long as he lives, he is mine," the banshee wailed, and the wind wailed with her.

"I am not giving him to you so that he can starve to death," George snapped.

"Come nightfall, my keen will destroy you," the banshee cried.

"Then it most certainly will kill the baby. You've already paralyzed him with fear," George retorted.

The banshee was silent.

"You don't want a dead human baby," George pointed out. "And it's not me you want to kill; it's Jozell."

"Yes," the Sad One whispered. "Jozell must die for what he did to me and my baby."

"But I'm not Jozell," George reminded her. "Let me leave here, and I won't bother you ever again."

The Sad One drifted down toward George. She stared intently at the baby. "That is not my child," she hissed. "Jozell murdered my child, and he must pay." She spun about and flew off toward the mountain. The wind died down.

Gently, George urged Perseus to turn about. The horse took a few tentative steps away from the banshee's kingdom, then, sensing a last chance, it galloped off at reckless speed.

Some hours' distance from the banshee's lair, George's right hand began to throb. Like a bug emerging from a chrysalis, his fingers began sprouting from the hand that the Sad One had maimed. The baby's legs grew back, too. George could not recall ever feeling so relieved in his life. That night, though, he dreamed he was begging in the streets of Darkon with the baby beside him, his hand again a stump, while the baby had eight hairy spider legs. He woke up covered in sweat and had to check both his hand and the baby's legs to assure himself the dream was false.

The baby would not suck, paralyzed as it was, and George began to fear for the child's health. The next day he rode Perseus hard until he finally came to a church. The priest laid his hands over the baby's head and prayed. Within a minute the baby was howling and shrieking. The priest fed him with goat's milk, which he sucked down with vigor. Then he slept with exhaustion, and George slept beside him. That night, George dreamed of the banshee tossing his baby down the mine shaft onto the piles of skeletons of other babies. He woke shivering and could not sleep again until he'd lit a candle and watched the child breathe.

The dreams returned each night.

Three days later, he stood before Soldest's wife and told her all that he had learned about the baby from the Vistana Aliza. The girl looked down in shame for her husband's crimes, but she met the ranger's gaze steadily when he asked if she loved the child, and she assured him that she did.

George handed the baby over to the girl. The child was quiet in her arms, but when she set him down to pour him a bottle, he wailed until she picked him up again.

George did not speak of the banshee or her kingdom. He just said, "Your child suffered much, Lady Soldest. I ask only that you never make me regret returning him to you. I will visit when I can, to be sure he is well. When he is old enough, tell him I will always be his friend."

"I will never make you regret his return; you will

always be welcome, and my son will know you are his friend," Soldest's wife assured him.

* * * * *

George Weathermay travels far and wide hunting evil, and many people think him fearless. Only a fearless man, they say, could survive the banshee wail of the Sad One. It is true that powers great and dark, powers beyond his ken, hold little terror for the ranger. There are everyday things, though, that stab his heart with an icy chill—seeing a master strike a young apprentice, seeing a child begging in the streets, seeing an infant's coffin, hearing a baby wail . . . especially hearing a baby wail.

Then he dreams of the mad drow spirit grieving for her lost baby and of all the babies others had left for her to claim.

When George Weathermay has these dreams, he visits Darkon to check on the son of Soldest. The baby is always well; he thrives in the care of Soldest's wife. Still, George Weathermay visits Darkon often, because the world is full of wailing babies.

Von Kharkov

Gene DeWeese

The only name he had ever known was Urik von Kharkov, and for a fleeting, exultant moment, he thought he had at long last gained his freedom.

In that moment he *felt* the life-force drain from Dakovny's body in distant Karg. He felt the grating of the stake against bone as Dakovny struggled to wrest it from his chest, felt even, for an excruciating instant, the driven blade that separated head from convulsing torso.

But in the next moment, as the flood of pain and exultation faded to a trickle, he realized that Dakovny's hateful power had not been lifted. It remained, smothering Von Kharkov's mind like a poisonous cloud, paralyzing his body until—

He screamed, more a snarl of the Beast he dared not summon than any sound that could emerge from his human throat.

But even as he screamed, he realized there was a difference, a vital difference. Yes, Dakovny's power remained, gripping him as tightly as ever it had, but there was no longer a mind behind that power. That had vanished with Dakovny's decapitation. The chain still bound him, but there was no hand to hold that chain. Not yet. Not until the one who was destroying Dakovny could complete that destruction, make it irreversible. Only then could he turn his full attention to his new slave.

With a strength born of desperation, Von Kharkov lurched into a stumbling run, forcing those grisly scenes in distant Karg into the background, demanding that his eyes, normally far keener than those of most of his other doomed brethren, focus instead on the world that surrounded him here, the dark and narrow streets of Neblus. When finally his vision cleared, he was nearing the graveyard that marked the far end of the tiny village. He could even see—or imagined he could see—the crumbling stones that marked the graves of the parents he had never known.

A sudden longing to spend a few final moments with them, to bid them one last farewell, was almost overwhelming, but he dared not pause for even a moment, no matter how much the sudden ache in his heart goaded him. His only hope—if hope indeed existed for what he had long ago become—lay in wasting not a second. Eyes were everywhere, looking out from behind every drawn shutter, riding every invisible current of air, concealed in every natural and unnatural shadow, and any of the creatures lurking behind those eyes could become a pawn of that other creature back in Karg as soon as it turned its full attention to him. Von Kharkov could only lurch on as the forlorn shadows of the graveyard slid past, the tendrils of fog that drifted among the stones a tantalizing reminder of his still-distant goal.

Beyond the graveyard, there were no roads, no paths. Only the River Tempe cut through the shadowed landscape, and even its dank waters grew more sluggish, as if reluctant to complete their journey into—

Into what?

If he didn't falter, he would soon know. Less than a mile ahead lay the edge of the world—the Mists. No one knew what they were, much less what became of one who entered them. Even Dakovny and others of his ilk claimed ignorance. All that was known was that no one who had been taken in had ever been returned.

But whatever lay within them, the Mists were Von Kharkov's only hope. He would plunge into them, not without fear but without hesitation. Whatever awaited him could be no worse than what he had endured in Darkon for more seasons than he could remember.

The graveyard dropped behind, its grip on him weakening. Ahead, a shrouded wood seemed to half emerge from the Mists themselves, and Von Kharkov wished desperately he dared assume the form of the Beast. Its senses were far sharper, and its lithe, clawed form could cover the distance in a fraction of the time it would take his human form.

But he dared not.

For the Beast, if it were allowed to emerge into reality, would know nothing of Von Kharkov or his wishes. It would not—could not—struggle as Von Kharkov was struggling now with every step. It was a mindless instrument of death and little else. It had killed and fed at the whim of Von Kharkov's master, and now that Dakovny was destroyed, it would unhesitatingly serve the whim of its new master.

If given the chance.

Von Kharkov's ebony skin rippled in a chill of revulsion as memories of countless awakenings swept over him, countless visions of shredded flesh, countless imagined images of his own features as they regained human form through a veil of blood. If only, all those years ago, he had been able to resist the lure of—

But you could not, Von Kharkov. You could not resist, and you did not.

A new voice echoed in his mind, stronger than Dakovny's had ever been. He stumbled, almost falling.

Resisting temptation was never in your nature, was it, Von Kharkov? That is why you found your way to Dakovny so quickly and submitted to his ministrations so gratefully. And look at you now, rushing headlong toward another of your illusory goals, not a worthwhile thought in your head.

The voice laughed, sending needles of pain through Von Kharkov's mind. *It seems I shall have to save you from yourself, then. After all, you are mine now. And your little machinations—you thought I didn't know? You thought you could hold your thoughts secret from not only your master but from me? That is delightful! Naive as well as impulsive and easily tempted! But as I was saying, your little machinations did give me the opportunity to eliminate an old enemy—at least eliminate him with less effort than I might otherwise have*

*had to exert. So you see, Von Kharkov, you did me a
favor, and now, in return . . .*

A pair of eyes, glowing red in the darkness, swooped
out of the air directly at his face, sending him reeling.
Others appeared, and he could see the shadows of bodies around them, hear the high-pitched chittering.
Ahead, at the line of trees that had emerged from the
Mists, larger shadows began to take shape, shadows
that snarled gutturally as they lumbered toward him
across the barren plain.

Desperately, he lurched to the side, toward the river. If
he were able to throw himself into the Tempe, no matter
how slowly it was running—

The Mists and the escape they offered were obviously
beyond his reach now, but the escape of oblivion might
still be attainable. It would even be preferable.

With every last ounce of his strength, Von Kharkov
plunged into the water.

Fool! the voice thundered in his mind as the water,
burning like liquid fire, closed over him.

Fool, he agreed silently as he forced himself to surrender, to simply wait as the pain burned brighter and his
consciousness guttered lower even as it tortured him
with visions of the Mists he had failed to reach.

* * * * *

Slowly, Von Kharkov's senses returned.

He was lying, not in the icy water of the Tempe but on
ground that was solid and utterly featureless. What—

The Mists! They were all around him!

They had not been a figment of his pain-racked mind!
They had been real! They had reached down into the
water itself and swallowed him up!

And for the first time since that terrible moment in
Karg, he felt hope. Not hope that he could someday be
human again—his humanity was irretrievably lost—but
hope that he could at least be free, free to think and act
on his own, but most of all, free of the horrors he had
been forced to commit again and again, whenever
Dakovny grew bored or wished for another enemy to be

destroyed in retaliation for some minor misdeed, either actual or imagined.

Surely even Dakovny's kind could not follow him here!

And the voice—

Von Kharkov smiled abruptly. The voice was gone. There was only silence in his mind. Only his own thoughts.

Eagerly, he leapt to his feet and looked around.

But there was nothing, only the Mists. He could see a few yards into them before they blotted out his vision, but that was all.

And the silence of the world around him was as complete as the silence in his mind.

He began to walk. But though he could see the featureless ground move beneath his feet, nothing changed. There was only the muffling whiteness of the Mists flowing by him. And the silence. Even his own footsteps were swallowed up in it. He could see his feet striking the ground, could *feel* them thud against it, but no sound reached his ears, ears that had once been able to catch the rustle of a single leaf as it drifted gently to moss-cushioned ground.

He ran, but even that was silent and dreamlike, and he began to wonder: Did this place have no end? Had he escaped into the Mists? Or simply been trapped by them?

He remembered the last word the voice had spoken to him, the word his own mind had echoed! *Fool* . . .

A wave of dizziness swept over him, and the Mists seemed to thicken and coil more tightly around him.

But only for an instant. As he lurched to a stop, the muffled silence suddenly evaporated, replaced by the rustling of thousands of leaves in the wind, the beating of wings overhead, the padding of a predator's feet as it stalked its prey through the underbrush—

And the Mists were gone.

A forest—a jungle!—surrounded him, with all its myriad scents and sounds flooding his senses.

Scents and sounds he was certain he had never experienced before, yet were instantly and intimately familiar. The spoor of a hundred different animals conjured up a hundred different images, each as detailed as if the animal itself were standing before him. The cries and flapping wings of a hundred birds, the muffled buzz of countless insects, the fragrance of decaying vegetation drifting up from the matted jungle floor, all assaulted his senses, screaming their familiarity. For a moment, the puzzle of that familiarity gripped him, but he quickly cast it aside. It wasn't important. All that mattered was that he was free!

Or was he?

A new chill of fear gripped him.

He stood perfectly still, listening not to the eerily familiar world around him but to his inner world. Ever since that long-ago night in Karg, there had not been a moment when he had been alone in his mind. The voice might not always be heard, but its potential had always been there, like a velvet cord looped about his neck, waiting to be pulled tight.

And Dakovny's eyes . . .

They were never seen, but they were always *felt*. Dakovny had been a constant presence in Von Kharkov's mind, just out of range, never touchable, but always there, watching, waiting, ready to take control at any moment, to grip the velvet cord and pull it tight in an instant.

Von Kharkov listened. With his ears and with his mind.

And there was nothing!

He was alone, truly alone, in his mind!

For a long time, that was enough. Like someone who has just emerged from years in a dungeon into the open air, Von Kharkov was euphoric with the simple pleasure of freedom, of looking at what he wanted to look at, of touching what he wanted to touch, of not having to constantly fight to cloak his true thoughts, his true intentions from what he had come to see as a hated part of himself.

Finally, more practical thoughts began to intrude.

Where *was* he? Was this world, wherever it was, nothing but jungle? Were there no people? No villages? No cities?

But the thought cheered rather than worried him. Villages and cities held only painful memories. It was Karg where he had gone to seek immortality, and where, to his everlasting regret, he had found it. It was in Karg and other cities of Darkon he had been forced to assume the form of the Beast and perform for his master, again and again.

Here in the jungle, there would be no vampire masters. No innocent victims to be tortured and killed for his master's idle amusement. Only others like the Beast, content in their mindlessness, never knowing—

A chill swept over him, moist and clammy, and everything was silence. It was as if every living creature within earshot had frozen, motionless, not even breathing.

Suddenly, his every sense was hyper-alert.

Something physically cold and damp brushed against his back.

Silently, he spun toward the touch.

And saw the Mists. For a fleeting instant, they swirled before him, and then they were gone.

A woman stood rigid in their place. She was young and beautiful and as hauntingly familiar as the land itself. Hair as black as night, sleek as—

He blinked the feline image of himself away before it could fully form. The sounds of the jungle returned.

"What is this place?" Her voice was a feral hiss. Her eyes narrowed as they focused on his face. "Who are you, and why have you brought me here?"

"My name is Urik von Kharkov," he said, "and I did not bring you here. Beyond that, I know no more than you. And your name?"

"Malika." Scowling, she looked around. "This is not Cormyr."

"Is it not?"

"You know it is not." Even as she spoke, he knew it was the truth. But how—

"This Cormyr is your home?" The simple syllables felt strangely at home on his tongue.

She nodded suspiciously. "And yours?"

"Darkon."

She shook her head. "That is not a land I know. How

do you come to be here?"

"The same as you, I would venture."

"You are not here of your own volition?"

"Not entirely. I wished to escape Darkon, but—"

"This is useless!" she snapped. She looked around. "Where is the nearest village?"

"There may not be any villages in this world."

"Do not be foolish. This is not the Great Desert. It is a forest, and all forests have an end to them."

"In your world, perhaps."

She laughed, but with a sudden edge of fear. "What foolishness is that? There is but one world. Even for sorcerers."

"I am no sorcerer."

"That is unfortunate. If you were, perhaps you could conjure up a meal. I had not eaten for near half a day when I was snatched here." She pulled in a breath. "I suppose there's nothing for it, then, but to set out. You have no suggestions regarding direction?"

"None."

She was silent a moment, then shrugged and pointed at random. "There. That is as good as any, I imagine." Abruptly, she turned and strode away.

Before she had gone a dozen steps, a sound emerged from the dense thicket ahead of her. Not a growl, but still a sound from deep in some waiting creature's throat.

It was a sound Von Kharkov had heard a thousand times welling up from his own throat as the change had begun and his consciousness faded.

"Wait!" he called after her.

A dozen yards away, she paused and turned toward him, frowning. She seemed unaware of the sound. "You remembered something?"

Behind her, the sound grew louder, more like a growl. Even she heard it then.

She had just turned toward the sound when the tangle of brush and vines exploded and a massive, jet-black panther emerged, its coat sleek and untouched by the underbrush it had just come through. Its green slitted eyes were tinged with red.

"Stay still," Von Kharkov warned her.

His own eyes locked with those of the animal. Slowly, his motions as fluid as those of the Beast, he moved toward her. She seemed as frozen in place as the animal.

Finally he was at her side. His hand on her shoulder, he urged her to move behind him. Silently, she obeyed.

The panther's eyes remained fixed on his as it crouched, as if preparing to leap, the growl rumbling deeper in its throat with each movement Von Kharkov made.

He took a step forward.

And another.

The growl became a snarl, then a hiss. The animal slashed the air with its claws.

A hiss emerged, unbidden, from Von Kharkov's own throat. His eyes remained locked with those of the panther, and for a moment it was as if he and the animal were linked—even more closely than he and the Beast had been. For a moment, he saw himself through the other's eyes, saw the feral snarl on his own face, almost as dark as that of the panther, his eyes even more piercing, more unblinking.

And then it was over.

Abruptly, the animal's entire posture shifted, from one of menace to one of submission. It slumped and lowered its eyes. Then it turned and vanished the way it had come, but in silence.

But as it vanished, Von Kharkov felt the Beast within himself begin to stir.

"No!" A strangled cry ripped at his throat.

"What's wrong?" The woman's voice came to him from a great distance, even though, as he turned, he felt her hand upon his arm.

He shook his head violently. He couldn't speak. He dared not. In his mind, he heard the Beast snarl. *What was happening?* There had been no voice in his mind, no command that the Beast come forth! There had been only that brief, intense link, and the Hunger had begun to rise.

The Hunger had come upon him countless times before, but not like *this*, not without a command from his

master! And here he had no master! It should not—*could*
not be happening!

But it was!

But he could control it!

Here, without Dakovny or another like him commanding the Beast to come forth, he could stop it in its tracks,
just as he had the panther! In Darkon, knowing he could
not disobey his master, he had never dared resist the
transformation. He had invariably surrendered, abandoning both resistance and consciousness as if simply
going to sleep. He had let the Beast assume control as
his body began the change. Only when his human form
returned had he awakened, his consciousness returning
from whatever dark recess it had hidden itself in.

But now he would not retreat! He would not give in! He
would fight, as he had fought—and beaten!—the panther.

Instead of letting his body drop to all fours when the
transformation had barely begun, he held himself rigidly
erect. But even as he did, he felt his body begin to
change. His skin started to itch unbearably, then burn,
and the fire went deeper and deeper until his very bones
were aflame.

Had it always been like this? he wondered. Was this
what he had blanked from his mind all those hundreds of
times before? Or was this only the result of his resistance?

Why was it happening?

He lurched uncontrollably, his arms flailing the air for
balance. The bones in his legs, still aflame, softened and
shifted and bent and formed new joints. The flames concentrated in his hips, then, and his whole body bent forward, as if pressed by a gigantic hand.

And he fell.

Reflexively, his arms—now his forelegs—took the
weight.

His whole body erupted in a new wave of agony, as if
his flesh were being eaten from his bones with acid.

And then the flame engulfed his face, and the world
melted and ran like candle wax as his eyes were transformed. When the fire faded and the world solidified

again, the jungle shadows were no longer places of concealment. To the eyes of the Beast, they were bright as day.

Looking up, he saw Malika. Her eyes were wide in terror, yet she stood before him as if frozen. "Go! Run!" he tried to scream at her, but only a snarl of the Beast emerged.

But that was enough. Whatever spell had held her was broken. She turned and ran, vanishing into the jungle as quickly as the panther had moments before.

Then the change was complete. As he emerged from the flames of the transformation, the Hunger was unbearable.

The Beast sniffed the air. Malika's scent was unmistakable, as were the sounds of her flight.

No! I will not allow you to do this!

But the Beast ignored him, as if he did not exist. It stood silently for a moment, as if savoring what was to come.

Then it padded after the fleeing woman. Its pace deliberate and unhurried, its step lighter and surer than Von Kharkov's had ever been, it unerringly followed her trail. Desperately, Von Kharkov struggled to rein the Beast in, but it paid no more attention to his efforts than it would to a light spring breeze. He couldn't even be sure it was aware of his existence.

But Von Kharkov was aware of the Beast, excruciatingly so. He could feel its muscles ripple as it padded on, could feel the dirt beneath its paws, could smell the jungle scents that assaulted its nostrils.

But most of all, he could feel the Hunger.

A Hunger he could not overcome.

Ahead, the scent and sound of the fleeing woman grew stronger.

He could not save her.

Or himself.

And then he was upon her.

And the real nightmare began as the Beast's jaws—*his* jaws—closed on living flesh.

*   *   *   *   *

It was like a thousand other awakenings: the blood, the shredded flesh, the feeling of satisfaction giving way to self-loathing.

But this time it was not an awakening. This time, he had not lost consciousness—had not been *able* to lose consciousness for even an instant. Instead, he had lived through it all, experienced every grotesque horror of the Beast's feeding frenzy.

And every detail was gouged deeply and permanently into his memory.

He could not forget a moment of the horror, could not force it out of his thoughts for even a second. Nor could he forget—or forgive—his own helplessness to stop it.

Fool! his inner voice exploded. *You were wrong! What the Mists held* was *worse than your wretched existence in Darkon!*

In a daze, he found a stream to wash the gore from his human form, but nothing could remove it from his mind.

After what seemed like an eternity of aimless wandering, he fell asleep on the jungle floor from sheer exhaustion, but even then, he gained no relief. His dreams, his nightmares, were virtually the same as his waking memories, yet more horrifying.

And even more real, more vivid.

Again and again he relived what he had done. And each time Malika died, her memories spread over the surface of her mind, just as her blood spread over the remnants of her body, and while the Beast devoured the flesh, Von Kharkov unwillingly devoured her mind, absorbed her very *soul,* until he knew his victim more intimately than he knew himself.

And then he was forced to kill her again. And again.

After the dozenth—or perhaps the hundredth—time, a new memory began to emerge from the horror.

He had done this before, the memory said. To this same woman or to another very like her.

Not here in this jungle world the Mists had thrown him into.

Not even as Dakovny's slave in Darkon.

But somewhere else, in a lushly furnished apartment in a city whose name and country he couldn't even guess at.

And with that amorphous memory taking root in his mind like a gangrenous wound, he awakened. The jungle still surrounded him. The scent of blood once again clung to him like a poisonous shroud, renewed and strengthened by the nightmare.

As if triggered by his return to consciousness, a pocket of Mists pulsed into existence barely a dozen yards in front of him. He felt a physical chill as it swirled before him, thickening until it was as opaque as the jungle around it.

Abruptly, the Mists took on a reddish tinge, and for a moment he was certain it was Malika's blood diluting the m and that her tortured body would be deposited at his feet when the Mists retreated.

But it was not the dark red of blood, he realized a moment later. It was brighter, a crimson so intense it almost glowed.

A crimson that, like the jungle, triggered an inexplicable feeling of familiarity. And horror.

Then the Mists were gone, vanishing as quickly as they had come.

A man stood before him, his black-bearded face knotted in anger, his overweight body wrapped from neck to toe in a robe of brilliant crimson.

A name leapt out of nowhere into Von Kharkov's mind.

"Morphayus . . ."

The man's eyes widened. For a long moment he scowled at Von Kharkov, then darted quick glances at the jungle around them.

"How did you manage this, Von Kharkov?" the man snapped. "And what is it you want? Whatever it is, be quick about it!"

"Your name is Morphayus?"

"As if you didn't know! Don't waste my time with foolish posturing! Just tell me why you brought me here and what you want of me. If indeed you did bring me here."

The man's voice—Morphayus' voice—grated on Von Kharkov's ears. And suddenly, he *did* know. He knew this place. He knew this person, this wizard. He knew—

In an instant, like the sky opening and drenching him in a downpour, his true past descended on him, burying him under the million details of a life he had not until that moment known existed.

A life before Darkon. A life in which the parents whose gravestones he had visited so often in Neblus did not exist except in his own false memory.

A life in lands called Cormyr and Thay, where that first killing had taken place, the killing that had been echoed in the slaughter of Malika.

And before Cormyr—

For an instant, it was as if he were confronted by a featureless wall that threatened to shatter and fall and crush him, but instead it became akin to the Mists, and shadowy images reached out to grasp him and pull him in.

And he recognized those images.

And he knew the truth about himself.

The final truth.

He had not lost his humanity, trading it for immortality that night in Karg when he had eagerly submitted himself to Dakovny. He had had no true humanity to lose, only a veneer, an illusion.

An illusion created by the creature, the wizard that stood before him now: Morphayus.

Before Morphayus had found him and created that illusion of humanity, there had been no Urik von Kharkov. There had been only a beast, a jungle beast. A panther, virtually a twin to the one he had just encountered and bested. A beast, living its life out in this very jungle to which the Mists had returned both him and Morphayus.

The wizard had found the beast and transformed it into a man. Into the *form* of a man. And he had supplied that man with memories of a past that did not exist.

And then, when it had suited the wizard's warped purpose, the Beast had been brought back—to wreak bloody vengeance on an innocent woman whose only crime had been to spurn Morphayus. A woman named Selena, who could have been twin to Malika.

For what seemed like an eternity but could have been

only a moment, Von Kharkov was lost, adrift in the vast sea of new and contradictory memories.

But then his eyes focused on the crimson-robed man who still stood impatiently before him.

Morphayus.

And he knew that only one thing mattered in all that churning ocean of newfound memories: his true nature lay not in the Von Kharkov shell but in the nameless jungle beast he had originally been. Had he been allowed to remain in that true form, here in the jungle, he would have lived out his life as the simple predator he was. All the senseless killing, all the pain and horror he and his hundreds of victims had undergone, was the fault, not of the Beast or of the Von Kharkov shell, but of the monster who stood before him, the wizard who had created this misbegotten half-human *thing* and set it upon its hellish course.

Morphayus, who had been brought here and put before him.

For the first time in his pseudo-life, Von Kharkov willingly—eagerly—called forth the Beast. This time the transformation seemed almost instantaneous, the flames of his altering body compressed into a brief pulse of pure agony of an intensity he could not have imagined.

And then it was as if they were one: Von Kharkov and the Beast. Von Kharkov's lust for revenge on Morphayus meshed with the Hunger that pulsed through the Beast, a Hunger that, he was now positive, had not been a part of his original jungle self but something the wizard had stirred into the mixture when the Von Kharkov shell had been created.

They leapt.

Together.

Von Kharkov felt the wizard's will grasping at them, trying to force them back, trying to control them as it had in Cormyr, as Dakovny's will had controlled the Beast so often in Darkon.

But the wizard's power was not great enough, not here on the far side of the Mists, and not against the two of them, united in their overwhelming desire for his destruction.

And they were upon him.

* * * * *

It was over.

Little remained of the wizard's body and robe but crimson tatters.

For the first time, the feeling of self-loathing did not come to Von Kharkov as he observed the Beast's—and, this time, his own—grisly handiwork. Instead, there was a feeling of grim satisfaction. He would never atone for what the Beast had done in the names of its masters, but at least he had put an end to the human monster who had been ultimately responsible for those horrors.

And here, in the jungle of his birth, with no perverted master to serve, perhaps those horrors would come to an end. In time, even, perhaps the Von Kharkov shell itself would fade back into nonexistence, now that its creator was gone.

Perhaps that was why he had been brought here by the Mists—or by whatever power lurked behind them, using them to manipulate people and animals and even wizards for its own, impenetrable purposes.

Or so he could hope, though he feared it was more likely just the opposite. No power with any pretenses of goodness or justice could ever have brought an innocent like Malika here only to be pointlessly and cruelly slaughtered as part of its obscure plan for Von Kharkov and Morphayus.

And with that thought, his mind was invaded by a rumble of distant laughter.

And he felt the Mists closing about him once again.

Sight and Sound

D. J. Heinrich

"Open the door!" I cried as I pounded on the massive, metal-bound aperture that separated me from my purpose; neither the wood nor the brass gimmals ornamenting its ebon surface moved. "Open, I say!" I shouted, my voice rising almost to a scream. "Open in the name of justice!" Again I pounded on the portal with rage.

Lightning cracked behind me, silhouetting the black rain drenching this land. The heavens rumbled back—the expansive, pernicious murmurs of an alien sky I had quickly come to hate—and jags of lightning snapped again, momentarily illuminating the cold, forbidding stone of Castle Blaustein. I stared up at the double doors before me, which were fully the height of two men, and beyond to the walls surrounding the citadel's entrance. Snarling stone gargoyles, tortuous crenellations of slate, and shadows of black iron remained branded on my inner eye after the flash departed.

Rain poured down in sheets, engulfing me, soaking my woolen overcoat. It clung unpleasantly to my fevered flesh. I raised my bloodied fists high above my head and glared up at the monolith before me, oblivious to the rain pelting my face and eyes. With a feral moan, I hurled myself at the doors, crying aloud, "Hear me, Bluebeard!"

Lightning responded above me, filling the night sky with white light and sound, nearly blinding and deafening me in its turbulent response. But my senses were abruptly riveted by the doors before me: They were *moving*.

My eyes bulged in their sockets as I strained to catch that minute movement. I know that only seconds must have passed before the doors swung open to grant my admittance, but time seemed somehow suspended then. I heard the creak of those massive doors swing back upon badly oiled hinges. I saw the faint glimmer of light flicker on the gimmals marking the doors as they swung inward. I smelled the dank decay of stale rushes and rancid candle tallow as the warm air within the castle greeted me; it was a false warmth, unpleasant to me even in my cold and sodden state.

I stepped forward immediately, intent on the manservant lurking beside the door, and entered the keep. "Show me to your master at once," I demanded imperiously.

The creature closed the doors behind me, sparing me not a single glance until he had done so. Then he turned his gaunt frame toward me, squared his shoulders, and nodded with a dignity I had not expected in this backwoods country. "My lord will see you now," was his monotone, tight-lipped response. For an instant his gaze met mine, then slid away, but not before I caught the yellow gleam of hatred for a man his better. He picked up a candelabrum resting upon a nearby table and proceeded across the hall's granite floor.

I followed the manservant through the castle's foyer, the size of which was utterly lost in the feeble light of two candles, to an expansive stair that curved upward then split and flowed into separate hallways. My guide took the left branch, and here the dim shadows receded before the light. I gave little thought to the thick carpets we traversed, the muted tapestries periodically adorning the finely papered walls, or the pieces of furniture placed here and there in the long passages. I cared not at all for the glimpses of silver and gilt I caught via the candlelight as we walked this otherwise unlit abode. My thoughts were possessed by the man I would soon confront, by the tales the villagers had told me, by the man who had—

Abruptly, the manservant stopped before an ornately carved door. He threw it open, stepped inside, and announced, "My lord, the gentleman you wished to see is here."

I strode forward swiftly, knocking the servant aside in my haste, and halted just inside the room. In my heightened emotional state, my senses were acutely attuned. In a single moment I took in the vast number of books, the cheerful fire in the grate to one side of the large room, and the comfortable, elegant surroundings. My gaze slid to and locked on the man slowly rising from behind a desk at the far end of the room. The valet proceeded to light more candles, bringing the dark room to more sensible illumination. I strode forward, impatient words forming on my lips.

"Lord Henredon, I presume?" interjected the man behind the desk before I could speak. His words—pleasantly spoken, with a casual, intimate intonation—took me aback. I paused before him, inexplicably disarmed by his easy, familiar manner. I had told no one of my real name in this land; had Lorel . . . ? My eyes narrowed.

My hesitation was slight, however, and I regained my composure immediately. I bowed my head, pausing a hair shy of insolence, and said, "And Lord Bluebeard—I presume?"

His left eyebrow arched in amusement, and his red, full lips twitched. His beard, as I had been told by the villagers, was indeed a shade of black with highlights that waxed blue in the light. He was a man of my height, though he easily outweighed me by nearly half my weight. His features were bulbous and dissipated, and I was suddenly sickened at the thought of his fleshy lips violating Lorel. His eyes, however, were alight with a cunning I knew instinctively to be that of a most dangerous man. He waved his hand—fat and pampered, with rings on three fingers—toward a chair, but I declined with an icy smile. Again his full lips twitched; he fell backward into the huge wing chair behind him, his great girth encompassed by the even larger seat. The manservant lit a remaining candelabrum and stood behind his master.

Bluebeard gazed at me and said, "You are very much

like your sister, Henredon." He smirked. "You have her eyes." His fat red hand smoothed his embroidered waistcoat, and his watch fob jingled.

I leaned forward slowly, splaying my hands across the intricate parquetry of the desk between us. I responded tightly, "You are mistaken, sir, as my sister was adopted when I was fourteen." I smiled back at him smoothly. "But that is neither here nor there, Bluebeard. What matters, of course, is Lorel. Where is she? I've come far to visit her, and I'd like to see her immediately." I kept my voice cool and my gaze bland.

The man's expression did not change, save for a passing flicker of his left brow. He returned my look, meeting my eye measure for measure, but I did not yield. Then Bluebeard gestured with one ringed finger toward my hands. "Pray sit down, Henredon. Your coat is dripping upon my table."

I raised my chin at his tone, but to take offense would be churlish. I nodded stiffly and said, "As you wish," as I sat in the wing chair behind me. Not quite as large or as elaborate as Bluebeard's own chair, it was nevertheless well padded, and the cushioning was welcome to my fatigued muscles. But I resolutely pushed away the memory of my long journey and turned to the matter at hand.

"My sister is here in this castle," I stated. "You have spirited her away from her home, Bluebeard, and I would speak with her."

Again that raising of his left brow, which I began to believe was a habitual manner with him. "Would you now?" He drawled the words, though elegantly. I was finding his speech and mannerisms sharply at odds with his appearance, for at first impression Bluebeard had struck me as a coarse and ill-bred man—a view that warred with his gracious words and abode.

I allowed myself a cursory glance about the room. The walls were lined from floor to vaulted ceiling with books. Inside the hearth, the fire cackled merrily, lending a welcome warmth to my chilled bones. The rug beneath my feet was thick and luxurious, its pattern intricate and many colored. Ponderous rosewood furniture completed the stolid tone of gentility and breeding. My eyes flicked past the silver and gilt candelabra and returned to the books. The scholar in me yearned to explore them, but I was not here in that capacity; I was here as a brother to find my sister—and perhaps, the gods forbid, to avenge her. When I had learned of the man with whom Lorel had eloped, I was caught in an emotion so deep, in a pain and rage so encompassing, it had carried me forward on this desperate journey. A spasm passed through my jaw, and it was with the taste of blood upon my tongue that I returned to my host.

I folded my hands, steepling two fingers as I did so, and stared at Bluebeard. "Yes, I would speak with my sister now," I drawled as slowly as he, "or I will have to believe that something has . . . befallen her." I smiled icily, then arched my brow in imitation. "And I cannot believe—as the townspeople would have me—that *this* wife, too, has met with some . . . misfortune, can I?"

His smiled reply was every bit as cool as mine. "But of course not, Lord Henredon." He laughed shortly, glancing away. "I can assure you, sir, my wife Lorel has met with no such . . . misfortune, as you call it—certainly nothing of the sort that befell my previous wives." His lips twitched.

Inwardly something constricting my chest loosened. Perhaps I had arrived in time to show Lorel the truth, to free her from this monster. Admittedly, the tales I had heard of Bluebeard warred with the image of the elegant gentleman sitting before me, but I could not discount my belief that he would soon grow tired of Lorel and that death would befall her as had his previous wives.

"Then you surely have no objection to my seeing Lorel," I said smoothly. I heard the sudden catch in my voice at my sister's name, and I prayed that Bluebeard had not.

He cocked his head to one side, as if considering my request, then gestured forward his manservant. "I have been remiss, Lord Henredon, in my duties as a host. Please, allow me to offer you some refreshment." His man returned, carrying a silver platter upon which rested two snifters of cognac.

Gratefully I accepted one, though I was determined to sip it but slowly. I leaned back in my chair as the fiery liquid slipped down my throat. "Lord Bluebeard," I said firmly, "I would see my sister now."

The man spread his hands wide, then stroked his silken beard with one, his gaze returning to me. "Ah, but I must tell you, sir, that I do have some objections to your seeing my wife."

My eyes narrowed. "What, pray tell—" I could not keep the sardonicism from my voice "—could those be?"

"Your insinuations regarding the . . . untimely deaths of my previous wives, for one," Bluebeard responded blandly.

I took a sip of the cognac, locking eyes with the man before me, and said slowly, "Sir, my insinuations are merely that—they are hardly accusations." I grimaced. "You have but to let me see Lorel, to speak with her, and I will know that you have been subjected to slander and false innuendo." Some nerve inside my mouth twitched, and I bit my lip. I did not blink. "However, if you do not produce my sister, Lord Bluebeard, I will be forced to believe you to be a murderer and a madman. As such, I would kill you." This time my smile was slight, though filled with the resolve that burned in my heart.

Bluebeard's brows both rose as he cocked his head. Then he nodded slightly and murmured, "And if I allow my wife to see you?"

I leaned forward. "Then I shall ask her to come away with me this very night, Bluebeard, for you *are* a monster!" I cried, unable to restrain myself further.

Abruptly the man threw back his head and roared. One meaty red fist pounded the desk, knocking over his drink, and coarse laughter filled the room. I felt my face flush, and I struggled for composure. When his laughter subsided, he stood, walked around the desk, and sat in the chair next to me. He leaned forward, his elbows resting upon his knees and his girth spilling out of the confines of the chair. His gaze was steady and even amused, though now tinged with a malice that matched the darkness of his beard.

"I find I cannot allow that, Lord Henredon," he demurred, the mask of elegance once more in place. He tidied a turned-over ruffle of one cuff. "I cannot have you take my beloved Lorel, leave my home, and spread such . . . slanders about me." One indigo brow arched upward.

I gritted my teeth and then, with slow, ineffable care, I leaned toward Bluebeard and gripped his velvet lapels with my hands; I saw his eyes widen at the affront I was committing. Then, with a violent effort I hauled him to his feet. I tightened my grip on Bluebeard's lapels, catching some of his corpulent flesh as I did so. Bluebeard winced, then shook his head at his man, moving toward us. The valet subsided. My host's expression was remarkably unconcerned, his brow unfurrowed and his eyes clear. And did I dare believe that his infuriating little smile still played about his fleshy lips?

Bluebeard tapped my straining knuckles with his hands and said, "Henredon! Is there really the need for this? Surely we can talk about this like gentlemen?"

Nonplused, I could not speak. He stared at me coolly, with a bland expression loitering in his eyes. The scent of sandalwood and bayleaf toiletries that he used upon his person assailed my nostrils in these tight quarters, and I found myself struggling to believe that he was less than the gentleman he portrayed to be. But I did not let my hold on the larger man relax.

"A gentleman would have let me see my sister by now," I said grimly, tightening my grip still further. This time he did not wince.

Bluebeard smiled thinly, his full lips compressing into a line. "An excellent point, Henredon, but I must make a point of my own in return." He tapped my chest. "But first, a gentleman would not have his host in such a position, Lord Henredon." A grimace of annoyance flashed across his face. "Please, this is a most ridiculous scene—will you sit down and let us discuss the matter . . . like gentlemen?" His voice was silken and smooth to my ears, but still I did not yield. He continued, "I can excuse your inappropriate actions as those of one who is overwrought by both fatigue and by the depth of his concern for his sister."

Reluctantly, I withdrew my hands. Bluebeard smoothed his clothing and silently gestured me to return to my seat. I did so shakily, rubbing my strained knuckles and watching Bluebeard as he leaned against his desk, one calfskin-booted leg crossing the other.

"Your point, Bluebeard?" I said shortly. "I am in no mood for any more of your civilities."

"My point is one that you have overlooked, sir," he drawled, "and that is that perhaps Lorel *wants* to stay here with me."

I pressed my lips together. "Then I shall discover that for myself, Bluebeard. Let me see her!"

Bluebeard held up one hand, the rings twinkling in the candlelight. "Not so fast, Lord Henredon. You've accused me of being a murderer. Whether my wife leaves with you or no, you are likely to spread falsities about me. I cannot have that."

I bit my inner lip, and my brows drew together. I shook my head impatiently. "If Lorel chooses to leave with me, or if she convinces me that she is truly happy here, then, . . . despite my better judgment, I shall leave. Either way, I give you my word I shall never speak of you to anyone." My eyes narrowed as I looked at the man lounging so casually before me.

"Oh, I believe that you *say* you would never speak of me, Henredon, but what do you offer by way of security? Why should I believe you?" His voice held a tinge of smugness that infuriated my already jangled nerves.

"Because *I* am a gentleman, and I give you my word," I said firmly.

"But I need more than that, Henredon. I need security."

"My word, Bluebeard," I replied coldly, "is my bond. It is security enough."

The man laughed outright at that.

I leaped to my feet. "Call Lorel to us here, now, and let us settle this! I give you my oath, I shall never mention—"

"How?" Bluebeard snapped. The single syllable boomed through the room. "How can you give me that oath, Henredon?" This time it was he who grabbed me; one massive red hand clutched at my throat. His grip tightened as he pulled upward on my neck, as if he were trying to wrench my head from my body. He almost pulled me off my feet, and I realized I had sadly underestimated the strength of the man. "How will you give me that oath, Henredon? How can I trust that you will not speak—to someone, someday?"

I gasped through clenched teeth, my hands struggling to pull aside the vise on my throat, "My word, Bluebeard!"

"Your word is not enough, Henredon!" Bluebeard shouted. His eyes bulged, almost matching the quality of his pockmarked nose and fleshy cheeks. "*I want your tongue!*"

"My—my *tongue*?" I managed to gasp. I could not breathe, and my vision was fading. "What . . . foul enchantment—?"

"No magic, my friend! Give me your tongue, or you shall never see Lorel again!" Vicious glee swelled his voice.

From somewhere within me I found the strength to struggle against the behemoth who held me. My hands circled over two fingers and bent them backward. A little more, I encouraged myself, and then—

Roughly my wrists were grabbed from behind and yanked away from Bluebeard's hands. The manservant brutally twisted my arms in their sockets, and together he and Bluebeard threw me back into my chair.

Bluebeard's thick hand now clenched my jaw. I winced in pain. "What say you, Henredon?" the man crowed. "Give me your tongue and you shall see your sister this night. If she wishes to leave with you, by dawn, then so be it. I'll even annul the marriage and you can have the trollop for yourself!" He sneered, and little flecks of spittle spattered his fleshy lips. "You've lusted after her all these years—what's the loss of your tongue to attain your heart's desire? Nothing less will I take, Henredon— nothing else will vouchsafe your word with me!"

The man's hand tightened, and I looked into those dark eyes boring into mine with such ferocity. Thoughts ran rampant through my fevered mind. I was a scholar; how could I exist without speaking? But then to the fore rose the thought of my beloved Lorel lying with this—this abomination, and I could not abide the vision.

"Yes," I croaked breathlessly. Fear gave way to anger, and I raged at him, "Yes! Take my tongue, you loathsome, ill-bred cur! Anything for Lorel—"

Bluebeard roared, "*Enough!*" He slammed my head against the marble top of a nearby table, sending the piece crashing to the floor. Blood trickled into my eyes, and for a moment I was blessedly dazed.

He wrenched open my jaw, and terror struck me. Despite my intentions, instinct overrode me and, bucking and kicking, I writhed beneath his and his manservant's hands. I freed one hand and struck at Bluebeard, but the hand was too soon restrained—I was no match for the two of them. Bluebeard forced his monstrous paw inside my mouth. I felt his fingers curl around my tongue, one descending down my throat. Bile and blood gurgled in my mouth, and from somewhere deep inside me—from a place I had no idea existed before this moment—a shriek of absolute, primal terror welled up within me.

I screamed without stop. The sound filled the room, blocking out everything, all thought, all emotion, even all sensation, until . . . there came the faint sound of something else—something so repulsive, so violently revolting I felt madness caress me at the sound of it. I screamed again to hide from that sound, but I could not: it followed me deeper, into that tiny part of myself in which I tried to hide and shield my soul. That sound followed me and perverted anything of me that had remained sane.

It was the sound of my tongue being ripped from its roots: the thin, shredding noises as muscle and tissue gave way under Bluebeard's insistence.

My scream turned into some misbegotten gargle, and above the noise I made I could hear the madman's laugh of malevolent triumph as he held above him the bloodied pulp that remained of my tongue. And as I collapsed into a hazy swoon, I thought I heard him say, "Your sister is in the adjoining room, Henredon. Be gone at dawn and your lives are yours. If not, they're mine to torment still more."

He paused, then added casually, "For now, though, I think my man should try to stanch that blood. . . ."

Truculent laughter filled my ears, and at that point I knew no more.

How long I lay unconscious I do not know. I awoke some time later in a sick and pain-racked haze. In desperation, I stumbled to my feet in the near darkness. My host and his servant were gone, and they had left me with but a single candle, not quite gutted in its holder. I put my hands to my face, then a low moan issued without volition from my throat and I was forced to swallow the blood that threatened to choke me. But I could spare no thought for my condition. My beloved Lorel could be my only focus—my only salvation from the atrocity Bluebeard had committed upon me—and I had to find her.

Vaguely I recalled those half words I had heard before my faint. I fumbled for my watch fob, but couldn't find it in my weakened state. Haltingly, I picked up the candlestick and looked toward the mantel, but there was no timepiece there either. I longed for a clock to tell me how much time I might have in which to find Lorel. Although I knew the night must be old indeed, I didn't doubt that Lorel would leave immediately with me. Despite what Bluebeard had done to me, my sister would see me and know instantly that I had come for her. She and I would leave this accursed castle, and I could converse with her with pen and paper at a calmer date. I had only to find her now, and all would be well.

I faltered toward the side door, recalling something Bluebeard had said about an adjoining room. I stumbled past the overturned furniture and broken bric-a-brac and nearly dropped the candlestick. At the door, I was overcome by a wave of delirium, and I stopped to lean against the cool ebon wood. I marshaled my forces. Now was not the time to stop; now was not the time to succumb in defeat. I swallowed reflexively, the gesture filling me with pain and horror. I had risked so much and given more; everything would be worth it to rescue my beloved Lorel. With renewed determination, I opened the door.

All was in darkness inside this room, and it took many moments for my eyes to adjust, even with the feeble light from my sputtering candle. Vaguely I discerned the outline of a huge, four-poster bed, its draperies drawn shut. Lorel? my mind whispered. Her name rose in my throat, but I stopped myself. I would not frighten her in her sleep.

I staggered to the bed and drew back a curtain. I held aloft the candle and peered inside. The bedclothes were rumpled, and I reached out gently and pulled them back. Oh, how I longed for the pale gilt glimmer of my sister's hair to shine back at me! But there was no such sight. My eyes searched frantically as I wildly pulled back cover after cover. Lorel—!

Behind me I heard a sudden whimper, and I whirled about. My candle fell to the floor, sputtered once, then died. I was in utter darkness, but remained calm as I waited for my eyes to adjust. Faint, predawn light illuminated a large window some steps before me. The draperies, thankfully, were drawn open, and I would know the moment of sunrise. I made out the thin white form of my sister huddled in her nightdress upon the window's seat.

Only a moment more, my beloved, I said to myself, silently praying Lorel could hear my thoughts. Only a moment more, and I shall show myself to you in this wan light, and you shall call my name in joy, and we shall be gone from this abysmal place.

I stepped forward.

"No!" Lorel screamed, throwing her white arms over her face and cowering in the window. "No! Don't hurt me! Don't come near me!"

I hurried to her and said her name—or, rather, tried to say her name. In the face of her pain I forgot my own, and her sweet name came out as a garbled groan. She screamed, and I knelt at her feet, reaching out to touch her. Lorel flailed her arms at me, her pale hair streaming across her lovely face, and she cried aloud once more. I spared a glance out the window: dawn was imminent.

I grasped her arms and shook her, perhaps a little too roughly. She hung her head and moaned, shivering palpably and whispering, "Don't hurt me. Please don't hurt me." Again, at the sound of her voice, I could not restrain myself and I tried to say her name.

Lorel struggled to pull free of me, frightened by the grotesque noises coming from my throat, and her cry of agony tore at my heart. Oh, my dear! I thought. Look at me! Look at me with those eyes of azure! Just one look, and you will know that it is I, your beloved. Look at me!

With one arm I roughly pinned her against the window so that she could not escape. Beyond her shoulders, outside, I saw the sun crest the hill, and I knew that dawn was at hand. With my free hand I brushed aside that gilt curtain behind which she was hiding—

Lorel screamed—

—and I gazed in horror at . . . at the bloodied, sightless sockets that marred my lovely Lorel's face.

The Judgment of abd-al-Mamat

Jeff Grubb

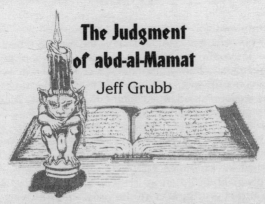

Eh? Visitors? I should have known my fire would have other effects than merely warding off the chill air. Come closer, friends, for no man or beast should be denied comfort on this night. Yes, my skin is duskier than yours, but it is better to be too dark than too pale, eh? Have no fear, my friend, for no ghul or ancient elder am I, but only a simple traveler, carrying his life on his back. Come closer.

A thousand pardons. You seem taken aback by my hand, or rather the stump where my hand should be. Alas, I wish I had a stirring tale to explain this malformation, but such is not the case. I was a simple thief, and for my thievery I was judged guilty and punished by the lopping off of my thieving appendage—a lesson to me and a warning to others. Such is the harsh justice of my home.

Perhaps I *do* have a story, then. Not of my personal judgment, but of judgment nonetheless. I come from the land of al-Kathos, a harsh land of hard judgments. I call upon the listener to turn a good ear to this tale, upon the scribe for a firm and learned hand, and upon Fate herself to guide my words as I tell them to you.

Al-Kathos is a land of sweeping arid wastes and burning sands. It is ruled by the powerful and evil Malbus, a ram-horned abomination who dwells in his Burning Citadel, commanding legions of hellish minions and dining on the flesh of those mortals he captures. However, it is not his tale that I now tell, and he must wait for another evening.

My homeland is also the land of the Sand Singers, luscious wraiths who lure the damned to their dooms with soft scents and honeyed tongues. But though they tempt, theirs is not the tale I tell now. And al-Kathos is the home of the jackal-headed priests of the Rotting Gods, yet even their story must stand aside for the moment.

For this is a tale of judgment.

In the land of al-Kathos there lived a great and powerful man, fair of face and strong of manner. His eyes glistened with a brilliance akin to the desert stars, and his name was abd-al-Mamat. He was thoughtful and wise, even in his youth, and spoke only when he had first thought what he meant to say, cutting to the heart of the matter and discerning truth from fiction.

Yet his role in life was determined not by what he was but by what he was not: for he was not born into high station. This abd-al-Mamat was the son of a slave, and though himself a free man, was considered of low birth and little worth. Were he the son of a sheikh, what you might call a clan leader here, all that followed might have been avoided. But alas, not a dram of noble blood flowed in his veins, and the luxuries of the nobility were denied him.

Yet his talent and his wisdom were recognized, first by his equals, and then by his betters, then by the tribal elders. Many came to seek his advice, and he thought carefully of each request, regardless of the seeker. He never said a word that he did not mean, for, as you know, braying is the mark of all asses. The word spread among his tribe that this low-born orphan, this son of a slave, was a font of wisdom and sound advice.

And at last, when the sheikh sought out a new counselor, which is called in al-Kathos a *vizier,* he came to abd-al-Mamat. The young man was honored and readily agreed to serve the sheikh with a glad heart. As the sheikh's advisor, he would sit near him at the head of the feast, at the side of his master, and offer counsel in all the sheikh's actions.

And that was enough, at first. As the young abd-al-Mamat grew to his maturity, he advised well and often.

Yet the excitement of his advancement, near the head of the feast, wore thin as abd-al-Mamat grew older.

Abd-al-Mamat could sit near the head of the feast, but not at the head of the feast; he could counsel, but he could not decide; he could advise, but not rule. Even the most foolish of the sheikh's brothers had more claim to tribal rulership than he, and should something happen to the sheikh, they would command, not he. And the sheikh himself would often have this thoughts muddled by wine or other pleasures and not heed his words, obvious and truthful though they be.

Late into the evening abd-al-Mamat would pace his tent and curse Fate for his lot. At first he would feel shame for cursing so, in that he thought himself a good man, and good men accept their Fate. Later he felt shame in that others might spy him cursing Fate, and so think less of him. And later still he would feel no shame at all, and wondered at the foolishness of his master.

And after that time he declined even to sit at the sheikh's flank, unless he was so commanded.

As a result, abd-al-Mamat was not present at the feast that was disturbed by the arrival of an exhausted horseman. The rider bolted into the sheikh's pavilion, still mounted, his horse foaming at the bit. Sitting pillows, tribesmen, and wine goblets flew in all directions as the rider spun in place near the center of the revelry.

The rider spoke in gasps, as if he and not his horse had made the long gallop. A merchant caravan from the Burning Citadel had been spotted not far away, he said. It had been in some battle, for it had a fraction of its legion of guards, and the survivors looked worn and bloodied. Should some further harm befall this weakened party, said the rider, then the treasures they carried would be free for the taking.

The celebration was electrified by the news, and the sheikh's brothers soon began arguing among themselves as how to split this as-yet-ungained treasure. The sheikh's eye lit with greed as well, but he summoned abd-al-Mamat. The vizier stamped his way to the sheikh's flank near the head of the feast.

The sheikh said, "A weakened party of merchants

from Malbus is in our lands, oh vizier—wounded, weakened, and bloodied. What say you to this?"

Abd-al-Mamat scowled at the thought of the ram-headed abomination's wrath and of what the sheikh said, and he asked no further questions. Instead, he nodded and said, "Go to them. The rewards will be great."

The vizier's fellow tribesmen gave a hearty shout, and as one, they tore from the pavilion to mount up and pursue the merchants. A large mob of them, touched by wine and dreaming of great treasure, set off at once, the sheikh and his brothers at the head of the van.

Abd-al-Mamat, standing among the remains of the revelry, watched with a puzzled look on his face as they departed. He watched the sheikh's party until they were mere dots on the horizon, and he shook his head. One of the sheikh's other servants stepped forward and asked why he looked so troubled.

Abd-al-Mamat said, "It is strange that there would be so much excitement for a simple mission to rescue some merchants' caravan."

The servant looked at abd-al-Mamat agog, and said, "They do not intend to rescue them, but to rob them. That was what the sheikh was asking."

Abd-al-Mamat's eyes widened, and he said in an ice-cold voice, "That is not what he asked. . . . I have sent our master into great peril! We must send a rider at once to stop them."

A rider was sent, but arrived too late to save the sheikh. He and his brothers and the flower of the tribe's warriors swept down upon the caravan, and the merchants in fear called upon the protection of their fiendish master. Malbus answered their call, for a tower of flame erupted from the desert floor. Of the fifty warriors who attacked, only the rider lived to tell the tale, and he only because he fled before the fire.

At the rider's return, there was a great lamentation among the tribesmen, and none cried louder than abd-al-Mamat. He publicly cursed himself for a fool for misunderstanding his master's words, and tore his garments in his grief. And yet still, surprisingly, he kept his wits about him and demanded everyone work at once to tear down the camp and abandon that which could not be carried easily. For, he said in a grim voice, the minions of the Burning Citadel might choose to slay not only those who attacked, but those who shared the blood of those who attacked.

And abd-al-Mamat's words were proved correct, for the minions of Malbus did pursue them. For seven nights and a night they traveled hard and fast, across the most desolate of the wastes, with the minions in pursuit. And those who faltered or who were left behind were slain by these minions, and their screams carried on the desert winds to drive the survivors onward. And throughout their flight abd-al-Mamat chose the correct and safest path. And if he felt anger or rage or any other emotion about the death of his foolish master, he did not show it.

When at last they reached safety and ascertained that the hellish minions of Malbus had abandoned their chase, the people gathered together to determine their own fate. The best warriors and leaders were dead, save for the sheikh's youngest son, who was not yet of his majority. Faced with such a blow to their very heart, many other tribes would merely have ceased to be, their families and clans wandering apart.

Some of the tribe felt they should disband and wander apart. Then abd-al-Mamat stepped forward, and, tears in his eyes, declared his failure, for his advice had cost them their sheikh and their bravest warriors.

And the people replied that he was not to blame for their sheikh's folly, and it was only through his wisdom that they did not all perish. Abd-al-Mamat bent his head in thanks, then, and swore to keep the tribe together, and to serve as regent until the young sheikh came to his majority, then step aside. And the people acclaimed that decision as the correct and just one.

And the decision was correct and just, for the tribe prospered. Abd-al-Mamat arranged the marriages of several beauties to the sons of other sheikhs, and strengthened alliances and trade. He mollified the agents of the Burning Citadel, such that the minions of Malbus no longer hunted them. And at last the tribe settled at the foot of the last spur of the Lost Mountains.

The tribe so profited from abd-al-Mamat's decisions that few, young or old, pursued any course of import in love or war or money without the counsel of abd-al-Mamat, vizier and teacher to the next sheikh.

And abd-al-Mamat could be seen trying to impart his wisdom on the young sheikh, a task that met with mixed results. The young sheikh was the image of his father in many ways, including an impulsive nature and love for rich finery, great feasts, and the attention of young women. The young sheikh also carried within him a savage temper, and on more than one occasion argued with his regent, winning his point only by reminding abd-al-Mamat of his place: the vizier was the son of a slave, and the youth the son of a sheikh. Abd-al-Mamat nodded in agreement and showed no ire, but instead served the young master as he had his old. The people flourished, and the youth depended on his regent to maintain and enforce the harsh laws of their people.

And it was at this time that abd-al-Mamat began to fully study all the old legends, both for the wisdom of their laws and the powerful magics that they described. And he received emissaries from Malbus, and some said from the jackal-headed priests of the Rotting Gods. Servants and slaves were sent to the far corners of the land, to return with musty tomes and ancient legends. Some did not return at all, and some returned silent, with their eyes purged from their skulls. Some said that this was a clear sign that the jackal-headed priests of the Rotting Gods had been involved. Those who said this said it very quietly.

And so it was: abd-al-Mamat sought further wisdom and tried to impart it on the young sheikh until only a few weeks before the young sheikh's majority.

At that time, the encampment was awakened by shouts and screams, though no one remembered afterward who sounded the alarm first. The daughter of an esteemed and wealthy elder of the tribe was missing from her tent, and could not be found anywhere in camp. The vizier was roused and organized a search, and in the search several noted that the young sheikh was not present.

They found the young sheikh, and what remained of the girl, in the young sheikh's quarters, and even abd-al-Mamat was struck pale by what he saw within those cloth walls.

The young sheikh was brought before abd-al-Mamat and said he knew nothing of what had occurred, though his robes and hands and face were smeared with her blood. He talked of being drunk on wine, of not remembering returning to his tent. He then gathered himself and proclaimed his innocence in a loud and proud voice. He claimed foul sorcery was responsible for this crime, and it should be remembered that he was the son of the sheikh.

Abd-al-Mamat heard the case, as he heard all such cases, and said nothing at first, his face solemn and pale, as if turned to gray stone. Then he rose and said he must consult, for as all know, a hasty decision is invariably wrong. And the people agreed and held the youth, waiting for the judgment of abd-al-Mamat.

The vizier spent seven nights and a night searching through his dusty tomes of legend and law and the ancient books brought to him by his blinded servants. He spoke with all who knew the young sheikh and the dead girl, talked to elders of other tribes, communed with the portents, publicly called on Fate to guide him. In the end, however, he returned to the sheikh's pavilion, his face wet with tears. There could be no doubt, he said. Abd-al-Mamat had to find the youth guilty of his horrid crime.

Under the laws of the people, one's punishment was as befits one's crime. A thief loses a hand, as you have clearly seen. A spy has his eyes gouged out so he may witness no more, and a horse-thief has his tendons cut, so that he may never ride a horse again. It is a harsh law, yes, but remember, al-Kathos is a harsh land.

So it was that the punishment for bloody and painful murder was to be tortured and killed, the process lasting several days. Abd-al-Mamat could have called upon another to oversee this lingering death, but shook his head and took the responsibility himself, blaming himself in the hearing of all for not teaching the youth better.

And the people saw the vizier overseeing the death of his young charge, tears in his eyes as he flayed his flesh and cut him into small pieces. And after the last breath left the shattered body of the young sheikh, abd-al-Mamat gathered the people together.

Abd-al-Mamat said to them, "We have no sheikh. no leader. We must disband the tribe and seek out other tribes with true leaders to follow."

And the people said: We have a leader, and his name is abd-al-Mamat.

And abd-al-Mamat said, "I cannot be sheikh. I am not noble."

And the people said: You are wise and just and stern and have chosen well when our sheikhs had failed. You have chosen the law over your own loyalties. You may not be a sheikh, but you are our leader.

And so it was that abd-al-Mamat became the leader of his tribe. He kept the title of vizier, serving only to counsel his people, but was sheikh in all but name. He sat at the head of the feast, and his advice was considered as law.

And if he was glad in his heart for the events of Fate, or felt guilt for his own role in those events, he never revealed it to his people. He kept his heart shrouded by duty and his secret face shielded by a stern and fair visage. It would be an easy matter to say that when the people left abd-al-Mamat alone in the pavilion of the sheikh, now his own, that a smile would crack the vizier's stony demeanor, that he would begin to laugh. But none could have witnessed this, and more remains to the tale.

The tribesmen became wealthier still under abd-al-Mamat's firm hand. The encampment at the base of the last spire of the Lost Mountains became first a village of tents, then a walled town of mud brick, then at last a city of stone. The pavilion of the sheikh became a beautiful granite Hall of Judgment, and in its central court the vizier sat on a throne of tortoise shell and agate and chalcedony, and advised and counseled, and decided for his people.

And the tribe did prosper in matters of wealth and

prestige, for the robes of their lowest castes were sumptuous and bedecked in rare gems and rarer pearls. Yet inwardly, they grew cold and remote from one another, always choosing to follow the wise advice of their vizier, careful not to violate his commandments.

And there were many commandments, for the vizier still paced his quarters, though they now be bound by finished stone instead of cloth and their floor covered with rich rugs instead of dirt. Again he cursed his Fate. He had made himself the servant of the people, as he had earlier made himself the servant of the sheikh, and as before, he found those he served to be unworthy. They had come to rely on him too much, such that they could not decide anything without his direct order. They were petty and quarrelsome and greedy and spiteful, and deserved nothing less than a stern hand of judgment to keep them from destroying all he had built for them.

One morning a man and two women appeared before him for his advice. The man had told each woman that he would make that woman his wife and take no other. The man could not choose between the two, for both were fair of face and heart, and each woman demanded he make good his proposal. The vizier listened with a stony glare, and wondered how it came to be that he, who had loved nothing but judgment, was called upon to settle such matters of the heart.

The vizier shook his head and said, "If the man cannot decide, then he will be split between the two women"—hoping that such a sentence would force the man to decide, or one of the women to save the man's life by abandoning her claim. Instead, all three nodded at the wisdom of the vizier, and when the man could still not decide, he was split down the middle, vertically, and each half stuffed and presented to each woman. And each woman spoke of the wisdom of abd-al-Mamat.

For his part, the vizier cursed the stupidity of his people, and his Fate that put him at the forefront of such fools. He wondered if the old sheikh, in the last moments of his life at the head of the deadly charge, realized he was among such fools, and could do nothing to change their direction. He, abd-al-Mamat, was no fool, and if his people called upon him to judge them, and approved of his iron-hard rulings, he would do so. He would counsel no longer, only order and demand. And judge.

And so he judged, and judged harshly, as harshly as the desert he once called his home, as commanded by tradition and his ancient tomes. A thief would lose a hand for her crime. A gossip would sacrifice his tongue as payment, and a snoop his eye or ear. And those who lost these organs would live still as symbols of the vizier's wisdom and the nature of the law. And the people would nod at his judgment and watch his ordered punishments, and then, cold-eyed and cautious, return to their homes. They became wealthy, but it was a cold wealth built on cold law, harshly enforced. Brothers shrank from warm greetings and strangers in the coffee houses eyed each other suspiciously, for none knew who would next fall victim to the judgment of abd-al-Mamat.

Now this would make a suitable ending for this tale, to simply say it has been such from that day to this. You have heard of a youth who remained unhappy even after becoming the head of the feast, and of a people who sacrificed their freedom for the leadership of one man. All gained what they desired, and all were punished for it. It makes it a suitable tale, but I fear it is not to be. There is more, and it deals with matters of the heart.

On the day after midsummer's eve, two mule-bound riders swayed into the city, leading a caravan of twenty camels heavily laden with carpets and casks of sweet-smelling oil. The man was tall and noble and had the look of one who had been touched by genie's blood, for his glance was penetrating and his smile (yes, he smiled, even at those he did not know!) was brilliant and sharp.

Yet his comely appearance was outshone by the appearance of his companion, a maiden whose face glowed with the beauty of the moon and whose eyes swirled and eddied with azure storms. She was bedecked in simple white robes and kept her face behind a demure veil, yet she wore her garb with the stature of a queen.

Abd-al-Mamat saw the maiden from his window and

was immediately smitten with her beauty. His heart (which some would think had hardened to a dull, inert lump by this time) leapt to his throat and pulsed there, sending a warmth through his entire being. He judged the maiden to be the most lovely creature he had ever seen, and vowed to win her as his bride.

Abd-al-Mamat sent a messenger to the merchant, bringing honeyed words of welcome and promises of great reward and trade. The messenger also inquired, discreetly, very discreetly, as to the maiden's relationship to the merchant. And the messenger carried out his mission and returned with a long face and a heavy heart: the maiden was to be the merchant's bride, and the two were very close. The merchant laughed at the suggestion that it might be otherwise.

And so Abd-al-Mamat sent a second messenger, this one bearing a chest filled with the finest gems and rarest pearls, to be laid at the merchant's feet in exchange for the maiden. This messenger too returned with a long face and a heavy heart. The merchant would not consider such a trade, and laughed at the suggestion that it might be otherwise.

And so Abd-al-Mamat sent a third messenger to the merchant, this one bearing a metal box. And in this box were the heavy hearts of the two earlier messengers. This third messenger was told to make no demand, but to merely show the box's contents to the merchant and wait for his response. This merchant too returned with a long face and a heavy heart, for the merchant looked into the box, and shook his head. He did not laugh and neither did he offer the maiden.

There was no fourth messenger. Instead, abd-al-Mamat's guards arrested the merchant and dragged him before the vizier for judgment. An old man, toothless and blind, accused the merchant of stealing an apple from his stand. The merchant laughed, though it was a wary laugh, and denied knowing of the apple, the old man, or the theft. Abd-al-Mamat listened and then made his judgment, quickly. He found the merchant guilty of theft and dictated that he must be punished according to the harsh rules of the desert. The merchant did not laugh at all now, but merely said, "If this is to be my Fate, so be it."

And the merchant was taken to the central square, and his left hand was chopped off, as befits the punishment of a thief. And the stump was burned and bound and the merchant sent back to his dwelling with the hope that both he and others had learned from his example.

That evening the third messenger appeared again with a metal box. And in that box was the hand severed earlier in the day. The messenger made no demands, but reported back to his liege that the merchant still refused to abandon his claim to the maiden. But the merchant no longer laughed.

And so abd-al-Mamat's guards arrived at the merchant's dwelling again and arrested him and brought the young man before the vizier for judgment. An old woman, deaf and weak of limb, accused the merchant of gossip, of spreading foul rumors about her and her husband. The merchant did not laugh, but denied knowing of the old woman, her husband, or the gossip.

Abd-al-Mamat listened and then made his judgment, quickly. He found the merchant guilty of gossip and dictated that he must be punished according to the harsh rules of the desert. The merchant did not laugh, but merely said, "If this is to be my Fate, so be it."

And the merchant was taken to the central square and the tongs and the awl and the curve-bladed knife were brought out, and his tongue was severed from its roots. And after the fleshy stump remaining was burned and bandaged, the merchant was sent back to his quarters with the hope that both he and others had learned from his example.

That evening the third messenger reappeared with the metal box, and in that box was the severed tongue. The messenger reported back to his liege that the merchant still refused to abandon his claim to the maiden.

And so once more abd-al-Mamat's guards came to the merchant's dwelling and arrested him and brought the young man before the vizier for judgment. This time the vizier himself was the accuser. The vizier noted that the merchant was maimed and lacked a tongue, and as such could no longer carry out the simple requirements of trade and barter. Yet he still intended to wed his maiden. To condemn such a beauty to apparent poverty, the vizier said, was the mark of a heartless man.

And the merchant said nothing in his defense, (for he had no tongue), and the vizier came to his judgment, quickly.

The merchant was taken to the central square before the great Hall of Judgment. And there abd-al-Mamat himself removed the heart of the man he found heartless, both as a punishment and an example to others. And if the people were shocked as their solemn leader held his bloody trophy aloft, none spoke out against it.

Abd-al-Mamat repaired to his hall and remained there, thinking, through the night. In the morning, he declared that the merchant's belongings had been abandoned by the departed merchant, and by the harsh law of the land were now the property of the vizier. Said belongings included the carpets, casks, and camels . . . and the maiden.

Even with the laws against gossip, the news of this announcement spread quickly through the town, and by the time the vizier's guards arrived to claim the maiden, she was gone. Some idle voices said she was seen climbing the last spur of the Lost Mountains, and so it was that she was seen there as the last rays of the sun faded from the sky. And she spread her arms wide and leapt from that summit, a black mote streaking against the blood-red sun.

She never struck the ground.

Some said (quietly) that she was blown aloft by wind; others (more quietly) that she had been seized by a great djinn; still others (quieter still) that she herself transformed into a creature of the air and vanished; a few (the most quiet of all) that both she and the merchant were touched by genie blood, and as such neither could truly be killed.

And here is another possible end of the story, for both the young lovers had gone on to greater rewards, and abd-al-Mamat was left cold-hearted and alone, his frozen spirit broken in the face of a greater bond of love. But, alas, that is not the end of the tale.

Abd-al-Mamat brooded for seven nights and a night, neither speaking nor eating. At the end of that time, he resumed his judgments of his people, and he was harsher than ever. The guards who had arrested the merchant were beheaded for not arresting the merchant when he entered the city. The gossips who warned the maiden of the guards' approach had their lips sewn together in tight stitches and as such starved. The third messenger was accused of stealing the vizier's words, and so lost only a hand, as I have lost mine.

The judgments did not stop there, for abd-al-Mamat's eyes and ears were everywhere. And wherever abd-al-Mamat looked, he judged, and wherever he judged, he found the people wanting, and issued his punishments accordingly. Soon the city was filled with the blinded, the tongueless, the orphaned, and the lame, such that those who were whole were viewed with suspicion and soon found themselves under judgment as well.

So it went for a year, and the city of abd-al-Mamat became known as the Wounded City and was shunned by travelers and caravans. And there were none within the city who were whole, for all had been found guilty in some manner or another, and punished as an example to all. None within the city, save the great and wise vizier, abd-al-Mamat.

So it was on the dawn of the day after midsummer's eve. The first warning on that day was a darkening of the sky from the north, a direction from which no storms normally came. The darkness rose as a obelisk of azure smoke, and as it drove down on the city, there was a low, metallic buzzing, as if it were made of mechanical insects. And as the storm broke over the walls of the city, the people saw that the wind carried not insects, but swords—great scimitars and daggers, cutlasses and tenwars and all manner of blades, which sliced apart everything in their way.

The city gates turned to dust in an instant before this sharp-toothed onslaught. The steel wind cut down those of the vizier's guards who stood and fought, and pulled those who attempted to flee into the streets, slashing them quickly to ribbons. The storm of whirling blades surged into the central court of the city, and up the steps, reducing the marble facade of the Hall of Judgment into mere motes of stone. There was silence for a moment, then the buzzing resumed as the unearthly wind pulled abd-al-Mamat into the central court.

The whirlwind passed over the vizier time and again, and with each passing collected a bloody trophy at the end of one blade. Abd-al-Mamat raised a hand to ward off the blow and had it severed at the wrist. He raised his other hand and lost it as well. Then the arms, the legs, and the features of his face—lips, ears, nose, eyebrows, and eyelids. Great strips of meat were pulled from his torso, and the vitals of his body were gutted by the great steel wind as well.

Yet abd-al-Mamat lived through his punishment and screamed for help from his guards, from his people, and from Fate. But no one answered, and he screamed until the means for him to scream were finally ripped from his ragged form.

At last all that was left was the skull of abd-al-Mamat, its lidless eyes still sharp, alive and silent within their bony housing. Then the steel wind carried off the remains of abd-al-Mamat, still twitching and alive. The wind of swords retreated into the desert and was never seen again.

And this, too, would be another suitable end for the tale, for the vizier of judgment was himself judged, they say, and found wanting, and punished by the harsh ways of the desert, and one could claim that the balance of good and evil was restored.

But alas! Such is not to be, for there is still more.

The time since the vizier's iron rule has not been kind to the people of abd-al-Mamat. Malbus, the ram-horned abomination, began to hunt the people again as animals, dragging them back to his Burning Citadel for his dark amusements. The Sand Singers lured off their men and women to nameless deaths. And the jackal-headed priests of the Rotting Gods struck at will, claiming the eyes of their captives. The people were leaderless and alone.

And, with none to rule it well, the city of Abd-al-Mamat fell apart. The walls crumbled and the fountains ran dry. The Hall of Judgment became a mere shell, housing those who would not leave the grandeur of their forefathers. And of the vizier's throne of tortoise shell and agate and chalcedony, there was no remnant left.

Many of those left would recall the harsh time of abd-al-Mamat and remember them as good days, at least for those who obeyed and knew the law. The fact that those recalling this were often maimed by that law was forgotten. And as time passed, these wounded remnants disappeared, leaving behind only tales and the empty shell of his castle as his testaments. So it was for a hundred years.

Then one of the sons of the sons of the sons of the vizier's followers found the first piece, there at the base of the last spur of the Lost Mountains, on the day after midsummer's eve. It was a left hand, still bloody and living as if newly severed from a thief's arm. The hand twitched and bled, yet it did not die, and the son of the son of the son of the vizier's follower thought it a miraculous occurrence. In his home, which was in the ruined Hall of Judgment, he made a small shrine for the bleeding hand.

The next year, at the same time and place, a lower left arm appeared, also bloody and alive, as if newly severed from a human. The son of the son of the son of the vizier's follower found it and brought it to the shrine as well. The hand and arm fitted together without a seam showing and could not be pulled apart, such that they became one part. The united hand and arm were kept in the Hall of Judgment as well, and people began to return to the city to visit the shrine and view this curiosity.

Then another piece appeared in the next year, and another in the third, always a new part that seemed recently severed from its host, and always on the day after midsummer's eve. An elbow, an upper arm, a bit of shoulder, the muscles of the neck, and so on. The son of the son of the son of the vizier's follower waited for each piece and fitted the living pieces together. And the collected pieces clung to each other as if they were one, and thrived.

And word spread among the other descendants of abd-al-Mamat's followers: the sons of the sons of the sons and the daughters of the daughters of the daughters, who knew of abd-al-Mamat only from their maimed great-grandparents sighing about a past golden age. The vizier was slowly being returned to his people.

Here we come at last to the end of my tale. It is an ending only in that this is all that has occurred so far. It is said that today the body is almost complete. It is said that only the skull, with its naked, screaming eyes, is missing. And when this last item is restored, the vizier will return fully to lead his people.

And the judgments of abd-al-Mamat will begin anew.

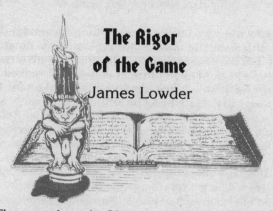

The Rigor of the Game

James Lowder

The game brought Oliver Arkwright to walk the harrowing roads of Sithicus, just as it had propelled him on other foolish journeys throughout his twenty-odd years as a gambler. To anyone who bothered asking, Oliver bluntly cited greed as his only motivation for such risky ventures. He knew better. The money purchased food and shelter and sometimes even companionship, but he'd realized years ago that he pursued a sharp's life solely for the thrill of tempting fate.

And he'd tempted it sorely on this trip. Since crossing the border from Gundarak three days past, Oliver had seen snakes as long as boar spears and slavering wolves with eyes that glowed like embers, even in the moonless murk of the Sithican night. He dispatched these threats as he did most living obstacles that stood between him and a game—mercilessly, with a lightning-quick flash of his falchion. But there were other things in the darkness as well, ghostly things that groaned and shrieked like the damned. Oliver suspected his sword would avail him little against such phantasms. Fortunately, the keenness of the gambler's curved blade was more than evenly matched by the keenness of his wits; he managed to elude the wailing creatures and even catch a few hours' sleep in dry gullies along the roadside.

Now, at last, he stood on the weatherworn threshold of his destination. It was a wayside inn very much like the myriad wayside inns Oliver had frequented in other, equally gloomy lands. The hulking two-story box slouched at the side of the road in the middle of nowhere, as if it had been traveling to someplace where it might share the company of other buildings, but lacked the resolve to finish the trek. And so it huddled on the forest's verge, defeated and forlorn. Only the inn's sign remained defiant. The miniature armor-clad knight affixed to the board clasped an embossed shield in one hand. In the other he clutched a long sword at the sky, ready to smite the very sun.

Oliver spared the knight the briefest of glances before he smiled with anticipation and strode to the door. The fatigue born of the past three days disappeared suddenly. In its place crackled a frisson of excitement.

That excitement dimmed only a little when Oliver discovered the door barred resolutely against him. When his first knock went unanswered, an uncomfortable dread began creeping up his spine. Had he come to the wrong place? He stepped back and again surveyed the sign. The knight's slate-gray armor and the badge embossed on his shield rekindled the sharp's hope—no, this was definitely the Iron Warden. And for all its forlorn appearance, the place wasn't deserted; eight tethered horses grazed to one side, and smoke curled languidly from the chimney.

His falchion drawn, Oliver closed on the portal once more. "Unless you want me to hack it down, you'd best unbar this door immediately!" He broke the answering silence by rapping on the wood with his sword's ornate pommel.

The stout door opened soundlessly on well-oiled hinges, and a large, bulbous head peered around the jamb. It was not nearly so silent as the door. "Bugger off!"

Oliver retreated a step. The bouncer's head was huge, at least twice the size of a normal man's. His mouth was a yawning, scraggle-toothed cavern, his bloodshot eyes two angry dagger slashes beneath a fiercely creased brow.

Brushing aside his initial surprise, Oliver adopted a practiced facade of road-weary impatience. "I was told a game is being played here. High stakes. One afternoon only."

The bouncer's expression remained fierce. "So?"

"So I'm here to play." A smirk crept across Oliver's lips. "Actually, I'm here to win."

With a flourish, the sharp swept back his travel-stained cloak and sheathed his blade. He then took up the small leather purse hanging at his belt. "There's an entry fee, I suppose," he said, extracting a silver coin. "Is this enough?"

"Enough to stop me from pounding you into the turf like a tent peg," the bouncer growled. He reached one beefy hand forward to snatch the coin from the gambler.

From what Oliver could see of the brute, framed within the inadequate bounds of the doorway, his body was completely in proportion with his huge head. The sharp remained impassive as the coin was wrenched from his fingers. He merely stood corpse-still and gauged the brute's agility. Just as he'd suspected, the bouncer fumbled with the silver as he drew it up to his eyes. Oliver was certain he could slice the man's head from his tree trunk of a neck before he landed a single blow. The knowledge cheered the gambler and made him bold.

"I suppose you don't travel much, so the coin's mint must be new to you," Oliver drawled. "The twined snakes on the reverse mark it as Souragnean. It was part of a haul I took aboard *La Demoiselle du Musard*."

The bouncer pocketed the coin and rubbed his nose, wide and nearly shapeless from being broken so many times. "Silver's silver," he said, clearly unimpressed by the coin's origin. "Now get walking, whiles you still got legs to carry you."

"I'm here to play in the game," Oliver repeated. "If you need to see more of my coin—"

The bouncer snorted. "I can see you ain't got enough blunt on you to buy your way in. The others brung theirs in chests."

Oliver held his left arm up, exposing the large diamond studding his cuff. "This little gem is straight from the duke of Gundarak's coffers. The silver it would take to purchase this beauty would fill five chests."

He twisted his arm so that the diamond cuff link flared in the bright, late afternoon sunlight. "Lovely, isn't it?" he lulled. "You'll never see another like it so long as you live." And while the beetle-browed doorman stared at the stone, Oliver stealthily slipped his right hand down to the hilt of his falchion.

"Watch his blade, Unthar," came a sweet, almost childlike voice from within the Iron Warden. "Master Arkwright's cuff links tend to precede his falchion into a fray."

The young woman who sidled past the bouncer matched her voice quite well. She was short, with girlish blond curls and round, cherubic features. The cotton dress she wore was the blue of cornflowers, trimmed with a fine white lace and cut to modestly cover her legs. A missionary's wife stranded in the wilderness. At least that was the impression she gave as she came to stand in the doorway of the derelict inn. Oliver knew better.

"Tisiphone," he whispered. The color drained from his face, leaving him as pale as a victim of the White Fever. And for the first time since entering Sithicus, the sharp was afraid.

Smiling sweetly, Tisiphone extended a dainty hand in welcome. "Glad to see you again, Oliver. It's been almost two years. I do believe that the game in Richemulot was the last time our paths crossed."

A vivid memory of Tisiphone flashed in Oliver's mind. The game had taken place in the fetid, dripping tunnels beneath the ruined city of St. Ronges. Guttering torches cast fingers of light and shadow over the grisly scene. Bloody to the elbows, Tisiphone straddled a twitching corpse. When the unfortunate man had attempted to palm a pair of loaded dice into the game, she'd torn his throat out with her bare hands. Oliver could still hear her laughter, still see the grin on her pretty face as she licked the gore from her perfectly manicured nails.

Gently Tisiphone hooked an arm in Oliver's and guided him across the threshold. "I'd heard you set yourself up a permanent game in Gundarak. I was surprised. You never struck me as the type to settle down for very long."

"I'm not. I only worked the taverns in Zeidenburg for the winter. Otherwise, I've been roaming." He glanced at the young woman. "Someone told me you'd finally run afoul of Renier's men in Richemulot and got yourself hanged."

She pulled down the high collar of her dress to reveal a smooth, milk-white throat. "Obviously you can't believe everything you hear. Tell me, what do you think of my place?"

From his vantage at the end of the long oaken bar, Oliver surveyed the taproom. It was poorly lit, but tidier than most, even rather homey. The tables were clean, the floor carpeted with fresh rushes. A small fire danced in the hearth that dominated one entire wall. The half-dozen men and women occupying the room gathered beside the flame, drawn like moths to the feeble, flickering light.

Oliver cautioned himself not to relax. If Tisiphone ran the Iron Warden, the pleasant facade most certainly masked something sinister. "Nice enough," he said noncommittally.

"I won the deed to the place a few weeks ago," Tisiphone offered as she poured a cup of blood-red wine. She slid the drink to Oliver and filled another cup for herself. "The man who lost the place to me inherited it when his father was killed by elves."

The sharp fought to maintain his guarded indifference. "Elves? I thought they were only a myth."

"I wish that were true," Tisiphone said darkly. "They avoid the main roads because of Lord Soth's patrols, but the hills and forests are full of them. They're monstrous things, feral and bloodthirsty. The tortures they use are more horrible than any you could dream up." She shuddered and took a long swallow of wine. "More horrible than any *I* could dream up."

The sound of Unthar shuffling across the rushes alerted Oliver to the bouncer's movement just as Tisiphone finished speaking. "If you want to be done by sunset, we gotta start," the brute said.

Tisiphone nodded curtly, and Unthar lumbered to the center of the taproom, where he withdrew a velvet cover from an elaborate dice table. A carved bone rail surrounded a long center of green felt. The center, in turn, was subdivided by thin lines of white paint into various betting areas.

"I welcome all of you to the Iron Warden. The game this afternoon will be death's-head dice," Tisiphone announced as she made her way to the dice-dealer's position along the rail. "For those of you unfamiliar with the game, it's a local version of craps, with two important variant rules."

She swept up a dice boat and emptied its contents—a pair of midnight-black dice with white pips—into her hand. "All Sithican dice have death's-heads instead of ones."

"How morbid. Now I know why I've never bothered to visit here before." The speaker was a heavyset man, well-dressed to the verge of foppery. He was the only one of the competing players that Oliver recognized, a money-hungry grifter by the name of Dorlon, whom he'd wagered against in Gundarak.

"You don't know the half of it," Tisiphone murmured. She rolled the dice between her thumb and index fingers until both death's-heads grinned at the assembled gamblers. "The icons figure as ones in determining a point to be thrown. But if you throw them as a double on a first roll, you're bust—completely. You turn over everything to the house."

Oliver scowled. "Everything?"

"Are you worried that I'm going to ask for your soul?" Tisiphone replied. Suppressed laughter made her voice a little shrill. "'Everything' means all the coins and jewels you brought into the Warden. That's all."

Tisiphone handed the dice to the closest player. The black cubes were passed from gambler to gambler, so each could check them for loading. While the dice were examined, she continued to outline the game.

"The other rules variation is just as simple: if a shooter rolls a natural—seven or eleven—the house gets a chance to kill it. I roll both dice. If they come up double death's-heads, the shooter loses everything. If they match the shooter's natural, his win is doubled."

The less-experienced gamblers bristled at the harsh irregularities, but Oliver found them enticing. The house always had an advantage in craps; the death's-head variations simply meant the risk of going bust was more threatening, more complete. It was rather like fencing with unbated foils, a practice Oliver still pursued from time to time.

"First shooter," Unthar grunted as he took up his post as stickman. He leveled a finger at a mousy woman with graying hair. "You got here first, you shoot first."

"Rules of the house, I assume?" Oliver asked. "Any others?"

"No," Tisiphone said brusquely. "No other house rules."

At Oliver's side, Dorlon chuckled and slapped him on the shoulder. "Were you expecting her to have some silly unspoken rule she could use to winnow the flatts from the sharps? Not everyone here has your experience, Arkwright, but I assure you that there are no flatts here to be gulled."

"Always learn the rules of the house before you put a penny on the green," Oliver said. "Only a flatt would balk at asking for them."

Dorlon sniffed effetely at the barb, shoving past Oliver and working his way to the opposite side of the table. He lingered there, next to Tisiphone, and waited for the other players to lay into Oliver. After all, the insult had been directed at them, too, since no one else had thought to request the house rules.

But the five shooters remained silent. From the distressed, nervous expressions on their faces, Oliver decided that Tisiphone had drawn nothing but flatts, wealthy rubes who'd soon find themselves bust. He smiled inwardly and plotted the course his wagers would take. If he played this right, he could draw off more than a little of their blunt with side bets before Tisiphone took her haul.

And the game soon proved Oliver right. The first Souragnean silver piece the sharp fished out of his purse was the last of his own money he had to lay down, and he won that back immediately. As the five flatts squandered their cash on foolish side bets, he steadily built a sizable hoard. Only Dorlon avoided his carefully considered wagers; the grifter knew full well that Oliver would never allow himself to be drawn into a side bet that wasn't to his advantage.

Within two hours, the novices had been driven from the game. The death's-heads grinned up from the table time and again, their eyeless gazes proclaiming ruin upon one player after another. And for each disastrous fall of the dice, Oliver felt his heartbeat speed a little, felt his caution dwindle. The rigor of the game was seducing him, as it always did.

Dorlon acquitted himself no better than the flatts, falling victim to the death's-heads just before sundown. As the foppish grifter pulled his fur-trimmed cloak around his shoulders, Oliver flipped a coin at him. It disappeared into the rushes at Dorlon's feet. "For the road home," the sharp said. "Maybe you can pay the elves to leave you alone."

The grifter took the coin and left without comment, but Oliver heard Unthar grumble a curse under his breath.

"Is there a problem?" the sharp asked coldly.

"Unthar rode with Soth's patrols once," Tisiphone explained as she scooped up the dice and handed them to Oliver. "He saw firsthand what the elves can do."

"Maybe you'll see them cut someone up," the brute rumbled. "You'll be real close and have to watch everything, all the blades and the needles. Then we'll see if you can joke about it."

Tisiphone glared at the bouncer. Oliver recognized the look from the bloody game in Richemulot. Her mask of sweetness had cracked just enough to reveal the horrible fury lurking just below the surface. But there was something else in her eyes now as well. Desperation, perhaps. Or was it fear?

"We have to close up soon," Tisiphone said at last. "Lord Soth's orders. The game has to be shut down by dark."

She was lying. Oliver had no doubt about that. And as he tried to piece together a reason for her fear and her obvious, desperate lie, he realized what was troubling the woman so: she knew she was going to lose.

"Fine," the sharp said. "Let's get this over with."

All afternoon, Oliver had avoided being the shooter as best he could. He'd passed the dice frequently, preferring instead to earn himself a better position through side bets and wagering alongside the house, fading the other players. Now, he heaped all his coins on a nearby table, capping the hoard with the diamond cuff links he'd won from Duke Gundar. "Everything on this roll," he said calmly, then gathered up the dice and threw them down the center.

The first die turned up a death's-head, and Oliver's guts clenched. He watched the other die spin wildly on a corner, for what seemed an eternity. A wave of despair washed over him. "Come on," he hissed.

The die dropped as a three.

"Your point's four," Tisiphone said, voice quavering.

Oliver rattled the dice confidently. He'd stood on the brink of ruin and come away unscathed. There was no way he was going to lose now. Fate was smiling on him, bathing him in a radiance that blinded the death's-heads to him.

Certain of his good fortune, he cast the dice again.

"Double two. Shooter wins," Tisiphone said. The words slithered from her on a ragged sigh. But before Oliver could even congratulate himself, she added, "I can't cover your wager."

"What?" he shouted.

"One of those cuff links is worth more than all the silver I took from Dorlon and the others," Tisiphone said.

Oliver stalked to her side. "You don't have anything else? No gems? Nothing hidden beneath the floorboards—besides the former owner, I mean?"

"I have the deed to the Warden. That's all."

The tears that began to course down Tisiphone's cheeks only hardened Oliver's heart against her. Did she think he was some bumpkin just wandered in from the fields to be swayed by such histrionics? "Then I suppose I'll just have to take the inn," the sharp said.

Shoulders hunched in resignation, Tisiphone took a rolled sheet of parchment from under the dice table. "This is the deed." She tossed it to Oliver. "The Iron Warden's yours."

"I won't be staying here. If you want to manage the place for me, we might be able to work something out."

"No, thanks," Tisiphone said. The tears were abruptly gone, as was the quaver in her voice. She signaled to Unthar. "Hurry. The sun's gone down."

"You're leaving?" Oliver stammered. "What about the elves?"

"I'd rather take my chances with them than with what's coming here," Unthar blurted as he retrieved two packed saddlebags from behind the bar and hustled one over each broad shoulder.

The curved blade of Oliver's falchion hissed like a serpent as it slipped from its scabbard. Sword raised before him, the sharp started across the taproom toward Tisiphone. "No one's leaving until I get an explanation," he said menacingly.

The inn's front door slid open then, revealing a tall, armored figure, black against the crimson and gold of the twilight sky. "No one is leaving until I have my turn at the table," it corrected in a sepulchral voice.

Tisiphone and Unthar dropped to their knees. "Lord Soth," they murmured, gazes downcast.

The Knight of the Black Rose walked slowly into the room. By the wavering light of the candles, Oliver could see that the ancient armor Soth wore had been scorched, as if blasted in some mammoth furnace. The intricate embossings of flowers and kingfishers that had once patterned its surface were scarred almost beyond recognition. The icon spared the most destruction—a rose on the breastplate—showed hints of its original crimson hue, but soot, or blood, had stained most of its petals black.

Soth's cape of royal purple swirled behind him as he moved, a banner borne up by ghost winds. At first glance, the cape appeared regal and richly embroidered. But as the knight got close to Oliver, the gambler noted that the fabric was bloodstained. Like everything about the lord of Sithicus, the cloak recalled distant victories, battles won for noble reasons long ago transmuted by fanaticism, honorable men long ago tainted by depravity.

The knight stopped less than a sword's length away from Oliver, disdainful of the gambler's naked blade. He regarded the sharp with eyes that glowed like wills-o'-the-wisp within the darkness of his helmet, then pointed at the parchment clutched in the man's hand.

"You are the owner of the Iron Warden," Soth said hollowly. "As stated in the charter you hold, this is the day of appointment. You will play me in a game of death's-head dice for the title warden of the Iron Hills. If the chain of office is yours after the contest ends, you will lead my troops this very night against the elves that dwell there."

A wretched groan escaped Oliver's lips. Tisiphone hadn't been fearful of losing. She'd been afraid that she wasn't going to pawn the deed off before Lord Soth arrived. She'd gulled him like the most pathetic of flatts.

As Lord Soth turned toward the dice table, another stranger hurried into the taproom. Clad in the finery of a court seneschal, he was no more than four feet tall from the heels of his iron-shod boots to the top of his bald pate. His muttonchop sideburns and thick mustache were the white of old bones. And while age had stooped the seneschal's shoulders decades past, it hadn't lessened his energy; he bustled after his master, a chain of office draped over one arm. "I have the warden's badge, mighty lord," he said. The words sounded like the creaking of ancient trees in a windstorm.

"Place it on the table, Azrael," Lord Soth replied.

Tisiphone came forward on her knees, her voice full of feigned sweetness and humility. "Begging your indulgence, Lord Soth, but if you won't be needing us for the game, we'd like—"

A blow from the seneschal silenced her and sent her sprawling into Unthar. "Lord Soth didn't ask you to speak," Azrael rumbled. He shook his fist in front of her bloodied face. "Open your yap out of turn again and I'll bash your teeth in."

The suddenness of the attack unsettled Oliver, but Tisiphone's reaction to the blow chilled the sharp to the core. She kowtowed to the dwarf, then crawled into a corner with Unthar, begging the lord's forgiveness all the way. If a barbarous, cold-hearted murderer like her knelt before Soth, what sort of infernal creature must he be?

"Come, Azrael," Soth said. "Let us appoint the new warden so the troops can begin their march to the Iron Hills."

The lord of Sithicus positioned the warden's chain of office on the green. "There is my wager," he noted as he snatched up the dice. "It is the only thing of value I have carried to the table." He tossed the ebon cubes almost as soon as he'd picked them up.

"Death's-heads," Soth reported without looking at the dice. "I've lost. The chain is now yours."

Oliver stared in horror at the twin skulls with their leering, rictal grins. The walls of the taproom seemed to close in around him, the beamed ceiling seemed to lower. He wanted to scream, but there wasn't enough air in the room to fill his lungs. After a moment, the gambler managed to gasp out a simple question: "I get a throw as well?"

Soth nodded. "Win and you earn your freedom. Since I have nothing left to cover your bet, I can offer you only that."

With trembling fingers, Oliver took up the dice. They felt like cubes of black ice, drawing the warmth from his palm, numbing his fingertips. He clenched his hand, but the cold only spread to his wrist. Soth's touch had chilled the dice, he realized. Cursing, Oliver flung them away.

"Seven," Soth said.

Oliver could hardly believe his ears. "I won," he breathed softly, trying to convince himself of his victory. The feeling began to flow back into his hand.

"Not yet," said the Knight of the Black Rose, reaching for the dice. "As dealer, I can kill the roll by throwing double death's-heads."

Soth's words took Oliver unawares, like an assassin's blade in a close alley. And when he looked at the knight, the gambler saw something that finished the murder of his hopes. The leather gauntlet had slipped away from Soth's wrist. The exposed flesh—what little of it remained—hung in scabrous tatters from blackened bones. Whatever the knight was, he most certainly wasn't alive.

Oliver knew then that any dice Lord Soth threw would turn up death's-heads. He was doomed.

"No," the sharp blurted before he even realized what he'd said. "You don't get a kill roll."

Lord Soth paused. "What?"

"H-House rules. I own the inn, I can set whatever house rules I want." Oliver tried to muster a more authoritative tone, but failed miserably. "You should have asked what they were before we started the game."

Snarling madly, Azrael charged at Oliver. As the seneschal scrambled across the taproom, his features flowed and blurred like an image viewed through a rain-soaked pane of glass. His face elongated. His nose and mouth lengthened into a snout. Hands transformed into paws that bristled with razor-sharp black claws. Arms and legs thickened until they resembled an animal's limbs more than a man's. And all over his body, coarse fur sprouted in a thick coat. Azrael's features and the striping of his fur marked him as a terrifying admixture of dwarf and giant badger.

Oliver managed to get his sword clear of its scabbard, but not even the sharp's battle-honed agility could bring the blade to the ready before the werebadger vaulted the dice table. Horror-struck, he stared at the mad thing leaping for his throat. A prayer flashed through his thoughts: let me bring my sword to bear before Azrael tears my heart out. At least then I might drag the creature down to death with me.

But Azrael never reached the gambler. As he passed over the center of the table, Lord Soth upended the heavy board and dashed him from the air. The bone rail splintered against the werebadger's skull. He landed in a heap, surrounded by shattered wood and torn felt.

"You're right," the Knight of the Black Rose said, as if the conversation with Oliver had continued uninterrupted. "I should have asked for the rules of the house before wagering."

Soth let the dice slip from his hand onto a chair. They came up death's-heads. "You see why I use this place to lure gamblers in, Azrael. They're much more clever than the drill-dulled military-types who would covet the commission."

The werebadger grunted and struggled to his feet. "And the gamblers you make warden live at least two or three days longer than anyone else you throw against the elves."

Cautiously Oliver backed toward the door, but Soth stopped him with a fiery stare. "You aren't going anywhere," the knight said.

"But the wager," Oliver began.

"Was more than paid when I saved your life from Azrael." Lord Soth recovered the chain of office from the ruins of the dice table. He held it up and examined it, then turned toward Tisiphone and Unthar. "The inn's charter states that, should the owner of the Iron Warden escape his duty, I am free to choose a replacement from the populace. You two will share the job. Azrael, get them ready to make the journey to Nedragaard Keep."

Unthar opened his cavernous mouth to protest, but Tisiphone silenced him with a somber shake of her head. "There's no way to beat him," she whispered. "Not when he makes the house rules for all of Sithicus."

As the werebadger herded the new wardens of the Iron Hills out into the night, Lord Soth faced Oliver once more. "You are confined to the inn," he said. "I will return in a few weeks—or perhaps a month—to play again for your service. Undoubtedly I will need a new warden by then."

Soth reached out and gripped Oliver's hands tightly. The chill that had radiated from the dice was a touch of the summer sun compared to the bitter, aching cold that Oliver felt in the death knight's grasp. His hands went numb quickly, but not before needle-sharp slivers of pain sliced into his flesh and began a slow, agonizing crawl up his arms.

"In case you have any ideas about gambling the deed away," was all Soth said before he abruptly whirled and strode from the taproom of the Iron Warden.

Oliver guessed the meaning of the knight's obscure statement even before he fumbled the dice into his pain-racked hands. But he had to test it, had to know for certain what Soth had done to him.

Wincing, the sharp spilled the dice onto a tabletop. Two death's-heads grinned up at him, just as they would each time Oliver Arkwright cast dice for the rest of his short life.

Cold, Hard Silver

Juanita Coulson

The beautiful young woman who stood on Baratok's western slope seemed disoriented, like one but recently wakened from a long sleep. In the foothills below and to her right were barrens dotted with pits, tailings, and workers' huts, which marked the location of rich silver mines. On either side stretched outliers of the vast Tepurich Forest. Beyond, at the mountain's base, lay Wagner Lake, its waters lapping the shores near the boyar's mansion and the adjacent village, pastures, and farmholds.

The scene ought to have gladdened her heart, for in times long past, Jezra was the Wagners' heiress. All she beheld belonged to her. But a terrible curse now forever divided her from kindred and home.

She gazed sadly at the bleak, autumnal landscape. Snow had come early to Baratok this year; even before the last leaves fell, deep drifts had accumulated above the mines and forest. The moon, at its zenith, reflected on a stark white wilderness and illuminated Jezra's silvery tresses and strange, pale eyes.

Bathed in pearlescent, unearthly radiance, she shivered despite her costly fur-lined cloak. Anguish contorted her exquisite face. Why was she condemned to wander endlessly through wintry weather, never knowing spring and summer? Why must she be alone and friendless? And why, no matter how warmly she was clad, was she always so *cold?*—as if knives of ice stabbed her to the very bone, never ceasing their brutal torture.

Suddenly her attention was caught by a faint glimmer in the forests below. Pinpricks of light moved slowly on an angling course from south to north, heading toward the mines.

Torches! People carrying brands to guide them in the woods!

After a moment of wonderment, Jezra realized this was the last night the miners would spend on Mount Baratok until spring. The torches probably were borne by the workmen's families, hurrying to meet their fathers and brothers dwelling in the hillside huts. It was most unusual for Barovians to be abroad at night, but she understood a yearning to see kin after a long separation. Tomorrow, the reunited families would return to the village. There the miners would deliver the results of a season's labor—a mule train loaded with refined silver—to the boyar's stronghold. That pattern had been repeated for generations on the Wagner estates. It was one she remembered well.

Hunger kindled in Jezra's heart, a hunger as intense as the perpetual cold afflicting her. To hear voices, to feel the touch of a hand, to know the warmth of a human presence . . .

Warmth!

It was a long way down to the forest, but nothing would deter her from reaching her goal. Wreathed in mist and moonlight, she started to descend Mount Baratok.

* * * * *

Five mercenaries and a half-breed Vistana woman climbed a narrow, twisting animal track. Towering trees, leafless silhouettes against the hazy, moonlit sky, swayed overhead. The glow of the travelers' torches cast eerie, wavering shadows, and creatures hidden in the surrounding blackness cried out sharply, startlingly. A thickening mist crawled like a serpent through frost-rimmed brush and deadfalls, obscuring the steep path.

"How can he see where we are going?" one of the mercenaries said, furtively indicating the darkly handsome giant at the head of their group.

"Need you ask?" the youngest fighter muttered. "He sees like a wolf or a cat, thanks to that damned enchanted sword." His tone sour, he added, "and because of it he wields powers none but the gods should own."

"Aye, but on this climb he is relying on the gypsy to guide *him*. And how trustworthy is she, after watching him kill her cousin?"

"As trustworthy as the spells he uses to control her and the rest of us," the young man said with smothered rage.

They spoke softly, but Lord Captain Hans Eckert overheard them. He halted abruptly and wheeled around. His height allowed him to loom over his men dauntingly. "Why do you chatter and drag your feet?" he demanded. "One would think we had never invaded enemy territory ere now. What has become of the boasting cutthroats I led against Teglan's forces and the maddened hordes of Dessiro? You were bold enough then."

"This . . . this is different, Cap'n," the eldest fighter said, "and that was another time and place."

For a moment, the handsome giant's expression grew remote. "Yes, another place . . ." Then he focused again on his followers and growled, "a place where you paid little heed to a storyteller's pratings. I *told* you to ignore that silly graybeard back in the tavern at the crossroads. Have we met any of the creatures he warned us about?"

"The . . . the wolf-thing that jumped us just after we started up the trail."

"The werewolf, you mean," Hans corrected him, scornful. "The *dead* werewolf. You saw my sword cut him down. Gods, how the brute yowled! And were any of you harmed? Did the man-wolf even touch you? No! Nor will *any* Barovian monsters, not so long as I wield this." He lovingly caressed the weapon's silver pommel.

Hate glittered in the black eyes of the gypsy at his side. "Warlock!" she cried. "If I could contact my people, they would warn the count of your presence here, and he would destroy you!"

"*Your* people, Lisl?" Eckert's mouth curved in a cruel smile. "But half-breed gypsies *have* no people. The Vistana tribes cast them out. True? Your stupid cousin revealed that, as he did so many other useful things before I washed my sword in his blood."

She gasped and pressed her hands to her heart. "Oh, Sebestyen, poor Sebestyen . . ."

"Best appreciate your current enslavement, or you can join him in his wretched, unmarked grave."

"Have you no decency left, Brother?" the youngest mercenary exclaimed. "Quit tormenting her!"

The giant's icy gaze shifted in his direction. "Ah! Lisl's chivalrous would-be protector is heard from. Still the moralist, eh, Wilm? You and she both learn slowly." Hans drew upon the enchanted weapon's power. A familiar sensation gripped Wilm and the gypsy, holding them fast while invisible whips lashed their bodies. The flogging left no marks, but the pain was very real. The three mercenaries cringed, remembering past occasions when similar punishment had been meted out to them.

Hans laughed as his victims' limbs trembled and their eyes bulged with silent pleas for mercy. Finally, with a negligent gesture, he released the sufferers and addressed them and his hirelings sternly. "Take warning: Waste no more of my precious time. All of you—*move!*"

Still shaking from her ordeal, Lisl stumbled up the path. Her master did not look back to see if his brother and the other men followed him; there was no need.

Ruthlessness was as much a part of Captain Hans Eckert's garb as the finely crafted wool, leather, and metal he wore. Like his men, he went well-armed, but no weapon they carried was a match for his blade. Its keen edge and sorcerous powers had cut down many a foe— most recently, a werewolf!

As he trod close behind the gypsy, his thoughts strayed to Wilm's impotent outburst minutes ago. Foolish, idealistic Wilm! Faithful to a boyhood vow, he had been his sibling's loyal lieutenant throughout their mercenary careers. Not even profound disgust with that sibling's ever more vicious behavior had made the young man renounce the oath. And now he *could* not; the sword's obedience spell bound him with unseen but unbreakable chains. No matter how severe the provocation or how much Wilm's conscience protested, he must never raise his hand against his master and must follow wherever Hans chose to go. . . .

Or did *not* choose . . .

The captain's smile faded. He had built a solid reputation as a mercenary leader who did not quibble over the amount of blood spilled or whether or not his employer's cause was just. And he had amassed considerable loot and acquired influence among kings and princes who hired him.

Then he came upon a dying mage in a castle's ruins. His vision failing, the necromancer mistook Captain Eckert for an apprentice who had been slain during the attack. With his last words, the mage entrusted Hans with an ensorceled blade and its secrets.

The captain's first spellcasting enforced lifelong obedience on those attending him—Wilm and the three veteran mercenaries. It even protected him from assassination while he slept. Next he concealed the blade within arcane shields, lest enemy wizards steal it from him ere he had fathomed all its powers, which promised to be enormous.

He proceeded cautiously, discovering the range of the sword's magic little by little. At each new conquest, each overthrown opponent, each new trick of the sword revealed, he grew more confident. In time, this marvelous weapon would put wealth, slaves, and perhaps a throne within his grasp, if he controlled his impatience and did not become foolhardy. And no one ever accused Hans Eckert of being a fool.

Steadily, surely, abetted by the sword, he ascended. Shrewd, calculating, pitiless to any standing in his way, he neared the heights. Within a year, kings who once treated him as a hireling would grovel before his majesty. . . . And then his dreams of glory vanished in impenetrable mist.

One moment he was about to capture an important stronghold, slaughter its inhabitants, and plunder at his leisure. The conquest would enhance his rapidly growing political strength.

But a peculiar fog separated Hans, his three veteran

fighters, and Wilm from the rest of the army. And when the mist lifted, the five found themselves in this alien realm, Barovia.

Initially unperturbed, Hans called upon his sword to help retrace their steps. In vain! The portal between his world and this one remained hidden. Evil gods and some sorcery far greater than his blade thwarted every attempt to escape.

How could this have happened? All his hard-won wealth and influence lay on the far side of that diabolical mist, and he could not reach them! The mercenary genius who had ensnared so many others was himself ensnared! Hans belabored the problem and brooded for days before he was forced to concede defeat.

There seemed no way out. So . . . he must adapt if he hoped to survive. This was, in effect, enemy terrain, and he must study it. Over Wilm's outraged objections to the shedding of innocent blood, Hans coerced information from isolated farm families and wayfarers and left the bodies for scavengers. He learned that Barovia harbored numerous fantastic and deadly creatures. And the mist that had trapped him was not unusual; such mists were all too common in this realm, and were rightly feared.

The wealth and reputation that could have kept Hans and his followers sheltered and well fed lay on the far side of that infernal gate of mist.

In the end, they stooped to robbery, always leaving evidence to imply that the thefts and murders were committed by renegade gypsies. Wilm, naturally, abhorred these despicable forays even as his brother compelled him to participate.

Inwardly, though, Hans, too, seethed with resentment. He was a master mercenary, a man on his way to great things. It was shameful to be reduced to common pilfering and throat slitting!

He *must* escape from Barovia. If he could not return to his own world, he would seek out other realms in this one—realms ripe for the sort of conquest Captain Eckert had perfected elsewhere. Once he left Von Zarovich's fog-shrouded land, Hans could create a domain of his own.

Wealth was the key, and for a time, he despaired of ever acquiring sufficient funds to fulfill his dreams.

When he first met Lisl and her cousin he did not fore-see the gypsy half-breeds' value to him. But *tuika* brandywine loosened Sebestyen's tongue. He began to boast of big plans for stealing an annual shipment of silver from the Wagner mines. Hans immediately saw the flaws in the clumsy scheme. And he saw how to correct them with the aid of his enchanted sword. The end result would be a masterpiece!

In drunken generosity, the Vistana offered to make his new "friend" a partner. Hans, however, had no intention of sharing. Resisting the takeover, Sebestyen forfeited his life.

Terrorized and grief-stricken, Lisl was easily bound by an obedience spell. She became an unwilling native guide to Barovia, particularly to this mountain trail. Once Hans had the treasure and was safely across the border, she would serve him in a more sensual capacity. And if Lisl failed to please, she would go the way of her cousin. Small loss; there were countless other women he could enslave.

Sebestyen had proposed an operation worthy of Captain Eckert's talents: an entire season's output of refined silver. His palms itched at the prospect, and he lusted to hold the lovely, argent metal, the shining foundation of his future private kingdom.

King Hans! He liked the ring of that, and soon it would be true!

The path had begun to fork and divide confusingly, sometimes dwindling to nearly nothing. He held his torch high, probing the darkness, staying to the main trail with difficulty. "How much farther to the campsite?" he demanded.

Lisl tensed at the sound of his harsh voice. "I . . . I do not know."

He seized her arm in a brutal grip. "Liar! Your cousin knew. But that map he sketched for me on the tavern's filthy tabletop was as muddled with wine as his brain. Sebestyen bragged that gypsies are familiar with every pathway in this realm. Prove it!"

He thrust her away from him so violently that she nearly fell. The Vistana rubbed her aching arm and dabbed at her tears with the hem of her shawl as she staggered on.

All about them now, trees thinned, scrubbier varieties replacing the forest titans of the lower mountain. Through gaps in the woodland wall, the journeyers saw open ground, a frozen desolation drenched in waning moonlight.

"Hope we is nearin' them mines," a mercenary wheezed. "I wants to get about killin' them pit workers and takin' the silver."

"Save your breath," Wilm said curtly, eyeing his bloodthirsty fellow fighter with distaste. "No telling how much farther he will make us climb. . . ."

But in fact, within fifty paces they reached the sought-for campsite. Five of the travelers sank gratefully onto the stone benches ringing an ancient fire pit. Hans alone was energetic, buoyed by anticipation. He walked to the northernmost edge of the clearing and gazed out at the barrens. Not far away stood miners' huts, securely shuttered against the night. With an evil smirk, he touched the sword. Lisl and the men watched him anxiously, sensing magic in the frosty air. Satisfied with his efforts, Eckert turned and said, "Gather fuel. Get a fire going."

"Will that not reveal us to them there on the slope, Cap'n?"

"No. Nor will our torches. I willed the miners to see and hear nothing beyond their doors. So you have no excuse for not working. Move."

They did, grumbling. And when the pit glowed with heat, they grumbled about the hard cheese and dried meat they had brought in their packs. Exasperated, Hans used the sword to lure two plump hares within reach, skewering the helpless prey. Content at last, the mercenaries butchered and roasted the game, devouring it noisily.

Wilm and Lisl ate little and sat apart from the rest. Clasping hands, they eyed each other sympathetically, mutual enslavement and hatred of their enslaver linking them. As a cold wind soughed overhead, the gypsy began to croon. The haunting melody gave the brutish mercenaries pause. Even Captain Eckert listened with interest.

"What is that song?" he asked when she finished.

"Regina d'Ghiacco."

He grimaced. " 'The Ice Queen?' That ridiculous Vistana legend of a beautiful spirit who prowls this mountain?"

"Jezra Wagner is *not* a legend," Lisl snapped. "She was buried in an avalanche long ago. Her spirit roams Mount Baratok and the lands about and seeks relief from the terrible cold that always afflicts her. If she touches you . . . it is death."

The veterans' eyes widened. Hans, though, spat an obscenity. "Ridiculous!" he repeated. "Who has seen this Ice Queen? You? And if she is such a menace, how has anyone lived to tell the tale after encountering her?"

Lisl shrugged. "I said you die only if she touches you. Some who saw her managed to flee before she got too close. Later, they returned and found their unfortunate companions frozen."

His laugh echoed through the clearing. "And you superstitious Barovians can think of no other way a man might freeze to death? If a fool gawks at a snow mirage until his blood congeals, that does not prove spirits exist." The mercenaries, encouraged by his explanation, nodded and chuckled.

Lisl insisted, "Jezra is *real,* and the gods help those who invade her ancestral lands, as we are doing."

Hans lashed out, slapping her hard. She fell back on the stone bench, her cheek reddening from the blow. Wilm struggled to rise and defend the gypsy, but could not; his brother crushed that noble impulse with a scornful glance and a touch on his sword.

"You seem to have an affection for her," he said, his tone mocking. "Very well then, keep her quiet. Share her naive beliefs in Vistana legends, if it solaces, so long as you are not noisy about it. As for me, *I* believe only in money. Not gold, precious though it is, for it is too soft for my nature. No, I will have a fortune fit for a king— cold, hard silver, enough to last me a lifetime!"

*   *   *   *   *

On the mountain slope, the beautiful young woman halted. She had been listening to a melancholy song issuing from the woods and wondered why it had ceased so abruptly. The ancient tune and the singer's sweet alto voice had been pleasing.

She wondered, too, why the journeyers stopped where they did. Jezra had assumed they would continue straight on to the miners' huts. Instead, they made camp on the border between forest and barrens.

No matter. Indeed, this was better. She would rendezvous sooner than she had expected.

Ever since she had begun her descent at twilight, she had adjusted her course to intersect with theirs. Now she would meet these people face to face. Her heart pounded with excitement. How she could speak to them, perhaps share her own songs with the woman she had heard earlier . . . and she could touch them . . .

The strange hunger in her breast worsened with every passing moment. She must hurry! Her pale eyes gleaming, Jezra headed toward the camp at the edge of the barrens.

*   *   *   *   *

A lopsided discussion was underway there, the veterans questioning, their captain sweeping aside every doubt expressed.

"But the count, the boyar's thief-takers . . ."

"No thief-takers will pursue us. Admittedly, Sebestyen's original plan would have drawn them like flies to carrion. He was going to recruit a gang of fellow half-breeds to slit the miners' throats. How stupid and clumsy! And entirely unnecessary!" Hans grinned and said, "Once the moon is set, we will simply walk over to the huts. At my command, the bespelled workmen will emerge from their hovels and load the silver on mules for us. We lead the pack train back here, then on down the mountain . . ."

"Leaving a trail of footprints and hoofprints a child

could follow," Wilm commented acidly.

Hans noted that his brother still held Lisl's hand. This deepening affection between them might explain the pair's annoying tendency toward defiance. He would smash Wilm's feeble little rebellion in due time. As for Lisl . . .

"You forget my sword's power," he said, gesturing grandly. "The mountain flank above the mines is heavy with snow, a weight that needs only a touch of magic to bring it down on them. The avalanche will cover everything, including tracks. To the boyar, it will seem an unfortunate accident. By next spring's thaw, when he discovers the truth, we will be far away—and very rich!" Hans sat back, his expression smug.

The mercenaries nodded approvingly. "Ai! 'Twil be a treat to see 'em squashed under all that snow!" one crowed, his mates slapping their knees and grinning.

Lisl shivered, and Wilm put an arm around her. "Come closer to the fire," he said.

"It is not . . . not that kind of cold. It is . . ."

"We still have a while before the moon sets," Hans interrupted them. "Amuse us, gypsy. Tell our fortunes, for fortunes we soon will have!"

Lisl shivered again and shook her head. Wilm pleaded that his brother let her be, but Hans demanded she obey. "I know you play those Vistana tricks, woman. I saw you reading fortunes for the tavern patrons. Read ours."

Reluctantly, she knelt by the fire pit and pulled a set of runes from her pocket, casting the engraved stones on the ground.

"Well?" the eldest mercenary exclaimed. "What do they say?"

"That you will finally have relief from the aches in your bones, an end to the old wounds that often pain you."

He looked surprised, then smiled. "A good fortune, that! No more pain while we and the Cap'n lounge about the foreign palace he will buy with that silver!"

"What about me?" another asked.

Lisl threw the runes again, her manner solemn. "I see you . . . elsewhere."

The man guffawed. "Elsewhere than Barovia, you mean. Far away! I will drink to *that,* once we are across the border with the loot."

The gypsy seemed about to add to the prophecy, but did not. Instead she cast the runes for the remaining mercenary. "A long journey for you as well."

"Not comin' back to Barovia ever, am I?" he worried.

"No. Not ever."

Wilm knelt beside her and whispered, "What do you foresee for us?"

She cast the runes carelessly and said, "Freedom."

"You have not read *my* fortune," Hans cut in. He chuckled at her surprise. "I need not believe this mumbo-jumbo to be amused. Throw the stones."

This time, Lisl peered closely at the runes' position, then stared at Captain Eckert. "I see silver. Cold, hard silver. You will have more of it than you can carry."

"Ha! It takes no arcane skill to predict that! Of course I shall have the silver," he said loudly, as if daring anyone to argue. "After all I have done to win it, I *deserve* that silver."

Lisl thought of her cousin. Wilm remembered scores of helpless victims cut down by his brother, as though those people were less than insects. The gypsy said tonelessly, "Yes, you deserve it."

Suddenly, a moan of agony stunned the group. Hans whirled around and watched in astonishment as a beautiful stranger rushed into the clearing.

She was a tiny, lovely woman dressed in an elegant habit, her cloak lined with the most expensive fur. Hair the color of silver flowed about her shoulders and exquisite face. Her eyes were an incredible blue, and they seemed to pierce the captain's soul.

Hans had never beheld such a woman. Fascination warred with suspicion. "Who . . . who are you? Where did you come from?"

"Where? I come from the mountain. My mountain."

"Yours?" He sounded inane, even to himself. His shock was now heavily tinged with apprehension, and he unsheathed his sword.

"I am Jezra, and all the Wagner lands are mine."

Briefly, she glanced at the others, then returned her attention to Captain Eckert.

"You are one of the count's spies, sent to stop me from taking the silver!" he shouted, raising the sword and ordering his men to attack. As alarmed by the unforeseen threat as he, the mercenaries hastened to cut down this intruder.

Compelled to obey his brother's commands, Wilm, too, started forward. But Lisl clutched at his arm desperately, holding him back. "Stay away from her!" she screamed. "She is death!"

If Hans heard the warning, he gave no sign. "By edge of steel or by my magic, you perish!" the captain exulted. "Become the ghost you claim to be!" His sorcerous blade slashed completely through the stranger's pretty neck.

To no effect.

The mercenaries struck her breast and belly and head. None of their blades drew blood.

Hans Eckert gawked at his sword and then at the woman. "This cannot be! It is impossible! The sword *must* kill you. I bade it take your life!"

"Why are you so unkind?" Jezra wailed. "I only want to share your fire, your presence. . . ." As swift as light, she darted at them, taking hold of each man in turn, pleading for understanding.

As she made contact, bodies were transformed instantly into glittering, crystalline ice. Three frozen corpses stood in the clearing when Jezra reached Hans.

The spirit touched him, and the touch became an embrace. Her small arms slid around his waist as she gazed up at him. "You are too handsome to be such a cruel man. So handsome, and so *warm*. No, please, do not pull away from me! Just let me hold you for a while." Sighing, she laid her silvery tresses against his chest and hugged him tightly.

Invisible manacles fell from Wilm's wrists. The compulsion that forced him to serve a brother grown hateful and murderous vanished like dew in a bright sunrise.

Dumbfounded, he stared at Hans and the silver-haired woman. She embraced a man of ice who held a sword of ice. As she at last withdrew a pace from the mercenaries' leader, an abnormally powerful gust of wind roared up the trail. It was preternatural, an angry god's breath, thrusting violently at the lifeless statue of Lord Captain Eckert. The crystallized form swayed for a long moment, then fell with a crash, shattering, and the magic sword shattered beside him.

Jezra was oblivious to this stunning conclusion of their embrace. She cried in ecstasy, "Warm! I am *warm* again." It was a prayer of thanksgiving, and she repeated it over and over, dancing among the remaining ice-clad statues she had made. The spirit sang joyously of spring and summer, things she had not known for centuries.

Lisl tugged urgently at Wilm's arm. "Do not listen. Her singing can drive mortals mad. Quickly! We must get away. Legends say that her joy when she steals warmth from the living lasts only a short time. Then the Ice Queen might seek *us*."

The young man sheathed his sword, and he and the gypsy sidled cautiously around the fire pit and hurried to the edge of the woods. "We can go to the miners' huts," Wilm suggested. "The spell Hans cast is broken for them, too, now."

"Yes! We will be safe there. Safe . . . and free." Reminded of the accuracy of her earlier prophecies, Wilm felt a chill snake down his spine.

They paused at the forest's edge and looked back at the camp. Jezra still danced there, leafless trees visible through her graceful, insubstantial face and body. Broken pieces of a steaming, half-frozen corpse and a now-useless mage sword lay at her feet.

"What of her?" Wilm wondered. "Poor specter!"

"She will return to the mountain," Lisl said. "Jezra spoke truly. The Wagner estates *are* her home, and she guarded their upland holdings from invaders tonight."

Wilm stared at his elder brother's remains. Moonlight gleamed on the frozen pieces, making them resemble a heap of sparkling coins. "You spoke truly as well, Lisl," he said. "Hans finally won his cold, hard silver, enough to last him through eternity. Come. He has no power to keep us with him anymore." Holding hands, the couple walked on toward the mines.

And Jezra Wagner, the Ice Queen, singing a paean to the warmth of life, danced out of the forest clearing. Bathed in silvery moonlight and momentarily rid of the terrible hunger that drove her, she began to ascend Mount Baratok.

Objets d'Art

J. Robert King

The invitation had mentioned "finest pheasant, reddest wine, and afterward, a tour of Marquis D'Polarno's famous art gallery." I had no doubt of the excellence of these amenities, nor of my enjoyment of them; but I'd not come for dinner or drink or paintings. I'd come for immortality.

Stezen D'Polarno himself met me at the door. He was dark and elegant in the way of Southern men, but his smile was fierce and cold as a cat's. His attire was much richer than mine: a blue brocaded jacket, ruffle shirt, red vest, white canons, and tall boots that might have been made for riding.

"Welcome, Professor Ferewood—and all the way from the Brautslava Institute in Darkon. I am honored. Come in. You've nearly missed the first course."

I bowed deeply, trying not to ruin the crease in my trousers. I'd struggled long to impress the line in the knee-worn wool and didn't want it stretched out just yet. Before I could rise again to speak, Stezen, hand extended, interrupted:

"Your study of mortality and its . . . remedies is quite well known to me."

He was a card player, this one, and had just revealed enough of his hand to draw me off. But these swarthy canasta cardsharps have nothing on Darkonian poker players.

"As, too, sir, is your art collection, and your own . . . dabbling in my discipline."

He smiled his cat-smile again, and the wry light that shone in his eyes told me my motives were duly noted. "Come in."

I bowed once more, shallowly this time, removed the cocked hat from my silver head, and stepped across the threshold. The moment I was fully within the huge crimson forehall—with its lush carpets, fine wall fabrics, satin draperies, black-marble stairs, and high and molded and bossed ceilings—I knew I must not let slip my awe. Keeping eyelids trimmed, I calmly relinquished my walking stick, coat, and hat to the servant who materialized out of nowhere. I waited until Stezen had stepped up beside me before offering some polite though reserved observations about the place.

With a wordless nod, he gestured me into the great hall, and I walked dutifully into it.

Though I had attended many of the richest colleges in Darkon, I had not seen so sumptuous a chamber in all my days. The place, though uniformly huge, felt dark and close due to the thick piling of red upon black upon red: candles and moldings, casements and floors, embroideries and vases. . . . My stoic expression grew less so as my eyes greeted marvelous appointment after marvelous appointment.

Stezen hung back half a pace, a smug look on his feline features.

No point in my masking it, I told myself: he could have *smelled* my amazement. We passed many gold-gilded paintings that I knew would be making Curator Clairmont drool. He might have come for the paintings, but I had not.

"As you might imagine, good sir," I commented as we approached the banquet table, which was decked with silver and hemmed in by a black crowd of carnivorous nobles, "the chance to converse with you about our . . . mutual interest is what I'm *really* hungry for."

His eyes flashed. "We will more than converse on that matter. But food first and philosophy following."

I drew back the proffered chair and was seated amidst the other carnivores. The impressive collection of noble folk around me seemed to know that I had delayed their meal, and they seemed to resent it. Some were acquaintances: the mousy and disheveled Curator Clairmont from the Institute, a burly oaf of a man named Krimean, a flirtatious former student named Lynn who must have gotten an invitation by way of the bedroom. Others were mere acquaintances, or total strangers: a chubby merchant couple displaying all the hackneyed gawd of their kind, a passel of women who seemed all too fond of touching one another, and a host of others that disappear into the depths of my memory now. In one way or another, though, I knew everyone's interest was doubtless piqued by the rumors of Stezen's elixir of life.

Mine surely was.

No sooner than I was seated, servants sailed into view, their hands bearing cargos of huge and steaming platters. The first of these was placed in the center of the table and uncovered: a giant roasted pheasant. By some culinary trick, the bird had been cooked with the feathers still on its wings, tail, neck, and head. The rest of the fowl had been plucked bald, then dressed with wine and butter and feathered with leafy spices of every variety. After roasting, the lifelike head and slender neck had been pierced by an ingenious and inconspicuous wire near the breastbone, which was driven right through the throat to the beak. By this contrivance, the fully plumed head was positioned in a gracious bow, its unblinking eyes regarding the feasters submissively. The wings and tail were similarly arrayed, so that my first impression of the bird was it had somehow submitted itself to the plucking and basting and dressing and roasting and piercing through neck and wings and tail so that it could now stand before me, willingly presenting its steaming back to be sliced open. And, presently, it was.

There came a similarly statued lamb, pig, veal calf, and other objets d'art for our watering tongues. All had been imported, clearly, for the food of Ghastria was notoriously ghastly.

Curator Clairmont, with old, thin lips well greased by the hunks of pig he'd been stuffing through them, spoke to me across the clatter of cutlery. "Ferewood, eat up." He winked. "You can wash it down with the elixir later."

This social effrontery did not go unnoticed by the others gathered, and not a few reddened about the temples to hear their hopes laid open so.

I was not one of them.

"Art is the only elixir I seek," I replied. "Do you speak of some other?"

The burly oaf Krimean interrupted Clairmont's response with a call for more wine, and in the meantime the fat merchant spoke through a chomping grin. "We're great patrons of the arts, you know. Many of Stezen's best artists were funded by us."

"Charming," I replied under my breath, not so much to the fat merchant's comment but to the fact that the flimsy girl Lynn was fairly crawling over our host as he finished his repast. I could see that I'd not have much chance to talk to Stezen during dinner: I'd need a riding crop to get the girl off him.

When the meal was well finished, we all rose to follow Stezen into his famed gallery. At that point, I made my way to the front of the pack, almost as close to our host as the clinging Lynn.

With a gesture, Stezen gathered us as a shepherd before a pasture gate and said, "What you all are about to see is the jewel of my crown—my love, my life, my joy. I'll not mar these gorgeous works with shouted commentary, for I wasn't there shouting when the artists crafted them."

A ripple of bemused laughter circulated through the clustered flock.

"But, please, my sweets, gaze and gaze and gaze at these, and converse with them and each other as you wish."

With that, he stepped backward, swinging wide the great black door that stood behind him. A gush of cool air spread deliciously over us. It bore with it the gathered fragrance of old oils and polished wood and gently burning lamps. The faint murmur of music also seeped out.

Following our host, we rolled slowly through the towering doorway, past the velvet curtains that eclipsed the view, and into another room of black-marble floors and dark red walls.

This place, though, had none of the palatial refinement of the rest of the estate. The walls were starkly crimson from some deeply plied pigment, and they met the black ceiling above and the black floor below without ornament of any type. On these walls hung paintings of the crudest sort—some on tablets of stone or wood, others on thick and fibrous reed-papers pressed together. A host of huge and unrefined statues populated the floors, and only now did we catch sight of the music-makers—bards with reed pipes and hand drums, who played tribal songs.

As my fellow feasters spread reverently into the hall, I maintained my close carriage beside Stezen. I cleared my voice and spoke: "Thank you again for the fine meal"—he waved this off—"but as I warned you before, the greater part of me still hungers—"

"Pray, what for—?"

"Or perhaps *thirsts* is a better term," I continued.

The chit of a girl interrupted, "Yes, I'm thirsty, too. Give me a drink, Stezen," but Stezen slipped a hand over her mouth.

I tried again. "You see, word has reached my circles that you have, in your travels, discovered some great elixir that might prove interesting to me." I cringed the moment these words were full-formed from my lips, for I knew I'd projected my bid and dealt Stezen the upper hand.

He knew it, too. "You are here for the *gallery*, my friend, are you not? For a man so interested in immortality, you seem rather uninterested in patience."

Ah, yes. Well played. I was fittingly chastised and would hold my cards closer from now on. But also I was encouraged; my host had just proved himself the sort of wily bastard capable of finding the fountain of life and hoarding its waters for himself. Fair enough. Now I had to prove myself worthy to drink.

"The art, yes," I replied quietly.

Even so, I did not turn my attention to the bizarre artwork about me, but rather to my fellow feasters. I watched their faces, their puzzled and disdainful faces, and saw the effect their arrogant ignorance had on

Stezen. Krimean, that great, burly oaf, even laughed in nervous bursts as he poked his head through a huge stone wheel. Though he and I shared the same opinion of this primitive junk, he and I did not share the same politick about it.

"Forgive my eagerness of a moment ago," said I to stall for time. "My eyes were so bent on immortal endings that I was blind to these mortal beginnings."

Stezen's close-lipped smile eased, and I saw that I had scored a point in this odd game we played. "Beginnings?" he asked with an innocence that ill-suited him. "How so?"

My mind struggled to lay hold of something useful— something about the state of nature, the mythic origins of our brains and the bestial seeds of our bones—some such tripe from the Brautslava ethnographer.

"Yes, beginnings. This room is full of perfect beginnings. If my colleagues at the Institute are not fools, I would say that the soul of art is the soul of us, and the soul of us is yet a primal, primitive . . . *beginning* thing."

Now the grudging respect turned to interested appraisement. "Your mind is sharp. I knew that from stories of you. But now I see that your eyes are their match." He gestured about at the room full of tribal masks and queer pottery and confused guests, many of whom seemed to sense a kind of explanation emerging between the two of us and were coyly drifting this way. He continued, "What piece, in this primitive collection of mine, would you say is greatest?"

Now I had to look past the bemused guests and at the art itself. Since all the pieces seemed equally crude and worthless to me, I decided in that moment to choose the first work that caught my eye, and think on my feet for a reason why.

"That monolith," I said, pointing at a huge, trunk-shaped stone that stood crude and erect in the center of the floor.

Stezen gestured me forward, and the nervous flock of sheep about us followed. "How so?"

I stroked my chin by way of stalling, then said, "Well, to start, it is stone. All things come from stone, I am told.

Indeed, one professor of ours claims that this world of ours was stone until the mounting up of corpses and feces gave us the rich black soil in which we plant."

We'd reached the monument now, and Stezen's cocked eyebrow told me he expected more. Fortune was with me, for I now saw that the shaft of stone had been rudely shaped into the general features of a man— a rather giantesque man—who leaned stupidly forward on his fat feet. That gave me an idea.

"The figure is human, but crude still, like a man made of stone who has just risen from the stony ground."

"Or risen from the ranks of beasts," Stezen added.

"Yes. And the fact that he is standing defines him from the stone and from the beasts. For stones and beasts do not rise up to deny the world its pull. He is, in that way, pushing away from the primal and fleshly to the final and empyrean."

"Perhaps," Stezen allowed. I knew then that my reading had been too devout for my host's tastes. He underscored this perception. "Or perhaps he is a great, leaning phallus, born up only by vague and violent and demonic desire toward divinity."

He was that sort of man, Stezen was. I coughed into my hand to hide my discomfort. Others imitated me.

Stezen's next words both thrilled and horrified me. "Well enough, my friend. I can see you still have a primal soul, as you so well said it. Let's hope each of these rooms of my gallery finds your being in an accord. If so, yet may we both drink together from the fountain you seek."

That was it—this game I knew we played from the moment D'Polarno's face appeared behind the door. At last the rules were spelled out. I had thought at first, seeing that feline visage, that ours would be a game of cat and mouse, me hoping for the cheese, and he for the fun of the chase—and perhaps for the kill. Then, as the banquet went on, as more plattered beasts came with compelled willingness to be eaten by us, I thought the game would be the subtler, deadlier match of wits, the fencing of intellects that would end in humiliation or death for one of us. But now I knew. This was not a game of bodies or of minds, but of souls. And I had the clear conviction that Stezen intended to prove me either a match for his spirit or another beast that, by a wire through the throat, could be bent in supplication to be, steaming, cut open.

The next room provided a welcome relief from the blood-red walls and the death-black floors. Here, stately silver-white marble filled the floor in elegant patterns of geometric tilework. The same polished stone covered the walls, supported at even intervals by columns, pilasters, and arches. Along the far wall ran a colonnade of massive stone drums, with larger-than-life statuary ensconced in niches along it.

The art here was also far more pleasing to the civilized eye: well-rendered statues in granite, frescoes of stately figures reclined at table, sturdy and supple black pottery with silver scenes inlaid upon them, stone friezes and reliefs of epic battles between men and centaurs. . . .

My fellow revelers either appreciated this stuff more—as I did—or masked their feelings more assiduously than before. I noticed that Krimean and a few others of the more overtly baffled or amused feasters apparently had been ushered out of the tour due to their disruptions. Unfortunately, prehensile Lynn still held on.

Despite this clear warning to scoffers, a few of the elite women who'd been clinging to each others' arms and disdaining males throughout the evening did not rein in their opinions in this new room. In fact, they openly ridiculed the masculine gods statued about, as well as the harsh *paters* of the domain where these artworks originated. They were likewise excused from the tour.

Meanwhile Stezen and I, and the pack of hangers-on we'd gathered, ended up before a rather grim example of the very oppression the women had ridiculed. The frieze was a lower fragment from a once-magnificent stone pediment, the whole of which could not have fit in this room. The carving showed a mother standing with head bowed, a swatch of her toga drawn up to shield weeping eyes. In the other loose folds of her robe, two small daughters clung fearfully to her legs. Their tear-ringed eyes had been bored deep by the sculptor, and they seemed connected by strong cords of grief to the third sister. This child was but an infant, and lay on its back, a leather thong piercing its ankles and wrists to bind them together.

I shuddered.

Stezen noticed. "Yes. I see you have not only the beast's bones and heart and soul, but the citizen's mind in you as well. I see that you cringe."

"And who would not?" I asked, though a moment later I could think of an easy handful who wouldn't and saw some of them standing beside me. "It is brutal," I explained.

"But well rendered," Stezen replied, "as is childhood."

This comment brought my mind back on its perpetually curving course, toward the subject of immortality. Sickened as I was by the display before us, I knew I'd best hide this feeling or choose to be ushered out with the rest.

"The artistry of this relief goes without question," I said in an imitation of distraction. "But, I must confess, the exact purport of the scene eludes me."

"As it should. Ours, though still a brutal society, no longer leaves girl children to die of exposure."

Now I saw it. The depicted mother and her two daughters, each of whom had no doubt narrowly escaped the thong through the heel, now had been forced by some grim *pater* to work this very crime on their sister and daughter.

"It's not art, it's butchery," muttered the plump merchantwife a little too loudly to her now-wary husband. Before the fidgeting and mustachioed man could cover his wife's errant comment, I jumped in to win Stezen's favor.

"Not butchery, milady, but childhood. As children we are the hopeless and powerless chattel of our parents, who may nurture or slaughter us, as the shepherd does the sheep. And as adults, we become the chattel of gods, who exercise the same rights."

Stezen was pleased: that much I could see. The merchant and his wife were not, and neither were the others.

The crowd thinned.

The next room was truly elegant, the flower of our time. It was lit by shimmering chandeliers and bedecked in gold traceries and moldings and bosses. The windows on all four sides of it were festooned with garlands and draped with the richest red-velvet curtains, which hung to the floor into pools of fabric. And the paintings and statuary were of the finest quality, the eyes of the subjects peering out hauntingly to follow all who walked past.

But that was not the only haunting thing about this room. I'd walked to the center of it before I realized that the windows could not possibly be on all four walls, for we had entered through one wall from a room of equal size, and would exit through the opposite to a room no doubt the same.

I wandered with Stezen and our dwindling group of followers to one of the windows that stood beside the door where we had entered. Peering out, I saw not the wall of the other room where it should have been, nor even the estate grounds I had walked through to arrive. Instead, outside lay a strange, moon-washed landscape of trees that roiled up like smoke or curdling milk into a mackerel sky. There were peaks of mountains out there that I knew stood nowhere in these lands, and were, themselves, impossibly tall and pointed. Glancing out another window on an adjacent wall, I saw a morning field dotted with grazing cattle.

With amusement, D'Polarno took in my amazement and trembling shock. He similarly noted the horrified gasps of the others.

One of those was Lynn, who'd finally found an impulse other than errogeny. "This place is unnatura-"

"Of course it is," Stezen broke in. "Didn't a single one of you look at the outside of this estate before you came into it? Didn't any of you notice that these rooms through which we have been walking could not possibly fit into my manor house?"

"Where are we, then?" Lynn returned angrily.

"Why, we are in my famed gallery, don't you know?"

"I'm going back," she cried. "I didn't want to come in here anyway." She charged back toward the doors.

"Oh," D'Polarno said innocently, "you can't go back.

They've barred the doors behind us."

"Others went back!" she shouted, pouting as she pushed on the unforgiving wood.

D'Polarno merely shook his head. "The only way out is forward. You are here. Why not enjoy the rest of the tour? Besides, you should not be so greatly disturbed by these windows that apparently lead to other worlds. Have you never seen magic before?"

"Of course not!" she cried, pounding like a child on the impassive doors.

"I have," I said, which was true, though I've never been sure why I said it. Perhaps it was because I was not yet sure what I thought of this place, and some part of me thought that if I got to speaking, I would be able to sort out my thoughts. You see, I was fearful like the rest, but these queer examples of Stezen's power only assured me that perhaps, beyond that next door, lay the goal of my quest, the fountain from which I might drink of eternity. So, frightened as I was, I still wanted to believe in him, believe in this all.

"I . . . had once made the acquaintance of an actual magician on the Brautslava staff—that was before the purges, of course. He was an illusionist by speciality, and showed me many simple spells that could account for such an illusion."

"Precisely," Stezen responded through wicked teeth. "Lynn, darling, think of these not as preternatural windows, but as paintings of a different sort—magical paintings, if you will."

But she would not be appeased; she shook the doors violently and shouted indecipherables.

It was then that motion in the corner of my eye drew my attention to the window with the moonlit trees. There! It was the merchant and wife from the other room, the ones who had maligned the relief sculpture. I knew it was they—he fidgety and fearful, she plump and vital—running away from us into the pitching and dissolving trees beyond the magic windowpane.

Despite myself, I let out a small yelp of surprise that, by virtue of its pitch or its fear, stopped the struggles of Lynn and drew her attention to the window.

"They *did* escape!" she shouted in desperate triumph. "See! They *did* escape!"

Next moment, she was running toward us—not actually us, but the great window. En route, she snagged a small granite statue from a wobbling pediment and brandished it in her tight fist as she ran toward the glass. The helmeted head of the warrior statue struck the window first, and the glass shattered like a thunderstroke. I backed away due to the sheer loudness of the event, and Stezen, too, retreated as though to avoid being struck by flying particles. Lynn turned a fevered, leering, hopeful face toward me, by way of invitation to join her, then ran the statue through the splinters and chips and triangles of glass that remained. Without another word, she jumped through the frame.

This window, clearly, was no illusion. I saw the girl scramble away across the grass-that-was-not-grass, looking back occasionally and squinting, as though she could no longer see the estate.

"Extraordinary," I commented unnecessarily.

"Exactly."

The subject broached, I felt I had nothing to lose. "Where, precisely is she now?"

"Why, in the painting," Stezen replied with mock incredulity. "Don't you remember my explanation?"

"Yes, that it was a magical painting, an illusion. But how could she break the glass if it were an illusion?"

"Are you saying illusory glass would be harder to break than real glass?" Stezen asked. "Come now. I'm beginning to lose faith in your deductions."

He was right. Clearly, if the magical window were easily conjured, a magical broken window with a girl running through it would just as easily be produced. Besides, I knew that I must not jar his faith now, so near to the goal.

D'Polarno had turned to address the remaining guests, some scant ten or so who'd not been weeded out earlier. Even so, these looked anything but the pick of the litter. They were uniformly wide-eyed and cringing, their faces a ghastly green that belied the bounteous meal they had eaten.

"And what shall it be for all of you?" he asked them. "Continue the tour, or bring it to a close here and now?"

As I had done throughout the evening, I rushed then to nail my coffin shut. "I, for one, am utterly fascinated and wish to carry this all to its conclusion." Stezen answered me with a wave of the hand that indicated that he had expected nothing else. Flustered to have been read so easily, I glanced away toward the window again, where servants of D'Polarno were already nailing boards into place.

"What of the rest of you?" D'Polarno asked in the silence that followed. "Continue, or quit?"

The man who answered for the host was a tall, hatchet-faced fellow who held his hat clutched tightly in his hands and blinked his large fish eyes often as he spoke. "Of course, we're enjoying the tour—to the utmost, sir, Marquis D'Polarno. But it's getting late and, well . . . I bet it would take a good few months to really apprec-"

"A few years," Stezen interrupted dryly.

"Yes, years, to really appreciate all that's here. So if we could call it a night and, perhaps, see the rest of the gallery next week some time?" Those standing around him nodded their appeasing agreement.

"Sorry," Stezen said, running his thumbnail beneath the nail of his little finger, "this is your one and only tour." He gestured to the crowd. "Come. The final room."

My heart leapt. If he harbored his fountain anywhere, it would be in this place. I needed only to step across the threshold to find out, and perhaps this would be my literal doorway to eternity. Inwardly upbraiding myself for standing still so long, I started forward, and reached the back of the anxious group.

The great black doors creaked open. Stezen, at the head of the procession, backed slowly through them. The cold that poured out of the chamber beyond reached me even at the party's rear, and I gasped slightly. My eyes stared through the portal to see a cavernous room all in black. Indeed, the floor and wall and ceiling were so lightless that they seemed to recede forever. No paintings here, only thousands of pieces of white granite statuary, only rows upon rows of poised figures, like the gravestones of a battlefield's dead.

In their center stood a magnificent and enormous fountain—*the* magnificent and enormous fountain. Its sprays and jets of water arced up higher than any ceiling I had ever seen. The base of the fountain was wide and white, and its waters a kind of pale blue, the only true color in the cavernous chamber. In the center of the fountain, a vast marble mountain rose, composed of columns and acanthus and countless statues in relief or full: griffins, snakes, cockatrices, scarabs, phoenixes, lambs. Most importantly, though, was the water, cascading through thousands of falls and chutes, rising again through piping and tubes only to spray out and fill the black firmament.

So mesmerized was I by this, so moved and affected, that I felt drawn forward across that threshold into the cold and windy and infinite place. I stood on the black floor, knowing it to be there by the pressure of its pushing back, but having the queer sensation that I stood on nothing. To relieve this distressing confusion of the senses, I let my eyes rise up the form of D'Polarno, standing on the floor before me.

He smiled his feline smile, gestured at the room about us, and said, "Welcome, Dr. Ferewood, to the Hall of the Eternities."

Only then did I notice that we two stood alone. The nervous flock of ten, who had gone through the gate before me, had dissipated into air. Well, not precisely air. By the path where I stood, I saw the tall, hatchet-faced, fish-eyed supplicant from the other room. He stood splendid in white marble, his hat still clutched tightly in those fists that would clutch nothing else, forever.

"Where are the rest of them?" I asked through a constricting throat. "What have you done?"

"They're around here somewhere," Stezen said with a laugh and a casual wave of the hand. That simple gesture took in a number of the guests: a woman in her flushed thirties, whose belly had just begun to show the child, now stone, within; a gap-toothed falconer whose staring eyes of granite had that wide and fierce and unblinking aspect of birds; a lady all done in furs whose heretofore and hereafter silent grace was augmented by sables, now elegantly spiked in stone. All statues. All dead.

Though Stezen paused for only a breath, his voice broke like a cannon blast on my musings. "I'd really begun to think I'd not find any of you worthy to drink from the fountain tonight—I thought everybody'd end up in one sordid scene or another in one of my paintings. But here you are."

"The rest aren't free?" I gasped. "The rest are in these sculptures? The paintings?"

"It is as I told you—as I showed you," replied D'Polarno easily. "You saw the merchant and his wife, and the duke in the magical painting back there. You see this one standing here like some granite rube, staring forever at you. . . ."

"You've turned them into—"

"Immortals," Stezen interrupted. He coughed into his hand. "Well, immortals of a sort. They're still very much alive, I assure you. But they've all been freed of their flesh and embodied now in stone. That's the best immortality I can offer to the common cut of man."

"All of them? Every last one of them? From Krimean, the oaf in the first room, to . . . to this one standing here now?"

Stezen just shook his head. His face wore a look of feigned surprise in mockery of me, and he said, "Of course, all of them. In the room of classic sculptures, didn't you notice those women clustered about in mourning? Remember them from the table, clinging to each others' arms? You yourself studied the monolith in the first room, studied it in great depth—commented on it even. Didn't you recognize that the statue you studied was Krimean?"

"You've killed them!"

"No." The response was curt. "No, I did not. I've told you, they are alive, only in bodies of stone, which will last them millennia, if not forever."

"But why, why did you do it?"

"They asked me to," Stezen replied simply. "You think you were the only one to come here seeking the fountain of life? Of course not. I sent the word out myself—carefully, restrictedly—to just the sort of people who would covet it and would have the stuff to make it this far and drink. But only you made it."

"Only me."

"Only you."

My avarice—my compulsion and passion for immortality—began again to take me over. At first I'd been shocked to discover the fate of my fellow revelers, then stunned in an attempt to puzzle out just what had happened to them all, then confused. . . . Now all my qualms fell away, as the hunter's twinge of sadness departs when the pangs of hunger set in.

"Only me," I muttered again stupidly.

Stezen nodded. "All the others sought immortality for fear of death. They feared the rending of their flesh, the ending of their minds. But you know immortality is more than that."

"Yes," I moaned, though I did not really. "I know."

"You know that immortality is about soul and being. You, like me, would sacrifice body and mind for it."

"Yes."

"For the others, it was a fashion. For you it is a faith. I gave the others the immortality for which they had asked. I offer another immortality—a higher, better immortality—now to you."

Already I was walking toward D'Polarno, toward the hissing, thundering fountain. He turned about and led me there, producing a leathern cup from within his vest, unfolding it, rounding it, and seating himself on the fountain's rim. I did the same.

The next words he spoke were almost lost to the roar of the water. "This libation will give you everlasting life, free you of the ravages to the flesh, free you of the frailties of the mind. It will transform you, fill you, allow you to transcend all that is petty and mortal. Will you drink?"

I nodded in mute reverence.

He dipped the leathern cup into the bubbling water, a

strangely crude vessel for so empyreal a drink, and lifted it, dripping, up to me. When a few drops struck my knee, the water felt cold and clear and magnificent.

"Drink," said he.

I drank. The taste was like nothing I had ever had before. The water was very chill, and when it went down my throat, it caused a sensation that I can only call an ecstatic burning. The feeling spread rapidly through me, reaching the tips of my fingers and toes, making my skin flush with its intense heat. It felt as though sparks were flying through my body, transforming it into a vital, trembling, invincible form.

I laughed out loud, and my voice was carried into the fountain and it merged with the water that had brought this unbelievable joy—merged and circulated and bubbled and danced. I was alive, as though for the first time ever.

"Welcome," said Stezen, "to the brotherhood of Immortals." He leaned toward me and, in the custom of his land, kissed me upon the lips. Then he raised his hand, brushed my jaw for a moment, and jabbed a steel-hard forefinger through my cheek.

There was a moment of horrible tearing, and I glimpsed my flesh splitting away like the shirt ripping from a man's shoulders. Then the ruptured skin of my forehead dragged over my eyes and brought crimson darkness to them. I staggered for a moment, feeling Stezen peel my body from me like the skin from an orange. Everything was violent jolting and liquid sloshing and lacerations rubbing. Flesh and bone and marrow, torn away from my soul.

Then it was over. It was that sudden. In a rushing cascade of slippery mortal flesh, I was defrocked of my body. But I—my soul—remained.

Though my mortal shell, my fleshly existence, has been removed, I am still here, a disembodied mind—the ghost in the gallery. All my time has been like this now, bodiless and eternal. I could not scream my rage to Stezen. I could not even see him to hate him. I have no eyes to see with. I have no ears to hear with. I have no skin, no tongue, no nose, no heart, no hands, no bone, no flesh at all with which to sense or affect the gallery around me. I am utterly alone, and utterly indestructible.

Since that time—how many centuries or minutes, I know not—I've realized how truly Stezen spoke. I was mortal and wished not to be. To become otherwise, all that was mortal in me would needs be purged. He did so. And now I know it was mortality, not immortality, that I had once loved.

So I tell my tale, in the vain hope that if there are others like me in this gallery, others whose beings have been stripped of their bodies, they might perhaps hear and let their souls weep. But mine is a vain hope. For I, myself, cannot hear their cries.

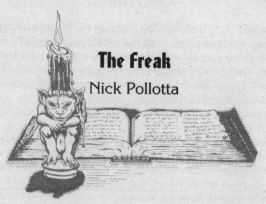

The Freak

Nick Pollotta

He burst from the dark forest, a twisted, ragtag figure frantically running along the rutted gullies of the old dirt road. A man fleeing for his very life.

In every direction, tremendous granite mountains dominated the horizon, looming large above the wooded valley. Sharply silhouetted by the star-filled sky and waning crescent moon, the somber, jagged monoliths stood silent and uncaring of what occurred below in the world of mortal men.

Though dressed in tattered clothes, the body of the running man was perfection: the limbs and chest of a young Adonis, strength and masculine beauty personified. But when a shaft of moonlight pierced the thick cover of trees and illuminated his face, it was clear that nature, which had so richly rewarded his body, had definitely not done so here. His grotesque features were the essence of nightmares.

Mottled, discolored skin. A flat, slit wound of a nose, like that of a rutting boar. One eye was three times too large, sans lashes and set above the other, with no regard for balance or function. His bulging forehead extended in irregular patterns as if the pressure inside was simply too much for the bones and his head was likely to burst apart at any moment. One ear was human enough, though of disproportionate size; the other was delicately pointed like that of an elfin child, a tiny pink flower growing on the side of the crumbling, moldy ruin of his face.

His hair, a dozen shabby hues, grew in tufts along his ragged widow's peak, and his crown was partially bald. He lacked a top lip entirely, and the bottom was too full by far, easily exposing his broken, gap-filled teeth. Even the jaw appeared to have been melted in a furnace, then randomly recast.

It was a face of horror, and that was what it radiated now. Raw horror.

Wheezing for breath, the grotesque mockery named Anatole the Freak glanced over a slim shoulder and stumbled into a rut in the hard-packed soil. Down he fell, gashing his lopsided chin on a sharp rock. The small pain went unnoticed as the deformed hermit scrambled to his feet, just in time for torches to appear over the low rise behind him.

They had found him. Now the panting hermit could clearly hear the loud crackling of the torches, the angry voices of his three hunters, the deadly pack of hounds—vicious, bloodthirsty brutes that liked to wound before eventually killing. The dogs were savage beasts, fit companions for the humans pursuing him.

"There he is!" shouted the burly man, swinging his bare sword.

"Murdering freak!" screamed the tall one, brandishing an axe.

Bullwhip in left hand, rope in right, the fat man added, "Sick 'im, boys!"

Anatole sprinted for the safety of the trees, but, released from their restraining ropes, the snarling dogs surged upon him in a instant. Seizing his bedraggled clothes in their teeth, they pulled the freak down to the ground, their great jaws snapping inches from fingers and eyes. Crying aloud in fear, Anatole covered his face with both hands, a meager protection from their lethal fangs.

"Why are you doing this?" he screamed in confusion. "I am innocent!"

"Liar!" stormed the overweight man, uncurling his weapon. In the darkness, his arm jerked, and a whip cracked across the back of the cowering recluse. His rag shirt split asunder under the stinging lash, and pain knifed into his flesh.

A shuddering gasp escaped his lips as the freak raised his hands in surrender. "Please!" Anatole begged, tears cascading down the twisted ravines of his cheeks. "I haven't left the swamp for weeks! I know nothing! Nothing! Tell me what was done. I'll prove my innocence!"

The bullwhip cracked again, and a sizzling and popping torch was thrust toward him, the flames nearly setting his stringy hair on fire.

"Shut up, monster!" screamed the man with the sword, flecks of foam staining his thick mouth. "We'll not listen to your lies anymore! You killed those people, and we know it!"

"Killed who?" he pleaded in bewilderment. "Who?"

Outraged by his refusal to confess, the workmen put weapons aside, and their fists pounded him mercilessly. Helpless beneath their iron blows, Anatole fell unconsciousness for awhile, lost in a red haze of pain. And when at last his mind cleared, he saw the three men standing tall above the slavering dogs, the rope leashes in their callused hands being knotted into a hangman's noose.

All the while screaming his innocence, the bloody hermit was kicked to his feet and shoved toward the woods. The night watchmen from the village had no intention of wasting time with a public trial or other legal foolishness. When the mayor and constable awoke in the morning, it would be over and done. A tree with a stout limb would be the judge tonight, and a dog's rope the jury.

Roughly, the laughing murderers hauled the weeping Anatole off the road. But as the stout boots of the killers stepped off the packed dirt, their leather soles crunched on loose gravel, the sound making the men pause. Lowering the torches, they saw an unknown road stretch out before them. What was this? The three men looked about in confusion. No other highway cut through the forest, and certainly none with crushed rock to stiffen the soil against the autumn rains. Theirs was but a poor village of farmers and fishermen.

With icy dread, the men watched thickening mists obscure the landscape, the ghostly fog moving with unnatural speed. A chill took them all as they saw a strange newborn cobblestone road physically stretch to the foggy horizon. And just below the crescent moon there loomed the black silhouette of a bizarre figure, the weird outline discernible by the complete lack of stars in the stygian sky.

At the sight, an awful hush engulfed the four, and even the dogs stopped panting in the eerie silence. It was as if all their ears had been stoppered shut with wax. Breath fogging from their open mouths, they saw the forest grow black as pitch, saw steaming mist rise from the ground everywhere. Rumbling storm clouds masked the moon, and a graveyard cold gripped them as, in growing horror, the would-be murderers realized that the far figure was coming their way at a full gallop.

Appearing and disappearing within the billowing tendrils of moving fog, the silhouette formed the familiar outline of a man on horseback, and the watchmen sighed in relief . . . until the surging clouds parted and the shimmering moonlight bathed the oncoming rider with nightmarish clarity. A man on a horse, yes, but unlike any this side of hell.

The horrible horse was impossibly large, heavily muscled as if for war, and moving faster than any noble's racing steed. The flaring nostrils of the mighty beast emitted blasts of white steam into the cold air. Its hide was the shiny black of oiled metal, its eyes wild and white, its sharp teeth distended and bared in a hateful grin. A burning spray of bright sparks erupted from every loud strike of the powerful hooves on the stony road. It was a beast of the Apocalypse. Some dark and obscene thing from the very depths of the Abyss itself.

The rider, bent low against the wind, was dressed in elegant finery, the clean white shirt and spotless black velvet jacket of a rich nobleman. His fold-top boots were of an ancient style, long out of fashion, his ebony and scarlet cloak spreading out behind him to completely hide the road beyond, as if it no longer existed. Sparkling among the somber apparel were spurs and stirrups of gleaming, polished silver.

As the noble approached, the watchmen cried aloud:

the evil figure possessed no head. None at all. His stiff white collar of fine starched linen encircled vacant air.

Misunderstanding, the watchmen waited for the newly dead body to fall from the saddle, waited for the victorious cry of the brigands who had slain him seconds ago beyond the rise. But with the reins held tight in his left glove, the decapitated man dutifully rode onward, ever onward with increasing speed. Then the empty shoulders turned a bit, and the stupefied villagers were pierced by the stare of eyes that were not there—or at least, eyes that were not in this land of the living.

In that same heartbeat, the ghastly rider drew a shining steel sickle from his voluminous cape. And in terrible clarity, the watchmen saw a single ruby-red droplet slide along the razor edge of the curved blade, cling to the needle-sharp tip, and then drop away, vanishing in the dark wind before striking the cold cobbles below.

The dogs cowering in terror, the would-be killers released their victim, who fell to his knees. Backing away, the watchmen moved with the restrained steps of shackled prisoners. The mounting cold had seized their joints with brutal force, congealing the blood that was so hot moments ago, making even the tiniest motion difficult. Panic-filled eyes were unwillingly pinned upon the approaching madness, this specter of death. Only their hearts moved freely, slamming inside their heaving chests.

"This . . . is impossible," mouthed the portly owner of the whip, dropping his weapon from limp fingers. "Impossible!"

And with those soft words, their hearing violently returned. Strident thunder, like a never-ending avalanche, boomed from the maelstrom in the tumultuous sky, the concussions wildly shaking the bare winter trees. And yet the approaching hoofbeats overwhelmed the fury of nature, seeming to physically fill the frosty air. The fiery pounding hit their faces with stinging force like angry, invisible slaps.

No thought of battle occurred to the watchmen. Escape was their only wish. Flight and survival. But their will to act was as frozen as their shivering limbs. All they could do was stand trembling, helpless as children, and watch primordial death enter their world.

The leering horse looming larger, more solid than the surrounding granite peaks; the dire specter galloped straight toward them. The tall man with the axe attempted to throw himself backward, to fall off the cursed highway, but it was as if he was nailed into place. His magic charms and good luck pieces were still at home instead of in pockets where they might have done him good. He tried a desperate prayer to the gods, but none seemed to hear.

In somber ritual, the phantasmal rider raised the lethal sickle, perfectly blotting out the slim sliver of moon, casting the small group of men and dogs in a freezing shadow of doom.

And then he was amid them.

Frantic, the dogs went under the charging stallion and were ruthlessly trampled by the great hooves, helpless as wheat before a thresher. The horse and rider exploded between the shaking men, the deadly sickle swinging back and forth with the rhythm of a clock pendulum. Shivering in his bloody rags, Anatole heard a whistling pass and saw red-tainted silver flash in the harsh moonlight. The freak stared agape, drooling upon his lopsided chin, as the heads and bodies of his tormentors dropped separately to the roadway.

Now the slayer was upon him, and the hermit closed his mismatched eyes, throwing a perfect arm before his hated face. There was only a scant meter of road between them. Yet the pounding hooves seemed to take forever to reach him, the deafening noise growing until it shook the universe. His stomach heaved as, large and powerful, the sickle swept past him with tingling nearness. Braced for death, Anatole dementedly imagined that several somethings flew past him, moving all around him, brushing near enough to disturb his matted hair and tug on his tattered clothes.

But nothing else happened. As the nerve-wracking seconds wore on, the hoofbeats receded and the sounds of the forest slowly came again. Crickets. An owl hooting. The rustle of leaves. Fearful of what new horrors might assail him, Anatole managed to force his one good eye open a crack.

There was nobody in sight. Even the mist was gone. The trembling hermit stood alone in a grassy field surrounding by lush forest greenery. Collapsing to the dirt, Anatole wept, his body shaking with exhaustion and the sheer joy of living. Alive. He was still alive! Gods above, had it been only a dream? Some wild fever vision brought on by near starvation? Or perhaps he had been beaten insane by the villagers. Yes, that must be the answer.

But shakily rising to his feet, Anatole the Freak noticed dark shapes lying motionless in the green grass: the horribly mutilated dogs, the fresh human corpses. The scene telescoped before him, filling his mind, almost smashing his sanity, and in that instant of crystallized reality, deep in his heart, a new type of fear was born.

Shivering again in spite of the muggy summer warmth, Anatole lurched away from the dead watchmen, forcing himself to stumble toward the dirt road. Once on relatively flat ground, the hermit sprinted through the fearful darkness, heading for the village. The mayor must be told. The people warned! This had not been a dream, but a living nightmare. The dreaded headless horseman of myth had come to their valley! What could they do? How could any of them hope to survive?

And most importantly . . . why had he?

*　*　*　*　*

Running. Running. A light flashed between the tree branches, then disappeared as the road rose and swept downward. A distant call of laughter was heard through the darkness, then the dirt road curved, and crackling torchlight washed over the panting hermit. Surrounded by a tall stone-block wall, the gates of the city stood wide and inviting, as if there were nothing to fear. The fools!

Dashing inside, Anatole glanced wildly about at the dim

houses, their facades illuminated by the flickering of street
torches. Who first? Anyone? A city guard? The mayor!
Turning right at the fountain, the hermit scrambled down
the brick side street.

Every shadow seemed to reach out for him; the sound
of a passing horse and wagon almost made him scream;
a bare tree branch swiped at him like a giant hand; eyes
seemed to peer from every eave. Clutching his throb-
bing head in both hands, Anatole spun about in a mad
circle, wasting precious minutes as sanity returned.
Imagination. It was all in his mind. He hoped.

The wooden outline of a shoe hanging from an iron
post marked a cobbler's house. Anatole rushed to the
door and banged furiously on it, then yanked the cord
for the upstairs bell. He could hear it clang within, but no
one came and no lights appeared. Despite the summer
warmth, cold sweat poured down his back. Anatole spun
and started to bolt, but paused midstep. Where next?
The city alarm bell for fires? Where was it? He had rarely
come this far into town.

Memories of screaming women, laughing men, and
children with stones rose to memory, but he forced
those phantasms down. They all hated him for his ugli-
ness. Mocked him! But it was still his village, his home,
and he must warn them. A breeze scented with fresh-
baked bread wafted along the street, and the clouds
parted, allowing the silvery light of the moon to bathe
the city in an unearthly blue. Wiping his mouth with the
back of a hand, Anatole thought of other nights, other
midnight beatings. The city constable, of course! But he
would be on his rounds, checking doors and locks. Was
there no place where he could find . . . the Dog 'n Bull.
Yes! Perfect!

His lungs heaving for breath, the hermit once more
lurched off and began racing deeper into the village. He
passed a dog rooting in some garbage, and it stared
curiously at him. A loving couple, arm in arm, strolled
eastward as he went west crossing a small bridge, but
they paid him no mind. Turning at the half-built library,
Anatole saw a brightly lit section of street, illumination
streaming from the windows of the Dog 'n Bull. Accor-

dion music sounded from within, mixed with laughter and pounding boots. As he approached, the double doors burst open, and out staggered a singing man who walked as if on a storm-tossed ship. The hermit passed him, and the fellow doffed a hat he was not wearing and started to say something, then went pale and backed away, white-faced and trembling.

The oak doors were warm and smooth beneath his fingers as Anatole shoved them open. Bright light and music washed over him, and he blinked, tilting his head away from the smoke-filled air to protect his bad eye. Tables jammed with laughing people filled the central room, a wooden wheel made into a chandelier hung from the ceiling, and half a pig was roasting in the huge fireplace. He shuffled inside and across the sawdust-strewn floor.

"Hey, stranger!" called out a man behind the bar, sliding a tankard of ale down the countertop to a waiting customer. "Welcome to the Dog 'n Bull! What can I . . . good gods above!"

"It's the freak!" shrieked a woman, and the music stopped. In ragged stages, all talking ceased and every head turned to stare. More than one person spit upon the floor, and several drew their belt knives.

"The mayor," wheezed Anatole, his throat bone dry from panting. "I need to find . . ." A half-filled container of ale was on a table near him, and impulsively the hermit grabbed the blackjack and drank deeply. The leather was warm to his touch and the tar lining gave the ale a flavorful tang. Then the mug was painfully slapped from his grasp.

"Aye, and we don't want you drinking from our mugs!" cried the bartender, towering above the cringing man. "I'll have to burn the thing now. That's nine coppers you owe me, freak!"

Shoving aside their chairs, men moved toward the hermit, their faces menacing scowls.

"They're dead!" he shouted over the growing rumble. "I saw it! They're all dead!"

The mass advance stopped.

"Who's dead, ya murdling goon," barked a squat

shepherd, shaking his blackjack until it sloshed over.

Fear tightening his belly, Anatole spoke fast. "Hans, Emile, and Angelo. He killed them all. Cut off their heads. I saw it! In the fields by the waterfall."

Cries of outrage and confusion.

"Cut off their heads?"

"Who did it?"

"Dead, ya say?"

"The horseman," he said, his voice a whisper.

The village tax collector pushed his way through the crowd, strode closer, and stood before the hermit, his thumbs jammed inside his wide leather belt. A belt Anatole's scarred back knew far too well. "What horseman? Speak fast, freak," growled the clerk.

"It was the headless horseman," said Anatole "He came out of the moonlight on a horse blacker than the night! And he had a silver sickle—"

But his words were drowned out by gales of laughter.

"The headless horseman of Hanover?" guffawed a serving wench. "Idiot, can't ya lie better 'n that?"

Another shouted, "And he attacked you in the middle of a field? Poppycock!"

"Even a child knows he can't leave da road," growled an elderly man in soldier's livery. "Ya dang fool."

Anatole's eyes flicked from one disbelieving face to another. "But it's true! And there was a road! It just appeared under us and the horseman killed everyone!"

"But not you," spoke the city constable from the mezzanine above the room. The tavern quieted as the blubbery man waddled down the steps, tucking in his shirt. A gale of feminine laughter came from upstairs and was quickly cut off by the closing of a pink door.

Three times his size, Brad Thalmeyer stood before the hermit and scowled. "You say the headless horseman came and killed three armed men, but not you."

"Yes!"

"Why?"

"I . . ."

"Well?"

"I don't know," Anatole said softly, lowering his head. Rough hands grabbed his clothing, tearing it from his body.

"Aye, but *we* know!" stormed Constable Thalmeyer. "Those three went to hang you for that gypsy killing. Now you return with this witless tale of galloping monsters and claim they be dead! If so, then you did it, not some children's ghost!"

"I swear!" began the hermit, but a hairy fist punched him to the floor. Something banged off his forehead, and ale splashed over his face, washing the wooden planks beneath him clear of sawdust. "Hold him," stated the constable, grinding a fist into the palm of his other hand. "I'll find the mayor and get us a writ of execution!"

"And a rope!" cried somebody else. "Truth, 'tis high time we got rid of this . . . abomination!" stated the school teacher, adjusting his spectacles.

"Who'll come with me, lads?" called the constable standing in the doorway, one great hand on the metal latch. "To help protect me from the horseman?"

A scribe rose from his table and laughingly joined the constable. "Here, Brad! I'll even help the mayor sign it, if need be!"

"Aye!"

As the double doors closed behind the laughing men, the tavern once more turned its attention to their captive. "What shall we do to make sure he don't escape us, lads?" called out a lanky herdsman, undoing a bullwhip from about his waist.

Cruelly, the crowd roared suggestions, but Anatole went still when he saw that the breath of the herdsman was foggy here in the warm tavern. Others noticed a sudden chill, too, and many shivered, drawing their clothes tighter about them. "It's him!" cried Anatole, cowering on the floor. "Gods, save us!"

The table lanterns died. The overhead candles puffed out. The blaze in the fireplace dropped to a low crackle of icy blue flame.

Outside the tavern, the constable and his companion cried out in surprise and fear; a sudden pounding of iron hooves filled the air like winter thunder, the steady, savage pounding of a racing warhorse. Then a large shadow eclipsed the window beside the door. The two men screamed in terror, screams cut horribly short.

Then the sound of the hooves faded away.

Silence reigned for several minutes, until the flames in the fireplace blazed up to full fury once more, making everyone gasp and recoil, dropping whatever they were holding. But no one moved to relight the candles or lanterns. All eyes stayed on the closed front door, and the only sounds were muttered prayers and hard, rasping breath.

Then some thick reddish liquid began to flow underneath the door and into the tavern. Knives were drawn by a dozen men; women pulled amulets into view. With slow, hesitant steps, the bartender lifted an ancient battle mace into view from behind the counter and moved past the patrons to place a gnarled hand on the latch of the front door. He pulled it open, and two headless corpses fell onto the dirty sawdust. The rest of their remains stayed outside in the middle of the street, black lumps half-hidden by blessed moonshadow.

Women screamed in terror, men cursed, chairs were overturned, and the trembling hermit released. The bartender backed against the wall and splayed his arms as if seeking support. Somebody started to cry, and another began to retch.

Levering himself to his feet, Anatole said nothing, but he winced as he moved his wrenched right arm. In response, a young barmaid wordlessly drew a fresh blackjack of ale and placed it before the shuddering hermit. Anatole watched the action, not understanding for a moment. He glanced upward at her, and she shied her lovely face away, but made a wiggling motion with her fingers. Eagerly, he took the mug in both hands and carefully drank the frothy brew. It was wonderful, fresh from the barrel, not the bitter dregs he usually stole from the drained barrels in the alleyway. Still cold from the cellar, the ale chilled his empty stomach, and he shivered violently.

On impulse, he placed the empty on the counter and pushed it toward the woman. Without comment, she refilled the mug and slid it back to him. Reveling in his good fortune, Anatole sipped his drink and watched as the people in the tavern whispered to themselves and moved away from him.

Over the leather rim of his blackjack, Anatole saw it in their eyes. In the faces of every man and woman present. A new emotion. Not disgust, not contempt. But something he had never seen before. Fear. Fear of him!

Hmm.

*   *   *   *   *

A few hours later, the mechanical clock in the church tower struck midnight, the reverberations of the great bronze bells rolling in somber majesty over the little village. Everywhere, in every house and store, hushed voices spoke of the bizarre events that had occurred. Most prayed that the night of terror was over. Surely five dead was a bountiful enough harvest for any hellish minion. But a scant handful believed differently, and they gathered in secret at the house of the mayor, clustered around a hand-hewn table of forest oak to speak of death. And life.

"The two of them are obviously linked," growled Mayor Ceccion, pouring dollops into the glasses of his guests. The three men sipped the vintage, taking courage from the sweet English brandy made of cider and molasses.

"Some sort of weird connection here," added Franklin. Rising from his chair, the stonemason glanced nervously out the side window of the second-story room. The brick street, well lit by torches, was deserted. He allowed the lacy curtain to drop back into place. "That swamp freak with his bastard face and this monster without a head. Ye, gods! No head!"

"And five good men dead," added Hecthorpe. The fat cooper frowned at the full glass on the table before him. One sip had been enough. Wretched stuff. "Two in the very heart of our town!"

At the head of the table, a tall, lanky man removed his ancient fisherman's cap and stuffed it into a back pocket of his weathered pants. "Aye, but what be this thing wanting?" demanded Captain Emett, tossing off the homemade brandy as if it were weak tea. He took the bottle and gave himself a proper refill. "Tribute? Revenge?"

"The dead hate the living," said the mayor softly, over the crackling of the fire, "because we can still hope and laugh. No other reason is necessary."

In silence, the men listened to the beating of their hearts and acknowledged the wisdom of the statement.

"Accepted. So, how do we stop this bedamned spook?" asked Franklin, rubbing his aching right wrist. The arthritis there usually pained him only with the coming of winter. "Can we kill the undead with pikes and axes?"

"Is he really a ghost?" pondered Hecthorpe, heavy brows lowered in thought. "Mayhaps it's only a magician's trick. A black bag over his head, something like that."

"A possibility," muttered Ceccion, taking his clay pipe from the mantle and lighting it from a candle. Now within a cloud of brackish smoke, he added, "But anyone who can slay men faster than reaping wheat is still a problem we need to solve quickly."

"No living man can behead others from the back of a striding horse," snorted the stonemason. "It be impossible! Not even I am that strong!" To make his point, the bricklayer flexed his arms and chest, the seams of his shirt threatening to burst apart.

"Agreed," puffed the mayor dourly. "So that brings us back to why this monster is attacking our town. The freak?"

Muttered agreements. There seemed little doubt on that point.

"So what do we do?"

"Kill him," said Hecthorpe grimly. "We have five dead on account of that misshapen man-thing."

Captain Emett slammed his glass down. "Aye! Keelhaul the creature!" snapped the fisherman. "Draw and quarter 'im!"

"Burn him alive is probably best," advised Hecthorpe, scratching his cheek. "That way his screams will tell the world of his death."

"And with him gone, that headless horseman should leave also!"

"Aye."

"Makes sense."

Tapping out his pipe, the mayor warned caution. "We shall handle the killing ourselves, with no help from others. Speed and secrecy are our best chance. Remember, the last men who tried to hang that abomination are being buried even as we speak," he intoned, the breath fogging from his mouth.

All conversation abruptly stopped as a wave of arctic cold washed over the large room. In heart-pounding fear, the men glanced about and saw that the table and chairs where they gathered were no longer in the den of the mayor's house, but now in the middle of a dark forest. Mountains rose on each side, forming a valley for the starry night overhead. And beneath them the decorative carpet was gone, replaced by a gravel road that stretched from horizon to horizon, from crescent moon to sea.

And then a silhouetted figure appeared on the distant, silvery ridge. A cloaked human without a head sitting on a great warhorse . . . which was galloping toward them down a cobblestone roadway.

Struggling to rise from their chairs, the village councilmen found that even the slightest motion was difficult, as if invisible chains bound them to the spot. Forcing hands into pockets, three of the four clutched their good-luck charms, and the men wrenched free of the paralysis and stood. Moving with slow desperation, Mayor Ceccion went to the corner where his weapons cabinet should have stood, and he fondled and fingered the empty air, searching for the wall rack with its steel sword and crossbow. But nothing met his urgent touch. Impossible! This must merely be an illusion. It must!

The strident pounding of iron hooves filled the frigid air, and faintly the terrified men could hear the ghostly rattle of plates and glasses somewhere else, far off in another place. Another world.

Cursing loudly, the river captain knocked over the table as a shield and the stonemason brandished a chair in one hand. In his mighty grip, even that simple stool should be a deadly weapon. Unable to rouse himself, the sweating coopersmith sat motionless, darting eyes betraying his terror.

Thundering ever closer, the leviathan horse bared its teeth in a ghastly rictus, and the dire horseman raised his sickle high, the curved blade eclipsing the moon, casting them all in soul-freezing shadow.

A scream trapped in his throat, Hecthorpe twitched helplessly in his seat. Franklin threw the chair, and it missed both man and horse. Captain Emett drew a belt knife, but it tumbled from spasming fingers. Choking on his rising gore, Mayor Ceccion dropped to his knees, praying for divine rescue. But in the lurid nightmare of black and silver, they all knew death was but moments away. Nothing could save them. Nothing.

The pounding hooves deafened them. The crimson-lined cape flared wide like blood-soaked dawn, and in a heartbeat, the protean pair was among them. The silvery blade flashed downward. The hardwood table exploded into splinters. Cries of anger were horribly terminated, and three grisly thuds sounded on the cobblestone road.

Standing at the edge of the roadway, unable to move back another step because of some unseen barrier that resisted his best efforts, Mayor Ceccion closed his eyes against the slaughter, and felt a white-hot pinprick on his throat. Tiny as the pain was, it shattered his silence.

"Forgive me, Lord!" he managed without moving his taut neck. "I beseech your mercy!"

Incredibly, astonishingly, he lived for another moment, two, three. The tiny prickling burned into his vulnerable flesh an impossibly long time. As painful seconds stretched into forever, all around him, Ceccion heard the gnashing and chattering of hundreds of teeth. The source of the feasting noise was unthinkable. Then the pressure of the sickle increased, warm blood trickled down his throat, and suddenly the mayor knew he was being asked a question. One for which the wrong answer meant instant death.

"On my honor," he wailed, tears flowing beneath his closed eyelids. "I swear none will be allowed to harm the f-frea . . . Anatole!"

And miraculously, the stabbing agony was gone. Blessed relief washed over the man as he slumped to the gravel road. The stentorian hoofbeats faded away, along with the stomach-turning sounds of chewing.

A wave of warmth from the crackling fireplace shook him to the core, and, daring to open his eyes, the mayor saw that the room was in shambles. Everything was smashed and broken or splattered with fresh blood. Even the beheaded corpses of his friends, even their clothes, were torn to shreds as if wild dogs had savaged the bodies. Gingerly touching his stinging throat, Mayor Ceccion saw his fingertips were stained red. But he still lived. He lived!

Loud knocking on the door finally penetrated his joyous thoughts, and weakly he staggered across the wreckage to throw aside the locking bar. Instantly, his neighbors rushed in, almost knocking the mayor down. But then his well-intentioned rescuers jerked to a dead halt as they saw the brutal scene of murder. A man stuffed a fist into his mouth so as not to scream. Another backed out into the hallway and headed quickly for the stairs. A scarred young woman in soldier's livery scowled and tightened the grip on her sword pommel.

Weeping and sobbing, Ceccion told his tale to the dumbfounded villagers, and soon the story spread like wildfire throughout the no-longer-sleeping town. The horrid news went from house to house in frantic, fevered whispers. The shocking warning of the hysterical mayor galvanized the frightened citizenry, first in a panic, then in terrified immobility. The headless horseman had struck again. So if you wish to live . . . do not harm the freak.

*   *   *   *   *

Sluggishly, Anatole stirred in his sleep, feeling oddly warm and comfortable. Something soft brushed his cheek, and the hermit sat upright in his bed to see that a nice new quilt of blue cloth and goose feathers was covering his rickety bedframe.

Swinging his legs to the floor, Anatole saw that the dirt floor of his sagging cabin had been swept tidy during the night. Arising, he blinked at the sight of actual cloth curtains on both of the windows of oiled paper. Incredible!

A tantalizing aroma caught his attention, and the hermit spun about to see that the upside-down barrel that served as his table was covered with an old linen cloth and piled high with a mound of food. Food! He rushed forward and dared to touch the unbelievable cornucopia, testing its reality. A loaf of bread not yet stale. An entire wheel of cheese with only a bit of mold on one side! A wicker basket of apples! A smoked roast of beef wrapped in waxed paper and greasy twine! A bottle of real wine! The smell of it all together was heady, almost narcotic. It was more and better food than he would normally eat in a year.

Wasting no time, Anatole sat himself down and began to feast, half afraid the bounty would vanish before his disbelieving eyes as he awoke from this delightful dream. After sampling everything, he settled in for a royal meal of bread and cheese, with an apple for desert. The beef he would save for a dinner celebration. He could barely remember what meat tasted like anymore.

Burping softly as fitting tribute to such a momentous feed, Anatole went to check on last night's fire and behold! next to his red-glowing, crude firepit was a rusty hatchet of steel. Wonders of wonders! It was a gift for a king! He owned nothing made of steel. It was impossibly expensive. Examining the tool, he marveled at its sharpness despite the thin layer of rust, and lightly cut a finger testing the edge. Amazing. He could probably shave with such a magical device.

Going outside to examine his prize in daylight, Anatole found a clean, dry suit of old patched clothes on a new clothesline. Placing the precious hatchet on the small wood pile, the delighted hermit stripped himself naked, washed with cold water from the trickling stream running through the bog alongside his ramshackle cabin, and dressed quickly. The grayish undergarments were soft as clouds. The mismatched socks thick and cushiony. Without any patches, the pants felt oddly smooth to his legs, and the oversized tunic was so loose and flexible that he wondered if he was wearing it correctly. The boots of stained brown leather rose to his calves, giving him a feeling of height and authority. They didn't fit very well, and the left heel was cracked, but who cared? They were infinitely better than his ancient sandals.

A plaintive moo sounded from his left. Behind some moss-covered scrub trees, the hermit discovered a scrawny cow tethered in the grassy clearing. Anatole was overwhelmed, tears of joy blurring his sight. How could all of this . . . why would . . . who . . . Turning about in wonderment, he spied a parchment note tacked to his battered door. Rushing over, Anatole gingerly removed the piece of homemade paper and struggled to read the printed message. His only schooling had been received sitting outside the window of a classroom and listening until the teacher chased him away. It was difficult, but as memory sluggishly flared, the block lettering began to make sense and the awful words written there pierced him like an arrow. These things, this junk, was a gift from the villagers. And with them, he would have 'no need to visit the town again for supplies. Ever.'

Casting aside the note like an unclean thing, Anatole felt a cold anger form in his belly, and his large hands closed into fists of rage. Damn them. Gods damn them all! So only their fear of death would earn him charity, eh? All he had ever wanted was to be left alone, to live a normal life. And all he ever received was beatings and starvation and hatred and scorn and . . .

As a clear, reddish dawn crested the vine-encrusted trees of the swamp, bathing the cabin in bloody light, his breathing became deep and steady. Plainly, after last night, the townspeople were so incredibly afraid of the horseman that they had decided to appease the deadly lord of the roadway by bribing the hated freak. And this is how they decided to buy his favor? Keep him in the stinking swamp? With a dying cow, stale food, and discarded clothes? This was payment for all the wrongs done to him? As a gift from friends it was staggering, magnificent. As tribute it was rubbish. Worse. It was garbage! An insult.

The noxious smells of the muck and mire mixed freely with that of the food and his soap-clean clothes. Anatole suddenly felt violently ill, and turned to retch in the bushes. Afterward, wiping his mouth on the sleeve of his new shirt, the hermit stood and stared with unseeing eyes of hatred at the burning sun. Well, now he was in charge, holding their very lives in the palm of his hand. In bitter satisfaction, the freak closed that hand, crushing its imaginary contents, and dumped the remains onto the ground. Offend me, he thought in ill-restrained fury, and my mysterious friend shall slay you like cattle. Like sheep!

Hitching up his pants, Anatole started across the string of rocks that bridged the bubbling mud around his little island home. In broad daylight, without a mask, he was going to go to town and walk about. And bedamn anyone who tried to stop him. Let's see how they like tasting fear for a change. The horseman had presented a bill to the villagers, and it was up to Anatole to collect it. In full.

*   *   *   *   *

Sternly ambling into the village, feeling angrier with every step, Anatole was shaken to be greeted with cheery hellos from the gate guards. Stumbling from surprise, he waved to them in return. Once past the city wall, the freak was endlessly called to by strangers and enemies alike. Everybody gave a smile, and it took the hermit awhile to realize that these were false expressions—mouths lifted in grins, but eyes cold and hard, brimming with darker emotions.

Going boldly down the main street, he spied that many windows slammed closed before he could look at the inhabitants of the houses. But when he saw them first, the people beamed, and some even called his real name. Astonishing. He hadn't known that they even knew his name! Anatole had never been called anything but 'freak.' At first the hermit hesitantly waved back, wondering if he had misunderstood the note. But slowly the duplicity of it all became clear, embittering his heart, and he stopped playing the fool in their game.

Some of the townsfolk halted dead in their tracks and openly stared at the hermit. Quietly, their neighbors pulled them aside and whispered into astonished ears, faces rapidly changing from disgusted surprise, to fear, and then to forced friendliness, neck muscles tight from the strain of cowardly grins.

In the center of town, the great square was jammed with people pushing heavily laden carts of produce, barrels of wine and fish and pickles, boxes of shoes, nails and bolts of cloth. It was market day. Everyone seemed to be yelling prices, and all arms were carrying parcels and packages of brown paper. As he moved among them, the shoppers parted, giving the youth a wide berth despite the fact that the market square was heavily packed.

Some youths lounging in an alleyway spied the disfigured freak, and one grabbed a stone, preparing to throw. With fearful cries, his companions wrestled the offender to the ground. "Are ye mad?" whispered one, straddling the chest of his struggling companion.

Another hissed, "Aye, want to die, fool?"

"Want us all to?" quietly demanded a third, trembling hands pulling the stone free and hiding.

In the bustling market, a mustachioed green grocer offered Anatole a huge, delicious-looking red apple. The hermit accepted with thanks, but noted that the fellow secretly wiped his hands on his apron afterward. The hermit dropped the fruit to the ground, where dozens of uncaring shoes trampled it underfoot.

"Get a canvas bag, ya walking dung pile," softly muttered a busy clerk, ladling milk into a bucket for a waiting customer, "and put it over that gruesome head before you sour my cream."

Somebody laughed, and a friend elbowed the fellow in the stomach, cutting the noise off.

Though the words had been whispered, Anatole heard them anyway, and he shied his disfigured head away in shame. Listening carefully, he could hear a hundred people talking at once in the square, all of them plainly, purposefully, ignoring him. Standing alone and isolated in the bustling crowd, the hermit sagged in defeat. Annoying the townspeople lacked the pleasure the original notion had offered, and with a sigh, the disfigured youth sadly turned to leave. This was not a good idea. Why should he act like them? Time to go back to the swamp where he belonged. At least they would never beat him again.

To all nine hells with the village. He would never return.

Walking briskly around a corner, the hermit accidentally bumped into a woman and child hurrying along, making them drop their purchases. The woman gasped at the sight of him; the child went stock still and stared with perfectly round eyes.

Shyly giving his most pleasant smile, Anatole bent over and picked up one of the packages, offering it to the little girl.

"You dropped this, pretty one," he said politely.

Stuttering in fear, the mother attempted to smile and say thank you, but the child screamed in terror.

"Mommy! Mommy!" she shrieked, hiding in the fold of her parent's skirt. "Don't let the ugly monster eat me!"

The package dropped from his limp hand. "B-but, ma'am, I was only—"

"Leave us alone!" sobbed the woman, lifting the weeping girl into her arms. "Get away, you filthy beast! Don't you dare hurt my daughter!"

What? Stunned, the hermit could only gape as the two hurried frantically away down the street. Was he truly that repulsive, even now, in these good clothes? He glanced at the bright noon sun, his old enemy who so clearly displayed his flawed features. And only dimly did he hear the reactions of the growing crowd of onlookers.

"What happened?"

"The swamp freak tried to hurt a little girl!"

"Eh? He attacked a child?"

"The dirty scoundrel!"

"Monster!"

"He's as bad as that horseman!"

"They're probably brothers!"

"Or his son!"

"Hear that? Da freak is the bastard son of the horseman!"

"What should we . . ."

"I won't stand for . . ."

"Never again . . ."

"I don't care what the horseman can do . . ."

"KILL THE SON OF A BITCH!"

On those words, Anatole went cold and quickly turned, just in time for a brick to strike him painfully in the chest. He staggered, and his shoulder smashed into a store window, breaking the glass. A glistening shard sliced into his arm, and a rivulet of blood flowed down his chest, marring his new clothes.

In absolute horror, the crowd gasped aloud and went motionless, an evilly grinning youth standing amid the terrorized adults. Pale faces looked everywhere, frightened eyes staring, every second increasing their panic as the whole town waited for galloping death to appear out of the thin air and strike them all. Stanching his wound, Anatole did not dare speak, also expecting the terrible slaughter to begin.

Oh, gods, not again. Not again!

But moments passed in silence, minutes, and nothing happened. Nothing at all.

Brandishing a meat cleaver, a butcher woman in a bloody apron snarled, "Look, all of ye! The mayor was wrong! That blasted swamp-thing has no magical protector."

A dozen voices spoke in outrage and hate. "So it was all a lie!"

"A trick of the freak!"

"There be no horseman!"

"Aye!" loudly stated a burly stevedore, gloved fists bunched and shoulder's bent in a fighter's crouch. "An' I say we end this charade now!"

Countless people everywhere took up the cry. "Kill the freak! Hang 'im! Burn 'im!"

As the crowd surged forward, Anatole dashed through an alleyway, clambered over a wooden wall, and landed in a pile of garbage. Uncaring of soiling his clothes, the youth fought a path through a tangle of thorny rose bushes and managed to reach the next street. He ran on.

On the other side of the buildings he could hear the noise of a growing mob; shouts for weapons, rope and pitch, tar and feathers, boiling oil and dull axes. Their rabid cries fueled his feet to greater speed.

Sprinting through the city gates, Anatole pushed aside the yawning guards and jumped over a pile of hay fallen from the back of a two-wheel cart. There were woods on each side, but it was sparse greenery and offered no real protection from the mob. As he forced his muscular body onward, he laid his plan of escape. North along the king's road to the big bridge, then he would jump into the river and swim with the current until reaching the east end of his swamp. Once there, they would never find him. And in the night, he would leave this valley forever. And he privately hoped the horseman would come that evening and kill them, one and all. The whole damn town.

Soon, the bridge was in sight, and Anatole felt a twinge of success before he heard the galloping horses approaching from behind. Throwing himself to the right, he scrambled for the trees, but a dappled mare cut him off, the hooves just barely missing his feet. He heaved sideways, but a whip cracked across his sore shoulder, slicing open tunic and flesh. Pain! Grabbing hold of the knotted end, Anatole pulled with all of his strength, and the startled rider came flying off his mount. Sprawling, the man struck the road flat on his face and went still. Too still. Anatole dropped the whip in horror.

The mob gushed through the city gates, and another rider called out, "Beware! He killed Raymond!"

Howling for vengeance, the crowd charged forward. Trying to flee, Anatole was cut off by the horsemen who now raced in a circle around him. The villagers rushed closer, and the hermit glanced everywhere, praying for a miracle.

That was when the sky turned purple, as if with twilight. Shouting their confusion, the crowd paused to stare at the dimming sky. This was impossible! It was but minutes after noon!

Anatole, too, looked upward and saw a slice of the blazing sun disappear into darkness, an encroaching black curve extending deeper and wider. What the . . . an eclipse! The moon was coming between the sun and the earth, giving them night in the middle of the day. But that was impossible! The moon was only a crescent last night. How could . . .

Ohmigodsno.

A few of the villagers turned to go back to the village, and staggered as they saw an empty road stretching out of sight to the distant sea. Ghostly echoes of crashing waves rose faintly.

Sensing this was his only chance, Anatole started to edge away, but could not step from the road. Something invisible, perhaps the air itself, forbid escape from the highway.

Now breath fogged from cursing mouths, and tendrils of thickening mist rose from the cobblestone road. As the lunar orb claimed the last of the sun, night enveloped the world. Stars appeared overhead, and mountains rose on each side of the dense, primordial forest. Clutching his misshapen head, Anatole felt his mind reel. Time and distance no longer seemed to have meaning. The world was warping around him like clay in the hands of a mad child.

And then the awful silhouette of the huge horse and its ghastly nonhuman rider blossomed on the high horizon, the savage pounding of the iron hooves rumbling the ground like an approaching earthquake, a descending avalanche.

As one, the crowd screamed in fear and fury. The horses bucked and threw their riders to the hard pavement, and one man cried out as he held his twisted leg, his mount charging off into the distance. Despite their terror, half the villagers stood motionless, watching death approach. The rest forced hands into pockets to grab good-luck charms or wards, and thus broke free of the paralysis.

Shouting orders, the village guards assumed a battle formation. Levers were cocked and a dozen crossbows twanged, sending a flurry of arrows through the cold air.

Neat holes appeared in the billowing cloak of the horseman, one arrow striking him in the shoulder, the shaft sinking to the feathered fletching. One bolt, particularly well aimed, lanced straight through the collar, notching the stiff white linen at the back of the neck.

In response, the rider drew a hand-held sickle from within his cloak, and the horse bared its perfectly square teeth, grinning like an exhumed skull.

More arrows and bolts were unleashed, with the same useless results. Again the soldiers fired, making the horse their target this time. The barbed quarrels jammed into the ebony flesh of the animal, and ribbons of red blood trailed behind the galloping nightmare beast. Illuminated by starlight, the silver ornaments of the headless rider twinkled like the firmament itself. Whitish steam poured from the flared nostrils of the behemoth horse, the thunder of its approach shaking the very stones in the road. And now there was something moving behind the giant horseman and his bedamned stallion. Flying black globes, which bobbed and gamboled in wild abandonment.

His back against the invisible barrier, Anatole could do naught but watch this final tableau of horror unfold. As if sensing the futility of conflict, three of the townspeople threw away their weapons and ran down the road toward the sea. But the rest bravely raised their swords and axes, preparing for battle.

The reverberations of the hooves grew deafening, and then the horseman and his mount were among them. Swords stabbed, and axes swung, missing, always missing. But the silver sickle rose and fell with inhuman accuracy, and headless bodies toppled over, gushing life fluid and smashing apart the orderly ranks of the mob.

Then the things aft of the pair came out of the fog and into horrifying view. They were heads. Disembodied heads sailing through the air like nimble cannonballs. Hair whipping in the wind, the dead snarled at the living, exposing teeth yellowed with age and cracked to jagged stumps. One even grinned humorlessly as it bit a soldier's arm, exposing bone. Anatole gasped. It was Hans! These horrid things must be the amassed victims of the horseman, now serving as his unholy minions. Dead, they had become mute slaves of their killer.

A standing man sliced the flying head of a woman apart with his sword, and the rest of the aerial servants changed course to converge on him. The snapping and gnashing of the hundreds of teeth almost drowned out his piteous wails of agony.

Wheeling about, the headless horseman galloped inches away from the sweating Anatole, his sickle killing frozen villagers to the left and the right, but not touching the terrified hermit. In the manner of carrion birds, the flock of heads followed their diabolical leader, sailing around Anatole as if he were a rock in a river. And then the freak understood.

He was the bait for the trap! The horseman wanted the whole town out here on the main road during the eclipse, where he could slay them in one great battle. A bloody harvest of lives to feed his lust.

Whips cracked at heads and horse. Swords parried. Crossbows twanged. Axes slashed. The sickle flashed and bodies fell.

Then from the cloying mists a different head appeared out of the darkness, that of a silently laughing woman. Her countenance was fiendish: slanted cat-eyes with square goatlike pupils, no ears, fanged teeth, mottled reptilian skin, and hair a nest of wriggling, hissing snakes that spit in fury at everything!

Moving directly before a stevedore fumbling to reload his crossbow, the eyes of the hideous head glowed greenish, and the man froze abruptly. Anatole could see that his eyes jerked wildly about, and his muscles bunched and writhed beneath his leather apron. Yet he moved not a bit. And the hermit realized it was as if the fellow's very bones had been fused into a single mass. Trapped on his own immobile skeleton, the helpless man could only twitch as the other heads swarmed around him, their broken yellow teeth biting and tearing and ripping him to pieces.

With a high-pitched whinny, the great black stallion once more charged through the pandemonium. The ruby-dripping sickle of the horseman struck like deadly

lightning. Arrows flew everywhere, striking nothing.
Breath fogged. Torches flared blue. Clothing was ripped.
Swords clanged. Screams. Oh, the screams! And the
horrible animal growls of the flying heads. It was chaos!
Madness!

Crying aloud in shame and fear, Anatole covered both
ears and dropped to his knees, trying to blot out the
massacre around him.

The slaughter seemed to last forever.

Eventually, Anatole roused from his stupor. Silence.
Moving almost against his will, the hermit rose and faced
the foggy roadway. It was a charnel house. Bent and
broken weapons lay abandoned everywhere. Decapitated bodies were piled atop each other. Only partially
obscured by the swirling mists, one stood directly across
the roadway from him, supported by the unyielding barrier like some hideous scarecrow. The head was nowhere
to be seen. Some of the villagers were torn limb from
limb, others split asunder, and each was ravaged by
endless bite marks, their tattered clothes in pieces,
exposing the chewed flesh underneath. A sob of anguish
wracking him, Anatole gulped a breath, and the coppery
stench of fresh blood filled his lungs.

Turning to be sick, the freak leaned against the cold
barrier still confining him to the death arena. His fault. It
was all his fault! The horseman had used him like a
worm on a hook, played him like a pawn . . . but no, for
he was still alive. He had not been sacrificed with the
rest. Unharmed and alive! Why? Because he had unwit-
tingly helped the midnight rider? Or perhaps, maybe,
even this darklord of the road could feel some small
measure of compassion and mercy for one such as he.

Then suddenly Anatole heard galloping iron hooves
once more. Turning, he saw the silver blade flash downward. Hot pain took him as the sickle brutally struck,
removing his good ear, gashing his normal eye, and slicing his disfigured face to bits.

Reeling from the attack, the youth vaguely saw a shaft
of golden sunlight appear, dispelling the graveyard
mists. The eclipse was over. Numb from shock, Anatole
heard the leviathan horse neigh a taunting laugh and

then canter away, taking its silent master back to whatever hell he had come from. Weeping aloud, the freak stood trembling amid the desecration, holding the bleeding ruin of his face in those perfect-perfect hands. He would survive, but made ten times more ugly than before, rendered unfit for even the lonely swamp by this departing 'gift' of his dark benefactor. Anatole would leave this place of death, leave his lonely swamp, find another dwelling somewhere. . . .

But would the horseman follow him, use him to bait another town? Dare he go anywhere to find a home? And suddenly, the broken youth knew the answer to his earlier question. Did hell have compassion and mercy? Oh, yes. Most certainly.

But in its own dark way.

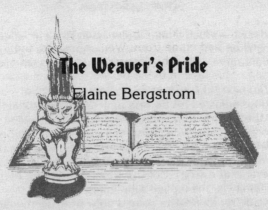

The Weaver's Pride

Elaine Bergstrom

Welse, guild weaver of Arbora, tried to hide his disgust at the acrid stench of the half-naked old Abber nomad who fingered through the goods in his shop. Did the nomads ever bathe? he wondered. Perhaps there were no pools of water in their lands. He had heard tales enough to understand the strange haunted looks in the eyes of those who dwelled there, and the stoic acceptance they had of their fate.

"It's fine cloth," he said slowly, hoping the nomad would understand. The nomad scratched his armpit, and Welse hoped he would pick something less fine, for above all else he prized the work he had done on the mauve- and plum-colored blanket. The red and white silken threads that ran through it gave it a delicate look and feel, one unsuited to a nomad's life. Welse almost hoped the man had brought nothing to trade, but it was unlikely. Nomads did not come to Arbora empty-handed.

A weaver did not deal with the nomads often. Usually the Abber nomads brought strange metals and gemstones from their lands, trading for the practical items they needed for their tribe. It always astonished Welse how unsettled, almost frightened, the nomads seemed among the orderly houses and tree-lined streets of Arbora, and how quickly they returned to the ever-shifting terrain of the country all of Nova Vaasa called the Nightmare Lands.

The Abber turned his attention to a pile of colorful scarves and skirts, reaching for them with his filthy hands. How much would Welse have to clean after the grimy man left? "If you show me what you've brought, we can agree on a price," Welse said with some irritation.

"You best," the nomad commented.

Welse adjusted his flowing tunic on his shoulders and tied the contrasting woven belt more tightly. Like all Arbora weavers, Welse wore his own creations. So did his wife, his daughter, and his four sons, weavers all of them. There was no family as prosperous in all of Arbora, and every bit of the wealth had been earned. "My family is," he replied with honest pride.

"Trade for this?" The nomad drew what seemed to be a dirty length of silk from the pouch on his belt and handed it to Welse.

When Welse examined it closely, he saw that the strand was actually a braided chain of perhaps a dozen thinner filaments that glowed with a strange silver sheen. He had never seen a fiber so delicate. He unbraided the end of the chain and examined a single filament, finding it incredibly strong, with an elasticity that astonished him. Though he longed to keep it, he handed it back to the nomad. "Nothing," he replied sadly. "Too small an amount. I am sorry."

The nomad grinned and pulled something else from the pouch, a glowing cocoon of the silver threads. He handed it to Welse. "More," he said. "Many more."

Welse looked at the cocoon. "Many more?" he asked.

The Abber smiled, his teeth surprisingly white and sharp for one so old. He held out his hands, indicating a pile half his height and as wide as his outstretched arms.

"We trade," Welse said.

The nomad returned the following day with two of his tribesmen. Each carried a pair of huge leather sacks. Welse had already cleaned out one of the great metal cauldrons he used for boiling silk. As the nomads emptied their sacks into it, the cocoons expanded, filling the container and overflowing onto the floor. Even here, before Welse had unraveled the cocoons, before he had a chance to use his skill on them, the strands were magnificent. Welse was almost certain that, if he closed the doors, the pile would shed its own silver light.

He paid the nomads in coin rather than goods. He was pleased to see that the old man purchased only his most durable weavings, blankets and clothing that would serve his tribe well through the winter—if there was a winter in that cursed land, Welse reminded himself. Later he heard that the nomads spent every coin he had given them to purchase knives, axes, and other tools. A strange people, Welse thought, yet they had brought him such an incredible find.

No one else in his family would touch this weaving, he declared, for he alone had the skill to work with strands so fine. He boiled a small amount of water and threw in the first handfuls of cocoons. As they hit the water and sank into its heat, Welse thought he heard the insects inside cry out in pain. Later, when he unraveled the cocoons, he found no creatures within, as if the strands had absorbed their spinners completely.

He spun the filaments together, threading his loom with them, then beginning the weaving. Days passed. Welse paused only when hunger made him weak or when Ronae, his wife, or Geryn, his oldest son, intruded to try to coax him to rest. He ignored them, and the intensity of his gaze made them retreat and leave him to his work.

When he'd finished, he had woven a thin cloth the length and height of *three men*. Welse hung it behind the counter in his shop and let no one touch it. In some lights it almost seemed to reflect the form of an admirer, and the shop was always crowded with people who came to gaze longingly on it then leave with another purchase.

But there were others who came as well. Some were coarse men who had no use for Welse's fine garments and who dressed in hides they had tanned themselves. Others were wealthy and purchased their clothing from the master weavers in Kantora and had no use for locally designed goods. The former made threats, the latter offers that weeks ago Welse would not have refused. Now, with a stubbornness his family could not comprehend, he refused to consider any offers.

One evening, Welse had left the shop in the care of his wife while he ran an errand. As he returned, he saw a crowd of people milling outside of it. Had someone taken his treasure? Furious, he pushed his way through the bystanders and went inside.

The body of a man lay across the entrance way. Welse's wife was on her knees beside it, still clutching the knife she had used to kill him. Though Ronae had borne him five children and worked tirelessly at his side, she had always had a gentle temperament. He crouched beside her. "Ronae," he called gently. "Ronae, what happened here?"

She pressed herself against him, trembling in his arms. Her breath came in shallow puffs, and Welse knew she was still in shock. "The man tried to steal the cloth. I grabbed the cutting knife from the counter and yelled for him to stop. And then . . ." She paused and hugged him more tightly.

He pushed her gently away, looking directly at her as he said, "You killed him. Had he been caught, others would have done no less."

"Yes, but he would not have died had the cloth not moved."

"Moved?"

"It moved, I tell you. I . . ."

"Hush," Welse repeated more forcefully. "Not a word about that." He sent Ronae home in the company of their daughter and answered the questions the authorities put to him. Afterward, he left his two oldest sons in charge of the shop and went home to get the whole story from his wife.

By then Ronae had calmed, or so her speech made it seem, though her story was no less fantastic. She said the thief had been standing outside, waiting until the shop was empty before coming inside. "He said he needed yarn, not finished goods. I went in the back to find the black and red he needed. When I returned, he was behind the counter, trying to untie one corner of the silver cloth. I picked up the cutting knife and threatened to stab him."

Welse could well imagine the force of her threat.

Though she had the strength to bear five children and would fight to the death to protect any of her family, mice gnawed at their bread because she didn't have the heart to set traps in the larder.

"He laughed and grabbed my arm, holding it back. I would have dropped the knife except the cloth moved."

"Was the door open?"

"No. And the cloth did not move like it would in a breeze. It rose as if the corners were on string and covered the man's face. He released his grip on me so quickly that my knife went in. Even after I cut him, he continued to pull at the cloth. When he fell beyond its reach, the cloth grew suddenly rigid as if trying to touch him. I dragged him away from it, and that was when he died."

"Ronae, you were hysterical. Listen to what you're saying."

"It moved! It sucked the air out of that man's body the way a vampire sucks the blood of his victim. Get rid of it, Welse. Get rid of the cursed thing before it destroys all of us."

Get rid of it? How could Welse consider such a thing when it was his most magnificent creation, such a product of his skill that he seemed to have woven a part of his soul into it? Poor Ronae was hysterical or she would never ask such a thing of him.

Welse lay beside her, comforting her until she slept, then returned to the shop. Dismissing his sons, he remained there all night, a sword in his hand, ready to kill any intruder. More than once, he dozed off, but always came awake the moment anyone left any of the taverns on the street or stopped in front of the barred shop door to tell another about the thief that Ronae had killed.

Ronae refused to enter the shop or weaving room behind it until the tapestry was sold. She ordered their daughter to stay home as well. Welse didn't mind. His sons listened to him. They agreed to take turns guarding the tapestry at night, always two together.

The agreement took its toll on everyone.

"Perhaps a wizard could weave a spell to protect the shop," Moro, his youngest, suggested after one of his nights at the shop. Though he was nearly thirteen, he still had trouble staying awake, even on special occasions.

"I'll have no magic here," Welse countered.

"But, Father . . ." Geryn said, going to his brother's defense.

"How long before some enterprising thief finds his own wizard and buys a spell to open our doors? No magic," Welse reminded them. "We'll protect it the way we always have," he said, laying a hand on the dagger he carried in his belt.

"Why protect it at all?" Geryn countered. "Prince Othmar's nephew offered you a fortune in gold. We could open a shop in Kantora with the money we'd get for its sale."

"No!" Welse bellowed. "It's mine! I will not part with it."

Geryn, who had done no weaving for days due to lack of sleep, looked from the dwindling stack of weavings to his father's stubborn expression to the cloth itself, hanging with such splendor on the wall. "Who needs a wizard when there's magic here already," he mumbled, softly so his father would not hear him.

Though the young men had been ordered to stand guard in pairs, Geryn consulted with his brothers. Afterward, one would watch the shop while the other went in the back to weave. In that way some of their stock was replenished. Welse, who usually kept accurate count of every scarf and shirt and tunic, did not seem to notice their appearance on his shelves or the shoddy workmanship of his exhausted sons.

Eventually all but Moro became accustomed to their nocturnal hours. The boy kept nodding off. Geryn would always partner with him. At first, he would come into the shop often to be certain Moro did not sleep. After weeks had passed and no one had tried to steal his father's treasure, Geryn began letting Moro sleep for a few hours each night in a chair close to the door, often pausing in his work to check on the boy.

One night, Geryn began a particularly beautiful weave in silk and flax. Caught up in his work, he did not hear the soft padding of feet outside the shop's back door, or the quickly whispered spell, or the creaking of the hinges as the door swung open. His only warning was a sudden draft of air that made him turn and cry out before a thief's cudgel knocked him senseless.

When Geryn regained consciousness, he lay in a square of light falling through the open rear door. Staggering to his feet and into the shop, he saw Moro sprawled facedown across the counter, one hand resting on his bloodied knife. "Moro!" Geryn screamed. As he touched his brother, he saw the boy's head had been nearly severed from his body. The body was cold, dead for some hours. Even so, the cloth was still in its place on the wall.

At first, Geryn thought his brother had managed to kill the intruder, but there was no sign of a body or any blood. With a heavy heart, Geryn tied off the work he had done and wrapped his brother in it. Afterward, he went outside and sent one of the street urchins to deliver a message to his father. When his parents arrived at the shop, he did not lie about what he had done.

Ronae knelt beside the body, stroking the boy's golden hair, crooning to him as if he were still alive, in pain and in need of comforting. Welse, on the other hand, displayed no emotion but fury, and all of it was directed at Geryn. "How could you be so foolish!" Welse screamed. "I gave you orders for your own protection. Everyone covets the cloth. You should have expected this."

"The walls are stone, Father. The doors and windows are barred. Only a sorcerer could have entered without my hearing," Geryn countered with no real energy. "And if the thief was a sorcerer, it might explain why he disappeared after Moro wounded him. If the man is still alive, he'll try again."

"And kill another of us, or perhaps two," Ronae said, her voice dulled by grief. "Sell the cloth, Welse, for the good of all of us."

Sell it! How dare she speak to him that way. How dare the others nod their agreement. "Never!" Welse bellowed. "I'll watch it myself, for it's clear I can't trust any of you." He moved toward the cloth, as if to protect it. As he did, he noticed a brown smudge in the corner and lifted it up to the light.

"Blood?" Ronae asked, thinking of the thief she had killed.

Welse shook his head and examined the spot carefully, the way a craftsman saw a flaw in his creation. The concern would hardly have been unusual had the son he loved so dearly not lain dead behind him. "The smudge seems to be a part of the cloth, some shift in the coloring. It looks like a face."

"A terrified face," Geryn commented, looking over his father's shoulder. "Two men have tried to steal it. Two have failed. Do you suppose the cloth protects itself?"

Welse looked at his son as if the boy had suddenly gone mad. "I created it. From now on I'll be the one to guard it," he said.

Each night, Welse positioned his chair in front of the cloth and sat with a knife in his hand, constantly alert for any sound outside the thick stone walls. Each day, he slept in the same chair while his remaining sons went about their work. Welse did not speak to them save when utterly necessary.

One afternoon when Geryn was alone in the shop, he saw an old man standing outside the open door, looking intently beyond Geryn to the cloth on the wall and Welse sleeping in front of it. The man was richly dressed in clothes from the northern lands and carried a tall, intricately carved walking staff. "Come in, friend," Geryn called good-naturedly. "See the wares we have for sale."

"Come out," the man responded, holding up a single golden coin.

With a backward glance at his sleeping father, Geryn did.

"You've had problems. Traders as far away as Egertus speak of some strange sorcery. I've come to help you." The man spoke so softly that Geryn had to watch his mouth move to understand the words. There was a persuasiveness to his voice, a persuasiveness so strong that Geryn forgot he should be angry at the rumors, or of being reminded of them by a stranger.

All he believed was that the old stranger was here to help him.

"I understand a sorcerer tried to steal it and failed. Such a foolish thing to do when it is clear that you desire nothing so much as to be rid of it."

"I do," Geryn answered honestly. As he did, the need to dispose of the cloth overpowered all fear of his father's wrath.

"You can have your desire, and he need never know."

"The cloth has cost us a great deal." Again Geryn confessed exactly what was in his heart.

"Of course. You care for your family. I understand. I would not own such a thing, but there are others foolish enough to want it and to pay well. I am generous. I could steal the cloth, but that is a dangerous thing to do. Far better to share what I have been given." He returned the gold coin to a purse on his belt then unhooked it and displayed its contents to Geryn.

Gold! Not as much as others had offered, but more than enough for a lifetime of comfort.

The man pulled a small corked vial from inside his cloak and laid it in Geryn's hand. "I will give you the gold now if you promise to follow my instructions. Tonight, when your father has his evening meal, slip this small bit of powder into his food. No, do not worry. It will not harm your father, only make him sleep soundly. In the morning, the cloth will be gone, and no one will know that you were involved."

Geryn looked at the coins and thought of the wealth.

"Spend it slowly, and your father will never know."

Geryn nodded and led the old man into the shadows beside the shop. There he took the money that was given, so thankful for the burden being lifted from him that he kissed the old man's hand before leaving him and returning to his work.

By evening, Geryn was certain that the old man was a wizard rather than a merchant, and a powerful one at that. Yet it was not only fear that made Geryn obey the man's orders. He wanted that cloth gone, and hopefully the curse that seemed to have fallen over his family would go with it.

So he did what was asked. No one saw him mix the powder in his father's stew. When Geryn left the shop a short time later, it seemed that his father already looked drowsy. Once home, Geryn hid the coins in his cupboard in the room he shared with his brothers and tried to forget they even existed.

The following morning, Geryn and his brothers were some distance from the shop when they heard their father's bellows of rage. Saying a quick prayer of thanks that his father was still alive, Geryn ran with the others, pushed past the crowd that had once more gathered in front of the store, and unlocked the door.

As Geryn expected, the cursed cloth was gone. What he had not expected was the terrible damage to the shop itself.

The bare wall where the cloth had hung was coated with dyes from the work room. The blankets he had arranged on the shelves by the door were scattered across the floor. The tunics that had hung on pegs in one corner were strewn above them. The boxes that had held hats and scarves were overturned and broken.

They heard metal beating against the stone walls and floors and ran into the workroom just in time to see Welse toss another cauldron against the wall. "Where is it!" he bellowed. "The doors were locked. Where has it gone?" He looked at each of his sons, madness clear in his eyes, in the tension in his arms, in the way his fingers were spread, ready to grab onto his vanished treasure. "You know!" he declared, staring at each of his startled sons. "Only the family has keys. Tell me where you've hidden it. Tell me!"

While his brothers stood silently, Geryn went to the back door, lifted the wooden bar and examined the door frame. When he did, he discovered that the wooden frame had been carved back far enough for the bar to be lifted from the outside. It would be as simple a matter for the thief to lock the door behind him as it would have been to open it. It occurred to Geryn that the wizard with the beautiful voice had taken great care to see that no harm came to Welse, nor any theft from the shop. "Father," Geryn called anxiously. "Come and see this."

Welse did and, as he began to understand that his sons had not stolen his treasure, he understood that he would likely never see the cloth again. He went into the shop and looked at the wall where it had hung. Tears flowed from his eyes. He began to tremble and fell to his knees in the center of the room where, with his face in his hands, he began to cry with deep, terrible sobs.

His father should have cried for Moro that way, Geryn thought. Instead he had reserved the grief for his lost creation. Though Geryn believed that his father was somehow bewitched, he could not forgive him for such misplaced sorrow.

*   *   *   *   *

Later, Welse let his sons take him home. For the first time in weeks, they ate their evening meal together. Though Ronae had prepared all her husband's favorite dishes, he did not notice. Some thief had stolen into his shop, crept by him while he slept, and made off with his treasure.

He could not stop his hands from trembling. He could not stop the rage growing inside him. And he would never stop searching until he found the thief.

His children went to bed while Ronae sat beside him, wiping the tears from his face. Finally, she took his hands and held them gently as she said, "It's over, Welse. It's better this way."

"Better?" he mumbled, unable to believe the words she spoke. As he began to understand, his face darkened with rage. His hands tightened over hers until she cried out in pain. "You did it! You paid to have it stolen while I slept."

She shook her head and tried to pull away, but his grip was too strong. An instant later, Welse, who had never struck any of his family, was beating his wife. His sons, drawn by her screams, rushed into the room and pulled them apart.

Ronae fled to her sons' room, but Welse followed, rage giving him a strength his sons could not subdue. She pressed herself behind the great chest of drawers

that held her sons' clothes, but he pushed it over. It fell
forward against the bed, the drawers opening, their contents falling out. "You took it! Admit it!" Welse screamed,
kicking the drawers out of the way and scattering the
clothes. As he did, he heard the clinking of the coins
Geryn had hidden, and he reached for the bag. "So they
paid you as well!" he bellowed to his wife as he lifted the
sack and felt its weight.

"Leave Mother alone," Geryn said. "A man paid me."

"You!" Welse turned and faced his son, showing all the
betrayal he felt. "Tell me why you did such a thing."

Now that he had told the truth, Geryn had a compul-
sive need to explain all of it. After the others retired, he
sat alone with his father and told him the story, taking
great care to make Welse understand that he had been
ensorceled.

"Where do you think the old wizard came from?"
Welse asked.

"From the look of his clothes and accent, Egertus, I
think."

"Excellent! We leave tomorrow to get it back."

Geryn felt some guilt for what he had done, but not
much. "I will not help you in this," he said. "The cloth
has brought us nothing but sorrow." He pushed himself
wearily to his feet and started for his room.

Welse stared at the fire for a moment, thinking of the
betrayal, the beauty of the cloth, the incredible wave of
fulfillment he'd experienced after weaving it. How dare
his son disobey him! How dare he disobey him still!

The blind rage Welse had felt when he'd first seen the
blank wall returned with all its fury. Later, he did not
recall pulling the dagger from his belt or moving softly
toward his son.

Blood was the first thing he saw—blood lying in a
black pool that glittered in the firelight; blood staining
the blade of his knife; blood covering his hands; blood
seeping slowly from the wounds in his dead son's back.

Understanding came an instant later. With a bellow of
rage for what he had done, Welse ran from the house.
He heard Ronae's scream, heard his sons rush outside,
calling his name. He stood in the shadows and did not

respond. He could never face them again.

With home lost to him, only one thing remained. He followed the road until it crossed the Ivlis River the second time, then headed north, drawn by the far-too-real pull of the cloth he had created. He did not stop to wash. Flies feasted on the blood soaking his clothes while the blood on his hands dried and flaked off as he rushed through the scrubby land in search of the treasure that called to him.

The pull of the cloth had grown so strong by nightfall that Welse stumbled on in the darkness. Eventually, he saw a campfire and, as he moved closer, a single man sitting beside it, wrapped in a blanket for warmth. Welse did not need to see the color of the man's hair, or his staff lying on the ground beside him to know that his treasure was there. With his dagger in his hand, Welse crept closer. One stroke, and the cloth would be his once more.

"You may put your blade away, Weaver. You have traveled far in pursuit of me. I will not struggle with you," the man said before turning to face Welse. "Come, friend, sit by the fire, and we will talk."

The man's voice was as Geryn had described. It had a beauty in its timbre that calmed him. Welse, still gripping his blade, did as the man asked.

"Eat," the man suggested, holding out his own bowl to Welse. "You will need your strength."

Welse pushed the bowl away and reached for the man's water cup instead. It has been hours since he'd crossed the river. When he had, he'd drunk deeply, then realized he had nothing to carry more water in.

"You were in an accident?" the man asked, his voice filled with concern.

Welse shook his head and pushed himself to his feet. "I dispensed some justice. You purchased a cloth that did not belong to the seller. I've come to claim it."

"Justice?" the old man questioned. "What did you do?"

"I killed my son," Welse answered honestly. As he did, he felt tears of grief begin to form in his eyes. He ignored them.

"Ah!" the man responded and sat up straighter. Welse, alarmed, held out his knife. But the man only pulled the bag on which he'd been reclining from under his back and handed it to Welse. "Have you brought the gold I gave to the unfortunate lad?" he asked.

"You knew he was stealing it. You helped him. In Arbora that makes you a thief as well, and your payment mine to spend."

The man appeared to consider this and decided not to argue. "Be certain it is what you seek," he instead suggested.

"I intend to," Welse growled. He unbuckled the bag and threw back the flap. The folds took on the yellow hue of the firelight, but there was no disguising the suppleness of the fabric, the smoothness of the tightly woven web-thin threads.

"I have taken great care with it," the man said. "You'll find it in perfect condition."

"And you've never owned such a prize, have you?"

"Owned?" The old man laughed, a soothing sound from deep in his throat like the purr of some great cat. "I would not purchase this for myself. Consider what possessing it has done to you."

As had happened to his son, the most gentle suggestion was enough to force Welse to focus honestly on his acts. He had terrorized his family, contributed to the death of his youngest son, destroyed his wares and . . .

As he thought once more of Geryn, he began to cry, then once more forced the feeling back, replacing it with what seemed like just fury. "I did what was necessary," he declared stubbornly, then pulled the cloth from the bag. "If it has been damaged in any way . . ." he began.

He never finished.

The cloth tumbled over his outstretched arm, but the folds did not fall to the ground. Though the night was still, the cloth moved, rising between Welse and the fire.

The cloth was so thin that, for a moment, he could see the flicker of the flames on the other side of it.

And within the weave itself, something moved. The brown smudge that Ronae had said looked like a face was indeed a face. The eyes were open and staring at him. The lips parted, rising at the corners in a leer of anticipation, of greeting.

This creature that had killed his youngest son now greeted Welse as an equal.

And Welse had killed the oldest.

Horrified, Welse tried to fling the cloth away, but it was already too late. The silvery folds covered him. The need of the fibers to absorb and possess sucked the breath from his lungs, the life from his body.

Though he saw the old man standing by the fire and heard him crying out in alarm, Welse could not answer, could not move. For a moment Welse thought he would die, but death somehow eluded him. Instead, he felt his body thin until it had no more substance than the smoke still rising from the fire. The cloth, so light and supple a moment ago, weighed down on him, absorbing his essence.

Bodiless, but not dead. Seeing, but unable to act. Welse watched the old man lift the cloth from the ground and pause to study his face as Ronae had done to the thief's face some days before.

"I have done no wrong," the man said, and Welse understood that he spoke to the cloth rather than to him. "And I will do no wrong in all the days I possess you. I hope the one who has paid so well for you has a conscience as clear as mine."

With a twisted smile, the old man added, "I doubt it."

There would be others, Welse knew then. Many others.

Welse would never lack for company, not here on these folds.

The Glass Man

William W. Connors

October 1
From the Journal of Julio, Master Thief of Hazlan

I have done it!

The rest of the guildsmen said I was mad to try, but try I did. Imagine how foolish they'll feel, especially that bloated Cordova, when I show them the treasures I have plundered from the wizard Hazlik's tower! So much for their superstitious fear and cowardice.

I can just hear them when I open my velvet satchel and empty the guild's cut onto the table in the main hall. "Julio!" they'll say, "This is incredible! How did you come by such magnificent pieces?" I'll smile and laugh and raise a great toast to my so-called peers. As each of them drinks, I'll tell them about the wizard's tower and laugh as the color drains from their faces. Oh, what a glorious sight that will be!

But I digress. I must get all the particulars down in writing so that none of this great adventure will be lost to me in the future. After all, even the great Julio must grow old. One day my hands will shake, my eyes will grow dim, and my memory will become suspect. I shall have nothing then but my journal to help me remember my youth and my days as Hazlan's greatest thief.

For many months now, I have studied the wizard's tower that stands some miles north of town. While it can be seen from the road to Sly-var, the details of the structure are impossible to ascertain until one moves closer.

The others laughed when I told them that I planned to do just that, but I was not swayed. For them, such a crime might be impossible, but I am Julio.

I knew the risk, of course. Only a fool would think that burgling the keep of a wizard is easy. But I knew also that there must be treasure within that twisted tower, treasure the likes of which no member of our Thieves' Guild has dreamt of. Thus, I explored the lands about the keep. For my efforts, I came away with a serviceable map and a good knowledge of what must be done to obtain entrance to Hazlik's keep.

With that done, I began to visit the shops and taverns of the town. With casual conversation, I found the places that the wizard's men visited when they came to Toyalis. Eventually, I arranged a casual meeting with one of them. It wasn't long before Julio's winning smile and keen wit won the trust of this lowly administrator. He was not a popular man, tending to be moody and having been disfigured by a long scar that almost split his face in two. When the time came and I asked him to make a map of the wizard's tower, he readily agreed. I promised him a share of the treasure that I planned to liberate, but his only reward was a dagger in the back.

Last night, when the moon was at its darkest, I moved in. With all the skills at my disposal, I reached the outer wall and began to climb. The old stones were worn and cracked with age, making the climb a fairly easy one. Half an hour after I had begun the ascent, I found myself perched outside an ornate oval of stained glass near the top of the tower.

I set quickly to work, extracting a small set of tools from the hidden pockets of my broad buckskin belt. It took me only a few seconds to defeat the primitive lock that held the glass in place. With a bit of disbelief, I pulled at the window. Much to my surprise, it opened easily. I had expected some enchantment to hold the portal against me, but there was no sign of any such wizardry. Of course, I was ready to deal with such a thing if I found it, but that would have been time-consuming and I was grateful to be spared the effort.

I daresay that I must have been grinning like a foolish

footpad when I slipped out of the chill air on the ledge and into the musty darkness beyond. I pulled the window closed behind me, taking care not to let it latch, and settled back while my eyes adjusted to the darkness.

As I waited, I tried to gather what impressions of the room I might. The air was thick with the odor of cloth, canvas, and mildew. Had I found my way into a simple storage closet of some sort? I certainly hoped not. Still, the ease of my entry suggested so. I risked a scrape on the cold stone floor beneath me and listened carefully to the way that the sound traveled in the room. The place was not overly large, but neither was it small enough to be a closet.

When at last my vision improved, I saw that my gamble had paid off. The room appeared to be a magical laboratory, though not one that had been recently used. There were all manner of instruments scattered about. Some I could identify, like the magnifying crystals and the various beakers full of chemicals. Others were totally alien to me. For all their possible worth, however, none of these things interested me as much as the wood-and-glass case that stood near the door to the room. It was the sort of cabinet that might be used to display valuables, and those were exactly what I was after.

Alas, my good fortune with the window was not repeated with the cabinet. It was too dark to see inside, so I could make out nothing of what lay behind the glass doors. Further, the lock was not as simple as that on the portal. In the gloom of this macabre place, I could not hope to pick it.

I decided to risk a light, for the lock would have been impossible to defeat without one. Thus, I withdrew a small object the size of a brandy flask from my belt and placed it near the lock. I slid open a panel on it, triggering a tiny spark, and allowed the minuscule lantern a moment to ignite. There was only enough oil in the small lamp to provide fuel for a few minutes, but with luck that would be all that I needed.

The work was slow, for the lock was an excellent one. In the process of picking it, however, I noticed and disarmed no fewer than three traps that had been set on the thing. Whatever was in this case had to be worth a great deal to merit such special attention. Finally, as the last of the oil in the lamp began to give out, I released the latch with a click that was entirely too loud for my taste. Then I opened the doors.

Inside I found exactly what I had hoped for. More than a dozen splendidly crafted bits of jewelry were displayed inside the case. The smallest was an ornate platinum ring that must have been worth twice the annual income of any man in Hazlan. The largest was a torque set with gleaming diamonds, whose value I could not imagine. More importantly, they each had the aura of magic about them. I cannot say how I knew this to be the case, but I did. As I lifted them gently from their resting places and dropped them into my small velvet sack, I could sense it.

As I have said, each of the treasures that I removed from the cabinet was magnificent. One by one, I claimed them, and in my heart, I felt the weight of gold in my safe growing and growing. If I wanted to, I could retire from thieving and live the rest of my days on the profit that I would realize from the sale of these items. To do so, however, would have been as great a crime as the theft of these treasures, for it would deprive the world of my talents.

When the twelfth item was secured, I snuffed the sputtering lamp and turned to go. Again, I waited for my eyes to adjust to the darkness. Then, as I stood there, I noticed something that I had not seen before. At first, I thought that it was simply an afterimage that remained with my eye from the glow of the lamp and the gleam of the wizard's valuables. Then, as my night vision sharpened, I saw that it was really there. Carefully, I crept over to examine it closer.

The item was a small disc, perhaps two inches across. It consisted of a polished crystal lens set in a silver frame that was etched with mysterious glyphs. The latter glowed ever so faintly blue in the darkness. I estimated its worth at a few hundred gold coins, as much for the delicate silver chain on which it hung as for the crystal itself. I almost decided to leave it behind, for there seemed no point in adding so minor an object to my collection. Something about the lens impressed me, however, so I scooped it up and started for the window.

As I slid the stained glass open again, I started to drop the crystal amulet into my velvet sack. Then, I decided that it was probably too fragile to store there, and I slipped it around my neck. I made certain that it hung inside my shirt so that the glow, minor though it was, would not give me away, and slipped quietly out of the tower.

My journey south to the main road and then west into Toyalis was uneventful. Certainly, the city watch was standing at the gates to search travelers as they always do, but I am Julio, and they never saw me pass by their posts. As the first rays of the sun began to brighten the distant horizon, I drew the door to my home shut behind me and raised a glass of brandy to the success of my little venture.

October 2nd
From the Journal of Julio, Master Thief of Hazlan

A most curious thing has happened.

I was on my way to the guild halls with my newly acquired treasures when a cold rain began to fall. As I was unprepared for such a change in the weather, I hurriedly ducked into the Red Robin. The prospect of a warm mug of cider by the inn's fire seemed far more pleasant to me than lingering in the embrace of a frigid autumn shower.

The place was not full, but neither was it deserted. The rain had driven in more than a few new patrons, so Andreas the barkeep was more than a little busy filling new orders. I caught his attention, dropped a coin onto the bar, and drifted back into a corner with a mug of steaming cider.

I had only just tasted my drink when I felt a sensation of warmth from the pendant I had liberated from Hazlik's tower. This quickly increased until I feared that it might burn me, so I slipped my hand inside my tunic and drew out the crystal. The glow of the thing, which had been no brighter than that of a firefly before, was as great as a candle now. Slender traces of energy, looking much like small forks of lightning, ran around the silver frame and the runes on the crystal.

Just then, the door swung open and a pair of burly men walked in. They wore the utilitarian armor of the town watch and carried the great hammers of those so-called public servants. As these two cast their eyes over the Red Robin's patrons, everyone in the room fell silent. I whispered a silent wish that they might be looking for someone else, but I knew this was folly.

As the last whispers in the place faded, a third man stepped through the door, between the two warriors, and into the light of the hearth. An almost audible shudder of contempt swept through the crowd, for this was none other than Kagliara, the sadistic captain of the watch. I did not have to think long to realize what business might have brought him out of his decadent office and into the streets.

"Julio!" he bellowed. "I want Julio!"

Sitting there with the glowing pendant around my neck, it was impossible for me to avoid his notice. Our paths had crossed before, and he knew my face as well as I knew his own twisted countenance. Resigning myself to the fate that was mine, I stood up. Why couldn't he be looking for that vulgar Cordova?

"Well?" roared Kagliara. "Where is he?"

I was about to speak, when the truth dawned on me. Somehow, he could not see me. Clearly, some magic was at work. My mind flashed at once to the crystal. I looked down at the hand holding it, but apart from the azure discharges of the pendant, it looked quite normal. I was not invisible . . . or was I? For all his talents, the great Julio is no wizard. I had never been invisible before and had no idea if I would be able to see myself when under the effects of such an enchantment. I decided to stay still and see what happened.

Andreas was the first to respond to Kagliara. He spoke in a hesitant voice that was hard to hear over the crackle of the fire, but his words were clear enough. "He was here only a moment ago. You could not have missed him by more than a few seconds!"

"Did anyone see him leave?" demanded the watch captain. No one responded, drawing a frustrated curse from Kagliara. He looked around the room once more, clearly oblivious to my presence. "The man who brings Julio to me will be well rewarded!" he hissed, turning to leave. With a powerful stride, he burst through the door and out into the rainy night. The brace of warriors spun crisply about and followed him out into the rain.

I let out my breath, which I suddenly realized I had been holding, and sat down again. I needed time to consider what this turn of events might mean. For instance, how long did I have before this magic wore thin and I was visible again? I did not know. One thing that I was certain of, however, was that I did not want to be in so public a place when it happened. I daresay that half a dozen of the Red Robin's patrons would have eagerly handed me over to Kagliara had they but been given the chance.

I darted into the night, welcomed by a crash of autumn lightning, and made my way back to my room. The wonders of this magical treasure threaten to overwhelm me, and I must consider how best to use this newfound power.

October 3rd
From the Journal of Julio, Master Thief of Hazlan

Cordova is dead.

Only great effort enables me to write in this journal today. I keep telling myself that by writing down what has happened, I will be able to make sense of it.

After a great deal of thought, I decided that I would use this new power of invisibility to rid myself of that worthless Cordova. For years now I have put up with his ridiculous boasting. How many times have I dreamt of drawing my knife across his fat throat?

Of course, Julio is a thief, not a murderer. I have never seriously considered taking the life of another. But now, with the power of Hazlik's lens, there was no chance that I would be caught. Why shouldn't I do it? I thought long and hard about the prospect. In the end, it was not a difficult decision. Cordova would die.

By the time I left my home, the storm had stopped. The cobblestones were slick, and the deep puddles held the rippling reflections of amber street lamps. To the east I could see only the faintest glow of the coming sunrise. There was a sharp chill in the autumn air, and my breath curled into small clouds that drifted slowly away into the night.

I moved quickly through the streets. Twice I stopped to pull the lens out from under my clothes and examine it. I told myself that this was only a precaution, but perhaps I hoped that the flickering traces of lightning around it would be gone, that its power had faded away. No matter, the azure fire had not dimmed. Indeed, it burned brighter than ever. By the time I reached Cordova's house, I was confident of my invisibility.

Slipping into Cordova's home was not difficult. After all, he was a forger and confidence man by trade, not a burglar. His locks and safeguards were easily defeated. Once inside, I made my way quickly through the garishly decorated rooms until I came upon my enemy sleeping in an ornate bed.

The room was dark, for the gradually brightening sky outside could not penetrate the thick curtains that hung across the window. Cordova's snoring was so loud that I almost feared that it would shake the foundations of the building and bring the place crashing down. Even in sleep he was vulgar.

I looked around the room and saw a lamp resting beside the bed. Stepping without a sound across the wooden floor, I lifted the glass from the lantern and drew out a match. I lit the match and then the lantern, filling the room with an even yellow light. I placed the glowing lamp on the table again, making sure that it cracked against the wood with a loud report. At first, Cordova did not appear to notice. Then, something must have registered in his deficient brain, and his snoring sputtered out. With a shock, he sat up and gasped for air.

"Who is there?" he cried.

I said nothing. It was satisfying to watch his head swing back and forth as he frantically looked around the room for some sign an intruder. His eyes were wide with fear, and rivulets of sweat seemed to have suddenly burst from his brow. As I slipped my knife from its scabbard, I saw in his bloated face the look that cattle must have when they know that the butcher's knife is coming for them.

I struck quickly. My blade sank deep into his chest, and as I withdrew it a wash of blood began to pool on the front of his white nightshirt. He did not cry out in pain, but gasped in surprise. His hands clutched at the wound and came away soaked with crimson. Twice more my dagger bit into him, and at last he fell back in his bed. Blood spread out from the wounds, staining the blankets and pillows.

As his life trickled away, I decided that it was time to show myself. He must not be allowed to die without knowing that it was I, Julio, who had sealed his fate. I removed the shimmering lens and placed it on the table, beside the lamp.

Then, something curious happened. Cordova, though he looked right at me, asked again to know who it was that had attacked him. He could not see me! But how could that be? I had removed the crystal. I must be visible. Perhaps his eyes had grown dim with the loss of blood! Bending low over the dying man, I grabbed his shirt and dragged his face toward mine.

"It is I!" I shouted, "Julio!"

There was still no sign of recognition in his eyes. The old fool hadn't seen me, and now he was unable to hear me as well. I dropped his almost lifeless body back onto the bed. This could not be! I would not be cheated of this moment! Cordova must know who had killed him. There must be some way that I could make my presence known to him.

Frantically I began to look around the room. Ah! I found it! Hidden away in the drawer of the table beside the bed was a stick of writing charcoal and several sheets of paper. I snatched out the stylus and one of the sheets, quickly writing down what I had said before, that it was Julio who had killed him. With satisfaction, I spun about and thrust the paper into his face.

He was dead.

Infuriated, I crushed the paper into a ball and hurled it across the room. Red rage swept through my soul, and I howled at the indignity. This could not be! I had finally rid myself, no, the world, of this offensive creature, and the fool had died ignorant of the hand that had killed him.

It took several seconds for my rage to pass. Suddenly, however, I saw clearly what had happened. I turned to look at the pendant, which seemed almost to mock me as it sparked and flashed. If removing it from my neck did not lift the magical aura from me, what would? The idea of being permanently invisible certainly did not appeal to me. But, no, it was worse than that. I was not only unseen, I was unheard.

I grabbed up the offensive lens and raced out of the building. My heart pounded in my ears, and the blood in my veins seemed to burn. When I reached my home, I burst in, slammed the door behind me, and bolted it in place.

October 4th
From the Journal of Julio, Master Thief of Hazlan

This is madness.

I do not know how much longer I will be able to write in this journal. My hands are shaking so badly now that I can hardly read my own words. How can I describe what is happening to me? With every passing second, my grip on sanity seems harder to maintain. Still, the world must know what has happened.

After my encounter with Cordova, I returned home and locked myself in. I quickly transcribed my experiences into this book and then fell upon my bed. Nothing seemed to make sense anymore. Fear such as I have never known tore at my soul. Finally, I slipped into an exhausted slumber and slept for several hours.

When I awoke, the sun was setting in the west and a

dark purple sky spread itself outside my window. Things seemed calmer now, and I was able to organize my thinking. As I knew little of the dark powers of sorcery, I decided that I must seek help. This done, however, I had no idea where to go. I knew no wizards or enchanters. After lengthy consideration, I resolved to seek out my fellows in the Thieves' Guild. Certainly there must be someone among that body who understood the weaving of spells and might be counted on to provide wise counsel. Slipping the shimmering lens into my pocket, I stepped out into the street.

While I expected the hall to be well occupied on this brisk evening, I had no idea that it would be as populated as it was. As I slipped inside through one of a dozen concealed entrances, I saw nearly every rogue in the city, from the lowest of the street thugs to the most dignified of confidence men. The great hall was packed.

I moved into the press of people, little caring if I bumped against those who could not see me. At the moment, stealth was not the object of my endeavor. If someone noticed me, so much the better. Indeed, I still had not considered what I would do to attract the attention of my peers or to explain my plight to them.

As I walked, my eyes swept back and forth across the room. The woman I wanted to see, Kassandra, stood near the front of the chamber. If anyone in the guild could help me, it would be she. I increased my pace.

Just before I reached her, she stepped onto an elevated platform and took her place behind an ornate lectern. Her delicate fingers lifted a small silver bell, and a shake of her wrist filled the hall with elegant ringing. At the piercing sound of this chime, everyone in the room fell silent. Even I, for all my pressing business, slowed to a halt in order to hear what she had to say. I suppose that I should have guessed, but my thoughts were not flowing smoothly on that autumn day.

"Listen to me, all," she said in a smooth, even voice. "I stand before you today with a sad announcement. Cordova, one of our most prominent and beloved members, has been murdered."

I almost laughed at her sincerity. Could it be that I was

the only one who had seen that bloated fool for the char-
latan that he was? Impossible. Others in the room must
even then have been struggling to keep from laughing at
the thought that Cordova had been beloved by the other
members of the guild. I attributed the widely spread
gasps of surprise and alarm as nothing more than polite-
ness on the part of Cordova's contemporaries.

Of course, to kill a member of the guild, even one as
unworthy as he, was to invite the ultimate penalty from
the assembly. Were it not for the cloak of invisibility that
I had employed, I should not have dared to attempt the
feat myself. After all, even the most clever of rogues
could not hope to escape the vengeance of five score
others, no matter how great the difference in their indi-
vidual talents.

"Who has done this?" came a cry from the crowd. I
must admit that the speaker sounded sincere. Perhaps
the bloated pig had managed to find one friend among
the guild. I supposed that the law of averages would
make even that unlikely event a certainty.

To my horror, Kassandra did not dismiss the answer as
unknown. Instead, she reached into her pocket and drew
out a folded bit of paper. Wrinkles and creases in the
creamy square showed that it had once been crumpled.
As she opened it, I recognized it as the frantic letter I had
written to Cordova in that failed attempt to make myself
known to him. In my panicked state I had not thought to
pick up the incriminating note. I could say nothing as
Kassandra began to read the vindictive words that I had
intended for only Cordova's eyes.

At last, the shock faded. I sprang forward and flung
my hand out. I would reclaim the letter and explain what
had happened to me. Certainly they would believe me if
I claimed that it was some spell of the wizard that had
motivated me to do the deed I had done. I reached the
front of the chamber just as the lithe Kassandra finished
her reading. My fingers curled around the note, and I
pulled it out of her hand.

At least, such was my intent. Imagine my surprise
when the paper was not affected in the least by my clawing grasp. I tried again, slapping wildly at it in an attempt

to knock it from her slender fingers. Again, there was no reaction.

I stood perfectly still for a moment. I struggled to control myself, aware that panic and madness were hovering on the fringes of my soul. Kassandra dropped the paper as murmurs of alarm rippled through the crowd. People began to shout, demanding that I be found and killed, but I paid no attention to them. My whole being seemed to be wrapped up in that tumbling scrap of paper. If I could do nothing to affect it, then I was already lost.

With every bit of mental effort that I could muster, I reached out for the incriminating note. It settled onto my hand . . . and stopped! For nearly a second it rested in my palm, the sensation of it racing like a mixture of pain and pleasure through my nerves. Then the sound of Kassandra ordering the members of the guild to find me and kill me broke my concentration. The paper trembled, passed through my fingers, and did not stop again until it rested upon the floor.

As the others moved out into the night, I moved with them. I could not stand the thoughts in my head. What would become of me? I could not imagine.

Then, a single idea became fixed in my mind. This diary would be my voice. I would record what had happened to me on the pages of this book and leave it where others would find it. Perhaps someone will discover a way to undo the terrible curse that has fallen upon me.

I returned to my room, arriving before any of the guildsmen had reached it. It took me no fewer that three attempts to lift the quill that I now write with. At last, however, I mustered the required concentration and set about recording my experiences.

I do not know how much longer I will be able to write. The effort of will required to keep the pen from slipping through my hand becomes greater with each passing second. In the end, I will simply . . .

Epilogue

A tumbling snow drifted down from the empty black of a midnight sky. Throughout the dark domain of Hazlan, it smoothed over the landscape with a delicate layer of white. The peaceful tranquility of this, the first snow of the looming winter, could not have been in greater contrast to the hectic rush of the townsfolk in Toyalis earlier that day as they made ready for the harsh hand of weather that would soon assail them.

The last bell of midnight tolled out across the countryside, and all was calm and still and quiet. Only one light broke the perfection of this darkness, and none of the domain's residents saw that, for it was perched high atop a stone tower, well away from the road that ran from Toyalis to Sly-var. This amber glow radiated from the laboratory of the foul wizard Hazlik, and his labors were not such that any of Hazlan's folk cared to know of them.

Cloistered away within his magically warded keep, the wizard moved to and fro about his workshop. As he drifted past trays of chemicals, shelves of arcane scrolls, and racks of unusual objects, his withered hands darted out to gather up various items. In the end, he came to stand next to a slender table over which a silken blanket had been draped.

Hazlik pointed at a small lamp that rested upon the table. With a sudden spark, it came to life and spilled an even yellow light upon the counter and the small crystal disc that lay upon it. The wizard leaned low over the crystal, allowing the golden light to wash across his gnarled face, almost bisected by a terrible scar.

Hazlik picked up the lens and cast a careful eye upon it. Clearly, he could discern more than the average man with his penetrating gaze. After several minutes of examination, he spoke. At the sound of his words, a quill pen sprang into action, recording what he said in a great book.

"Final notes on experiment twenty-seven dash thirteen. As in my twelve previous attempts to pierce the border ethereal and escape from this demiplane, the subject has broken up and become trapped in an incorporeal form. There is no reason to believe that this procedure is without hope of success, however. Perhaps I am taking the wrong approach. In my next experiment, I will alter the balance of astral and etherial vapors. If I am correct, this will enable the subject to regain a corporeal form with only a minimal effort. After all, there is cause for hope. This subject resisted fading from existence for fully forty-eight hours longer than all previous subjects."

Dark Tryst

Andria Cardarelle

Marielle circled the campfire in slow, liquid steps, idly fanning her skirts as she moved. At the far side of the fire she let the strength dissolve from her legs and sank to the ground, alone. The low flames formed a curtain that separated her from the others of her Vistana tribe, those few who still lingered, not yet ready to surrender to sleep. No one paid her any heed. The dancing had ended, and the last strains of the fiddle had faded, drifting into the night sky like missive spirits sent from the fiddler's hand to a distant realm. The youngest gypsies had already succumbed to the music's spell; toddlers now snoozed in their mothers' vardos, while the older children lay haphazardly in the shallow sleeping pit lined with moss and blankets, sheltered by the circle of gypsy wagons. Marielle could hear one of the old dogs snoring beside them.

It was a queer autumn night. The leaves of the bone-white birches ringing the camp had already paled and begun their death rattle, yet the air was warm and moist. It reminded Marielle of a story her elder sister had once told. The land was like a creature, Magda had said, a slumbering fiend, breathing long and languid breaths. In summer, the beast exhaled, spreading forth the heat of its abyssal fires. In winter, it drew back its breath, draining warmth from the world. Marielle wondered what event had stoked the furnace for this brief autumnal surge.

Restless, she picked up a stick and stabbed at the

campfire. A fountain of sparks erupted, dancing ever higher into the night sky until at last they blinked and went out amongst the blanket of stars.

She turned her gaze to the others of her tribe. It was as if she were observing them from a great distance—as if they were real, but she, like the sparks from the fire, were somehow temporal and fleeting. Sergio, the tribe's eldest male, had spread his broad haunches across the rear step of his wagon. His billowing white shirt was open to the waist, exposing a sweaty mat of peppered gray hair. Three other men sat beside him on log stumps, whittling sticks and puffing on pipes. They murmured in deep bass tones so as not to disturb those who slumbered, occasionally chuckling at some private joke.

Annelise and her mother huddled beside a wagon nearby while Annelise nursed her newborn. Their faces were round and golden, forming the perfect trinity of mother and child, child and mother, mother and child. The tiny creature suckling hungrily was the only baby born to the tribe that year, but it was Annelise's third. Marielle wondered if she herself might ever know this joy. But there was no suitor in the tribe she fancied. Nor did anyone fancy her.

No twist or hump rendered her form imperfect; no angry marks marred her luminous skin. She was sinewy and smooth, with bewitching black eyes and long raven hair. But any desire she kindled among her cousins was tempered by fear or superstition. Dark, lovely Marielle. Better to look but not touch.

She had already killed once, some said, though none called it murder. Sergio had bespoken her to a cousin, a self-important simpleton whom Marielle despised. Before a fortnight had passed, the boy had died in his sleep. Sergio proclaimed that Marielle had inadvertently cast the evil eye upon him. No one dared to want her thereafter. Only Magda's threat of a curse had protected Marielle from harm.

But now Magda was dead. Marielle's last direct blood tie with the tribe had been severed. Magda's lover, a half-blooded Vistana named Sean, had been cast out of the tribe upon her death. Marielle wondered how long it would be before she suffered the same fate, before fear of her own wrath subsided and was overshadowed by Sergio's growing contempt.

Her tribe was small and insular compared to others in the land. By choice, they lived austerely. They formed few alliances and crept like shadows through the forests, struggling to escape the notice of malevolent forces. Magic such as Magda's drew unwanted attention, claimed Sergio. She had been more than a gifted seer. She knew how to draw upon the powers of the moon and could use it to weave spells upon those who wronged her. Marielle bore the same blood; the same power lurked in her veins. It was only a matter of time, said Sergio, before her presence would bring misfortune to them all.

Marielle moved closer to the fire. Her flesh grew hot, yet she did not move away. The flames offered the only comfort against the cold she felt within. She drew her skirts above her knee, first the gauzy red apron, then the green silk below, revealing a sleek and graceful limb. Her skin gleamed. She closed her eyes against the flickering light and imagined that her entire body began to melt into the fire.

Without warning, the vision took a path of its own. Her lashes fluttered apart. The scene around her had faded to black; her tribe and the wagons were gone. The fire still blazed as she sat before it. A single flame lapped gently toward her. It became a man's arm, white and cold. The arm lashed out, and the hand grasped her ankle, freezing her in place. Upon one smoke-white finger was a silver ring with a large ebony stone, flashing white, then black as the hand softened its grip and began to caress her skin, rising toward her thigh.

Marielle shut her eyes hard. When she opened them, slowly, her tribe and its wagons had reappeared. She gasped and sprang away from the fire, staring at the flames in disbelief.

A woman's voice called out to her softly. "Did you burn yourself, Marielle?"

It was Annelise, ever patient and kind. She alone gracefully tolerated Marielle's presence.

Marielle shook her head dumbly. She looked up and met Sergio's disapproving gaze. His companions stared too, eyes aglow in the night. They blinked in unison, unflinching.

"Just startled by a spark," Marielle lied. "I fell asleep. It's time to retire."

The others nodded, then turned their attentions to themselves. Marielle walked to her vardo and slipped through the back door, closing it gently behind her.

The tiny chamber was pitch black. She lit the lamp hanging in the corner, flooding the vardo with its amber glow. The wagon's opulence belied Marielle's low stature, for it had been Magda's before she died. A small portal was cut into each sidewall, one a mosaic of indigo and scarlet, the other leaded and clear. The arched ceiling had been painted to look like the night sky, with a smattering of bright yellow stars spread between three gilded and carved beams that spanned the roof like ribs.

A small mirror hung on every wall, not for vanity's sake, but for reassurance—to confirm to Marielle that she truly existed. She sat upon the narrow padded bench that doubled as her bed, examining her leg. It ached, but bore no mark.

Marielle spread a thin blanket across the bed and peeled off her clothes, then put out the light and lay down. Shadows played across the tiny windows overhead, echoing the dance of clouds across the moon. For more than an hour she lay there, listening to the sound of her own breathing. Her heart raced. Sleep was impossible.

Finally, she gathered the courage to recreate the vision, to imagine it once more so that she might come to understand its meaning. Magda's powers of inner sight had been uncanny; at times she could detect the remotest sign and discern its portent. In contrast, Marielle's skill was raw and undeveloped. Even when she unraveled an image and found its truth, she might not know whether it was a guidepost to the future or a glimmer of something past.

Marielle pulled the blanket away from her body. The moonlight shone through the leaded window, flickering upon her skin like an ivory fire. Slowly, she closed her eyes.

The white hand slid up from the vardo's floor to the edge of the bed—an albino python, forearm snaking behind. The skin was smooth and hairless, gleaming like translucent marble. The nails were hard and pale gray, like steel.

For a moment, the fingers touched her ankle tentatively, probing, exploring. Then they drew tight like a noose. Upon the ring finger was the ebony stone. In her mind's eye Marielle stared into the gem. It was a black pool, calling, drawing her beneath its surface to the mysteries below. Marielle felt herself slipping into its cool depths. She drank in the liquid. A silver heat flared in her lungs, then spread to the surface, rolling across her breasts and belly in a wave that came suddenly, then disappeared.

The hand moved, so slowly at first that she failed to notice its progress. The fingers slid like silk along her leg. When she pulled her focus from the ebony pool, she saw that the ring and the hand had reached her knee. The fingers were spread wide. The arm was now draped along her calf. The hand inched forward like a spider, drawing the arm behind it.

A chiseled shoulder appeared, then a man's dark and shining mane. The shadows on the floor shifted and changed, and she saw a masculine figure crouched beside her bed, completely unadorned. His head was bowed, concealing his face. The hand continued to snake across her leg, rising to her thigh, drawing the man to his knees. A storm of black hair slipped across her ankle. Hot breath caressed her calf, and she felt the brush of his lips. The hand crept onward.

Marielle caught sight of a mirror upon the wall. It flashed red, as if afire. Mirror to the soul, she thought. The hollow cold within her had waned, staved off by the ever-building heat.

Then the night gained a voice.

"Damius . . ."

The hoarse whisper came not from the man, but from every corner of the vardo, echoing softly.

In the whirlpool of shadows above her, a shape appeared, the barest outline of a face. The darkness slowly relinquished its hold, and a pair of steel-gray eyes emerged, shadowed by a dark, heavy brow. Features took shape around them—pale, chiseled, and strong. It was his face, of that she was sure. Deep within the eyes, a flame began to burn. The lips parted, wide and pale.

"Say my name," he whispered, "and make me real."

She did not have to answer; the night did it for her. Once more, a whisper echoed throughout the vardo, rising from every corner, vibrating through her.

"Damius . . ."

Her lips silently mouthed the word. The face lowered to her own. Her lids sank lazily as his lips brushed hers. When she opened her eyes, the vision was gone. It was as if a lifeline had been cast out to her from the darkness, then pulled away as soon as she dared to grasp it.

For a moment she simply lay there, contemplating the dream. Who was the man? Was he even a man, or merely some message in a man's guise?

The moonlight pulsed upon her skin. Marielle knew the heavenly orb was nearly full, swelling with power. On such a night, Magda had told her, certain herbs could be gathered to make a brew. When drunk, the concoction would sharpen and guide a Vistana's inner sight. Sergio, of course, would not approve of such a harvest. It was bad enough that Marielle held such powerful magic within her, but to enhance it—to perform the rites that summoned spirits who wove tales of moments future and past—that he had forbidden since Magda's demise. Of course, Marielle had disobeyed him before. He did not have to know it this time.

She rose and drew on her clothes, wrapping a red silk shawl around her shoulders. Then she slipped out into the night.

Yuri sat by the embers of the fire, ostensibly keeping watch. But his head was bowed in half-slumber, and Marielle's footsteps were too swift and soft to rouse him. As she crept past the sleeping pit, the ancient yellow hound shifted and moaned. Marielle put a finger to her lips, and the dog sighed, then went silent. In three swift and fluid strides, she was free of them all. The forest closed in around her.

Beyond the tangle of birch and brush lay a deep stand of pines, an army of tall black sentries. The wind surged through the heavy, feathered branches, sighing. The scent of the pine was intoxicating, and she drank it in like wine. Her senses blurred. Yet, without question, she heard the trees whisper her name: "Marielle . . ."

Swiftly she moved onward, bare feet padding across the dense carpet of needles. She knew the pines would not hold the treasures she sought; their fallen needles kept all other flora at bay.

Soon the pines gave way to oak, and the forest floor was cloaked with moss and rotting leaves. She scanned the ground for the precious herbs. For a moment, she felt someone watching her and paused to search the shadows for the source. Perhaps she merely hoped it was true. Both the herbs and the watcher eluded her.

She descended a slope into a low, damp valley where the wood thinned and was dotted with clearings. A warm mist filled the hollows, rising like steam from the soil. The vapors snaked round her ankles as she walked, swirling softly. Marielle paused to remove the shawl from her shoulders, wrapping it around her waist. Then she continued her search.

At last, she spied a patch of the rare plant she sought most: the moonflower. Each tiny white blossom formed a cup, bent upward to drink in the light. Marielle removed the shawl and spread it upon the ground, then tied the ends to form a pouch. Carefully, she began to gather her treasures. In all, there were fewer than ten.

Again, she felt the eyes upon her. Fear danced along her spine, mingled with anticipation. She rose slowly and turned.

The man from her vision was standing before her, but a few paces distant, his back against a tree. He was the embodiment of midnight. The white, chiseled face shone like the moon itself, framed by the wild mane of shiny blue-black hair. His clothing was fine and foreign in appearance—a white silk tunic billowing across the broad shoulders, a black sash at the narrow waist, black trousers tucked into shining black boots upon his long, slender limbs. Tendrils of mist floated around his body like faithful servants.

For an eternity, neither soul moved. Then Marielle dared to speak.

"Who are you?" she asked quietly, as if afraid another might overhear their conversation.

"I believe you already know," he replied. He smiled, revealing a glimmer of white teeth.

Inside Marielle, a spark flared. He was toying with her, a cat with a mouse, and she sensed she was no match.

"Damius," she whispered.

He nodded. Suddenly, he stood behind her left shoulder, his breath upon her ear.

"Yes—Damius," he whispered.

She froze, staring forward, not daring to turn. The space between them was palpable.

"What do you want?" she asked.

"What you want," he murmured. "I am your slave. Did you not summon me?"

"No," she replied.

Without warning, he had shifted. Now he stood to the other side. She did not move.

"No, then," he answered slyly. "As you would have it."

"You were in my dream. I did not invite you," Marielle protested gently.

"Nor did I invite you into mine," he whispered, words flowing as easily as the mist. "Yet here you are."

She started. The fog swirled around them. Was she really a part of his dream, or was he merely toying with her?

"Are you not real?" she asked.

His hand reached out to stroke her cheek. The softness of his touch was agony.

"What do you think?" he asked in turn.

"That you are danger itself."

"Perhaps to some. Never to you," he replied.

The distance between them narrowed. Only inches before, it was now no deeper than a layer of skin. Still, it felt like a chasm to Marielle. Pressure rose in the void.

"What do you want from me?" Marielle repeated.

"It is I who must ask that of you," he said.

Marielle paused. "And if I want you to leave me?" she asked.

"Then I would go. If that is truly your desire." Again, his breath pulsed upon her neck. "But I think it is otherwise."

She did not, could not, answer. He moved closer, and she felt him against her. One arm came round her waist in a gentle caress. Involuntarily, she pressed herself back into his embrace.

"Shall I go then?" he asked, mocking her.

A voice within her struggled to say yes, but it was too distant, too faint. A storm had begun to rage through every tissue in Marielle's body, and its fury drowned all reason. Hot tears spilled from her eyes.

"No," she answered.

She felt her clothes slip to the ground, piece by piece, trailed by a tiny snowstorm of white blossoms. More than mere flesh had been exposed. But she did not care.

* * * * *

At dawn, Marielle was awakened by the cock's crow. She lay in her vardo. Her memory of the return was faint, clouded by the intensity with which she recalled the sensations that had preceded it. A ray of sun pierced the white window and fell upon her face. Instinctively, she rolled away from the light. Her legs and arms felt weak, her body heavy with exhaustion. She had no wish to rise anyway; her dreams held more interest than the day. In moments, she slept again. The dreams did not come.

When next she awoke, someone was rapping on the door. A woman called out.

"Marielle?"

It was Annelise. Without waiting for a response, the young woman opened the door and stepped inside.

Marielle groaned.

"Are you ill, Marielle?" Annelise asked, standing beside her. "It's well past midday. We assumed you were off wandering or gathering wood, but when you didn't reappear, I decided to check on you. Sergio will be wondering why you haven't risen."

Marielle drew the blanket over her head. "I'm fine."

"Then why not get up?" Annelise persisted, mildly annoyed.

"All right, because I'm ill," said Marielle. "Or I was. I'm better now. I'll be up in a moment."

"I'd help you dress," said Annelise, "but I've got to get back to my baby." She paused. "It looks like you did burn yourself last night, Marielle. Your leg has a mark."

Marielle opened one eye, following the gesture of Annelise's hand. Sure enough, a red streak lay upon her thigh.

"It's nothing," she said.

"Well, it's not bad, but you should be more careful," Annelise chided. "I don't suppose you will, though."

Marielle sighed. The woman was tedious. "No, I don't suppose I will."

Annelise did not hear her reply. She had already stepped through the door and closed it behind her.

Marielle rose and pulled on her clothes, then stepped out into the daylight, squinting. The sun was not bright, despite her reaction. Gray clouds hung low in the sky, promising a heavy rain. Three boys were playing with a stick and ball while a dog bounded beside them, yapping. The sound hammered through Marielle's head.

"You don't look well, Marielle." It was Annelise, back again. This time, she held her baby to her breast. Her concern was genuine, if not deep.

"Perhaps I'm not," replied Marielle. She gazed around the camp. She could not bear the thought of remaining there through the day, and hungered for the night to return. "I think I'll go for a walk. It might refresh me."

"Now I know you're ill," said Annelise. "Can't you see a storm is coming? The weather is about to break. It'll hardly do you good to be soaked to the skin."

"I won't be gone long," Marielle answered. Without looking at her companion, she turned and walked into the woods, thinking that perhaps she might never return.

If she found him, she thought. If the previous night had not been a dream after all. She hurried through the pines and down into the valley, seeking out the spot in which they had met, in which they had lain together. He had promised he would return. Rain began to fall softly, and she broke into a run.

When she reached their trysting place, water was pouring from the heavens. The sky was black, relieved only by brilliant lightning, which tore across it like a jagged blade. Thunder filled her ears. She pressed herself against a tree. With each stroke of lightning, she scanned the clearing, desperately seeking any sign of her lover. He did not come. In time her legs collapsed, and she slid to the wet ground, huddled against her knees. So she remained for hours, tears diluted by rain. Still, he did not come.

Finally, Marielle rose, calling out his name. Perhaps he was lost in the tempest, she thought. Lost, just as she. She stumbled into the forest. The earth turned to deep, gluey mud. In the darkness she misstepped. The mire closed in around her, pulling her downward, swallowing her to the waist.

Again, she called out, then three times more. The mud rose to her chest. She flailed desperately, clutching at nothing. Her face and shoulders sank into the mire, and the mud muffled her screams. Then a hand clamped hard on her wrist, drawing her from the grave just as the world faded to black.

* * * * *

When Marielle regained consciousness, she found herself in a great cavern, lying on the ground beside a campfire. A black, scratchy blanket covered her body. She rose quickly, then hastily pulled the blanket around her. She was nude, and not alone.

Around the fire sat a dozen gypsies. All had blue-black hair and skin as pale as the moon, like Damius. In their ebony clothing they resembled mourners, while she herself played the role of the dead. They gazed at her calmly, unblinking, with eyes the color of steel. A young woman beside her touched her arm. Marielle flinched. The cold fingers stung her like frozen metal upon bare, wet skin.

"You have nothing to fear," murmured the woman,

white teeth flashing. "Nothing at all."

Her words brought no comfort. Marielle looked about the cavern, searching for Damius. The chamber was immense, with corners draped in shadow. She could barely make out two passages, though where they led, she could not see. A smoke-filled alcove lay on the opposite side of the cavern, and within it another small fire glowed. A trio of elders sat around the fire. Only their stooped posture and their silvery hair described their age, for their white skin appeared smooth and unlined. The pale hair glowed against their black robes; in the dim haze, it was as ethereal as the smoke. One of them turned and met her stare. The eyes flashed yellow, then looked away.

A knot of fear took root in Marielle's stomach. By instinct, she pulled her legs close and clutched the blanket more tightly, withdrawing into a fragile, futile shell.

"Where is Damius?" she asked quietly.

"Very close," said the woman at her side. "But you are safe here with us. Is that not true, Niro? Play a little music to soothe her while we wait for Damius to return."

She nodded to a man opposite the fire, and he drew a shining black fiddle to his chin. Ghostly strains issued forth, filling the cavern. Marielle felt the music piercing her soul, and indeed, it put her at ease. Such beauty was not to be feared.

The woman beside her hummed the melody softly for a moment, calming Marielle further. "Damius told us you were near death when he drew you from the mire," she said. "Your body is weak. Drink this, and you shall mend."

She offered a cup filled with dark, bitter tea. Marielle drank it down dutifully, then set the vessel aside. The white faces swam before her, smiling faintly, each a copy of the other. She sank limply to the ground, twisted like a rag doll in lazy repose.

The roof of the cavern swirled overhead. Wet, glistening red lichen covered the stone, pulsing in the firelight like a living organ. Stalactites hung from the ceiling. Tendrils of smoke and mist caressed each glittering and jagged point, unhurried as they sought their escape through some hidden chimney in the rock.

"Yes, rest," said the girl. "I am Lizette, sister to Damius. He will come to you soon."

"Damius," Marielle echoed, tasting the name upon her tongue. Her eyelids sank, unable to bear their own weight. She heard a shuffling beside her, as if a small crowd were drawing near.

*   *   *   *   *

When Marielle opened her eyes, Damius sat at her side, stoking the fire. He turned and smiled, sensing her gaze. The white teeth shone like pearls.

Marielle struggled to cast off the vestiges of sleep. Damius reached out and stroked her face, tracing her jaw, brushing her lips. His fingers conjured a thin line of heat upon her skin, a tiny snake of sensation that wriggled down her neck and across her body even after his hand had lifted. Her strength slowly began to return.

"I'm sorry I was not here when you first awoke," he said. "I was gathering more wood to ensure your warmth."

Your touch alone is enough, thought Marielle, but she didn't say it. The rest of his tribe still looked on, as quiet as ghosts.

She rose to her elbow, pulling the blanket close.

"Where are we?" she asked.

"At my family's camp," he replied. "Our vardos are outside. We take shelter in this cavern when the storms come."

Marielle looked at the faces gathered round. Half were male, the others female. Their resemblance to Damius, and each other, was uncanny. A few, like Lizette, appeared young, perhaps no more than twenty, though Lizette herself was no longer among them. The others seemed roughly the same age as Damius, which was indistinct, somewhere past thirty, yet still prime. There were no elders among them; the silver-haired gypsies in the alcove had vanished. Nor were there any children. Perhaps the young and old had left the cavern and retired to their wagons.

Lizette reappeared, carrying Marielle's clothes. "They are dry now," she said. "I washed out the mud."

Marielle thanked her and took the bundle, then looked around for a place to dress.

"Shall I go outside?" she asked. "The storm seems to have lifted."

Lizette and Damius exchanged glances and smiled faintly.

"It has not yet gone," said Damius. "We are very sheltered here, and the sounds of the heavens can be difficult to discern. You can dress in the shadows." He motioned toward the alcove where the elders had sat. "Lizette will stand before you, if you have decided to be modest."

Marielle rose and crossed the cavern. The elders' campfire had faded to ash and glowing embers, but its acrid smoke still filled the small chamber. Marielle turned her back toward the others. Lizette took a position behind her, watching as she pulled on her skirts and then her blouse.

"You are very lovely," said Lizette. "You needn't be shy among us."

The remark made Marielle uneasy. She quickly tied her shawl around her hips and returned to Damius. He wrapped an arm around her shoulder and kissed her neck.

"Let's go out into the woods," she whispered.

He smiled. "We will break away later when the storm has fully passed. But for now, my tribe would like to welcome you. We do not have many visitors. And one so special as you is rare indeed."

Lizette stood beside them.

"Damius," she said softly. "You must ask her."

"Not yet," he replied. "Soon."

"Ask me what?" said Marielle.

"It is not important now," he answered. "It can wait until after the dance."

The fiddler once again lifted his instrument to his chin and began to play, spawning a dark, hypnotic melody. The five women beside the fire rose and formed a circle. Each held a black silk scarf in her hand, tracing circles in the air.

Lizette stepped into the shadows, then returned with a small bundle. She unveiled its contents slowly: a drum with a livid hide, a pair of slender white sticks, and a string of tiny silver bells. She passed the instrument to the man seated beside the fiddler, then tied the bells around her ankle. When she had finished, she stepped into the circle of dancers.

The women began to move slowly with the music, hips swaying, arms writhing like charmed white serpents to the fiddler's dark tune and the drummer's sensual beat. Their black skirts swirled in the shadows, layer upon layer of silk and gauze fluttering about them like crows' wings.

Lizette left the group and approached Marielle. "Come and dance with us," she said, extending her pale hand. Her eyes were lowered seductively, and a faint smile played on her lips. "Come and dance with me."

Marielle hesitated. Damius's arm slipped from her shoulder, and he leaned in close. "Yes, join her," he urged softly.

The fiddler picked up the pace. The women opened their circle, and Marielle stepped to the center. A tempest of arms and silks whirled around her. Each body entangled her for a moment, then set her free as another took its place. Lizette joined her in the vortex and grasped her hands. They began to spin as one, turning round and round until Marielle grew dizzy and her legs felt weak. The music reached a crescendo, then stopped abruptly. Marielle and Lizette collapsed to the ground, exhausted. The dance was done. The five women nodded at Marielle and disappeared into the shadows, leaving only Lizette and Damius beside her.

Damius stood. "I must see whether the storm has lifted," he said. "I will return shortly." He bent and kissed Marielle on the cheek. "I enjoyed the dance," he whispered. "I hope it pleased you as well."

Marielle started to rise and follow, but dizziness overcame her.

"Stay with Lizette," said Damius. "And keep her company." When Marielle turned her head, he was gone.

"Yes, stay with me," said Lizette, lying at Marielle's side. She leaned over and kissed Marielle on the knee. "Damius has kept much about you hidden. Tell me about your tribe."

"There is little to tell," Marielle replied, withdrawing her leg. "I'm sure it would bore you."

"Not at all," said Lizette. "We meet so few others when we travel."

"My tribe also keeps to itself."

"Are there many of you?" asked Lizette casually.

"Twenty-seven," Marielle answered. "Twenty-eight with the new baby."

Lizette paused. "The baby . . ." she said softly. "Such a gift. If it is healthy . . ."

"It's quite so," Marielle replied.

"And so it should be," said Lizette. "Tell me, how old is this child?"

"Not yet a month."

"So sweet," murmured Lizette. "Is the mother young?"

"Just seventeen. But already she has three children."

"That must be very nice for her," Lizette said evenly. "And is the father handsome, like Damius?"

"Handsome," Marielle replied. "But not like Damius."

"No, of course," added Lizette. "Not like Damius. Are there no other babies but this one?"

"No. Only one child was born to us this year. Why does this subject interest you so?"

"Surely you must have noticed that we have no children ourselves," Lizette replied.

"I thought perhaps they were simply sleeping."

"No, not sleeping," said Lizette softly. "Gone from our midst. Ours is not a fortunate tribe, Marielle. We have been cursed with barrenness. But perhaps, you yourself might change that, should you decide to remain with Damius."

"He has yet to ask," Marielle replied.

"But he will," said Lizette, rising to her feet. "And you will say yes, won't you?"

Marielle did not answer.

"Of course you will," said Lizette. "It was meant to be."

Damius returned and announced that the storm had

ended. Lizette said good-bye to them both, disappearing in the shadows.

Damius took Marielle by the hand and drew her to her feet. Then he led her into the passage from which he had come. As their path rose, so too did the mists, until Marielle could see nothing around her. Damius gripped her hand tightly and bade her not to let go. They walked for what seemed an eternity. Marielle heard a strange sighing all around her. Then the fog grew less heavy. Trees took shape. They were in the forest, at the clearing in which they had met the night before.

Damius drew her close and kissed her fiercely on the mouth. Desire flared within her as if she were nothing but dry tinder and he the spark. She slid her hand beneath his tunic.

"Tomorrow," he whispered. She felt him press an object into her hand: the ebony ring.

"I must ask something of you, Marielle," he said. "And your answer will seal our fate." He took the ring and placed it on her finger. At once, the silver band contracted, fitting her snugly. For the first time, she noticed the small white stones encircling the ebony gem. No longer beautiful, the ring appeared to be a mouth. Damius stroked the side of the gem three times. A tiny barb rose from the center, forming a sharp and eager tongue.

Marielle gasped.

"Lizette told you of our plight, did she not?" Damius said. "We are childless. It is a curse that you alone can lift. Draw a drop of blood from the baby in your tribe tonight, and bring it to me here. No one must see you draw the blood, else your efforts will be spoiled. It is a small thing we ask. Yet it means everything to my tribe, and to us both."

Marielle began to protest, but he raised a finger to her lips. Then he pulled her tight against his chest and whispered into her ear. "Do this for me, Marielle, and I will come to you tomorrow night and always. Fail, and I can never return." Before she could answer, he stepped away and disappeared into the mists.

Marielle stood in the clearing, dazed and alone. She

stared at the strange ring upon her hand. The barb had withdrawn. The white stones had vanished. Damius's words echoed through her mind: Fail, and I can never return.

She tugged at the ring. To her relief, it slipped off with ease. For a moment, she thought of throwing it into the brush. Then, tears welling, she tucked it into a small pocket within her skirt and began the walk back to camp. Morning broke, turning the woods from black to dull gray. By the time the familiar vardos came into view, the sun had begun to burn away the mist. The women in the camp were stirring, building a fire and preparing the kettles.

Marielle walked toward her wagon. Annelise intervened, a phantom from nowhere. Marielle brushed past her, but the phantom followed behind.

"You look dreadful," chattered Annelise. "What happened to you?"

Marielle cringed at the sound. She did not want this attention, nor could she bear this concern.

"I took shelter in a cave during the storm," she replied. It was, after all, the truth.

"I warned you not to leave when the sky was so threatening," chided Annelise.

"So you did," replied Marielle. "But I am all right, as you can see."

"Even Sergio was wondering where you were. If you had not come back soon, we might have begun a search."

"Sergio has not bothered himself with my whereabouts before," said Marielle wearily.

"That's not true, Marielle. But in any case, we are leaving soon. Sergio has decided to break camp tomorrow. I thought you'd like to know."

Marielle did not answer. Annelise clucked her tongue and walked away.

The hours of the day passed slowly, as if in a dream. Marielle completed her chores by reflex. All the while, she watched Annelise and the baby, and thought of the task Damius had set before her.

Sweet, unsuspecting Annelise. Marielle could simply

ask to hold the baby, she knew, and Annelise would comply. Then the deed would be easy. Still, Marielle hesitated. It was only a drop of blood, a tiny prick, she told herself. But she sensed it meant more. How could she do this thing that Damius asked? Yet how could she not?

The afternoon faded. Marielle thought of Damius, and an unbearable longing took shape within her. It fed on her strength like a parasite, pressed hard against her chest, twisted around her heart.

As the sun sank past the trees, she seized her chance. Annelise was seated at the rear of her wagon with her baby while her toddling young sons wrestled before her. The middle child stumbled and fell, then began to cry. At once, Annelise went to his side and examined the damage. Blood streamed from a rip in his trousers.

"Let me help you," Marielle offered. "I can take the baby while you see to Nicolai."

She extended her arms. Annelise thanked her and presented the baby, completely absorbed in her injured son's plight.

Marielle stepped away. Then she drew the ring from her pocket and slipped it onto her finger. At once, it tightened to fit. She stroked the side three times, just as Damius had done. The barb sprang forth, and the stones at the edge of the ring appeared, a circle of tiny teeth, forming a macabre grin.

Marielle pulled the white blanket away from the baby's smooth, chubby leg. She had to choose the site of the wound carefully; otherwise Annelise might see it. She probed the cocoa-brown folds of flesh just behind its knee. Then she inserted the barb. The baby shrieked.

"What now?" asked Annelise, her voice rising with irritation. "No sooner do I get one son settled when the next begins to cry."

"I'm not sure," Marielle replied, struggling to remain calm. "You know I haven't got your touch, Annelise. Perhaps he just misses you."

Annelise patted Nicolai on the head, then turned to Marielle and held out her arms. Marielle released the writhing bundle to its mother, who cradled the baby and began to coo. Still, the creature wailed.

"This is strange," said Annelise. "Surely you must have noticed something."

"I did see a black fly," Marielle replied. "Perhaps it stung him."

"Oh, my poor, poor dear," said Annelise soothingly, searching the baby's limbs for signs of a bite. She spied a red mark behind the baby's knee and kissed it. "That nasty fly. Mama will make it better."

To Marielle's relief, the baby quieted.

She tucked the ring back into her pocket. The deed was done. Now, she need only wait until after dark. Just a few hours. Then she would slip away, never to return.

The hours dragged. The baby slept peacefully. Finally, Marielle bid the others good night and climbed into her vardo. She gathered her treasures—a few pieces of jewelry, a carving made by her father, a miniature portrait of Magda, crafted by an artisan years ago. Then she placed them in a makeshift sack. When she was certain only Yuri remained by the fire, she slipped out and entered the forest.

Damius was waiting at the trysting place, surrounded by mist. He held out his hand.

"The ring," he commanded. His voice was deep and calm.

Marielle pulled it from her skirt and presented it. He smiled faintly as he took the ring and laid it before a large granite rock in the clearing. Then he drew her into his arms.

"Say my name," he whispered.

"Damius," she murmured, drunk with anticipation.

Marielle felt her clothing melt away, one piece at a time, just as it had when she met him before. Then Damius too was naked, a pale statue carved from stone. A yellow flame burned deep within his eyes, mirroring her own internal fire. He pulled her to the ground.

The mist grew heavy and wet. White hands slithered across her body, leaving a trail of searing heat wherever they passed. The cool mist melted upon her flesh and formed tiny streams that raced toward the ground. Damius's pale skin merged with the fog, blurring, until only his shiny blue-black hair remained distinct, sliding across her torso. Marielle sank her fingers into the silken mane. She was delirious, adrift upon an undulating sea of moss.

Then she heard a woman's laughter nearby, soft and faint. She turned her head toward the sound and glimpsed a ghostly figure. Lizette was crouched before a granite rock. She was naked and white, with a mass of gleaming black snakes for hair. Marielle tried to call out, but the words caught in her mouth. Damius groaned above her.

Lizette lifted a tiny object from the ground and held it aloft in the moonlight. It flashed white, then black. She clutched it toward her breast, and it became a small, squirming creature, wrapped in a glowing white shroud. Lizette laid the bundle upon the rock. The mists swirled, consuming the form. When the fog parted, the offering had vanished. Damius, too, was gone.

Lizette stood in the clearing, smiling slyly. "Marielle," she intoned. "I say thy name, and make thee ours."

Then she too departed, drifting away into the night upon the sound of her own laughter.

Marielle was alone and cold as the dead. She lifted her hands toward her face. The fingers had turned black. Though she had never seen this sign before, she knew its meaning. Black hands marked those who had wronged the Vistani.

Then the screaming began, distant and faint. She rose, drawing her garments around her. The screams grew louder. They seemed to emanate from within her own head, yet she knew the voice belonged to Annelise. An image took root in Marielle's mind. She raced back toward the camp. She had to know if her vision was true.

When Marielle reached the tribe, Annelise stood by the fire, her face twisted and red with grief. In her hands lay a bloody shroud. The other members of the tribe stood around her. As Marielle approached, Annelise turned and held out the bundle. A tiny arm fell away from the cloth—limp, shriveled, and black.

"Devil!" rasped Annelise.

The other members of the tribe formed a line beside

her. Annelise's mother stooped to the ground and picked up a stone, then flung it with all her might. Marielle felt a sharp blow against her forehead. Blood flowed down the side of her face. Another rock struck. And then another. Marielle did not lift her arms to protect herself. Warm blood filled her eyes, shutting out the mob before her. When the fourth stone crashed against her skull, she sank to her knees and cried out in agony.

She could not see the mists as they rose up from the soil to envelop her battered form. Yet somehow she felt them within, as they transformed her to nothingness and lifted her in their ethereal embrace. When at last they drained away from her body, the scene around her had changed. Her tribe was gone. So too were the stains upon her skin. She was pale and unmarred, glowing white like the swollen moon overhead.

Before her lay the mouth of a great cavern. Its walls were red and glistening. In her mind Marielle heard the faint cry of a baby. She passed her hands over her hard, warm stomach, and knew that the curse had been lifted. From deep within the cavern came the ghostly strains of a fiddle, summoning her forth. She walked toward the sound, ready to greet her new tribe.

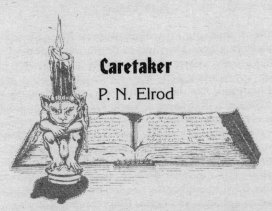

Caretaker

P. N. Elrod

"It is too dangerous, Lord Vasili," they said, using the name I'd provided them since my real one was often a burden when dealing with the general populace. "There are many perils in the night. Please stay here with us and be safe." They'd gathered close to each other in the doorway of the Vallaki Inn, not one of them daring to put so much as a toe past the threshold now that the sun was well down.

"The night doesn't trouble me," I truthfully replied, shrugging on my cape as I strode into the empty street. "Any perils may look out for themselves." My cavalier manner shocked them. Though too polite (or fearful) to say it, I could read in their faces they thought Lord Vasili a fool or a madman for venturing forth into the dark. Having been both at one time or another, I took no offense at their opinion. I even found myself laughing a little at their sincere concern for my well-being as I swung up on the lead horse of the four harnessed to a great black conveyance bearing the Von Zarovich coat of arms. "Have no worries on my behalf," I added, gesturing at the device. "I serve Strahd von Zarovich, and he always looks after his own."

At this, two of them surreptitiously made a sign meant to protect one from the evil eye. The others shifted uneasily at the reminder of Barovia's lord, though they could thank him for putting gold in their pockets for their goods, which were now packed away in the coach. This was the attitude that inspired me to occasionally adapt another name when traveling. My reputation was such that any business I wished to personally conduct was always severely hampered. The people either were terrified or overwhelmed me with ceremony, or both. Better to allow them the illusion that they were dealing with Lord Strahd's able envoy, Vasili von Holtz, rather than the dread Strahd himself.

One might question why I even bothered to attend to so humble a task as purchasing certain supplies for Castle Ravenloft, but the fact was that I enjoyed the distraction. The night air was good—when I bothered to breathe it—and the horses needed the exercise. Besides, as the merchants had correctly pointed out, there were dangers in the night . . . but who better to deal with them than myself?

With their fears settled, or at least momentarily distracted, I was about to depart when one of them pointed at the western sky with awe. It was lighted up as if the sun had reversed course to make an unorthodox return. Clouds hanging over the area reflected a hellish orange glow back to the earth.

"A fire," she murmured. "And a big one. What can it be?"

"It's miles away," opined another. This was confirmed when someone ran to the top floor of the Vallaki Inn to get a better look.

"What's out there?" I asked, standing in my stirrups, craning my neck with them. I knew Barovia well, but had not been west of Vallaki for several years.

"Farms, Lord Vasili," someone answered. "The fields must be afire. There are clouds. Perhaps some lightning struck the ground and . . ."

I left them to futile speculations and whistled my horses up. Within minutes I was clear of Vallaki and heading west at a steady trot. Crossing the fords of the Luna River, I noticed with dismay that the fire glow did not seem perceivably nearer, indicative of its distance. How far? Five miles? Ten? The horses were too slow for my curiosity. Throwing a silent command into them to ensure they would steadily continue along the road, I stood high in the stirrups again, this time grasping the ends of my cape and throwing my arms wide. My body began to rapidly shrink; color faded from my vision, but far away objects grew sharper and more easily discernable. Clothes and skin blended, transmuting into silken fur and the delicate span of wings; the west wind caught their black folds like a sail. With an effortless rush, I rose high over the rattling coach.

The laboring horses left far behind, I sped on toward a vast tower of smoke pushing itself against the clouds.

A fire indeed, and a bad one.

Acres of nearly ripe wheat had already gone up, and a broad arrowhead of flame marched relentlessly east, driven by the wind. It might burn itself out, but the last month had been unseasonably dry, so that seemed an unlikely chance. Vallaki itself could be spared for being on the other side of the river, but not so for the miles of farmland in between.

When the smoke became too thick to see, I wheeled back, swooped down to the road, and resumed a man's form again. One breath of the choking, ash-filled air blowing from the inferno convinced me not to try another. My eyes stung and streamed freely as I considered what best to do.

To magically control the fire was my first thought, but instinct told me my influence would be insufficient for the task. My second thought was for the weather. I glanced up. The clouds looked promising; at least I had something to work with. Checking through my pockets, I found a small pouch of incense. It hardly seemed enough, but I had plenty of fire to light it, there were some sticks lying about, and I knew the words of power to . . . my heart sank. I had everything necessary for the magic but *water*.

In order to create rain, one must have water, but if one *has* water, then the rain is hardly likely to be necessary. Of course. It made perfect sense. To whatever fool had designed the spell.

I put the incense away in disgust, then retreated as the stifling wind carried a phalanx of sparks toward me. It was pure reflex. On my left hand was a ring capable of providing me with a certain amount of protection against fire. Its pale stone cast a cool blue radiance about me even now. Well, I couldn't keep retreating all the way back to the Luna. If I could trust that there were farms ahead, then I'd surely find a well or stock pond to complete the requirements of my spell. I had only to go forward.

Into the fire.

Clenching my left hand into a fist, I grimaced at the ring. Yes, its magic would stave off the harsher effects of the blaze; I well knew that in my *mind,* but putting aside so primal a fear is much easier said than done.

Then run fast, Strahd. Run very, very fast.

It might have helped not to look, but even I had not that much control. With walls of flame booming on each side, horrific heat, and smoke dense enough to cut into bricks, I sprinted down the exact center of the dirt road, fervently wishing the damned thing were wider. I could have moved more quickly in the form of a bat or a wolf, but wasn't sure if the magic of the ring would function as well, if at all, under such a change. This was not the time for experimentation.

I pulled my cape high in a feeble effort to protect my head from the worst of it and raced on. The racking heat beat hard on me, worse than any forge, worse than any midsummer sun. I would melt from it or flare up like an oil-soaked torch, twisting and screaming as . . .

Stop whining and run.

It bellowed like a living thing. It *was* a living thing, consuming all life in its path and leaving death in its wake. Raging and roaring, the wind of its voice threatened to pound me into the ground for daring to challenge its power over the land.

Through. I'd gotten *through.*

The burning wall was behind me. But not the heat. That rose up from the roasted earth, curling about my body as if to yet sear me. The ring helped, but I'd pushed its limits. My hands and face were red and stinging, but not too badly. They could be ignored; I kept moving.

I'd known that the vanguard of the blaze would be my greatest danger, but once past its barrier there would be a relative respite since the grass and wheat would have been quickly exhausted as fuel. Had this been a heavily forested tract, with tall trees capable of burning for hours, I'd have never attempted it.

Striding forward into a charred and reeking world, I viewed a sorry landscape, utterly black except for bright spots where it still burned or an unexpected patch of green that had somehow escaped. Ahead, partially concealed before by the smoke, was a farming village—or rather its corpse.

It hadn't been much before the fire, and was less than nothing now, just a few wretched hovels crowded together on each side of the road. The thatch roofs were gone, but the wooden frames and beams were still aflame. My attention, however, was focused on something far more riveting. Scattered in the ruins and along the road were the bodies of the peasants who had lived here. Young and old, some so burned I couldn't tell man from woman, but others nearly untouched. These latter told me that the fire might not have had a natural origin. For without exception they'd been cut down by sword or by arrow.

Slaughtered. Murdered.

The smell of their blood hung thick in the hot air. My drowsing hunger, ever a light sleeper, came fretfully awake.

But I had no time to attend it. Every minute's delay meant the fire spread a few more yards. Multiply that by its breadth . . .

I dashed to a waist-high ring of mortared stones that marked the remains of the village well. Its low roof was burned away; the four poles that had supported it were smoking stumps that had to be kicked down so I could get to the opening.

Bucket and rope were missing, but I'd expected as much. I sat on the edge of the stones and swung my legs around, easing myself into the well. Its rock sides were hot to touch, but not uncomfortably so, growing cooler as I descended; my hands had no difficulty maintaining purchase. Down I went, until my boots splashed into the debris-clogged water. I went lower in order to thoroughly soak the bottom of my cape, but when I began climbing back up, something tugged at it, pulling strongly.

Thinking that the edge had simply caught on something, I turned to shake it loose and nearly lost my hold on the wall from the surprise. Clinging to the hem were two small fists belonging to a thin child not more than ten years old.

Dumbfounded for all of two seconds, without further thought, I reached down and grabbed one stick of a wrist and hauled upward. The waif instantly wrapped arms and legs around my body in a death grip. The extra weight was negligible; I climbed back to the top quick as a spider.

Once out of the well, I took a look at my partially drowned rat. It was a girl, if one might draw conclusions about the dripping rags that served as a dress. Her bone-white face was puffed from tears and blank with shock, and it took no little effort to peel her from my waist and set her on the ground. She took one terrified look at the village, another at the body of a woman slumped near the well, then fastened herself around my legs and started wailing.

Grief has its place and purpose, but hers was a decided impediment to my urgent business. I pushed her an arm's length away, stared hard into her eyes, and instructed her to be quiet and go to sleep. Her weeping hiccupped to a stop, and I lay her limp body onto a bare patch of earth for the time being.

That distraction dealt with, I drew the incense from my pocket, found a brand of wood, and commenced the work of casting the spell I'd planned.

This was no light undertaking; I wasn't even sure of success, but after several minutes' work, the first tremors of power began running through me like the hot blood of battle fever. Squeezing a quantity of water from my cloak was the final step. I shouted the last words completing the spell at the sky and clapped my hands overhead. Raw power leapt from them, shooting up until its dark purple aura was lost against the clouds.

Nothing visible happened for a time, then I detected a shifting in the gray billows above, like a great animal rousing itself. They roiled and writhed in harrowing silence, then a kind of pale mist suddenly obscured their details.

Rain struck my upturned face.

It was better than I'd hoped. Such magic is difficult to manipulate; sometimes the results of alteration are as impossible to predict as natural weather. But this time I'd brought about a steady soaking downpour that hissed and steamed among the flames, gradually smothering them. I was well satisfied.

Free now to turn my attention to the child, I spent some moments waking her and more still gently opening her mind up to questioning. Because she was so young, and thus had little understanding of adult things, it was a tax on my patience to correctly interpret her answers into something comprehensible.

As far as I could judge, hers had been an unremarkable village, like hundreds of others dotting the valleys of Barovia. All had been at peace until the arrival of perhaps a dozen or so strangers who blithely announced they were taking the place over. When the elderly farmer who acted as burgomaster dared to question this, they cut his head off. After a few days of plunder and play, the new landlords grew bored and began the butchery, ultimately setting fire to everything. The girl had only survived because her desperate mother had dropped her into the uncertain safety of the well at the last moment.

I glanced at the woman's body. There was a fearful gashing on her back and shoulders. Sword wounds.

By the time I'd gotten this much from the girl, my conveyance was approaching in the distance. The downpour had apparently extended at least to the edge of the fire and likely beyond, else the horses would never have kept coming. I welcomed it, stopping and turning them until they faced east toward Vallaki. Since the back was crammed with boxes—including a special one large enough for a man to lie in—I put the girl up front on the driver's bench. She was alert to the point of being aware of her surroundings, but unable to offer much reaction. Crouching miserably in the rain, holding hard to the seat, she stared at me with neither expectation nor fear.

That counted for something. I firmly ignored the temptation of her blood while drawing my cloak around her slight body. Its heavy wool was wet, but would keep her warm enough until she reached Vallaki. I had more work ahead of me, anyway, and wished to rid myself of its encumbrance.

"The coach will stop at an inn," I said to her. "Tell the people there that Lord Vasili commands they care for you and the horses until his return. Understand?"

She nodded. Having imparted the instructions with a slight mental nudge, I could trust that she would readily pass the message on in a clear manner. She would be well fostered.

As the horses and wagon lurched over the now muddy road with their new cargo, I turned to the west, arms once more spread to ride the wind, and began to search beyond the burned area surrounding the village. Six hours later, after backtracking a sodden and nearly obscured trail originating in a wheat field, I discovered them camped high up in the foothills of Mount Baratok, to the north. Bandits they were, by the look of them, though it would not have mattered to me if they'd been nobles or slaves.

They'd sheltered in one of the caves piercing the limestone there and, from the piles of refuse thrown about, had evidently been in occupancy for quite a period prior to their invasion of the village. My small body hanging easily from the slender branch of a nearby tree, I settled in to listen to the men on guard.

Their talk was instructive, giving me to understand they'd not only murdered and done the arson, but from their high perch commanding a fine view of the valley, had taken rare delight at the fiery show. How disappointing that the rain had put an end to it; some were still grumbling over the ill luck hours afterward.

They were predators, but careless ones. A predator myself, I well knew the joy of the hunt, but also the responsibility, and to wantonly kill all your prey means your own death as well.

Particularly so in their case. Barovia was *mine*, the land, the peoples, mine to do with as *I* pleased. I would tolerate no interlopers despoiling *my* property.

Strahd von Zarovich looks after his own.

Abandoning the tree, I flew away, out of their limited sight, and became a man again, eyes and ears—and other senses—alert to all that lay around me. I became aware of a pack of wolves living not a quarter mile distant and put forth a silent call for them to come. In a remarkably short time I was surrounded by a number of their great, shaggy bodies. Grinning and panting, they bumped and fell against me to express their affection, nipping each other in their excitement and making soft yips and growls of greeting. I fairly basked in it, but not for long. At a soft word of command, they quietly followed me, threading through the trees like ghosts.

We stopped well outside the nimbus of light from the bandits' campfire. While the wolves remained hidden and waited, I slipped forward and made a slight noise to attract the attention of one of the men. They'd been in Barovia long enough to be cautious; instead of one coming to investigate, I had three to deal with. No matter.

Swords drawn and keeping within sight of each other, they crept forward into the trees, muttering cautions to be careful, treading on dry leaves, and otherwise announcing their intrusive presence to anyone or anything with ears to hear. I stood in the deep shadow of an elderly oak until the man I'd chosen came even with it, then reached out and plucked him from his feet without a sound. Pinning his arms with one hand and with the other clamped firmly over his face, I swiftly retreated with my prize. He kicked and flailed, ultimately vocalizing a strangled noise, but this was well muffled and brief for lack of air. My palm both covered his mouth and pinched his nose. His friends heard nothing.

Now was I well rewarded for holding my hunger in check against the girl. Her young blood would have hardly provided for me so well as this feasting. Ecstatic, I ripped into his throat with my corner teeth, releasing the life-giving fountain of his blood. Thus did I feed, swallow after swallow, like a drunkard draining a cask of ale in one draught. When finished, I let the man's limp and empty body fall at my feet, then stepped over him to pursue his friends.

They'd grown both bold and fearful. Having determined he was not where he should have been, they called his name, hesitantly at first, in whispers, then more loudly as their alarm and annoyance increased. Again, I waited until another came close enough and dealt with him in the same manner as his fellow, holding him easily despite his best efforts to escape.

The last man, realizing that things were very much amiss, fled back to the camp. Or at least tried to do so. The wolves took it as a sign to strike and were upon him before he'd gone two steps. And so as I crouched over one man, supping on his blood with even greater relish than before, my pets tore the other to pieces, making their own evening's banquet. His shrieks of terror and agony provided suitable music for our gathering.

As a rule, I do not encourage the wolves to feed on humans, lest they become too fond of an easy hunt and abandon their natural prey of deer, but on this occasion, I judged an exception might be allowed, since it would bring about the desired effect of putting the fear of all the hells into the hearts of the rest of the bandits.

Hell. Now *there* was an idea.

Leaving the wolves to their meal, I returned to the edge of the camp to observe the progress of things. Nine or so men had emerged from the cave, wide-eyed and quivering as they faced the part of the woods where their companion's wrenching screams (too quickly over, alas) had sheered through the darkness. All had armed themselves. Most had swords, but a few had arrows nocked and ready in their longbows. Despite their fear, they looked as hard and as experienced as any soldier that ever had served with me in days long past. Even so, I could have charged into their midst and taken on the lot with no great inconvenience or danger to myself.

But that felt wrong, somehow. An antic humor had seized me; perhaps it was inspired by the reviving flush of fresh blood, but I was of a mind to tailor their punishment to suit their crimes.

Though wolves frequently howl to work themselves up for a hunt, I was able to persuade them to break with habit and set up a truly hair-raising clamor for the entertainment of these spoilers. As the pack was a large one, the row was not only petrifying, but nearly ear-shattering because of their proximity.

The men did not remain petrified for long, though, and almost as one retreated into the shelter of their cave. The opening was rather narrow; it was most amusing to watch as they all fought to jostle through at the same time. Once within, two of them held nervous watch, peeping out from the cave mouth like frightened birds in a nest awaiting the snake's unstoppable approach.

Neither noticed my small winged shape flitting across the abandoned camp to lightly land on the rough stone arch of the entrance, well over their heads. Using tiny claws to grasp equally tiny irregularities in the rock, I clung tightly to its face and listened and observed.

The chamber where they sheltered was fairly large, and I sensed another deeper in. Relinquishing my hold, I few over the men to reach these areas, guided by the subtle differences of sound echoing back to my extremely sensitive ears. Past the first room, I made a quick circuit of the second before lighting on the dusty floor to become myself again.

This second room was just as large, and with a little quiet—so very quiet—exploration, I discovered a crevice leading even farther into the earth to others. This was of interest to me, since I was always glad to know about places that might offer safe refuge for the day. I'd have to make a thorough investigation of this place sometime soon.

It was a dead cave, this portion of it, anyway, since no sound of trickling water reached me, and no bats clustered along the ceiling. Bats prefer a very humid incubator for their young and for those times of the year devoted to hibernation; a disappointment, as I might have employed them to further bedevil the men. However, there had been bats roosting here in the past, the remains of their now dry droppings layered the uneven floor to a depth of several feet. Well and good. I would find excellent use for it.

Picking up a small quantity of guano and cupping it in

one hand, with the other I fished out a packet of sulfur tucked away in a pocket. Combining the two into a little ball and urgently whispering the necessary words to bring forth the power was the work of a moment. The ball took on a feeble blue glow that warmed gradually to green, yellow, red, and finally to a pure and brilliant white. As the colors supplanted each other in turn, the thing grew in size until it was nearly two feet in diameter. With a final word, I gently placed this highly lethal globe on the floor and lost no time commencing the change back into the form of a bat.

"What's *that?*" cried one of the men. He'd been drawn to this second chamber by the white light, and he and the others stood rooted with awe as they gaped at my transformation from man into animal. I have been given to understand the process is not an especially pleasant sight to witness, and doubtless this was a contributing factor to their shock. The delay was happily received by me, though, for I am rather vulnerable for the duration of the change and preferred not to have to deal with the complications of an attack from them while so occupied.

But once finished, I darted up out of reach of their blades. My movement prompted them to move in turn. One of them had recovered sufficiently from his surprise to take a swipe at me with his sword. I felt the wind of its passage ruffling my belly fur when I had to dive low in order to slip into the crevice that would take me deeper into the cave.

Thoroughly stirred up by this, some of them seemed determined to come after me, to challenge my unnatural threat. They'd have been better advised to retreat, to leave the cave altogether despite the wolves outside. But they angrily insisted on trying to follow me while the others paused to examine the gloriously beautiful ball of light I'd left behind on the floor.

Not for long. In order to prevent just such a retreat, I'd arranged for only the absolute minimum of time it would take for me to change and escape before the power within the globe finally burst forth. And burst it did, far exceeding my expectations. Confined as it was by the relatively close walls of the chamber, the blast was vastly more intense in its destructive force than it should have been—that, or my progress at spellcasting was more improved than I'd lately suspected. Of course, the very combustible bat guano lining the cave may have had something to do with it.

I flew as fast as I could, veering sharply to the side to avoid the fiery storm blowing through the crevice. Not fast enough. The wild, burning wind rushing in caught up with me, sending me tumbling helplessly end over end until I finally crashed hard into an utterly unforgiving surface.

Then I couldn't seem to move at all. Great billows of roaring flame rolled over my frail body, smashing me flat. I felt the fire eating away at the parchment-thin membrane of my wings, and screamed, adding my tiny voice to the shrieks of the men in the other chamber. A broken winged thing, I writhed, twitching and snarling as the heat seared us all together. But as bad as it was for me, they had it far, far worse.

The last wash of it passed, though, and I lay still and panting from the pain. Nearly deafened, I was still able to discern the low roar of fire and their last pitiful screechings as it consumed them. But I had no pity, not for these careless butchers. They'd despoiled that which was mine, and they were paying the price of it.

Damnation, but it seemed I *also* was paying a price. Even as I reveled in their deaths, I felt the nearness of that dark presence to me as well. It pressed close as a lover, caressing, seeping into my mind and heart, trying to persuade both to surrender to its embrace.

No, not this time. Not—

In one sickening wrench, my hold to a solid form was torn from me. For several panicked moments I feared I was dead . . . truly dead, for I floated formless and free, drifting like a cloud.

Or a mist.

My addled thoughts sorted themselves, and I realized what had happened, that I'd abruptly changed form without consciously initiating it. I must have been very severely hurt indeed to bring about such a drastic alteration. Flowing over the singed floor, I sought out some cooler, more hospitable place in which to recover.

I found a spot deep within the cave that seemed safe enough and ventured to resume being myself again. Though my clothes were in less than respectable condition, my body was quite whole and healed. But I was still very shaken and had to sit on a convenient mound of rock or fall over. I needed rest, it seemed.

My inner sense of time informed me that the dawn was hardly more than an hour away. If I hurried, I could beat through the sky with the west wind adding to my speed and make Vallaki in time to reach my traveling box.

Oh, but it was hardly worth the effort. Tomorrow night would do just as well. Then would I return and take possession of my horses and coach and perhaps see how the girl was being treated. Then would I climb the devil's pass, as the Svalich Road is called on this side of Mount Ghakis, cross through the ancient Gates of Barovia, and finally wend my way to the peace and sanctuary of Castle Ravenloft.

As I grew calmer with these soothing plans, I noticed the thick stench of burned meat and fat oozing in on the disturbed air of the cavern. The bandits were all dead, of that I was sure . . . if not by the fire, then by the wolves.

My work was finished. But at what price to me? I might have killed myself with this prank.

Careless, Strahd, careless. I thought, with dour chagrin. *It's not the done thing to exterminate yourself along with the vermin, you know.*

But they, at least, would trouble the land and people no more.

After all, Strahd von Zarovich looks after his own.